REV[illegible]E
OF A
QUEEN

Book Two of the Black Hallows Series

By G.N. Wright

COVER DESIGN: Outlined with Love Designs
EDITOR: Samantha Bee & J Wheeler
PUBLISHER: G.N. Wright via Amazon KDP

DEDICATION

This is dedicated to every person who took a chance on my first book baby. Thank you for taking the leap with me you bunch of Rockstar's.

TRIGGER WARNING

This is a full-length romance that is the second book of a dark romance series. It contains brief references to sexual assault, violence and other themes that some readers may find triggering.

Contents

Revenge is the raging fire that consumes the arsonist.

- Max Lucado

Prologue

Two and half years ago

All I feel is pain and all I see is blood. Fuck, it's like the night that shall not be named all over again. At least at the end of this, I will have a whole new reason for living, but fuck it hurts. Why does no one tell you that? I mean they do but, fuck them, they aren't trying to force a fucking melon out of their vaginas right now! I should not be doing this. I try to concentrate on my family's words, but the pain just seems too much.

"You have to push, little rose," Helen's smooth, motherly voice hits my ear as she strokes my head with a cold compress. Such an angel.

"You've got this, Ells Bells," Asher says from my other side while squeezing my hand.

I look down and see Arthur talking with the head of the OB-GYN Department, yes, the Chair because he and Helen would only allow the best for me. God, I love them, I hope they know that. He looks worried and is nodding rapidly at whatever the other doctor is saying to him. He looks at me and gives me a small smile. I know whatever they're saying isn't good, I don't have time to think about it before I scream out in pain. Both Arthur and the other doctor rush towards me, their panic-stricken faces are the last thing I remember before darkness descends.

I feel groggy and my throat is coarse and dry. I try to move but my body feels weird, lifeless almost. No not lifeless, more like weighed down, fuck, am I tied up? I start to panic but when I open my eyes I am greeted with the most beautiful sight in the entire world.

My best friend sitting in a chair, his shirt open, cradling our new-born daughter to his bare chest. He must hear me try to move because his gaze snaps up and meets mine. He smiles in pure relief when he sees my eyes open and locked on them. That look in his eye, the one that I've become accustomed to seeing since that awful night is nowhere to be seen. For the first time in months, he looks happy, hopeful, determined. It looks good on him.

"You gave us quite the scare, Hells Bells," he sighs, looking back down at our daughter.

I start to ask him what happened, but the nickname throws me off, "Hells Bells?" I question him in a drowsy tone, wondering if I misheard him.

He laughs, "Yeah you know like Ells Bells, but now it includes the hell you give me," he winks as I laugh a little, taking in my surroundings. What the hell happened?

"What happened?" I question him.

"Bunch of shit," he shrugs his shoulders like it's nothing. "There were some problems, so they had to rush you into surgery for an emergency c-section," he says

grimly. Ah, that explains why I feel slightly out of it and can't move properly.

He stands and I panic but somehow, he has already mastered how to hold our daughter perfectly. He walks over to the bed and bends down so he can show her to me.

"Baby girl meet our daughter," the pride in his voice is crystal clear. He no longer sounds like a fifteen-year-old boy, with the weight of the world on his shoulders and a mountain of regrets. No, he sounds like a man, a father, a hero, someone who is determined to make all of our enemies burn.

He passes her over to me, gently placing her in my arms and in an instant my whole life changes. I look down and see the most beautiful baby in the entire world. Long blonde lashes, fanning across her eyelids, a small button nose, and rosy lips puckered up like she is asking for a kiss. She has a dusting of blonde hair covering her head and a slight blush to her cheeks. She is absolutely perfect, and I know straight away that I will protect her with everything I have got and if that isn't enough? Well, then I will get more, I will give her the world and take out anyone who gets in our way.

Asher joins me on the bed, and we sit there just staring at her for lord knows how long until the door opens. I look up and find Helen peeking round the door.

"Ready for some visitors, little rose?" she asks gently, and I smile.

"Of course, come in, come in," I reply excitedly. Helen comes into the room followed by Arthur and Zack, all of them not paying me any notice, as they all stare at

the beautiful little bundle in my arms. Silence surrounds us as they take in my daughter and appreciate the light shining through the darkness that has brought us all together.

Arthur breaks it when he looks up at me and asks, "You okay, kiddo?"

"I don't know, am I?" I toss back at him with a smile, desperate for his medical expertise.

He smiles knowingly, understanding my need to know everything but he just nods, "Of course you are, you smashed it."

"Yeah, you did good, sis," Zack adds, smiling down at me as he drops a kiss to my forehead. "She got a name yet?" he questions, and I falter. I hadn't even thought about it.

I look at Asher and he just shrugs leaving it to me, I look down at the perfection in my arms until it comes to me.

"Everybody meet Cassie Royton," I say with glee and I hear Helen and Arthur gasp.

"You don't have to do that, kiddo," Arthur starts, sounding choked up but I cut him off.

"I know, but I want to. You guys mean the world to me and I would be lost without you," I don't think they can ever appreciate how much I needed them when we first met. They healed me in ways I didn't think possible, showed me what true loving parents looked like. "And besides this is the safest thing for her, so I don't wanna hear any more about it." I am not letting the demons of that night ruin this special moment for any of us. Fuck them to the fiery pits of hell. This isn't about them; this is

all about the tiny perfect girl in my arms. "Now come and meet your granddaughter."

They smile as tears gather in their eyes and even Zack's look a little watery. Asher just smiles nodding in total agreement. I pass Cassie over to Helen so she can have her first cuddle with her new grandbaby, and we all sigh in content.

"Can I just say something?" Asher speaks up getting off the bed.

"You're not gonna propose, are you? Because regardless of what happened today, she is too young for that," Zack replies, the tease of a smile on his lips.

Asher scoffs as he mutters under his breath "Dick," before saying louder, "You know it's not like that between us."

I shake my head with a smile, "Ignore him, Ash, go on."

"Elle," he starts, and I know from the use of my name that whatever he is about to say is going to be serious, he takes a deep breath before continuing, "I promise you now, they will not get away with what they did to you. I will make them pay. I will do whatever it takes before letting anything happen to you or our daughter. I know we don't really get into stuff like this, but I want you to know, you are my best friend, my only friend really. I love you and our child, and I will protect you both with everything I've got, always."

I swipe the tears from my eyes, unsure of what to say, so I just nod and respond, "Always."

Present

He knows, Marcus knows.

Until recently, the only people who knew Cassie's true identity were in the room with me the day she was born. Lincoln found out on a whim, but I trusted him to keep her a secret. Keep us all protected. This is different.

Inside all I feel is panic, pain and more panic but outside I remain stoic, calm, completely collected. It's something I have practiced with Zack over the last few years, one of the many things he has taught me. Keep your emotions off your face and out of the hands of your enemies. *Panic is what gets you killed.* Not that Marcus is my enemy, but at this moment, he definitely isn't my friend either. He's a new threat to me and my daughter's safety. So, I shut it all out and concentrate on only the things I can control, Cassie.

My biggest secret, well my second biggest, is staring up at Marcus like he's her favorite person in the entire world. Instead of the joy this moment should bring, all I feel is heartbreak. His, mine, ours.

I should have learnt by now how fast everything can change in this town. You think I would have become accustomed to that three years ago, when I was raped by someone, I thought I could trust, and escaped this town with a brother I didn't even know existed.

I always knew coming back here, back to him, would be hard, but I never imagined it being like this. I thought his hatred of me would outlast anything else he could ever feel, but I was wrong. Things between us blurred so fast I could barely keep up, but one thing I knew for sure is that I was never going to be ready for this moment.

It's strange that the panic I felt in the past is nothing compared to now. Back then, I had nothing to lose, they had already taken everything from me, so leaving for the unknown did nothing. Now though? Now, I have everything. Everything and more, all packaged in that tiny human with the perfect rosy lips, sparkling blue eyes and light blonde hair.

I could see it coming before it even happened. Marcus was so angry over what he thought he was seeing with Zack that he didn't hear the door fly open, but I did. I felt my entire body flinch when she called out to me, I could see Marcus looking around to see who she was talking to.

He never would have imagined this scenario when he wondered where I had been for the last few years. I'm sure he has conjured up plenty of stories, but this wouldn't have been one of them. He had no idea that while he was mourning his father and building his new life, I was birthing my best friend. She knows him but he doesn't know her. She loves him but he will never love her, not when he finds out who her father is, no matter which one he finds out about. I can see the shock, confusion and anger written all over his face. I wish there were something I could do to change things, but I can't.

He stands frozen as Cassie puts her arms around his legs and looks up to him. She's usually a very wary kid, knows not to speak to strangers and only interacts with people close to us, but Marcus is an exception. Yes, they are strangers to each other, but that doesn't mean she doesn't know him. I have been telling her stories of us ever since she was born. I didn't know how to be a parent at fifteen, so when she would cry at bedtime and refuse sleep, all I could think to do was talk. I would tell her endless stories about Marcus and I as kids, as she got bigger and started to understand I would show her pictures. She became obsessed, and the older she got, the more she loved the tales I would tell of the King and her River.

I have no clue what is going to happen next, but I know one thing for sure, I can't do this alone and neither can he. I pull out my phone and dial, Lincoln answers on the second ring.

"King," his sharp no nonsense tone hits my ear.

"I need you at the house, he knows," is all I say before ending the call and shoving my phone back in my pocket.

Marcus is still glaring between Cassie and I in shock, a thousand unanswered questions no doubt screaming at me inside his head, so I do the inevitable.

"You should come inside," I say simply, stepping towards him. I tug on Cass's hand and pull her to me. She turns and jumps up into my arms, snuggling into my neck. I breathe in her scent and it gives me the strength to deal with whatever is going to happen next. I turn and start towards the house not bothering to check whether Marcus is following or not.

"I'm so sorry, sweetheart," Helen says to me and I shake my head immediately.

"Don't be," I reply, I know what a little fireball my daughter is and how unstoppable she can be. She takes after me in that way.

I push the door open and head straight to the living room and everyone follows. It's clear that apart from Cassie, everyone is as on edge as I am. Thank god for children and their resilience and naivety. I sit on the sofa and pull her close on my knee as she rattles off all the things she saw on the drive home.

I watch as Zack comes into the room, offering me a grim smile in what I am sure he hopes offers comfort, but I am too far gone for that now. I feel so out of control of things, that I don't know how to get it back.

Arthur and Helen follow and they both look worried, but I offer them what I hope is my own reassuring smile as we wait. He takes so long that I almost think he's left, but eventually, Marcus makes his way into the room. His eyes are everywhere but on me as he takes in my home. I see his distaste from here, it's perfectly clear how he feels about wealth since he lost his. Not that he is low on the food chain by any means, but it's more what he feels this type of wealth represents. If only he knew the pure hearts in this room and what their wealth did for me.

He stands awkwardly in the entrance of the room, like he doesn't know if he is ever going to take another step. When his eyes finally hit mine, I feel it, that connection of ours, like a rope binding us together and for a fraction of a second I think everything might be okay. Then, his eyes turn cold, that bond between us no longer strong enough to hold us together. How did we get like this? Just last night I fell asleep next to him and woke up in his arms. Feeling safer than I have in years. My head was shouting at me not to let him in, but my heart didn't listen. I was too shellshocked from the orgasm he gave me. Add that to the fact that his touch doesn't turn my blood to ice like most people's does. Instead, it starts a fire I wish I could pour an accelerant on. I know I can never do that again, I let my guard down with him, and look at what happened. He now has my biggest secret in his hands and pure hatred for me in his heart.

"Wanna sit down?" I finally manage to find my voice as I gesture to the empty sofa across from me, as Cassie continues on with her stories. Marcus looks unsure but eventually moves at a slow pace taking the seat I offered. It's like everyone in the room relaxes just a little, but I know it won't last long. Things have changed, and we will never be the same again.

Chapter 1

MARCUS

S*he knows me.*

That's the only thought that is swirling around in my mind. Not the fact that Elle somehow has a daughter or that somewhere that daughter has a father. A father who has had my Ells and given her everything I promised I would. No, I refuse to think about either of those things. The only thing I can concentrate on is that this little girl knows me, and Elle kept it from me.

Elle King has a brother.
Elle King has a daughter.
Elle King is a liar.

I don't know how long it's been, but I know I haven't spoken, not one word. It's like I am mute and don't know a single word of the fucking dictionary.

Last night, I had Elle curled up in my arms, and I was happier than I have felt in years. Now, I feel like a bomb has dropped on my world, ensuring the casualties will never be the same. Elle invited me inside after my mind exploded. I had no choice but to follow her. My heart is beating so hard against my chest I feel like it might just rip right through my rib cage, no matter how deep of a breath I take, my lungs are screaming for air.

I am sitting frozen on the sofa, watching as the little girl speaks a mile a minute telling Elle about a trip she has taken with her grandparents, whoever they may be. Elle is listening intently, while stealing glances at me every few seconds, like she is expecting me to make a scene. Which isn't too farfetched considering what just happened outside.

We aren't alone either. Her so called brother is sitting next to her glaring at me intensely, the older man and woman are hovering with worried looks on their faces. I can do nothing but sit here in utter disbelief at how this day has turned out.

I knew Elle had secrets, but I never imagined this. She hasn't spoken to me directly since she introduced Cassie, invited me inside, and told me to sit down. She looks how I feel, confused, worried, devastated, far too many emotions for me to even register them all right now. I can tell she is trying to hide her feelings, but I know her too well for that. The tension in the room grows the longer we sit listening to the little girl's tales. I have no idea how old she is, but she can't be older than two or three. She is so small, and her words come out quick and not properly pronounced, telling me she is still young. I am trying not to think about what kind of timeline that puts her birth on, was Elle pregnant before she left town? Is that why she left? Who the fuck was she having sex with at fourteen years old? How the fuck did I miss this?

Just as I conjure up the only person who could be her father, he appears, like my mind summoned him. Asher Donovan. *Asher fucking Donovan.* He didn't ring the bell, so clearly, he is comfortable enough here to get past security and be let in. He rounds the corner, and just as I want to ask the question out loud and break my silence, Cassie beats me to it.

"Daddy!"

That one word cracks my already broken heart. Fuck. I never knew something could hurt this much. I bring my hand to my chest and rub against it, like that could take the pain away. When in reality, I don't think anything will ever ease the pain.

Asher spots me immediately, frowning as he takes quick stock of the rest of the room, gauging the situation. His face sets into a firm grimace until Cassie barrels towards him. He opens his arms for her, and she jumps into them, like she has done it so many times before. I guess she has.

"Hey, how's my best girl?" he says in a strained soothing voice as she nuzzles into his chest, his eyes back to being locked on mine.

"Good, Daddy, miss you!" she replies.

"I missed you too, little angel," he answers her and it's the softest I have ever seen him be. Their interaction is bittersweet. I can practically taste the betrayal on my tongue. Elle King isn't the only liar in this room. Finally, I find my voice as I shake my head in disbelief.

"She loves Asher," I mutter with a scoffed laugh, more to myself than anyone else.

"What?" Elle says to me, even though it's clear from the look on her face she heard exactly what I said.

I clear my throat and speak up, "You love Asher, he's your family, that's what you said to me right? You said you cared about me, but you couldn't be with me and when I asked about him," I practically spit as I motion to Asher, "You said he was your family and you loved him. I guess I didn't take that literal enough did I, little King? Or should I say, little traitor?"

"Careful, Marcus," Asher warns me with his arms still wrapped around his daughter.

I swing my gaze to him. "And you," I laugh, "You are a good actor, pretending to be my friend as kids--"

"I was your friend," he interrupts.

"Yeah, before or after you took my girl and your dad killed--"

"That's enough," Elle cuts me off. "Helen, can you take Cass to clean up for lunch please?" The pleading note in her voice calms me some as I remember there is a little girl here, I mutter fuck under my breath.

She offers Elle a sympathetic smile, "Of course, my little rose."

The woman, Helen, leads Cassie away and the older gentleman follows leaving just me, Elle, Asher, and her brother. I wait until they are out of the room before I continue with my eyes still locked on Asher.

"You looked me right in the eye and said there was nothing going on between the two of you, that there never had been. I, being the fucking idiot I am, trusted you. You think I would have learned my lesson after what happened the last time a Riviera trusted a Donovan," I spit his last name at him in disgust.

Asher's frown deepens in confusion, he swings his gaze to Elle, like there is something else going on here. I see the subtle shake of her head and am about to ask about it when an unexpected voice cuts into the room.

"Brother," Lincoln's wary tone drawls at me.

I snap my head around and see him and Jace standing in the entrance of the room, "The fuck are you doing here?" I ask.

Lincoln swings his gaze to Elle but before either of them can speak, another excited squeal comes as Cassie barrels back into the room.

"Superman!!" she yells out.

WHAT THE FUCK!?!?!?

She knows him. Cassie knows him and is using Elle's nickname to greet him. Which means he knows her too. What the fuck? Jace is standing next to him looking as shocked as I am as he takes in the scene before him with wide eyes. At least there is one person in this fucking town that hasn't betrayed me.

Cassie curls her arms around Linc's legs as he pats her head, "Hey princess," he says with a small smile, then looks at me with a tight expression on his face like he is trying to convey some sort of message to me. Well fuck him.

He looks to Elle and briefly nods before turning to her brother, "Zack," he greets him.

"Lincoln," he replies with a nod.

Oh, this just gets better and better, not only did he know about Cassie, but he knew about her brother too.

The cogs in my head are turning and it's like a lightbulb goes on in there when I realize he just called him Zack.

I break my silence again, "Zack? As in Zack Zack?" I look back and forth between the two of them but settle on Zack when I realize who he is, "You're Zack Royton."

He flicks his gaze quickly to Elle and back before answering, "Yes."

"How?" I can't even form another word. I'm too shocked.

Zack Royton, tech billionaire and our fucking boss is somehow Elle's brother. It wasn't even on my radar to think about him when she referred to him by name outside. Now? Now I need to know how she has a brother, a brother I knew nothing about, and how that brother is somehow who I work for.

Elle speaks now, "Zack's birth mom is Sarah King," she says with a look of disgust before she continues, "She gave him up when she was young and he was adopted by Arthur and Helen," she adds, gesturing to the older couple who have re-entered the room.

"Well, fuck me, this is the last thing I expected to find when Lincoln told me we were coming here princess," Jace says, breaking the silence that followed Elle's statement.

"Watch your fucking mouth Conrad," Asher snaps at him and I doubt the irony is lost on any of us that he is calling Jace out for swearing in front of Cassie, while he does it himself.

Cassie gasps, "Bad word, daddy."

"Daddy?" Jace almost shouts in shock, choking on a laugh before he takes in the room and reads the serious tension on everyone's faces. Yeah, not the fucking time for jokes brother.

"Well fuck," he adds.

"Last warning," Asher snaps at him as Cassie shouts, "Swear jar!"

I stand and start to pace; I can feel the anger in me pouring out into the room and clearly it doesn't go unnoticed. Zack leans forward and speaks to the little girl.

"You hungry squirt? I got you some spaghetti."

She squeals, "Yes, uncle Zaaa! I love sgetti," she replies excitedly.

"Well, come on, let's go get it," he bends in front of her so she can climb on his back. He nods his head at the man and woman, and they all exit the room together leaving just me, Elle, and the guys.

She turns to the guys first, "You guys should sit, I have a feeling this is gonna take a while," she says grimly.

Asher sits next to Elle and it just makes the anger inside me burn, as Lincoln and Jace sit in the space next to where I just vacated. There is an awkward silence until I can't wait any longer for her to start, so I start for her.

"How does she know me?" a hundred questions on my mind but that feels like the only one I can voice. I know I need to ask about Zack, about her and Asher, and about my dad, but the only thing I can think about is that little girl.

Elle releases a breath as she stands and leaves the room, just when I think about going to follow her, she returns with a large book in her hand. She passes it over to me and it's only then I realize it's a photo album. I recognize it immediately from when we were kids, she was obsessed with this thing, always adding stuff to it.

I flip through it and countless memories assault my brain, there are hundreds of pictures of us in here. Right back to when we first became friends all the way up to the summer she left. After that, it continues with pictures of me that I have no idea how she got, but they are all in order from after she left, to as recent as just before she came back. I shut it and take a deep breath; I have no idea how to process all of this.

"She wasn't a good sleeper when she was born and the only thing that would settle her, is if I told her stories," she shrugs. "I didn't really have anything to say that wasn't about us."

"Us?" I cut her off with a mocking laugh, "What fucking us is that Elle?" I snap at her throwing my arms out as my rage continues to take over.

"Marcus," Asher growls.

"Don't even fucking start with me, Donovan, you fucking backstabbing piece of shit!"

"River, please," Elle pleads.

"I bet you just fucking laughed at me, didn't you? I trusted you both, and you paid me back by sneaking around behind my back and lying."

"Brother," Lincoln's voice pleads with me, "remember what I said, remember who the real enemy is."

I laugh, "Oh I remember, brother," I spit back at him. "You told me to trust her, to be there for her. All the while you were in on all her secrets. Guess it's a day full of betrayals, huh?"

"You need to tell him, Elle," Lincoln says pleading with her, but her eyes remain on me.

"Tell me what, Linc? About who I can and cannot trust, think I can work that out for myself." I am so furious I can't even think straight, I need to get out of here and away from all these liars.

"Marcus," Elle tries again but I cut her off ignoring the desperate and pleading look on her face.

"No, the one thing I know about this town is that you can't trust a Donovan, and from the looks of things, this house is full of them," I bite back at her and her face immediately changes. She no longer looks desperate or pleading. No, her face changes entirely, completely shutting off her emotions to me.

"You were right," I continue, "I should have stayed away from you and trust me from now on I'll listen," with that I turn and leave the room without looking back.

I should have taken her up on every one of her warnings, she told me time and time again she didn't come back for me, that we couldn't be together. I was just a fucking blind asshole unwilling to listen. Well, message received, little traitor. Loud and fucking clear.

Chapter 2

ELLE

For the second time in this shitty town, my life has been blown up. The first, I never saw coming, the second, I have been trying to avoid since the minute I got here. Fuck. Fuck. Fuck. What the hell do I do now? Should I have told Marcus the truth? No, that would have been stupid. No, not stupid, suicidal. The boy who stole my heart when I was five is now a man whose job it is to protect people from the Donovan's. How would he feel if he knew the only person left, he cared about had already been ruined by them? They already took Michael from him, it's better he thinks I chose them over him, rather than that they took me too. I might not be dead like his father, but they killed something inside of me that night. The only reason my heart continues to beat is because I got something even bigger from them in return, my daughter.

I watch him walk away and force myself to be a shell, burying the pain until I feel nothing. An empty void of no emotions. I have done it before, and I can do it again. It's as easy as breathing for me. The room is deathly silent, and I can hear Cassie's voice filtering in from the dining room, as she happily chats away while eating her lunch. The innocence of children always astounds me, she has no idea the carnage that has just been left in her wake.

"Does someone wanna enlighten me to what the fuck just happened?" Jace's voice breaks the cold tension of the room, and I have to huff out a laugh because if not, I might just break down. Another innocent soul tangled up in this mess. I won't bring him into this, I don't know why Lincoln brought him here, they must have been together when I called, and he rushed over here without thinking. That's the only explanation I can think of.

I glance at Jace and swing my gaze between him and Lincoln who is staring at me tight lipped. I can tell by the look in his eyes that he isn't happy with me. He has always wanted Marcus to know about Cassie and now he does, he thinks I should have told him everything. Maybe I should have, but Marcus pretty much said it himself, he sees me as a Donovan, he was never going to listen to what I had to say.

I remain just as tight-lipped as Lincoln because the last thing I need is another Rebel in on one of my secrets, while their leader is left out in the dark. I look to Asher who is staring at me, when he realizes I am not going to say anything, he does it for me.

"It doesn't concern you," he snaps as he swings his gaze round to him.

"Oh sorry, Daddy, are you in charge *now*?" Jace growls back at him, sarcastically, but it's far from his usually playful tone, he's pissed off at me too. Well join the fucking club, pretty boy.

"Careful now, Conrad," Asher responds. I can tell from his flat, smooth tone that he has gone to his dark place, and things are about to go south fast if I don't step in.

I jump to my feet, "Look, pretty boy, I'm sorry Lincoln dragged you here," I say looking pointedly at him before turning back to Jace, "but this doesn't concern you. It can't concern you, but I need to know what you saw here today, won't leave this room."

His serious glare at me shatters. I can tell straight away that I've hurt his feelings. He stands abruptly shaking his head, "I really thought you knew me better than that, princess." He turns to leave, smoothing is long hair behind his ears, when I call out to him.

"Jace," I say a little desperately, but come up short trying to find more words for him.

He stops without looking back, "Your secrets are safe with me, princess. I never rat on my family," his tone almost makes me break. I want to tell him, I want to pour out my secrets until he drowns in them, but Marcus needs him more than I do. He is the only one who didn't betray him in his eyes. We all watch him leave, and then I sit back on the sofa and take a deep breath.

"What the fuck happened, baby girl?" Asher says, taking my hand in his, like he can sense I need the comfort, even though I can tell from his voice he hasn't left the dark place. He sees this as a new threat to Cassie. It will be a miracle if I can pull him back from this ledge. He is always doing everything in his power to keep Cassie hidden and out of his family's hands. Now that two more people know of her existence, he is going to be worse than ever, especially when those two people are South Side Rebels.

I blow out another breath before I try to explain how this happened, where do I even start? “He was here when I got home, or he followed me,” I shrug. “I’m not totally sure. All I know is I went to get lunch for everyone with Zack, and when we got back and started unloading the car Marcus appeared.” I scrub my eyes over my face, “He thought Zack,” I pause and my nose scrunches in disgust at just thinking about what Marcus thought, “He thought that Z and I were together.”

Asher snorts aloud, “Of course he did,” before adding under his breathe, “Stubborn fucking Riviera men.”

“And let me guess, he hit Zack?” Lincoln muses knowing how much of a loose temper his brother has.

“Erm actually, Zack hit him,” I cringe a little at admitting that. I know Marcus will be pissed about that too when he lets himself calm down. I see a smile tug at Linc’s lips before I continue, “He was distracted, but then Cassie came running from the house calling out to me.”

“Fuck,” Lincoln replies quietly as silence descends on the room again. *Fuck indeed.*

“Why didn’t you tell him the truth?” Lincoln asks after a few minutes.

“Are you fucking dense?” Asher snaps before I can even form a response.

“Care to elaborate?” Lincoln replies not affected in the slightest by Ash’s outburst.

“You just saw why she didn’t tell him the truth, something I’m sure you see every fucking day. Marcus is just like his father, a hunter for justice, he is too hot headed to handle the truth."

I sigh, Asher is right, and I elaborate, before either of them can continue, "Telling him the truth would be the same as signing his death certificate," I reply grimly. "It's better he hates me and Ash thinking what he does now, rather than knowing the truth and going after Greg alone." Which he would, he wouldn't even think, he would happily give his life to avenge mine and that is something I won't allow.

Lincoln doesn't disagree with me like he has before, he has seen how Marcus has no limit when it comes to me. We have a special bond, or at least we did, I fear that's over now. I saw the way he looked at me before he left, like I was the lowest of the low. Who can blame him? He thinks I left him after fucking our best friend, had his child, and that I came back here to be with him. That's all he will ever see when he looks at me now. He won't see Elle King, the little girl he used to wish upon a star with, no, he will see Elle King, the traitor, and the liar.

Cassie saves any of us from having to say anything further when she comes running back into the room clutching a piece of paper to her chest.

"Where did River go, Mommy?" her excited, innocent curiosity cracks my heart.

"He had to go, baby," I say trying to keep the emotion out of my voice, but I can tell it doesn't go unnoticed by the two guys left here with me.

Her face falls, "Oh," she replies softly before perking up, "will he come back?"

I should lie to her right? I should keep her innocent, pure heart intact and let her think the world is all sunshine and rainbows. Is that what a good mom would do? As much as that seems like the right thing to do, I just can't bring myself to do it, so I tell her the truth.

"Honestly, baby, I don't know if he will," I reply in my softest tone and her face shuts down.

"Oh," that one tiny word shatters me, and just when I think I will be okay, she runs over and hands me the piece of paper clutched in her small hands, "This was for him," she adds before running back off to where she came from.

I watch her go before looking down to see she has drawn two stick figures holding hands with crooked smiley faces. It's something she has learned recently, which is quite advanced for her age. She usually draws herself, Asher, and I over and over again and makes me write our names, but this one is different. There are just two lone figures by a river and it's as clear as day that it's meant to be her and Marcus. My heart cracks worse than ever. How do you explain the harsh reality of the world to an innocent child?

Chapter 3

LINCOLN

I watch as the emotions on Elle's face come out in full force. It's the most emotion I've ever seen her show before and it's not good. The look on her face is heart-breaking, it's a look of pure devastation. I can't help but wonder how bad this look would have been when she was fourteen and had her innocence stolen. Hanging around the other two Rebels means I rarely get my hands dirty and turn to violence, I left that part of me in my past. Yet, I can't lie and say I don't have murderous thoughts about the low lives that did that to her. That my palms don't itch to be coated in their blood, a feeling I know well, a feeling I miss, crave even.

I don't know what has made her so strong, well I guess I do, it's that beautiful little girl that just walked out of the room. Seeing her hurt little face at Marcus being gone, honestly makes me want to punch him, even if I do understand him. He's hurting, at what he thinks he knows, and I added to that hurt by betraying him. He probably won't forgive me, but I can't change that, and I wouldn't. Changing that would mean betraying Elle, hurting her, and Cassie and that is something I will never do.

I watch as Asher burns a hole through the piece of paper in Elle's hands. I can see how like me he is. His mind never stops turning, his thoughts a constant distraction. I can understand that completely. My focus is protecting my family. His sole focus is on the only two people that matter to him. We would do anything we had to in order to protect them.

I wonder if he's jealous of Marcus. They say they don't have that type of relationship, but I can't help but be curious about him. The dark prince of the Donovan name. Does he want her? Or were they telling the truth and it really isn't like that between them? They are as close as family, which given their situation, makes perfect sense, but everything about him is an enigma. He is a Donovan after all, so what makes him different from his family? He is just as psychotic and dark as they are. Yet, I know the eyes of a sadistic murderer, and he doesn't have them. He is just a boy trying to survive this town and the devils that run it.

I look back to Elle as she takes a deep breath, I know her well enough now, to see her shields going back up. She allowed herself a quiet moment of weakness, a moment of mourning, for something Cassie will never have, and now she is shutting it down. It's impressive really, makes me wonder if this is something natural to her or something she has learned, or should I say, been taught?

I can tell that nothing more is going to be discussed here, she is still pissed off at me for bringing

Jace, but I didn't even think about it. It's probably the first time I've not thought about doing something. I just got her panicked phone call, while I was grabbing lunch with Jace, and the tone in her voice had me flooring it here before he could even register what was going on. I know Jace and trust him implicitly, but I would never purposely betray Elle's trust, I hope she knows that.

"Is there anything else you need?" I ask gently.

Asher is the first to reply, "I think you've done enough," he snaps, and I roll my eyes, making him narrow his eyes at me. I ignore him and focus on Elle as she finally looks up at me.

"No," she says with a soft smile. "Thank you for coming but no, you should go. He needs you more than I do."

I huff a dry laugh, "I think the days of him relying on me for anything are over," I reply with a grim smile which she returns. She understands, I took a risk for her by keeping her secrets from Marcus, now I will pay the price but it's a price worth every penny. "Just call me if you need anything," I say, nodding to the two of them before I turn to leave.

I knew I wouldn't get away without a warning from Asher. I hear him behind me but don't react. Before I make it to the door, he is grabbing me and pinning me to the wall by my throat. Fuck. It isn't the first time someone has had me gripped by the throat but it's the first time I have more than fucking liked it. His touch elicits something in me that I rarely feel, need, pure carnal need. What the fuck? The last thing I need, is to be lusting over a fucking psychopath who may or may not be in love with his best friend.

His grip is firm and tight just how I like it, it makes me realize how long it's been since I have fucked anyone. Trust me when I say there aren't a lot of guys around here that I would let into my bed, even for just the night.

"Donovan," I say as casually I can manage.

"I am only going to say this once, Blackwell, so let me make myself perfectly clear. Marcus and that other lost boy in your sad little crew are your responsibility. If you or they step out of line and become a problem, I will not hesitate to neutralize you."

"I'm not scared of you, Donovan," I try to keep my voice smooth and calm, but his closeness is intoxicating. Like Icarus flying too close to the sun. A touch from him is like a touch from the devil, like molten lava, dark, burning, and branding. I feel my cock hardening in my jeans and if he moves any closer, I am sure he will feel it.

He laughs a sinister laugh as he leans in closer to me, "I've dealt with bigger threats than the South Side Rebels," he uses his free hand to poke at my chest as he continues, "you are a blip on nobody's radar," *poke,* "I will revel in making you scream if I need to," *poke.*

"And who makes you scream?" I reply before I can stop myself, that dark look in his eyes taunts me. I think about the few encounters we have had with each other, I barely took notice of him, other than being Donovan's youngest son, before Elle got to town. I mean yeah, I dug up his entire life and could tell you every school grade he's ever earned, or how he works out in the same place every weekday, but it's all shallow stuff. Nothing of real interest to tell me about him as a person. No, that comes with our interactions between Elle. I have watched him closer than ever.

People think that Elliot and Greg Donovan are bad men, and they are. They're truly evil and only live for power and money. Asher Donovan is moulded by the two of them, except much worse. Because he isn't like them. Asher doesn't care about his money, doesn't relish in his power. No, he lives for family, for love, and to protect these two girls. There is nothing more dangerous than that.

"None of your fucking business," he snaps back, before taking a deep breath. "Don't underestimate me, Lincoln. You think my father and brother are bad because they commit their crimes in the light of day, but you've seen nothing. The shadows of the night hide my crimes and when I bury a body, it stays buried. I don't care who I have to bleed out, as long as the blood doesn't belong to those two girls in there."

"On that we can agree," I reply honestly. "You can trust me," I add, even though I know that is the last thing he is going to do. I thought when Elle welcomed me into the fold and I found out about Cassie, he would soften up to me, but I was wrong. Asher Donovan is a fucking vault; I'll be lucky if I ever break through.

He laughs, "I trust nobody. Trust is earned and you have done nothing to earn mine. That being said," he finally releases his grip on my throat, I should feel relief, but I don't. I watch as he looks around to make sure we are still alone and then he reaches into his pocket and slams something into my chest. I rush to grab it as he pulls his hand away before it falls to the floor. I don't let my gaze leave his but from touch alone I can tell it's a USB. "For your viewing pleasure only," he adds, and I cock a brow at him, he huffs another breath. "Elle has enough on her plate today, so you look into this alone for now. Don't make me regret this."

He doesn't wait for my response before he turns and heads back towards where he left Elle. I don't waste my time leaving the house and climb into my SUV before I adjust my still painfully hard cock. Fuck, where the fuck has this come from? That is so not going to happen, for so many reasons.

1. He's Asher fucking Donovan.
2. He's straight.
3. He's a fucking psychopath that would murder me in cold blood if the right mood struck him.

I put the car in drive and leave before I get myself into any more trouble today. I put Asher Donovan out of my mind and bring my thoughts back to the other man who's also a thorn in my side: Marcus Riviera.

I enter the loft and find Jace coming from down the hall where Marcus' room is, he sees me instantly and offers me a sad smile.

"He's not here," he says even though from the silence it's obvious. If Marcus were here things would be loud, there would be shouting, fighting, breaking, and drinking. Lots of drinking.

I head straight into my office and turn on my laptop and check my tracking program. I created it over a year ago, the guys and I have been using it ever since. We have it programmed into our phones and cars, even his bike. They sync up with a program on our phones and a chip in our watches, we can use both to set off an SOS if need be. I click onto Marcus' name and they are all black. Fuck. Green means everything is okay, red means we are in trouble, and black means they aren't on which right now means only one thing. Marcus has gone off the grid.

Chapter 4

ELLE

It's been a week. A week since Marcus walked out of the house, with my biggest secret, and nobody has seen him since. I'd like to say things have been fine without him, but that would be a lie, everything is a fucking train wreck. I'm angry, the two remaining Rebels are lost, and Asher is downright insufferable. Don't even get me started on his pathetic band of merry followers at school, the boys think it means open season for their chance at top dog, and the girls are heartbroken that their King isn't here to pine over.

It's Monday lunchtime, I'm on edge but settled into my new normal of eating lunch at the Rebels' table. Marcus might be gone but Lincoln and Jace have barely left my side. It should be annoying, but I'd be lying if I said it was. It's actually quite nice, relaxing even, to know that no matter where I am, someone has always got my back. I understand now what Marcus found in his brothers, that he didn't have before on the North Side. I mean yeah, we had each other, and he tolerated Ash for me, but he never really had that friendship with guys, that brotherhood where you always have each other's backs.

He found that in his Rebels, and then I came back and ruined it. How much more am I gonna take from him?

Now that both Linc and Jace have become privy to the other half of my life they have become a fixture at the Royton household. With Marcus gone, we have taken to having dinner together for the last four nights. It's probably stupid to invite them further into my life, especially considering Jace still doesn't even know half of the truth, but I couldn't stop it. Cassie asked for Marcus for three days straight before I caved and invited Lincoln back over to appease her slightly. With Linc came Jace. There was no point shutting him out anymore, considering he knows about Cass and unsurprisingly they have quite the little friendship going.

Jace is still pissed at me for not trusting him. Not about the fact that I didn't tell him, but the fact then when he found out I asked him to keep it quiet. Like it was a given for him. He doesn't understand why I had to ask, and I get it. He has been telling me I'm part of their fucked up little family ever since I got back to Hallows. But what he doesn't understand is how hard it is for me to trust people with my secret. Cassie is everything to me and the more people that know about her the more danger she is in.

I flick my gaze around the cafeteria, and I see about fifty percent of the student population watching us but pretending they aren't. They are all wondering where their King is, and what his absence means. I grind my teeth at the fucking bullshit high school drama that I know is going to unfold. Last week people were cautious, but now that we are into the second week of school without an appearance from Marcus things are going to get complicated. Someone is going to mess with the power balance, I just have to wait to see who it's going to be.

The bell rings signalling the end of lunch and everyone starts to move.

"We doing dinner at Casa De Royton tonight?" Jace asks, and the guilt overtakes me immediately knowing Linc and I have revenge plans tonight.

With all the commotion of Marcus finding out about Cassie, I completely forgot that the reason Asher came to the house that day was because he said he found something. Something he then trusted Lincoln with, before me, but tonight we deal with it together. Asher will resume his usual role of Cassie's protector while Lincoln and I check out the intel.

I look to Linc who is happily leaving me to deal with this alone, he is firmly on team 'everyone should know the truth'. *Dick.*

"Actually, Linc and I have stuff to do tonight so--" I start, and he cuts me off, gesturing his hands into the air like he doesn't care, but I know he does.

"Say no more, princess," he replies as he turns to walk away.

"Fuck," I mutter to myself as I turn back to Linc, he just shrugs and turns to take after Jace.

"Meet you out front later," he calls over his shoulder like a condescending dick. Like I don't know that's where he will be. Between him, Ash, and Zack, I'm not allowed to drive myself anywhere.

Once the cafeteria is empty, I finally make my way to leave, but when I get into the hallway, they aren't deserted like I expected. No, instead practically everyone in the school is crowded around something. What did I just say? I knew it.

I move to the bank of lockers on my left and use a ridge on one of the bottom ones to hoist myself up so I can get a better view at what is going on. I find Jace and Lincoln surrounded by a few guys from our shitty football team. A team that wouldn't dare to approach the Rebels under usual circumstances, but with Marcus gone they think they stand a chance. I get it, Lincoln is the computer geek and Jace is the jokester, Marcus is seen as the threat of the three. God, these people are dumb fucks. Even without Marcus, these two could take on the five of them and more and come out on top. They are all an equal threat in their own rights.

I count five guys in total, but one is front and center and it's clear he likes to think of himself as the leader of this band of clueless assholes. He's tall and built but nowhere near the level that Marcus or the guys are. He's got dark hair and dark eyes and a stupid fucking shave in his eyebrow that he thinks makes him look sexy. Spoiler alert it doesn't. I move closer and start catching the gist of the conversation.

"What are you gonna do, Lincoln, throw your iPad at me?" he taunts, and a few people laugh. I can see the divide already forming. A bunch of students surround his little crew and that tells me that there are a lot of snakes in this building that don't support the Rebels. This is going to become a problem unless it gets shut down and fast. I ignore whatever Lincoln responds with and look around until my gaze settles on a girl close to me. She is standing back and looks like she has no interest in whatever high school politics are being played out right now. My kinda girl. I move towards her until I am next to her and give her a nudge, she startles and then her gaze meets mine.

"Who's the douche?" I ask flicking my head towards the guy who is continuing to talk a big game to two very amused Rebels.

"Chad McCormick," she replies quietly.

I just nod as I bring up the program on my phone that allows me to run his name through it. It's a program Zack came up with that features every person in this school, both student and faculty. It houses every piece of information on them, from birth certificate and school records to medical reports and dirty secrets. Basically, anything we could use against them or could be used against us. When I have what I need, I pocket my phone and nod my thanks to the girl who offers me a smile, like she knows exactly what I am going to do. Ha, she really has no idea.

I move stealthily around the crowd until I am leaning on a row of lockers that has a space between the two opposing sides with a clear view. I miss whatever Jace just said to the guy, but I don't miss him sliding on a pair of knuckle dusters and I have to smile. My little pretty boy has good taste in weapons.

The prick starts again, "You really think the two of you can take us?" he says loudly and puffs out his chest, like he thinks that will make him seem scarier. I stifle a laugh.

“What about me?” I say loudly, in a bored tone and every eye turns at once to look at me, no one noticed me before now. I ignore the grimace on both Lincoln and Jace's face in favor of the asshole with a god complex.

“Do I not count because I have a pussy?” I muse even louder and see a few people on our side snigger.

“What is Marcus’ whore of the month gonna do to me?” he replies coolly, I see the tension pouring off the Rebels, this isn’t just about a petty turf war now, it’s about disrespect.

“Oh, come on --” I pause for dramatic effect, enjoying myself here for the first time since Marcus left, “Sorry what's your name?”

“Really, whore? Almost two months here and you don't know my name. What’s the matter? Do you only get wet for Rebel cock?”

I smirk and he looks confused, “Oh, I know more than your name Chad McCormick, son of Barbara and Colin McCormick and that's the problem.”

“Yeah, well the only problem you should be concerned with, is that you can't keep your legs closed!” He snaps back and the only people that laugh, are the four guys stupid enough to stand with him. Everyone else is dead silent. They sense it, feel it.

“Yeah, and you can't keep your dick clean,” I reply smoothly, pulling out my phone and sending a mass text to everyone here, “Chlamydia three times really is impressive, I wasn’t aware Hallows High had any over achievers.”

The dings of everyone’s phone spurs him into action, “You fucking little cunt,” he goes to lunge towards me when I pull the knife from my thigh, giving zero fucks about anyone seeing. He falters immediately and I smile, a sinister smile channelling my inner Ash. Men always go for women when they think they are weak.

I slide my finger along the edge of my blade, "Just because Marcus isn't here, doesn't mean we will allow for any misdemeanours," I say calmly before throwing my gaze at everyone still watching. I look back to Jace and Lincoln and nod and it sets them both into motion in perfect synchronization. They take out two of the five before anyone has even realized they moved. Then move onto the other two, leaving their pathetic little leader for me.

I put my knife away and he smiles like he thinks he can take me without it. Stupid fuck. He hasn't seen me pull a Jace and slip my black jewelled duster onto my fist. I prowl towards him and when he reaches to grab me, I dodge it effortlessly before throwing my fist into his face. I hear a crack so loud that I'm sure I'm not the only one who heard it. When he falls to the ground, I relish in the fact that I chose heeled boots to finish my outfit today and slam my heel right into his dick and he screams out in pain. I bend down and grip him by the hair and whisper loudly into his ear.

"Don't fuck with the Rebels, we bite."

I realize what I am doing, I am cementing myself as part of them. They had already taken me in but I tried to push them away. I am starting to see that they might need me like I need them. But this isn't about me, it's about Marcus. He has built a life for himself here, not the life he deserves, but a life that will get him what he wants, and I won't let anyone take that from him. If that means stepping into his crew and becoming one of them, then so be it. I doubt any of this high school bullshit will affect my personal plans for revenge, so it's not an issue.

"Your King may be gone, but your court is not, now everyone fuck off to class." I have barely finished the sentence before everyone begins to scatter. Once the hallways empty, I turn and head towards the main entrance, I need some fresh air and I feel the Rebels behind me like I always do when I exit the school.

I keep walking, not stopping until I reach my sanctuary on the bleachers. It's barely a minute before Lincoln and Jace drop down beside me. We sit in silence until Jace breaks it with the playful tone I have missed hearing from him directed at me.

"Do I need to start calling you Queenie now, princess?" he asks, and I scoff.

The two of them burst out laughing when I respond, "Fuck off."

When they stop, he turns to me again, "You didn't have to do that, princess."

I shrug, "It was no big deal--" I start but he cuts me off.

"It was a huge deal," he begins, looking at Lincoln and then back to me, "every person we encounter comes to us for a reason and that reason is never pure, it's always bullshit. Trying to wet our dicks, smoke our stuff or just use us for some shit they can't do themselves," he says as he pulls out a joint and lights it, breathing in deeply before blowing back out. "No one has ever done anything for us just to help us," he adds.

I scrunch my face up in confusion as ever since I got here, all I have heard from everyone is how important the Rebels are around here. I suppose I never stopped to think that even with a band of followers, you could be lonely. Yeah, they have their loyal crew members, but that's when I realize that's all they are, just workers. They aren't friends with anyone but each other.

"That's sad," I finally reply and they both just shrug.

"We make it work," Lincoln adds solemnly, slipping his glasses on and tapping away into his iPad, no doubt just arranging ways to make the disloyal pay.

"Well, Marcus is gonna come back to his Kingdom intact and a Queen for his side," Jace laughs but the mention of Marcus pushes me back to reality.

"You mean if he comes back," I respond quietly looking out into the distance of the hills.

"Yeah if," he replies sadly.

Chapter 5

ELLE

After the exciting events of today, a stake out with Lincoln feels pretty chill. I have gotten very used to our evenings spent in his SUV, spying on targets, and eating snacks. He likes to pretend he doesn't enjoy the fact I constantly bring him snacks, but I see him eat them, when he thinks I'm not paying attention. I do it to try make him smile, I never see enough smiles from him and even though Cassie manages to draw a few from him, he always has a tension about him. That increases tenfold when he's at the house, especially when Asher is around, I have yet to get to the bottom of it.

The intel Asher shared with him before me was about the docks again, except it gave us more than we knew last time. Elliot Donovan does ship girls there, but he only uses the docks to send girls to buyers or receive them, he stores them at another location. A location we just so happened to be looking at right now.

It's a warehouse that looks disgustingly close to what I remember of where they kept me that awful night, but on a much smaller scale. I know exactly where they kept me when they took me, I know the way, the layout down to every last square inch of the place but it's too well guarded. There isn't one loophole in the place that we have been able to find to give us an in. Not like the place we're at now. This place is just off the radar, but it's clear from the lack of security that he doesn't care about this place as much as his main place.

"Seems quiet," Lincoln breaks the silence.

"Yeah," is all I reply. We've been sitting here two hours, and no one has come or gone. "Let's go in," I add.

Before Lincoln can even respond a dark voice hits my ear, "Don't even fucking think about it, baby girl," Asher says into my earpiece and I roll my eyes.

"Ash, it's a fucking ghost town out here, we need to get in there and see if there is anything we can use."

"Have you lost your fucking mind? I am not going to willingly let you walk back into a den of fucking demons to be taken again, have you forgotten my father put a fucking bounty on your head?" he snaps at me.

"Donovan's right, we don't know what's in there," Lincoln adds coolly, although it looks like it pains him to agree with him. Fucking traitor.

"You're supposed to be on my side, remember, dickhead?" I respond.

"No, I am on the side that keeps you safe."

I huff and roll my eyes, "Well, considering Ash isn't here to stop me, and Zack pays you to keep me safe, I am going in whether you like it or not. You can either wait here or come with me," I don't wait for a response before I jump out of the SUV and start to make my way towards the warehouse. I hear both his and Asher's curses in my earpiece, followed by his door opening and closing quietly behind me.

I am being a bitch, but I don't care. I want to move forward with my revenge plans now more than ever. The quicker I am done with Donovan and his sick band of merry perverts, the quicker I can take Cassie and run from this town again, and this time never look back.

I draw the gun from my waist and don't have to try too hard to stay hidden when it's practically pitch black out. I wait until I get close, then I use a tree for cover while I wait for Lincoln. Once he reaches me, I nod towards the cameras on the outer warehouse and he nods in acknowledgement and pulls out his phone to run interference. I thank the gods every day for his and Zack's technical abilities. I mean I have learned a lot myself but having someone to take care of it for me is amazing.

"What's the plan here, King?" Linc whispers into the cool night air.

I look around checking again we are alone before answering, "The plan is to see what's in there and then I don't know," I shrug.

Lincoln does his own sweep of the property with his eyes before looking back at me, "Wanna blow it up?" he asks, and I smile at him. I knew there was a reason I kept him around.

"Don't fucking encourage her, Blackwell," Asher spits into our ears and Lincoln smiles at his tone, it makes me wonder something that I don't have time to think about right now.

Lincoln ignores him and pulls out his phone and taps away quickly before putting it away and I look at him in question, but he doesn't elaborate apart from saying, "Let's go."

I calm my breathing and take one last look at my surroundings before nodding at Linc and moving towards the warehouse.

Once I reach the entrance, I glance back at Linc and he signals that he is going to check around back, which is a good idea. Although it seems like no one is here, we don't want to be caught off guard. I open the door quietly and peek my head round and am greeted with a very poorly lit hallway. I slip inside and close the door behind me. I hold my gun tight by my side and stick close to the wall, as I move deeper into the hallway. I come to the first door and take a deep breath readying myself as I open it and step inside. Thankfully, it's empty but that doesn't make me feel any better, it's practically a mirror image of the room I was kept in. There is a dirty old mattress on the floor stained with blood and lord knows what else and a bucket in the corner. I take a deep breath and ignore the hundreds of images that are trying to force themselves into my brain. This is exactly the type of situation Zack prepared me for.

I leave the room as quietly as I entered and check four more, finding them the same but also empty. As I move towards a fifth, I hear a commotion further into the back of this place and know immediately that Lincoln has encountered someone. I rush to find him when I hear footsteps close by. Asher obviously hears the struggle and starts shouting down my earpiece, but I zone him out. I can't respond without giving away my position to whomever is almost upon me. So, I ignore him and push myself into the shadows as the guy enters the hallway, I see him pull out a cell phone and know it's now or never. I have to take him out before he calls for backup.

He doesn't even sense me until the last second, as he goes to pass me, he is so close he must have felt my breath but it's too late. When he turns towards me, I have already pulled the knife from my waist, forgoing my gun, in favor of a quiet kill. I quickly slice right across his neck, even with all the training I've had, I'm impressed. It's clean cut and perfectly deadly, forcing the life out of him in only seconds. He never stood a chance; the only downside is the blood spurt that has just sprayed all over me. I don't need a mirror to know I look like fucking Carrie right now. I catch his body as best I can even though he's heavy as fuck and slowly lower him to the floor. My only friend is stealth right now.

Asher's voice is still blaring in my ear when I quickly respond our prearranged safe word for everything's fine, "Donuts," I whisper into my wire and it calms him straight away as he mutters, "Fucking donuts," back to me and I smile. He was the one who insisted on having code words for situations like this, he wasn't impressed when I insisted on coming up with them. 'Donuts' for everything's cool and 'Crab Sticks' for a cry for help. It still amuses me now as I get to use one.

I move further into the building when footsteps start coming towards me, I pause before the corner and ready myself for another attack. As the figure rounds the corner, I dart my knife out but my arm is quickly slammed backwards to the wall.

"Fucking hell, King!" Lincoln shouts, before taking in my appearance, then he quickly looks over my shoulder at the dead body behind me before looking back to me, "You okay?"

"Didn't you hear her say fucking Donuts?" Asher snaps into our ear and we both laugh at him drawing more curses from him. I notice a little blood on Lincoln's cheek, it's nothing in comparison to me but it looks weird on his usual perfect appearance.

"You okay?" I return his question.

"Four threats neutralized," he responds like it's nothing to kill a man, let alone four. His eyes are a darker shade of green than I am used too, and I can practically see the tension rolling off of him.

I just nod before he continues, "We don't have much time before someone else might check in, so we need to be quick," he says quietly. "You check the rest of this hallway and I'll check the remaining rooms at the back," I nod more in response.

"Five minutes King," he adds before taking off into the darkness. I search the remaining rooms but find nothing but more fucking sex slave rooms. It fucking sickens me, how many there are, how many girls will have been here. I take that sickness and pour it into my vengeance. I will make every single one of these sick fucks regret the day they ever took a girl against their will.

As I make my way back towards the front entrance, Lincoln appears carrying a black duffel bag that definitely isn't ours. I don't bother asking questions now, we need to get out of here. We exit and make our way back into the trees when a whistle close by draws our attention, causing me to draw my gun in quick succession, only to be greeted by the last face I expected here.

"Pretty boy? What the fuck are you doing here?" I ask, taking a deep breath and trying not to think about the fact I almost just shot him in his pretty fucking face. I look to Lincoln and even in the dark I can tell by his face that this is his doing. Fuck's sake, what the hell is he playing at?

Asher's voice curses in my ear for what feels like the hundredth time tonight, I ignore him again. I swing my gaze back to Jace as he replies, "I came to blow shit up," he says holding up the two bags in his hands and I realize Linc called in him for this.

I turn back to Linc, "Really you brought him into this to blow shit up?" I say in annoyance.

Linc just shrugs, "Rebels have each other's back, you're one of us now, it was time." Ash fails to stay silent at that and mutters "Oh great, she's a Rebel now too, just fucking perfect," but Linc ignores him and continues to say, "You're part of the family and this is Jace territory, he's our pyro specialist," he says like it's nothing.

"Pyro maniac more like," I mutter under my breath thinking about how he blew up my jeep on the first day of school before raising my voice, "Fucking fine just be quick about it," I snap.

"Damn, princess, didn't think you could get any hotter than that throw down today, but this bad ass, covered in blood, psycho killer look is really working for me," he says with a wink.

"I'm not afraid to add your blood to the mix, Jace Conrad," I snap back in exasperation, but he just laughs offering us a mock salute, before disappearing into the night. Linc and I make our way back to his SUV and I cringe thinking about getting in there covered in this much blood. He must sense my thoughts because he leads me to the back of the car and pops his trunk. A little light inside illuminates us slightly better and he rifles through a bag pulling out some clothes.

He hands me a black shirt, "Wipe your face with this and then strip," he says casually.

"Strip?" I croak out as Jace reappears.

"What the fuck does he mean strip?" Ash roars into my ear and I cringe.

"Relax, Donovan, I'd much rather see you naked than King. She's covered in blood and I need to dispose of her clothes," Lincoln answers him smoothly.

"In your fucking dreams, Lincoln."

Linc is saved from answering when Jace cuts in, "Oooh, perfect timing," he says, wiggling his eyebrows at me.

"Fuck off," I respond but still feel myself pausing. I look at the two of them and then feel stupid. Lincoln is gay, and as much as Jace jokes, I know he doesn't actually look at me in that way, he is too loyal to Marcus for that.

I slip off my boots and my pants, followed by my shirt until I am standing in nothing but a black sports bra and black panties. I feel both their eyes on me, but I know, it's for one reason and one reason only, they can see my scars. The couple on my legs are artfully disguised by the dream catcher tattoo across my thigh, you wouldn't notice them unless you knew they were there. The ones on my stomach are a different story. Some are minor, they look like they are a faded scratch, but there are two prominent ones that are red and jagged. It's clear to anyone that sees them what they are and where they came from. Neither of them say anything as Lincoln passes me some sweats and a hoodie and I slip them on. As soon as I am covered, I feel less vulnerable, having my body on show doesn't make me feel vulnerable but people seeing my scars does.

Lincoln takes my clothes and places them in a trash bag, I know I can trust him to dispose of them properly. We all climb into Linc's SUV and still nobody says anything, if only it could have stayed that way.

"Was it Elliot or Greg?" Jace asks suddenly and I almost choke on my own breath.

"I'm sorry, what?" I stutter, the panic causes my voice to come out squeaky and high pitched.

I hear Asher mutter something in my ear, but I can barely concentrate on whatever he just said. My heart is beating too loud.

"The scars, Elle. Was it Elliot or Greg? Which one of them is Cassie's father? I'm guessing Greg," he says with no emotion, staring out from the back seat at the warehouse in the distance. I look to Linc in a panic, but he is just staring at Jace like he doesn't even know him, and I know he hasn't told him anything.

When I don't reply, mostly because I don't know how to, he continues, "I had a sister," he speaks softly, and I turn my focus on him. "She was two years older than me. She went missing when I was eleven," he pauses, looking at Lincoln and then back to me. "Greg Donovan raped and murdered her."

I am frozen in shock, I don't know how to respond but he pushes on, "I have been watching them for years, learning what I could, paying for information about them. You think I don't know who this warehouse belongs to? Whose blood that was on your clothes?" He looks at me closely and continues, "You came back to this town on a mission, I saw it in your eyes that day we met on the steps and every day since. You've been hurt, burned, and now you want your revenge. So, who was it, princess?"

I see the darkness in his eyes that I recognized the first day we met, the darkness he hides with smiles and flirty lines. He is beautiful but damaged, he needs all the family he can get, blood or not. I reach out and squeeze his hand in mine before I close my eyes and take a deep breath "Greg. It was Greg," I whisper in response to his earlier questions.

He just nods, having clearly already come to that conclusion, "I'm sorry I kept it from you," I add.

"We all have secrets and reasons for keeping them, Elle."

"Well, your secret is safe with me," I say with a tight smile.

He just shrugs before saying, "Everyone has their own demons. It's up to us, if we let them win," with that he presses a button on the device in his hand and the warehouse explodes with a loud bang. The flames look as high as the sky in the darkness of the woods and the orange glow lights up all our faces.

He is right, everyone has their own demons, and he shares his with me. Another damaged soul, another dead girl at the hands of Elliot Donovan, and his fucking rapist son. They may have won so many battles, but they won't fucking win the war.

Chapter 6

ELLE

Betrayal. It's a bitter feeling. It grips you in the pit of your stomach and twists until you are sick with it. And that's how I feel, sick. Sick and lost. The emptiness caused by Marcus' absence grows every day and sharing secrets with the remaining two Rebels only increases it. I am digging myself into a complicated hole that I fear I won't be able to drag myself out of and what's worse? I'm not sure I want to.

Marcus uncovering my biggest secret has pushed him even further away yet drawn his brothers closer than ever. Having them in my secret life makes me question whether I should have told Marcus the truth when he met Cassie. Should I have just ripped off the band aid and let my secrets bleed out? The reasons for keeping him in the dark don't even seem like reason enough anymore. Sure, Cassie is my biggest secret, my biggest weakness, but do I really believe that Marcus, my River, would do anything to put her safety in jeopardy if he knew the truth? I can't decide on that risk though unless he comes back.

Another week passes with no word from him and I can't help but worry. It's Monday again which means it has been just over two weeks since he found out about Cassie. Two weeks, it's nothing in hindsight, such a short insignificant amount of time. We went three years without seeing each other, yet somehow these two weeks seem like a lifetime. That's two weeks of him holding my life in his hands and he doesn't even realize it.

I am riding shotgun in the passenger seat of Linc's SUV. The three of us have taken to riding to and from school together every day. Seems they find it pretty pointless to drive separately now, I mean I never understood why they did anyway, not since I found out they fucking live together, stupid boys.

I am grumpy as shit thanks to stupid period cramps and I pray to the gods that while Jace grabs us some coffee, he also picks up snacks too. While we wait for him to get our stuff, I grill Lincoln on any update about Marcus.

"What do you mean he wasn't there?" I say in exasperation.

"Exactly what I just said, King. He wasn't there. That was the last safe house he could have been at and it was empty."

"Well, did it look like anyone had been staying there?" I push him.

"No, but this is Marcus we are talking about, he knows how to cover his tracks."

I groan, scrubbing my hand over my eyes, "That isn't helpful, Lincoln," but he just shrugs his shoulders.

"I'm trying everything, but he's smart, ditching the trackers and taking a bunch of cash is just the start, he knows how to keep a low profile."

"What if he doesn't come back?" I ask him, voicing my true fear aloud.

Linc looks over and sees the emotions that I know are showing on my face, he reaches out to squeeze my hand, "Then he's a fucking idiot."

I offer him a small smile and gently squeeze his hand back as Jace climbs back into the car, "Fuck, it was busy in there," he complains as he struggles inside with a bag and tray of drinks. He shuts the door and shuffles over to the middle seat in the back and pops his head between us.

He hands Lincoln something white and red that definitely doesn't look like a black coffee and then I know what's coming.

"For you, princess," he says, with a smile as he hands me an iced drink.

"Pretty boy, what the fuck is this?" I say snatching it from his hand.

He gleams with mock innocence, "It's an iced white mocha with toffee nut and almond milk."

"In what world did you think I would want this and not my Americano?" I fume at him but take a sip anyway and groan. Fuck that's good.

"Good right?" he preens at me with glee and I curse in my head.

"Fine yes, it's fucking delicious," I say in exasperation, "But I am holding you responsible when I fall asleep during Mr. Keating's class later."

He just laughs and thrusts a little bag at me and when I look inside, I find muffins and cookies which I immediately reach for.

"Forgiven?" he says, wiggling his brows.

"Always, pretty boy," I say, around a mouthful of a blueberry muffin.

"I knew you couldn't stay mad at this face," he says, picking up his own cup housing lord knows what.

"Do I even wanna know what yours is?" I ask him.

"Mines a double chocolaty chip Frappuccino, you know for my sweet tooth." He flashes a flirty smile at me, and I reach out and turn his cup towards him, showcasing the phone number of the side.

"Is that the smile you gave to get this?" I roll my eyes.

He looks down noticing what I am referring to and smiles. "What can I say, the ladies go wild for me," he replies, and I scoff in fake disgust.

We continue back and forth, laughing and joking, and it feels good to have this sort of friendship again. The kind I had with Asher and Marcus before that fateful night. It feels nice, normal, and completely comforting. We pull into the parking lot at the school and Lincoln finds his usual space. I'm still teasing Jace about his coffee girl, when we hit the parking spot and out of nowhere. He chokes on his drink, spits some out, and some lands on my pants.

"Jesus, pretty boy," I hiss, "These are my favorite jeans." I scold him, until I see he is paying me zero attention. I follow his gaze to see what's distracted him, only to be met with the last sight I expected.

There, in all his South Side glory, is Marcus Riviera waiting on the front steps. The King overlooking his court, awaiting his knights. Except the spot usually saved for a Queen is currently occupied. WHAT THE FUCK?

I can feel Lincoln's eyes on me, but I ignore him in favor of Marcus who is looking right at me, like he doesn't have a care in the world. That insufferable tug of a smirk pulling at his stupid kissable lips.

"Has he lost his fucking mind?" Jace voices my thoughts. "What the fuck is he doing?" He adds.

I unclick my seatbelt and reach to open the door, "Let's go find out," I say through gritted teeth, trying hard to keep my smile in place.

I climb out of the car without waiting for their response, slamming my door and theirs soon follow suit. I have no idea where Marcus has been or what he is playing at, coming back unannounced, and not alone but I'm about to find out.

With Jace and Linc flanking me on either side, we walk over to him together.

"River," I nod at him, as the guys reach out their fists and Marcus hits them both, like he hasn't been AWOL for two fucking weeks, and this is just a normal Monday. There may be cracks in their relationship right now, but they are smart enough to know to leave that behind closed doors. When they are in the public eye, they show a united front, it's admirable.

I ignore the girl pawing at his chest and keep my stare on his eyes, trying to decipher the look I see there. I look for any indication to how he might be feeling towards me, but it's like I am no one to him.

"Ells," he nods back casually, like this is our normal everyday greeting.

"Where have you been, brother?" Lincoln questions, but Marcus doesn't break my stare, when he responds, "Just around."

"But you're back now?" Jace asks looking between the two of us, all of us actively ignoring the girl he's got his arm slung around.

"Obviously," Marcus drawls out.

I need to cut the shit, "Marcus can we talk a sec?" I ask, then look pointedly at his guest before adding, "Alone."

"Anything you have to say to me, you can say in front of Cherry," he says with a preening grin like he is enjoying having the upper hand.

Cherry. Did he just say fucking Cherry? Is he shitting me right now? He really wants to play these games with a girl who has a fucking pornstar name.

I scoff in a way which I am sure highlights my distaste perfectly, "I highly doubt she could keep up," I say, putting emphasis on the word highly and both Lincoln and Jace grunt a laugh.

But Marcus isn't fazed, "Oh, you have no idea how good her stamina is, little traitor," he smirks with a wink and she giggles.

Gag. I don't know what's worse, the fact he is doing this, or the fact I am actually fucking jealous of the stupid bitch. Fucking Cherry. Wonder if her blood is as red as I'm imagining. Maybe I'll make her bleed and find out. I imagine four different ways to gut her insides before I do what I do best and slam it down deep inside me and smile.

"Oh, I'm sure I can imagine," I say, with as much friendliness as I can muster.

I turn my attention to her for the first time. She is quite pretty. I'll give her that, I mean, of course she is to land a place on Marcus' arm, but she is ruining it with the caked makeup piled on her face. She's got blonde hair with a yellow tint that only comes from cheap hair dye and is wearing a skin-tight dress like this isn't fucking October.

"Do you charge by the hour, Cherry? If so, how much for some privacy?" I ask sweetly.

She giggles and it's the most irritating sound in the world, "I don't get it," she says, like being dumb is sexy. I huff, "No, you really don't," I huff with a humorless laugh before concentrating back on Marcus "So, this is how it's gonna be then?" I ask him.

"I don't know what you mean," he says with a smug smile like he knows how much this is getting to me. Curse this prick to the fiery pits of hell and his fucking bimbo too.

"This is how you're playing things," I confirm.

"You'd know all about games wouldn't you, Elle?" He snaps back, losing a bit of his cool and I smile my first genuine smile. Oh, he wants to fucking play.

"Game on, River," I give him my best game face and push past them both and enter the school.

Lincoln is the first to catch up with me and I don't even let him speak before I whip round and get in his face, "I want everything on her, Superman, fucking everything. I wanna know where she eats, where she sleeps, where she fucking works, everything."

He just nods, accepting my crazy, and already tapping away on his tablet. I know I'm being irrational but fuck it I don't care. How dare he! How dare he fucking disappear after finding out my biggest secret and then have the audacity to rock back up to school like it's just a regular Monday, with a slut by his side no less. I mean she could be Virgin fucking Mary for all I know but my irrational period brain has taken over and she gives zero fucks.

Marcus Riviera is a fucking asshole. A stupid, sexy, dumb as fuck, fucking asshole!

Well, if this is how he wants to play it then so be it, as long as he keeps what he knows to himself then he can do whatever the fuck he wants. I mean, this is what I always wanted, right? To push him far enough away that he finds happiness with someone who isn't me. So why don't I feel happy right now?

Chapter 7

ELLE

I suffer through the rest of the morning watching her paw at him during all the classes we share, and I swear to all the gods, I deserve a fucking medal for not spilling blood. That doesn't mean I didn't conjure up several creative ways I could gut them both and make their bodies disappear. Fuck, I have never felt so stabby! I don't do this. This stupid high school bullshit of being jealous of a girl who is with the guy I like, is fucked up, so why the fuck can't I stop?

I think I am doing well until lunchtime arrives and I make my way to the cafeteria and find her perched on his lap at the Rebels' usual table. I grind my teeth so hard; I don't know how they haven't cracked in my mouth. Oh, I really want to make someone hurt right now. Surely if I've got to bleed today it's only fair that someone else should too. Is it rational to kill someone for touching the boy you love, even though he hates you? Would I get away with it with so many witnesses? Can homicide by hormones be my plea?

No, now I am definitely being irrational. I can't kill her. *Yet.*

I feel the presence of the two Rebels, who aren't pissing me off, by my side and suddenly feel a little more ready to sit at the table with him. It's funny how the two Rebels I didn't know before coming back here are the ones giving me strength now. It hits me then how much I care about them already. Fuck. I have spent so much time concentrating on keeping Marcus in the dark that I didn't stop them from sneaking through my defense until I knew I would bleed for them too.

"I have what you asked for," Linc says, cutting into my thoughts.

"And?" I reply, desperate for him to tell me anything that would make killing her acceptable. Just any fucking dark mark against her and I won't hesitate.

"Cherry Daniels, seventeen, lives with her Mom in a trailer, barely scraping by in all her classes, works nights at the gas station over on Evergreen, has a younger sister named Daisy."

"Any red flags," I plead with hope, but he shakes his head. Fuck, nothing warranting her death apart from the fact her hands haven't left Marcus' body all morning. Which, if you ask me, is a valid fucking reason all on it's own.

"This is bullshit," Jace cuts in.

"How so?" I wonder out loud, as Marcus glowers at me with a fucking smirk on his arrogant perfect face.

"Come on, princess, use your eyes," he says, leaning in close to me. "See, how he isn't touching her?"

"She's sitting in his fucking lap, Jace," I snap back angrily, struggling to hold onto my temper.

"Yeah, she is, but look at his hands, they're nowhere near her. He isn't burning a stare into her head right now," he says, as he comes in closer to my side putting his hand on my shoulder.

He's right. Marcus isn't touching her. She's in his lap, stroking her hand up and down his chest but his hands aren't on her. One hangs down by his side and the other grips the table and his eyes are solely focused on me.

"That could mean anything," I say weakly.

"Care to test that theory, princess?" Jace replies with a gleeful tone.

"What do you mean?" I ask, turning to focus on him and without warning he pulls me close and tucks my hair behind my ear. My eyes shoot wide in panic until Marcus' voice booms across the cafeteria before I can even take another breath.

"Hurry up and sit down," he shouts, sounding pissed.

Jace smirks at me and I can't help but return it.

"Hear that tone, princess? I can feel his jaw tensing from all the way over here and all I did was touch your hair," he laughs, as he puts his arm fully around my shoulders and starts towards the table, "Come on, this is gonna be fun."

We approach the table slowly; I feel every eye on us as we take our seats. I choose the seat directly across from Marcus and both Jace and Lincoln forego the chairs next to him and sit on either side of me instead. It feels like a bold statement.

Marcus snorts a laugh, “Asher not enough for you, you had to take Jace too? You already got your claws into one of my brothers, now, you’ve got both I see,” he says, cocking his head to the side like he is trying to assess the new dynamic here. Good fucking luck with that, I have barely worked it out myself.

“You’re the one who left us without a word, Marcus,” I say trying to stay calm while also imagining breaking every one of Cherry’s fingers. She is still lazily dragging her fingertips up and down his torso and I squash down the feeling of snapping each one.

“Oh, and you’d know all about leaving, wouldn’t you?” he replies with a smirk “I just took a page from the Elle King playbook.”

“You're being ridiculous,” I say in exasperation, as I rub circles on the ever-increasing pounding in my temples.

“You three are the ones acting all cosy,” he snaps, finally losing a bit of his cool.

“Because we are *friends*,” I sound out the words slowly to insinuate how dumb he is being before adding, “And that's really rich considering you are practically getting a fucking lap dance from little miss porno here,” I grit back.

“It’s Cherry,” the girl in question pipes up, like the worst thing I just did was not get her name right. I am not usually one for tearing into other girls but right now I am too mad to care about female solidarity.

“I literally couldn't care less,” I snap back at her.

But before she can even defend herself Marcus cuts in, “She’s hardly a pornstar, just because you opened your legs at fourteen doesn't mean everyone else does!"

Bang. His words hit me like a fucking gun shot as they smack me right in the gut. I feel both the guys tense next to me at his words, but I feel nothing. I stand up so quick, my chair falls backwards and the clang of it hitting the floor halts the entire cafeteria, until every eye is on us.

"I'm done," I say simply, I can't sit here and play nice with him, not if he is going to spout shit like that. Anyone else would receive a knife in the fucking crotch for those kinds of comments. One more word like that and he will be lucky if he's even got a dick to get up for fucking Cherry here. I am ready to get fucking stabby.

"Well, that was easier than you are," he replies smugly.

Before I can even respond Jace jumps out of his seat and drags Marcus across the table by the collar of his jacket.

Unphased by him Marcus adds, "Woah, King, that pussy must really be good, if it can get a reaction from our resident playboy here," a devilish smirk curving his lips. The punch is so fast I barely see it coming, Marcus definitely didn't. The force of it causes his head to swing to the side and blood to spit out of his mouth.

"You can be a real fucking asshole, Marcus," Jace seethes at him but Marcus just laughs and that's when it hits me.

I bend down getting close enough to smell his breath, "Are you drunk?" I ask him in a low tone so only me and the guys can hear.

"None of your fucking business," he spits back at me, only enhancing the whiskey on his breath. Fuck. I huff out a breath as I stand and look to Lincoln, "Take him home, he needs to rest."

Lincoln nods and leans down to help him up, ignoring Marcus' attempts to push him away as he mutters traitor under his breath. Once he is on his feet, he goes to lead him away when Jace stops him with a firm grip on his arm.

"One day, you will learn what that was for and you'll wish I would have done worse to you," he says, through gritted teeth before he looks at me and nods as he walks away.

I watch as they leave with Cherry running after them. Fuck this Monday!

Chapter 8

JACE

The rage I feel is something I haven't felt in a while but fuck if I am not burning with it right now. Never in all the years since we met, have I ever wanted to hurt one of my brothers until just now. We aren't brothers by blood but by choice. Our connection runs on a deeper level. We can communicate without words. Always on the same page, same wave, same team. Until now.

Marcus and Lincoln saved me from myself. After my sister was raped and murdered by that fucking scum of the earth, Donovan, I was spiralling. Drinking and doing more drugs than any child should, but they came along and gave me what I was missing: a family.

Losing Rachel left a hole in my heart that can never be filled, but with Elle around, well damn, if I don't feel a little better. Yeah, she's fucking beautiful but it's not her face that draws you in, it's everything. Her heart, her presence, her fucking badass nature. She has been through shit that no one should have to endure and come out stronger on the other side. Just thinking about what she has gone through and survived makes me want to bleed for her. I know she won't replace my sister but having her around gives me something to live for again. I want to help her get her revenge on them all until there isn't a threat left that could hurt her or Cassie. She is the perfect missing piece for our little fucked up family and I can easily see the love between her and Marcus.

How Marcus doesn't see it, blows my mind. Her heart and soul fucking beats for him yet he is too fucking stubborn to accept it. I get it, I do, what he thinks he knows and how he found out, he must be losing his mind. But how does he not want to dig deeper and see the bigger picture here?

He is so fucking dumb, the way she looks at him, a lesser man would kill for that. That kind of love and adoration, a love that is so fierce, she is willing to push it away to keep it intact. He is too busy worrying about little Donovan to see what is right in front of him. Pure unconditional love. The kind that only comes around once in a lifetime, if you're lucky.

I stalk from the cafeteria on the lookout for something, anything, that can kill this rage inside me. I head to Elle's safe haven on the bleachers and spark up a joint. Weed is the only drug I allow to course through my veins these days. I take a few drags and am grateful when the effects start to calm my body. I pull out my phone and start scrolling through social media to distract myself.

It isn't long before I find the perfect one I'm looking for. Taylor Kennedy looking fine as fuck in her Hallows Prep uniform. She has posted a picture where someone has caught her off guard and she is laughing, her lips full and luscious, the sun framing her perfectly. Damn, if that girl doesn't turn me into a walking hard on. Her defiant green eyes stare back at me and I just imagine what it would be like to see those eyes looking up at me, as she took my cock in her mouth. Damn.

"Pretty boy, if you're gonna start jerking off, I will stab you," Elle's voice cuts into my perving and I smile, looking down at her as she climbs the steps to the top of the bleachers.

"What makes you think I'm gonna be jerking off up here?" I reply with glee.

She snorts, "Please. I know you well enough by now to know that pervy look in your eye," she says, getting closer before trying to peek at my phone, "Who's your next target anyway?"

I click my phone shut before she can see I was lusting after her only friend, "No one important, princess," I say with my usual jokey attitude and she frowns.

"That's just sad," she replies, like she feels sorry for me which is laughable. What is there to feel sorry for? I am an eighteen-year-old male who is getting more pussy than most guys will see in a lifetime.

"What? So, should I fall in love and watch them with someone else instead?"

"Ouch. Harsh, pretty boy," she throws herself down beside me and leans her head on my shoulder.

"You know I'm only teasing," I say, putting my head on hers and it feels exactly how I used to do it with Rachel. We sit in comfortable silence knowing words are pointless right now. We are both upset and pissed off with Marcus and talking about it won't change that. He is going to need to sort this one out himself.

The bell rings but neither of us move and I can feel the tension still pulsing out of her and I can no longer bear it. I sit up and she jumps at my quick movement and looks at me with a slight frown, so I just hold out my hand for her to take.

"Come on, let's go," I say with determination.

"Where to?" she asks but takes my hand anyway and I love that she is putting her trust in me. Fuck knows what I did to deserve it but I don't question it either way. She is exactly like Rachel in that sense, it's probably what dealt them both the shitty hand of Greg Donovan.

"We are ditching, you need cheering up, and I need chilling out," I say simply, and she just shrugs and follows me down the bleachers. It isn't until we reach the parking lot that I realize Lincoln took our only mode of transportation, fuck.

Elle isn't fazed though she just laughs and pulls out her phone and dials someone.

"Hey, I need a ride home now, can you come get me? You're the best, see you soon."

"Who the hell was that?"

"Ash," she says simply. Oh great, we are inviting the little psycho to join us. Perfect. "And why did you presume we were just going to your house".

She laughs loudly before catching her breath enough to reply, "Oh please, pretty boy, don't think I haven't realized that the number one girl in your life right now still needs parental supervision for everything," she says, with a smile and I smile back.

Damn it, she caught me. Of course, I was suggesting we go to hers and see Cassie, that little girl has me wrapped around her finger already just like her mommy. It feels good to be around girls again in a family sense and not just for mindless fucking.

"What?" I say with a shrug, "Can you blame me?"

"Of course not. She's perfect," she says with a huge smile and it's only ever that big when she is talking about her daughter. I smile back because it really is infectious.

We don't wait long before Asher Donovan pulls up in a blacked-out car and jumps out to open the passenger door for Elle.

He nods at me with a grimace, "Conrad."

"He's coming too," Elle says before she gets in and the look on his face is funny as fuck, he really does hate us Rebels. I flip him off before I jump into the back seat and spread out like I own it and his face is still set in a grimace when he climbs back behind the wheel. I offer him my smuggest smile when we lock eyes in the mirror.

On the drive back to the house, Elle fills him in on everything that went down this morning. He looks as murderous as always which for some reason just makes me laugh. By the time we arrive, my excitement at seeing mini-Elle has increased tenfold. What can I say, there's just something really enchanting about seeing the world through the eyes of a child.

It's just another thing I don't understand about Marcus. How did he just walk away so easily, without falling in love with the little version of his best friend. I can't help but feel sorry for him, no matter how fucking angry I am at him right now. Because when he finds out the truth, and he will, I know him well enough to know that. He is going to hate everyone but no one more than himself.

"He's a fucking idiot," Donovan says as we pull up to Elle's house.

"For once we agree on something, Donovan," I say with a smile and then flip him off one more time before climbing out ignoring his chastising of Elle about hanging around Rebels too much.

Elle just laughs him off as she climbs from the car and heads for the door and lets us in. We follow her through the giant hallway and into the main living area. I have been here more than a few times now and still I am astounded by the amount of wealth here.

I have more than I ever imagined I could, now, in terms of a home, cars, and stuff, but I am still not used to it. I'm not like Marcus, I didn't grow up with any sort of wealth. I barely lived hand to mouth as a child and Rachel and I suffered together. Our parents were a pair of crackheads, who were more concerned with their next high than their children's wellbeing. So, standing in a house worth millions, that is just something I don't think I will ever get used to.

It's the same feeling every time we get paid by Zack. Don't get me wrong, I love all the illegal money we have coming in under the table too, but something about that legitimate payment hitting a real bank account does something to me inside. Makes me proud to know I can afford more than basic necessities now. I wish Rachel were still alive to experience it with me.

We find Helen sitting on the sofa reading to Cassie and they both look up and smile as we enter.

"Mommyyyyy!" Cassie squeals as she struggles to rush off the sofa to run to Elle. When she dives into her arms it hits me in the heart every time. This is what a mother should be like: loving, attentive, and willing to burn the world to the ground for their children. I see that in both Elle and Helen. I only wish I could have been as lucky to have someone like them as a parent instead of the shitty hand I was dealt.

Helen immediately starts fussing over us asking if we need anything, offering us snacks, and drinks. I can't help but feel happy about it. She is no relation to me; she barely even knows me but the way she mothers over me makes my heart light and happy. A feeling I am becoming accustomed to for the first time ever.

Cassie turns to Donovan next and I swear it's the only time the ice around his cold, dead heart thaws. For her and only her. Okay, maybe Elle too, but mostly Cassie. I wish I could say I didn't understand him, that I didn't relate to his psychotic nature, but I do. Knowing what happened to Rachel, what his brother did to her fills me with a rage I can't even describe. So, to be in his shoes and have witnessed the aftermath with Elle, got her out of there, only to find out they had left her pregnant. I can't even imagine how psychotic that would make me.

I see it on his face every time I look at him. That rage, that pure unfiltered murderous look that tells me he will level this fucking city for these two and not have one single regret. How he holds onto that level of anger and doesn't plant a bullet in the skull of his father and brother every day he sees them is beyond me. But he does and it's all for them, kind of hard to keep a hatred towards him.

Cassie finally looks to me and in an instant all my anger and rage from the day disappears when she screeches my name.

"Jaceeeeee!" She shouts as she clambers down from Asher's arms.

She bundles her arms around my legs, and I reach down, lifting her up into the air and throwing her above my head while her giggles filter through the air.

"Careful!" Asher snipes at me and I just laugh causing him to curse under his breath.

I ignore him in favor of Cassie as I bring her down and ruffle her hair, "How's my favorite little lady?"

"Happy!" she shouts excitedly and makes me smile wider as I look at Elle, Helen, and even Asher as they all share the same smiling expression at her words.

"Well, we can't ask for better than that, can we, mini?"

Chapter 9

MARCUS

I wake to water being dumped onto my head and jump up to find Jace leering down at me.

"Time for school, asshole," he says, with a scoff as he steps over me and my eyes follow him to find Lincoln looking at me with distaste too. He just shakes his head and they both disappear into the garage and it isn't long before I hear the rumble of an engine as it takes off. I guess it's time to get up. I stand with a grumble trying to ignore the pounding in my head. I lost track of how much I drank yesterday, hell, how much I drank in the last two weeks. The only answer I know, is a fucking lot. I ignore my soaked t-shirt and head straight into the kitchen for coffee and aspirin, my only salvation right now, and feel the buzz of my phone in my pocket. I ignore it in favor of the coffee and then head to take a shower.

Looking in the mirror I see a reflection I barely recognize. Looking back at me isn't the man I am used to, the leader of the Rebels, the King of the South Side. No, the only thing I see is a broken, betrayed boy. I haven't shaved since Elle ripped out my heart and stomped on it, so I'm rocking an unusual amount of stubble.

I grimace at the sight. Everything hurts. My head, my back, my fucking heart. I put up a good defense yesterday, but I would be lying if I said I still wasn't hurting like fuck over everything that happened.

I thought leaving town when Elle dropped the bomb of Cassie on me was the perfect solution. I still can't believe it, Elle King is a mom and not only is she a mom but her kid's dad is none other than Asher fucking Donovan. Fuck, just thinking about them together makes my skin burn with jealously. However, disappearing didn't work, out of sight but definitely not out of mind. She was all I could fucking think about.

I came back to town with every intention of acting like she meant nothing to me. I rocked up to school with my pride back in place and a girl on my arm, yet it still didn't deter my little King. No, instead of being deterred, she fought back with that smart mouth and what I hope was a fucking joke with Jace. If not, I think I might murder my own fucking brother. Watching him touch her should not make me feel the way it did. I am fucking done with her. She is, what I thought she always was, a liar and a traitor.

I shower quickly and throw on some clothes and grab my jacket off the floor on my way out, opting for my bike. My phone buzzes again as I go to swing my leg over and I remember I still haven't checked it. I pull it out and see numerous texts all from the same person. Cherry.

CHERRY: Can't wait to see you baby!
CHERRY: What are you doing?

CHERRY: Wanna come over?
CHERRY: Are you picking me up?
CHERRY: I'll guess I'll see you at school

Fuck me. I knew picking a girl to show Elle I don't need her wasn't really my best idea, but fucking hell. I didn't think about how this would pan out. Now not only am I dealing with Elle and her lies, but also a clingy fucking girl, who thinks she has finally locked down a fucking Rebel. Things are just going from bad to worse, but can I really back down now? I saw the way Elle looked at her yesterday, how her hand would flinch to reach for her knife every time Cherry's hand stroked down my chest. I shouldn't have enjoyed it, but I did.

I could tell she wanted her gone, but if she is going to play games with Jace, then I need a partner to go toe to toe with her. Who is a better candidate than Cherry? Honestly, probably fucking anyone but it's too late now. I pocket my phone and get on my bike and head to what I am sure is going to be another fucking awful day. My little King wants a war. She'll get one.

It isn't long before I get to school and am both exasperated and excited at finding Cherry there waiting for me. I don't want to use her like this, but I don't have a choice. She thinks she has a chance with me, but I can't even touch her without feeling like I am betraying Elle in some way. After what she has done, how fucked up is that?

I think about ignoring her until later, but then I spy Elle sitting on the hood of Linc's SUV, with both Lincoln and Jace by her side. Seeing my brothers flank her like this would have made me happy before, now it just pisses me the fuck off. So, I do what any self-respecting, scorned male would do, I act like I don't fucking care.

Cherry only sweetens things when she sees me and runs at me as she shouts, "Baby!" before throwing herself at me until her body is flush against mine. I will for my body to react, to have even a flicker of a fucking erection to anyone that isn't Elle but nothing, nada. I am starting to think he is the biggest traitor of all. What kind of dick only gets hard for a fucking liar?

I shutdown my thoughts and begrudgingly put my arms around Cherry, at the same time I lock eyes with Elle. She looks murderous. I shouldn't be giddy about that but I am. That feeling lasts all of two seconds when I see Elle go to slide off the trunk and Jace grips her thigh to keep her in place while speaking closely to her so only they can hear. *Oh fuck no.*

I grip Cherry to my side and storm over to them before I can even think about it.

Jace cuts in before I can even speak with a sarcastic tone, "Morning, brother," he says with a smile. For the first time ever, the word brother sounds like an insult instead of an endearment and I fucking hate it. This isn't us, this is not what we do.

Before I can even respond he turns his attention to Cherry and continues, "And good morning to you too, Miss Daniels. So nice that Marcus here has finally got himself a girlfriend," He says with a smugly sweet smile aimed at me.

He gets his intended reaction when Cherry squeals loudly, "I know! I just can't believe how lucky I am that he finally noticed me."

The way she says finally has me swinging my gaze her way considering two days ago I had no idea who she was. I don't have time to think about it any longer before Jace continues on, "Yeah, love really is in the air round here," he replies to her as he swings his arm around Elle. "Isn't that right, princess?"

Elle is staring at me intently, like she is willing me to stop these childish games and just talk to her, but we are too far gone for that. We aren't Ells and River anymore, we stopped being them when she started piling on the secrets and lies. There is no going back to how things were before, there is just before and after. Now, we exist only in the after. I do my best to ignore the obvious attempt to rile me up, but Cherry doesn't help things.

"Oh wow, you two make a gorgeous couple!" She says complimenting them like she didn't get called a pornstar by Elle, just yesterday.

"Yep," Jace says, popping the P obnoxiously. "I saw what was right in front of me and snatched it up," he adds as he glares at me and I snort.

"Good luck keeping hold of her, liars get bored easily," I respond with a smug smile and she frowns before schooling her expression and locking her eyes on Cherry who just scoffed in outrage at my statement.

"Excuse him, Cherry, he's forgotten the manners I know his father taught him," she says with a sickly-sweet smile and I tense at the mention of my dad. Oh, is she really going there?

"Well, only you know why he isn't around to keep me in check, little King," I bark back at her and I see her tense from here before she lets out a low breath and looks to my brothers.

Ignoring me, she speaks to them, "Come on, let's go to class," she says before sliding off the hood and barging past me and ending our verbal sparring. I try not to feel the pang in my chest as she walks away from me but it's there, just like it always is. I turn back to my brothers who look at me with disappointment in their eyes. It just confuses the fuck out of me, but I don't have time to decipher it before they leave to follow after her.

I don't know what stings more, watching her walk away from me or watching my brothers go with her. I don't know when it happened but it's here right in front of me, I wanted a Queen and now my brothers have got one. I always knew she could be, but I guess I was wrong about who her King would be.

Cherry cuts into my thoughts as her hands slide up my chest and it takes everything in me to suppress a flinch.

"Wanna skip class? I bet I could think of something more fun to do," she says, smiling up at me, in what I am sure is her best seductive smile, but it does nothing for me.

I don't hesitate before I shake out of her embrace and turn to follow after my lying Queen. "Rain check, Cherry," I throw over my shoulder without looking back at her.

The only thing on my mind is getting to the bottom of whatever is going on with Jace and Elle. As if thinking about her and Donovan wasn't fucking bad enough. I stalk after them pushing people out of my way as I go and giving zero fucks about any of them. Now is not the time to be dealing with any bottom feeders vying for attention. No, the only person getting my attention today is my beautiful, little liar.

I am going to watch every move she makes until I uncover the rest of her secrets. If she can lie about having a child and a relationship with Asher fucking Donovan, then I'm sure there are plenty more truths that need to be uncovered.

I watch her, them. Taking note of every movement and filing it away. Lincoln is his usual serious self, and he looks like he is talking to them both sternly about something and Elle is growling at him while Jace just laughs. Lincoln shakes his head before giving Elle's shoulder a little squeeze and heading off to class.

Jace stays behind and whatever he is saying has Elle laughing. It makes me want to paint these shitty hallways with his fucking blood. She grabs books from her locker and nods her head my way indicating where her class is. Before she turns to leave, Jace locks eyes with me over her shoulder and pulls her into a hug with a smug smile on his face before dropping a kiss to her head and turning to leave.

Elle watches him for a couple of seconds before turning my way, her smile from Jace still lingering on her lips. A smile she used to save for only me. She doesn't notice me at first even though the hallways are emptying quickly. I use that to my advantage and fall in with a group of people heading the same way as her. As we get to a set of double doors, some freshman stops to keep the door open for her and she flashes him that same smile and I can no longer take it.

"Spread your legs for him too?" I snap and the freshman looks at Elle apologetically before scrambling away. Pussy.

She takes a deep breath before answering me, "What do you want, Marcus?"

Oh, so we are back to Marcus now. "I want you out of my school, Elle," I reply with as much emphasis on her name as possible.

"Well, that isn't happening. Anything else I can help you with?" she snarks back at me.

"I don't know. What's the going rate for North bred whores these days?" and she flinches at the word whore. I feel a bit like an asshole, but then I remember how she broke my heart and I squash those feelings down quick.

"Call me a whore one more time and you will regret it. I promise you," she says slowly through gritted teeth.

I mock a laugh, "Is that a pinky promise?" I say holding out my pinky finger to her.

Her eyes don't leave mine as she reaches out and snaps my finger back quicker than I can pull it away. I feel the snap but don't allow her the reaction of my pain. I smile gleefully as I grab her and push her back against the wall ignoring the pain as I curl my fingers around her arms to hold her in place.

"Remember when you said you were already broken, little King?" I whisper leaning in close, so my words are delivered right against her ear. I feel her skin break out in goosebumps beneath me "Well, I'm gonna test that theory."

"Come for me or my family and you won't live to see another day, Marcus," she replies coolly, and I don't miss the undertone of the threat.

"You're dumber than I thought if you think I'm scared of Asher Donovan," I snap back at her, losing some of my cool.

Before I can even feel her move, she has my arms gripped in hers and has flipped me around and pushed my face against the glass of the doors with her trusty knife at my throat. Fuck that shouldn't be hot, but it is. The fact she has just handled my six-foot two body into submission without even breaking a sweat is impressive.

"All the men in this town really need to fucking learn that I am the real threat around here," she spits through gritted teeth. "Last warning, Marcus. You're either with me or against me."

"And if I'm against you?" I ask trying to ignore the raging hard on I am now sporting.

She releases me and steps back allowing me to turn around and take her in from head to toe. The look on her face is completely murderous and sexy.

"Then prepare to fucking lose," she says before she turns and leaves me alone in the hallway staring after her.

Chapter 10

ELLE

This week is a fucking shit show. The fact I haven't spilled blood in Hallows High's fucking hallways is a miracle within itself. I have been towing the line between calm and chaos all week. The only time I allowed myself to slip was when I broke Marcus' finger on Tuesday. Not my best reaction in hindsight, but he's lucky that's all he walked away with. Now I know what it feels like to stab a guy in the dick, the urge to do it again is strong. You'd think the love I have for him would make dealing with him easy, but in fact it's the opposite. What is it they say about a woman scorned?

Everywhere I turn, I have to suffer through watching Marcus with his fucking girlfriend. At least that's what everyone is calling her. Every time I hear it, I imagine different ways to murder her. Not like any of this is her fault, my rage is firmly directed at Marcus, but of course the gods cursed me to love him too much to hurt him. What kind of sick sense of humor do they have? Pair that with the fact that Jace has entangled me in some sort of fake boyfriend situation with him and it's safe to say I am going fucking stir crazy.

After I threatened Marcus the other day, he has been hellbent on being in my line of sight any chance he fucking gets. I am growing more than tired of it. Thank fuck it's Friday because having to endure your period and high school bullshit is definitely some new sick kind of torture, that I don't enjoy.

I choose to forgo the cafeteria for lunch. If I have to suffer through one more day where Marcus gets a fucking lunch time lap dance, I might just fork my own fucking eyeballs out. Thankfully, the guys understand my need to flee and have agreed to ditch the rest of the day with me, in favor of hanging out at home. We are going out tonight, so it gives us time to put some plans in place.

Cooking up revenge plans is still at the forefront of everything, and there has been a lot of shit going on since we blew up Elliot's warehouse. We have noticed an increase in his men poking around the South Side asking questions. We have been keeping a low profile, aka not killing anyone else, while still doing required recon work. Being patient is shitty as fuck, when all I want to do is bleed out every fucking rapist I come across, but we have to think of the bigger picture.

Tonight, we are hitting the old warehouse on Riverside again for another party. We have a little business, but the outing is mostly for pleasure. Apparently, Jace thinks I need to 'chill', like it isn't his fault I am so on edge. The little show he has been putting on for Marcus all week has me worried that he might slit his throat in his sleep, I mean it's not like they don't share the same house. When I said this to Jace, he just burst out laughing and told me that I still don't know anything. Whatever the fuck that means.

I told the guys that they are welcome to join me at home, but that I will be getting ready at Taylor's. I have endured far too much testosterone this week and I need some girl time, thankfully they agreed.

Asher will also be joining us tonight, I hope, I have barely seen him this week which in part is my fault, I guess. His father has all their men on a tight leash after the unfortunate fire and that includes bringing Ash to heel as well. I would gut Elliot just for the way he treats his son.

The house is quiet when we arrive. It's Friday afternoon so Zack is at the office and Cass has gone with Helen and Arthur to visit the twins again. I make a mental note to plan to tag along with them soon. It's been a couple of months since I have seen them and I'm starting to miss the two of them.

The guys follow me inside and up to my room, they aren't strangers here anymore, and it's nice to see how comfortable they are around me and my home. I guess it's nice for me too. This is what I crave with Marcus, this easy friendship where we can just hang out like old times. It hurts my chest when I think about how we will never have that again.

Lincoln takes a seat at my desk as usual while Jace just dives onto the bed, into my mountain of pillows. "Damnnnn, princess. I will never get used to how comfy your bed is," he says in appreciation.

I pick one of the pillows that he has knocked to the floor up and throw it at him, “You won’t be spending enough time in my bed to get used to it, pretty boy.”
He clutches his chest, “You wound me,” he says with a smile. I roll my eyes at him as I climb onto it and lie next to him.

It’s funny, when I came back to this town, the only person I was comfortable with having in my room was my family, yet here I am with two of the South Side's most dangerous guys, and I feel nothing but content.

“So, what's the plan tonight?” Lincoln asks, breaking into my thoughts.

I shrug and then sit up onto my elbows so I can look at him, “Not much, superman. Ash says Elliot is still out for blood for what we did, so we keep a low profile for now.”

Jace snorts, “Yeah like the low life prick ever keeps a low profile,” he says through gritted teeth showing a rare side of himself.

Now that I know about what happened to his sister Rachel, everything about Jace Conrad makes a lot more sense, the jokes, the joints, the girls. All of it is an attempt to block out losing the only family he had. I get it. I know what she went through, but I live to deal with it. If it weren’t for Cassie, Ash, Zack, and the rest of my family, I would have joined her in death at my own hands.

I reach out and grip his hand in mine and squeeze it, “Don’t waste your breath on him, pretty boy. When the time comes, I will paint the walls red for what he did to her.” I don’t have to say his sister’s name for him to know who I mean. He uses my grip on his hand to pull me towards him until I am cuddled into his chest, I panic slightly but squash it down because I know he needs this.

He pulls back and looks down at me, “Elle King, I will be by your side to watch him bleed out, all the Rebels will,” he declares, and I frown slightly at the reference to Marcus.

I scoff, “Yeah, I’ll be lucky if Marcus doesn’t kill you first, the way you are pushing his buttons.” Both he and Linc laugh out loud at that.

“Princess, come on, look how much fun we have had riling him up this week. I am surprised he hasn’t bashed my face in yet.”

“He doesn’t care, that's why,” I respond and they both laugh again.

“Elle, for someone so badass, you really are such a girl,” Linc says, and Jace nods.

I climb off the bed in a huff as Jace goes on, “His eyes have not left you once this week. Either to watch you or make sure you are watching the show he’s putting on.”

“Cherry might not be a show,” I say weakly.

He dives off the bed and drags me to the mirror, “No red-blooded male in their right minds would give up on this,” he says gesturing to my reflection before turning me to face him. He grips my cheeks, “Listen to me, Elle King, and listen good, you were made for that boy. The sooner you both pull your heads out of your assess and realize that, the better things will be for all of us.”

“I hate to say this, but Jace is right,” Lincoln chimes in. Jace smiles big like the cat that got the cream before spinning me around to face them.

“Of course, I am, now let’s see how else we can push his buttons,” he says, releasing me and going into my walk-in wardrobe. He ruffles around in there for a few minutes before he comes back and places some stuff on the bed.

“I’m not a doll you can dress up, Conrad,” I say to him, then curse inwardly at the outfit he has picked, it’s kinda perfect.

He has laid out a red lace bodysuit that is sleeveless and cuts super low at the front and is backed by a peach material so you can’t see through the lace, but it still has the illusion of being able to. He has paired it with fitted black velvet pants and some strappy black heels.

“You were saying,” he says smugly, when he sees my appraisal of the outfit.

“Fine,” I huff back at him, “But only because I can hide my knife in those pants,” I say, and he laughs.

He pushes me towards my en suite while landing a little slap on my ass and I squeal. “Now go get that sweet ass pampered so when you see him tonight, he won’t be able to resist you any longer.”

I roll my eyes, “I’m not trying to seduce him,” I mutter, but it doesn’t sound too convincing and I just stalk towards the bathroom as Jace turns back towards my bed.

“Oh, and pretty boy?” He turns back to me with a nod, “Touch my ass again and you will be bleeding out on this carpet," I say with a smile before turning and slamming the door shut behind me, cutting off his roaring laughter.

Regardless of Jace's joking, it doesn't stop me from washing my hair and shaving and moisturizing from head to toe before I pack my stuff up and head over to Taylor's. The Rebels drop me off, of course, before they head home to change, telling me they will be back soon to pick me up.

Thanks to my constant texts to Taylor alerting her to all my high school drama she is completely caught up on what is going on and instead of offering me support, all she's got is jokes.

"What? All I'm saying is fake or not, if Jace Conrad was offering me some of that, I would climb him like a tree," she giggles before knocking back a shot.

"Trust me, Tay, I am sure if you ask, he would be more than willing," I say, licking the salt off my hand as I try my first tequila shot, ignoring the vile burn in my throat as I swallow and suck a lime.

She laughs at my scrunched-up face before answering, "Yeah, something tells me I am not ready to ride that Rebel rollercoaster. I'm not really into one and done, yanno?" She says shrugging her shoulders.

I place my hand on her arm so she looks at me, "Trust me, in a town like this one, the Rebels are the last thing you should be worried about." She frowns, giving me a look like she wants me to say more but she knows me well enough to know I'm done.

"Okay, one more shot and we hit the road. Your boys will be here any minute."

She doesn't hesitate to throw it back before adding "Fuck, it hurts my throat."

"That's what she said," Jace's voice cuts into the room and we both jump.

"Jesus fucking Christ, pretty boy, didn't anybody teach you not to sneak up on two girls?"

"How did you even get in here?" Taylor adds.

Jace gleams at her slowly taking her in from head to toe and I can see her blush from his appraisal, "Oh, I am a man of many talents, sweetheart."

Lincoln walks in behind him, "You girls ready to go?" He asks, in his always serious tone.

I take the both of them in too and see they are both dressed casually smart and looking as hot as ever.

"Damn, princess, I knew that outfit was made for you," Jace cuts in making me look at him, "Marcus isn't gonna know what's hit him."

Taylor replies, "Me, if he doesn't fucking man up," and I have to laugh at her feisty attitude inside a 5ft 2 package.

Jace crowds in close to her, "Oh, I like a girl who knows how to fight back," he teases, before reaching behind her to grab the bottle of tequila and knocking some back before offering her a wink. The sexual chemistry between the two of them is practically visible so I cut into it and suggest we get moving.

The boys ride in the front so I sit in back with Taylor and finish off the bottle of tequila. I wish I could say I was just having a night as a typical teenager but, in honesty, I need the liquid courage for whatever tonight may bring.

Chapter 11

ASHER

I am clouded by darkness and cloaked in death. That is what it feels like every time I step foot into my father's house. No, the devil's house, built on bodies and coated in the blood of the innocent. I don't call it home, it isn't. The only home I know is the one where my daughter lives. My sweet, innocent baby girl. Too pure for this world. The stuff I would do to protect her, the stuff I have done. It is limitless. There isn't a person in this world that I wouldn't kill to protect her and her mother. The only two people I genuinely care about in this fucked up thing I call a life.

She has that pure innocence in her, children always do. They don't know the depths of evil until it is thrust upon them. I used to be innocent just like her. Innocent and unaware of the horrors happening in my own backyard.

My father, for all intents and purposes, appears to be your perfect upstanding member of society. People know him as the face of business and hefty donations, not the leader of an illegal sex ring or a gun and drug dealer. He is a King in both his public and private life. By day, people adore him and tend to his every whim. By night, he is feared, and he meets his needs with blood and pain, just not his own.

My brother, Greg, is the worst of the worst. Calling him a rapist and a murderer doesn't do justice to the crimes he's committed. Everyone fears him, even my father sometimes. He is a loose cannon, a wild card drawing unwanted attention. People in our circle are always watching him, worrying about what his next move will be. My father has men keeping tabs on him, always ready to clean up his next mess.

Where Greg is a wild hunter, I am a stealthy predator. His loud and brash actions, the perfect cover for my quiet and controlled ones. Greg and my father hunt little girls. But me? I hunt them. Stalk them in everything they do. They don't even realize that when they invite me to the table, they are dining with a traitor.

A killer is what was needed to take them down, so a killer is what I became.

I changed that night. The night I don't name. The night I don't even try to think about. Thinking about it is just dangerous. The rage that courses through my body when I remember the blood on her, well it doesn't bear thinking about. When I do, I think about how it will feel when I coat myself in my family's blood. I want to drown in it as I watch them choke on it.

I sit at the table in my father's den perfectly prepped for another one of his meetings. It's a large circular black table that has gold veins intertwining around the legs. The top is glossy and smooth, it houses three chairs around one side and four around the other. This is where his true business occurs. The only people in here are the ones he trusts. I sit to his left playing the dutiful son as Greg sits on his right, the place of our father's heir. I sip the smooth clear liquid from my glass that is the only vice I allow myself. Something to take the edge off and allow me to be here and remain calm. I sit silently. Watching. Listening. Assessing.

We aren't alone here tonight. Across from us we have his band of loyal followers.

Steven Baizen, Rolland Atkins, Joseph Kavanagh, and Carter Fitzgerald. All of them, like my father, are upstanding members of society housing dark and dangerous secrets. Baizen is Captain of the Hallows Police who has a liking for underage boys and illegal contraband. Atkins runs a pharmaceutical company and happily provides the drugs to help my father subdue his victims. Kavanagh is a criminal lawyer which, I think, speaks for itself, he is always on hand to dig these men out of any mess they might make. And Fitzgerald is your typical double-crossing politician, high up on the food chain and low on morals. Safe to say there are a lot of powerful men around this table. Men who look at me as just a boy. A boy sitting in these meetings to learn the ropes of his father's business, to one day be by Greg's side as he takes over. They have no idea that this boy is the last face they will ever see.

I know everything about all of them. Where they live, where they work, what they like, and what makes them tick. Who they are married to and who they spend their nights with. Every aspect of their life is under my microscope. I have spent the last three years watching their every move and every mistake. Cataloguing it all for my own future gain. When we decide it's time for them to pay, they will be dead before they even breathe our names.

"What did your boys find, Cap?" Elliot's voice booms across the table to the Captain of Police.

"The explosion didn't kill your men, they were dead before it happened," Baizen replies, scrubbing at the scruff of beard on his face. He's a disgusting fat bastard who I will take no remorse in killing.

"How?" My father grits through his teeth at this new information.

"Shot, sliced, gutted. You name it and they got it," he muses, and I take note of the new information. Five men were murdered that night. One by Elle with a knife right across the throat and four by Lincoln in what seems to be very versatile methods. How interesting.

"This can't be a coincidence," Greg interrupts. "First the Octopus disappears without a trace, and now this? Someone is after us." I force my eyes not to roll at how obvious his statement is. Fucking cunt.

"In our line of work, someone is always after us," my father replies. Oh, father you have no idea how true that is.

"And what about King's girl?" Atkins asks. I can hear my heart beating in my head as I try to control my emotions and refrain from gutting every fucker at this table.

Greg laughs, "What? Do you think some broken bit of pussy is capable of getting one over on us?" He asks with a snort and the guy shrugs. My blood boils at the callous referral to my best friend. It takes a lot of self-control to not react and enforce the varying levels of violence I am imagining towards him.

"Who else?" He says tentatively, not wanting to piss off the wild card Donovan. I have to cover my smile; if only they knew that the only Donovan they should be scared of, is me.

"Literally anyone," Greg replies, with another laugh but is silenced when my father raises his hand to shut him up.

"Regardless, we leave no stone unturned. I will look into the girl myself," he says sternly, and I stiffen slightly.

"How will you do that? The boy?" Fitzgerald asks nodding his head at me and I feel slightly hopeful that maybe he will leave it to me but of course life isn't ever that easy.

"Of course not, I will find her myself," he grunts back.

"Where?" Greg asks with that sick little gleam in his eye, and I have to stop myself from putting a bullet in his skull right then and there.

My father smiles. It's cunning and full of malice, "Oh, don't worry about that." He put a fucking price on her head for fuck sake, was that not enough? Will it ever be enough?

I barely hear the rest of the discussion as my sole focus is on how he knows how to get to Elle. I do everything I can to protect her without alerting it to my family and when I can't, that is where Zack takes over. Except now it isn't just Zack, it's also the fucking South

Side Rebels, well two of them at least. Did they lead my father to her?

Does he know where she is? Or is he just bluffing? Has he already had contact with her, and she just hasn't told me? I mean it's not like people don't know she is back in town. Marcus fucking named her as his fucking Queen loud and proud and the way the Rebels flock around her, there is no way she is flying under the radar. No, impossible. I might fucking despise them, but it seems Elle has them wrapped around her finger like she does me. I know they won't hurt her, I don't know how, but I just do. I grind my jaw just thinking about them. Marcus was bad enough, always trying to keep her for himself, he never understood how all I ever wanted from her was friendship. I am not infatuated with her like he is.

Now it isn't just Marcus though, it's the other two as well. That fucking pathetic playboy Conrad and their pet hacker Blackwell. I don't know who I despise more. That's a lie, I do. Marcus is blinded by love and his current tantrum will pass. I know him well enough to know that. He will eventually learn the truth and then I will have someone else who will want Donovan blood just as much as me. We won't be allies in any way, but we will have the same goal. Avenge Elle and that is good enough to keep him in my good graces.

Conrad has his own demons to chase. Elle told me what my brother did to his sister and the only reason he hasn't killed him yet is the same reason I haven't. Patience. Patience and planning. Killing with reckless abandonment would only end in my own demise. So instead, I wait, plan and plot. I do this so when I finally strike there will be no loose ends left to deal with. Hallows will be painted in the blood of monsters and my girls will finally sleep peacefully and protected.

Blackwell is the only one I haven't figured out yet. No demons that I can dig up. No family either. He is just void of emotion and his skills with a computer mean he has left nothing behind for me to dig up about him. The only information I have about him are the tidbits I have picked up from listening and tracking him and Elle on missions. Which summed up is that he is loyal, capable, smart, and gay. I loathe that I know nothing about him. That and the fact that Elle just blindly placed her trust in him, just like Zack. It pisses me the fuck off. All three Rebels annoy me in different ways, but Lincoln Blackwell gets under my skin more than the others.

When the official meeting concludes, one of my father's whores' wheels in a drinks cart and that is my cue to leave. I have no desire to watch a girl be beaten and raped repeatedly. The horrors of what happened to Elle are imprinted on my mind for all eternity. I have never looked at a girl the same way since that night.

I head to my room to get changed. I am still wearing my Hallows Prep uniform and need to lose it before joining Elle and her merry band of Rebels at the warehouse on Riverside for a 'chill' night of fun. Whatever the fuck that means. I shower and change into dark jeans and a fitted Henley, I throw a holster on and place a gun on either side because regardless of how 'chill' the night is, I don't go anywhere unless I am armed. I learned the repercussions of that lesson the hard way when I had nothing to protect Elle with and I won't make that mistake again.

I throw a jacket on over my ensemble and leave my room, closing and locking my door behind me and start down the hallway and spot Greg hiding in the shadows as I round the corner.

"And where are you going?" he steps out of the shadows and I feign a jump and pretend I didn't know he was there. Just another game of shadows and mirrors.

"Out," I say, holding his gaze firmly but making sure the hate I feel for him is hidden behind the impassive mask I wear around my family.

"Business or pleasure, little brother?" he asks.

I smile a light smile, "Oh now, Gregory, you know I leave all the business to you. You're dad's heir after all. So why not indulge in the pleasure only?" I say sweetly with a laugh like we are in on some inside joke together.

He laughs and moves to clap me on the shoulder, and it takes everything in me to not rip his arm clean off his body.

"You not pounded enough of those Hallows Prep holes yet? They are easy prey; don't you want more of a challenge?" he asks.

"Oh, I like the challenge of working my way through every one of them," I say with what I hope is a smug enough grin, like I am showing off my conquests.

Clearly it works because Greg laughs, "You should have told me, I would have taken a bet to see who could complete it the fastest."

I fake a laugh in response in favor of telling him that raping girls against their will wouldn't count and then slicing his throat. No, laughing is better for now.
He smacks my back three times, "Well, go on then, don't keep all that pussy waiting, boy. The girls always go wild for Donovan dick."

I nod, then head down the stairs imagining every way I am going to cut into his skin and bleed him out before planting a bullet directly between his eyes. I think about harvesting all of his organs into jars and gifting them to Elle.

Hmm maybe I do need to 'chill.' Yeah right. I won't fucking chill until the only people alive with Donovan blood running through their veins are Cassie and myself.

Chapter 12

MARCUS

The warehouse on Riverside is somewhere my boys and I have frequented regularly for the last few years. It doesn't have a name or hold any loyalties, it's a free for all, in terms of the invisible divide in this shitty town. Tonight, I don't stand with my boys as usual, no the only person on my team tonight is fucking Cherry. And that's only because she thinks tonight will end with me *fucking* Cherry. Spoiler alert, it won't.

I used to love coming here. Indulging in shitty beer and easy pussy. Now, I'd rather shoot myself in the fucking dick than be here but it's all part of the game. A game of Kings. A game where I don't understand the rules, the players or what the outcome should be. But still, I play.

I wouldn't even be here if I didn't have to be, but I do because they will be, she will be. I heard Jace talking loudly about it as they left school at lunch today. Making plans and sharing jokes, seeing them together does something to me. Something I don't like. I always hated her friendship with Asher but that was when I was a fucking punk ass kid who would do anything to make her mine. Now I'm jealous for other reasons. I don't want her lying traitorous ass, but I want back what she has taken from me. My brothers.

They are the only family I have left, and I can't lose them, regardless of how hard I wanted my fist to meet Jace's jaw this week every time he touched her. Seeing them with her, protecting her, it burns something inside of me and confuses me. They know her truths just like I do and yet instead of hating her with me and taking my side, they are on hers. Why?

I can't help but think I am still missing something but what other secrets could she be keeping from me? Nothing as big as a secret fucking love child, I'm sure. That doesn't make the need to peel back her layers and allow her truths to pour out any fucking less. I feel powerless around her and that's not a feeling I enjoy.

I have asked myself why I even care, and I am yet to figure out the answer. She lied, more than lied, the secrets she kept from me are fucking astronomical, so why should I care what she does or who she does it with? We aren't Ells and River anymore; she has made that perfectly clear. She was making that clear from the moment she stepped foot back in this town, I was just blinded by what I thought was fate. It wasn't fate that brought her back though, it was fucking family, just not mine.

I knock back a piss warm beer and clench my fist around the red cup with the need to feel the burn of whiskey in my throat. I have drank so much in the last few weeks I am surprised my liver is even still fucking intact.

"You want another, baby?" Cherry's voice comes from my left and I have to fight to cringe when she calls me baby. I am nobody's fucking baby, least of all her's. She hasn't left my side since we got here and, in all honesty, she is irritating the fuck out of me and is a big reason why I am always a one and done guy. This is the shit I don't want, a girl hanging off my dick and crowding my every move. The fact she is already like this when I haven't even let her wet my dick means she never will. Fucking her would take her from a clinger to straight up stalker. I have already got one girl who wants my soul, I don't need another.

I stand pushing her off my body and tell her to stay there and head over to the makeshift bar to find my own drink. I don't even know why I am fucking here, she isn't, my guys aren't, so what is the fucking point?

I manage to snag a bottle of rum, not my first choice but better than warm beer so I twist off the top and knock some back. When I bring it back from my mouth, I lock eyes with the last person I want to see. Asher fucking Donovan.

He is sipping from a pristine crystal glass and I honestly wonder where the fuck he got it in a place like this, without bringing it himself. I wouldn't put it past the fucking psycho to do something like that.

He nods his head at me like we are friends and then pushes his glare past me to survey the room. I watch him eye every fucker in here, assessing them, noting their tells, anything that would give him an insight into them. Is this how he did it? How he took Elle from right under my nose without me being any the wiser. I push down my rage as I imagine all the secret rendezvous they must have had, the images of them fucking so much that he knocked her up. I squeeze my fist so tight I am surprised the bottle doesn't break.

"Fuck you doing here, Donovan?" I spit at him.

He makes a show of wiping his face before responding "Trust me, Marcus, I am asking myself the same thing."

"Waiting for your girl, I guess," smiling smugly, but he doesn't react, so I continue, "Only is she even your girl anymore considering she is now on the arm of a Rebel?"

"What do you want Marcus? I've had a long day and I am not in the mood to deal with your petulant childish ways right now," he replies, knocking back the clear liquid in the glass. Vodka, I'm guessing.

He still hasn't brought his stare back to mine and it pisses me the fuck off, game on prick. "How's the family today, Donovan?"

Finally, his eyes lock with mine, a look that tells me he would murder me where I stand if I push him too hard and, boy, do I want to fucking push.

"Careful, Riviera, don't think because of what feelings Elle has for you that I won't put you in the ground here and now if I felt like it," he grinds out to me, before looking back out into the room. I watch as the corner of his mouth tilts slightly into a smile and I don't have to look to know who has drawn that emotion from him. She's here.

I turn and come to lean on the wall beside him as we both look over to her. If moody and dressed down Elle is hot, well then drunk and happy dressed up Elle is a fucking volcano. She is wearing some form of red netted top that barely holds in her fucking tits. It tucks down into black velvet pants that are so tight they might as well be fucking glued to her. She has forgone her usual combat boots for stilettos and fuck me they make her legs look long and thick. The kind you want wrapped around you. Her hair is long and straight down her back and her lips are painted red. Fucking flawless.

She is holding onto Taylor's arm as they laugh at some inside joke and Lincoln and Jace come up behind them. When she feels their presence, she looks to them and smiles even bigger like they are her whole world.

"That smile could be yours if you pulled your head out of your ass," Asher cuts into my appraisal of her and I curse inwardly at being caught.

"Yeah, whatever, I don't fuck people I hate," I shrug and take another sip of rum.

He laughs, a rare thing from him, "Hate? Is that what that look was?"

"Yes, pure hate." I grit out.

"Please," he snorts." You have many feelings towards Elle King, always have, but hate isn't one of them."

"I do hate her I..." I start to reply but he cuts me off.

"No, you don't. You hate that she lied. Hate that we lied. That for once Elle and I are the ones with a secret and not you. You don't know what it's like to be on the outside looking in, to be the one left in the dark."

"Except, I'm not in the fucking dark anymore am I, Donovan? Your secrets have a fucking beating heart, now don’t they?” I spit the words at him, barely containing my cool.

He pushes off the wall, “Careful Rebel, I won’t allow any threats to my family.”

“I’m not scared of you, Donovan,” I reply, and he laughs.

“Stupid of you really,” he says with an eye roll. “But no, it’s worse, you're afraid of that pretty little blonde with the black blade, because no matter which side you fall on now, she will cut your heart out and keep it as her own. You just need to decide how she will do it.”

Before I can respond I feel her presence, my missing part.

“Everything okay here?” She asks, I flick my gaze to her as she looks between Asher and I.

“Yep,” I reply, popping the P. “Everything’s fine, traitor, just catching up with your boy here,” I add with a smile and she flinches ever so slightly looking to Donovan. He is just standing silently observing with that stupid fucking impassive face of his.

“Traitor?” Taylor’s voice interrupts us, I see Elle freeze.

“Don’t worry about it, Kennedy,” I say with a huff and then decide to play another game as I lean in close and slowly check her out, “Looking good, btw,” I add licking my lips.

She looks at me with a frown before laughing loudly, “God, you really are fucking dumb, Riviera,” she shakes her head, snagging the bottle of rum from my hand with a wink and then turns back to Elle.

“Come on, Smell, let's leave these two measuring their dicks, we came here to have fun,” she doesn’t wait for Elle to respond before walking away, heading back over to where my brothers are now sitting, their glares burning into my head. Elle looks at me for a second before releasing a breath and looking to Donovan.

“You coming, Ash?” she asks him, with a tentative smile reaching her hand out to him and I tense at the offer.

Asher stares at me and then smiles smugly, taking her hand and linking their fingers together, “Always, baby girl.”

They walk off together, and I watch them go as they join Jace, Lincoln, and Taylor sitting on a couple of leather sofas in the corner. When they reach them, Jace keeps his glare on me as he pulls Elle down next to him and puts his arm around her. A move that I thought would provoke Donovan, but he just takes a seat next to Linc not caring that Elle is now snuggled up to a Rebel. A Rebel that isn’t me. Not that I care. Except I do, I really fucking do.

I grind my teeth before grabbing another bottle of fuck knows what and head back over to Cherry, who, shocker, is still sitting where I told her to wait. I roll my eyes, are girls really that dick desperate that they will just fall at the feet of any guy who gives them the slightest bit of attention? I almost feel sorry for her, but I shut it down. She has one purpose and one purpose only. Make me forget about Elle. So why can’t I pull the plug and let her do it?

Chapter 13

ELLE

The self-control I am exhibiting right now, should win fucking awards. I have never possessed so much of it in my entire life, I didn't even think it was possible for a person to have this much, let alone me. Watching Cherry grind her ass into Marcus' dick on the dance floor like it's an Olympic sport has me wanting to plant a bullet in her pretty little skull. Over the top? Maybe. Do I give a fuck? No.

He is drunk as shit, that much is clear. It's like he is in competition to see how much he can drink before he fucking passes out. Watching as his hands grip her waist has me hoping it's before they move this fucking sex show to his bedroom.

"If you stare any harder, you are gonna pop a vein," Lincoln cuts into my thoughts. I scowl at him.

"I hate to agree with the help, but he is right." Asher adds on. I grind my jaw hard.

"Yeah, well, excuse me if I'm not into fucking sexual voyeurism."

"Don't knock it until you've tried it," Lincoln adds, and both mine and Ash's gaze snap to him. Linc just laughs when I raise my eyebrows at him. I realize he is drunk too, for the first time since I have met him, he seems a little lighter. Like, he is actually having fun for once and not taking life so seriously.

"You are letting your jealousy cloud your judgment, princess," Jace adds pushing forward from the sofa so he can lean into me.

"Look what they are fucking doing, pretty boy," I snap back at him, the anger flowing out and Taylor laughs at that. I flip her off, but she just laughs harder.

"I am," he replies, "Look at how his hands grip her waist, how he pulls her body into his and how his eyes are on you and you alone," he adds talking low and close, putting on our own little show in return. I try to keep my emotions at bay, but I know for sure I am failing, as I watch him sway with her to the music.

I watch him and his stare is so intense I can practically feel it on my skin as he sways with her to the music. His eyes are so dark they are practically black, and his grip tightens every time Jace leans into me. I frown because I really am confused at this point and Marcus smiles at my expression like he knows he is winning this fucked up game of chess we are involved in. Well, game fucking on.

I jump up and hold my hand out for Jace, "Come on, pretty boy, let's dance."

He looks at me confused slightly before showcasing his megawatt smile and taking my hand, letting me pull him up. He leads me onto the dancefloor, not too close to Marcus but close enough that he has a clear line of sight to us. I knew there was a reason I liked Jace so much.

He spins me around and then pulls me in, so I am in the same position that Marcus has Cherry. My back is against his firm chest and we sway in time to the music. The song isn't one I recognize but the beat is smooth and bold meaning grinding is the perfect dance to match it. I have never danced like this with anyone in my life, so I am praying Jace is better at this than me.

I try to lose myself in the music, but it isn't long before I risk a glance at Marcus. His glare is so intense, I think if he could, he would rip Jaces arms off my waist with his mind alone. I can't take the heat, so I turn in Jace's arms and throw my arms around his neck and drop my head to his chest.

His arms curl around me and rest on the top of my ass.

"Remember what I said about touching my ass, pretty boy," I say with a laugh.

"Oh, princess, you love me too much to make me bleed," he replies, looking down with a smile. "Besides," he leans in to drop his voice to my ear, "You should see Marcus' face right now, he looks about ready to fight me, or fuck you. Don't know which, doubt he even does."

I glance over my shoulder and see he has spun Cherry to mirror Jace and I, I grind my teeth as he slips his hands over her ass at the same time Jace grips mine. Not a move I would allow from anyone usually, but I know how invested Jace is in pushing his brother to the point of no return. I'm just not sure what happens when we get there.

I turn back to Jace, "This is a dangerous game we are playing, pretty boy." I look up at him and he smiles.

"Story of our fucking life, princess, now wanna seal the deal and kiss me?" he asks, wiggling his eyebrows at me and I laugh.

I laugh looking around, "I think I'd need a little more liquid courage for that," I finally say.

"Seems like someone has already beaten you to that point," he says, through gritted teeth and I look back up at him to see his stare over my shoulder. I follow his gaze and freeze.

I watch as Cherry reaches up and kisses Marcus and all the joy, I felt a minute ago, playing him at his own game, evaporates.

I push Jace back and he releases me immediately after witnessing the same thing I just did. He looks more shocked that I do. I leave him standing, staring at the two of them and push past everybody and make my way outside. I turn down the same alley Marcus cornered me in last time I was here and walk all the way down it until I hit a metal fence. I grip it tight and try to control my heart, it feels like it might burst right out of my chest.

I am fighting to try to catch my breath so I can smooth out my heartbeat, but it feels all too much. A feeling I have never felt before churns in the pit of my stomach. Is this what jealousy feels like? Like true jealousy and heartbreak seeing your guy with someone else. Fuck. It hurts more than I thought it would.

A noise behind me has me spinning around quickly to see Marcus stalking down the alley towards me, he doesn't even get to speak before I slap him hard across the face. His head swings to the side before he looks back to me slowly. I am panting so hard trying to catch my breath, but it doesn't come.

He takes one last step forward closing the distance between us and then before I can even second guess it, I slam my lips against his. He freezes at my attack before he grabs me hard and pushes me back into the fence, returning my kiss with everything he has got. It's exactly like when we kissed at the club. Hard, punishing, reckless. The kind of kiss that leaves a stain on your soul. I know I shouldn't, but I can't seem to stop myself. It's like my head and body aren't in sync anymore, my heart for sure fucking isn't. His touch against my skin is scorching.

His hands reach down and squeeze my ass and he uses his grip to pull me up against him, so I have no choice but to wrap my legs around him. He swings me from the fence into the wall and pushes further into me, his hard on hitting my core, and I moan into his kiss. I slide my hands into his hair and tug hard and he growls ripping his mouth from mine.

His dark black stare collides with mine assessing me. I'm drunk, he's drunk. Are we really doing this? Just when I think he is going to pull away he crowds into me again.

His hands cup my face, "Does he kiss you like this, little traitor?" He whispers to me as his lips just barely graze mine. I daren't answer and I doubt he really meant it for me to answer. His hands slide down my face onto my neck before he slides them to my chest. He looks down and watches his hand trace over both my nipples as they harden under his touch and glare. He pinches them both causing me to moan slightly before he tightens his fingers on them and pulls until I am sure I could orgasm from that alone.

I don't think before I grab his neck and drag his mouth back to mine and he comes willingly. I have no idea what game we are playing now, when not even five minutes ago we were both grinding into someone else. But when his tongue tangles with mine I find myself not caring as much as I should.

His hands push down my body until he finds the button of my pants and rips it open with both hands before pushing them down slightly. I pull back and so does he and he pauses. Even drunk, he is stopping to ask for permission, and I give it to him with a nod. I unwrap my legs from around him and slide down until I am pressed back into the wall on shaky legs. He looks down and then curses.

"Fuck," he says as he takes in the red netted top I am wearing as he realizes it's actually a bodysuit, "So fucking sexy." He says with a groan. He traces a finger along my seam, and I shudder at the light contact. He drags it back and forth until I am soaking through the material onto his fingers and I can't take anymore. "River," I say breathlessly and his eyes snap back to mine.

"Feeling needy?" He asks with a sexy smile, "Want to come for me, Ells?"

"Yes," I say pleadingly before I can even think about it and he doesn't waste any time pulling my bodysuit to the side and gliding his fingers through my slick folds. He pushes down into my wetness and gathers it as he drags his fingers up to my clit and circles it in quick motions until I am panting and moaning against his hand. Fuck!

My drunken haze means I can only think about what he is doing to my body and nothing else. He pushes a finger inside me and brings his thumb to my clit, working me over until I am moaning loudly, and not caring who might catch us out here.

He slams his lips back against mine and pushes his tongue in my mouth and kisses me ravenously capturing my moans. His hand moves faster and faster until I am practically writhing against it and the wall, until I begin to shake. One last flick of my clit and I am coming hard all over his fingers and he pulls his lips from mine and groans as he watches his fingers pump inside me a few more times as I ride out my orgasm.

I sag against him and his stare comes back to mine and just for a moment everything feels right, how it should be. There is no tension or hate, just two people who care about each other, but as usual, nothing lasts forever. I feel when he slaps his mask back in place as he rolls his shoulders before pulling his fingers out of me and I gasp as he drags them past my clit, he smiles a smug smile before shoving them into his mouth and sucking them clean. Fuck, that shouldn't be so hot.

"Mmm, who knew traitors could taste so good?" He says with a wink as he awaits my retaliation, but I know how drunk Marcus likes to play now.

I reach for the fingers he's just taken from his mouth and suck them into my own. His stare turns dark again as I drag them fully into my mouth before releasing them with a pop.

"Nope, just tastes like pussy to me," I say with a smile and I see his jaw tighten.

"Yeah, I've tasted better. I should get back to Cherry and compare," he fires back.

I reach down and cup his still hard cock, squeeze, and he gasps in surprise slamming his hands to the wall either side of my head. I'm surprised too because I don't know what is making me so brave. Note to self, tequila makes me handsy.

I lean in close, as I squeeze him again, and feel him shudder against me before I whisper into his ear, "Touch her again, Marcus," I say before pulling away and ducking under his arms and walking backwards out of the alley my gaze still on him.

"I dare you," I add before turning away from him and heading back inside.

I get back into the warehouse and allow my heart to finally stop racing as I let the music calm me down. What the fuck was that?

How did I go from dancing with Jace to grabbing Marcus' dick? And I let him finger me, AGAIN! Like seriously. I am a sane person. Okay, so I kill people sometimes, but I still consider myself to be someone who is calm and responsible, someone who always thinks through their actions. So why the fuck did I just do that? It's like anytime my body has alcohol in it and Marcus is around, I suddenly lose my mind. Absolutely no more drinking for me.

Just as I think that Taylor comes up to me and hands me a shot. “You look like you need this girl,” she says. I don’t even hesitate in knocking it back.

“Thanks Tay, you have no idea,” I say with a wince letting the alcohol burn.

I look back at her and she is staring at me with a smile, “What?” I snap and her smile just grows wider.

“Might wanna fix your lipstick,” she replies with a cheeky smile. Fuck.

She hands me a mirror and I take in my flushed cheeks and smeared lipstick. I look different, wild, satisfied, comfortable. It’s not a look I see on myself often and I don’t want to allow myself to think about what it means right now.

I give the mirror back to Taylor, she nods, and we push our way back inside to the guys, who as I approach, I see all have a frown on their face. I follow their stares and find Marcus back with his arms around Cherry. When he notices me staring, he raises his glass with a big smile as he uses his other arm to pull her closer.

Oh, he really wants to fucking play. Well, get ready for check fucking mate.

I don’t even think before I drag Jace to me and kiss him with everything I have got. I feel the shock in his body before his arms mould around my body and he kisses me back. There are zero sparks, no lust, no tension, even as I slide my hands into his long hair. The kiss itself is great, even with my limited experience I can tell how skillful he is and I can see why the girls throw themselves at him but apart from that, I feel nothing. Nothing except payback, especially when I hear the smashing of glass and a few people yelling. I pull back and Jace speaks first.

"Princess?" he asks, with a mixture of a smile and a frown.

"Yeah?" I reply tentatively and suddenly feel super awkward.

"As much as I enjoy hot girls throwing themselves at me, that was really fucking weird," he says, and I burst out laughing.

"Yeah, pretty boy, sorry about that," I wince slightly, as I pull back and find Linc, Ash, and Taylor all staring at us with varying expressions from shock, annoyance to amusement.

Jace just throws his arm around my shoulder and drops his usual kiss to my head, "Don't sweat it, it clearly had the desired effect," he says with a laugh, as we both turn to look at the destruction Marcus left behind.

"Let's go home," I say and they all nod.

Not exactly the 'chill' night I expected.

Chapter 14

MARCUS

I wake up feeling sick and disorientated. Fuck knows where I am. The last thing I remember is seeing Elle kissing Jace. Fuck. I thought the images I had conjured up of her and Donovan together were bad enough, but this is so much worse. Seeing it with my own eyes fucking stirred a madness inside me. I completely lost my mind and instead of punching my own brother because I didn't trust myself not to kill him, I punched through a window instead. Then stalked home to pick up my bike and drive it to wherever I am.

I have never been so reckless. Reckless and broken. How can you hate someone with every bone in your body but then love them with every beat of your fucking heart?

My head is so fucked up, but I am far too hungover to be able to deal with it. I sit up and rub my eyes, desperately trying to clear the ache in them, but it's useless. That pounding feeling spreads right across my temple and round the back of my head. Fuck. I want to stay in bed, but I can't today for one reason and one reason only. It's my dad's anniversary.

Three years. Three fucking years since he was shot and killed by that fucking animal Elliot Donovan. Now my father was far from innocent, I am sure he had plenty of skeletons in his closet, ones I don't even know about but as far as I am aware, he never killed an innocent man in cold blood. People who say time is a healer, talk fucking bullshit, three years and it still feels like yesterday. Time hasn't helped me with shit.

I make my way to the bathroom in this place and attempt to flick on the light and it's only then I remember there is no electricity, it's probably cold as shit in here too, but my hangover is overpowering my senses. I can't feel much else. The window allows some natural daylight to filter in, enough for me to see my reflection in the mirror. I look like shit, pure and simple. I still haven't shaved so my usual light dust of scruff is practically a full-on beard and the circles under my eyes are almost as dark as my coal-colored hair. Grief really is a killer. Not sure if I am grieving my dad or the future I will never have with Elle, but it doesn't matter. Both left me behind without looking back.

After taking a leak, I splash some water on my face and go back into the living room to retrieve my leather jacket and head out the door. The daylight is harsh, and I find myself wanting to turn around and go back inside to sleep some more but trying would be useless, I'm too wired. I just need to go see my dad and then maybe I should get back out of this hell hole of a town.

I climb on my bike and go on my way. The air whips past me in quick succession as I guide the bike in the direction I want to go. I love my bike, I love feeling the power beneath me, knowing just one wrong flick on my wrist could end it all. Probably a little sick to think of it like that but it keeps me on my toes. I push through ignoring the rain as it starts to fall and make my way to the gates of Hallows Cemetery.

It's funny, isn't it? It doesn't matter how much money you have, where you're born, or who you're born to. When we die, all our lives amount to the same wooden box, in the same mudded hole, with the same concrete stone above us. Doesn't matter how different we all live; we all decay the same.

I swing my leg over my bike and lean it against a picnic table next to a bunch of other cars. The rain is really fine and it's soaking me through but the cold bite of it is a welcome touch to my burning skin. I don't bother to even look where I am going as I enter the cemetery, I don't have to, I know the way to my dad's stone by heart. I spent every day out here for weeks after he was buried. The pain of losing him and losing Elle was something I didn't know how to deal with, I guess considering how hungover I am right now, you could say I still don't.

I reach his stone and release a deep breath. Looks the same as always. Beautiful, clean, and expensive. I still wonder now who paid for his funeral costs after all our funds were taken, but it's not important. Whoever it was, I will never be able to repay them.

I do my usual and head past his stone until I am round back and take a seat. His stone is so big I can easily lean my huge frame against it. Add that to the fact that he is buried around the edge of this place, it offers me the privacy to grieve in peace. I pull out a crumpled joint from my pocket and light it, inhaling deeply. Hopefully, it will numb me from the pain that pumps through my body. I don't know how long I sit there but I must have drifted off because I don't hear her approach and it's clear, she doesn't know I'm here when her voice hits my ear.

"Hey, stranger," Elle's sad tone pierces through the soft drizzling rain. "Sorry, it's been a while, but I am sure you're watching me and know what I've been up to," she adds, with a little scoffed laugh.

I daren't move, I don't want to reveal my presence and deal with our issues today of all days. So, I remain completely still and silent. I hear a shuffle and I can tell she has moved closer to the stone.

"I know you told me not to come back here," her voice is lower now but still perfectly clear, meaning I was right, she has moved closer, probably bent down in the mud, "I'm sorry I didn't listen, but I couldn't. I hope you understand. They had already taken so much from me that I was barely surviving until a heartbeat changed my life," her voice is straining, and I can tell she is barely holding back tears.

"I wish you could meet her; she would adore you, and I know you would look out for her like you did me," I hear her sniffles and deep inhale like she is forcing herself to keep her emotions in check. "God, you have no idea how much I wish you were here, wish you could see the things I have done, see the amazing man your son has become. Marcus, my beautiful River, you should see him, Michael. You would be so proud of him. He's a little lost right now, and I wish I could help him more but it's too dangerous. He already knows too much," her voice cracks when she says my name and it takes everything in me not to move to comfort her.

"I think I could have survived if they only took from me, but then they came for you, took from him and I can't, I just couldn't ignore that. I've done things, things you wouldn't be proud of, but I don't regret them. Every move I make is to keep my family safe, to keep her safe. I won't let them get her."

Her statement gives me chills and starts an inferno of rage inside at the same time. What the fuck? What is she talking about? Who? Elliot? What has she done? What was taken? More questions without answers. Except the answers my brain is conjuring up make my skin crawl, no that's not right, it can't be. Did Elliot do something to her? No. She would have told me, right? We're best friends, we told each other everything. She would never keep a secret that big from me, except she already has, hasn't she? We aren't best friends anymore. She pushed me away. No this is just more of her lies and mind games, it has to be, the alternative is too fucking sick even for someone like Elliot Donovan.

She doesn't speak for so long that I would think she has gone but I didn't hear her move, so I know she is still here. I can feel her like she is part of me and just as I am about to give in and go to her, she speaks again.

"Anyway," she says, dragging out the word forcing a cheery tone to her voice that sounds so fake it almost doesn't sound like her. "These are for you, I know orange is a weird color, but I didn't pick them out," she laughs, "but I hope you like them."

"I'm sure he'd love them, princess," the dark sinister voice causes my entire body to flinch, I'd know that voice anywhere.

Elliot Donovan.

I know I should move, make myself known and face him like a man. I have been waiting for an opportunity like this ever since he murdered my father. To come across him somewhere quiet and secluded like this is a rare occasion and I could use it to my advantage.

Except I have nothing but my hands as weapons and as much as I would love nothing more than to make him bleed, I also want to see how the dynamic is between him and Elle. She made her distaste clear for her parents when they came to school for her and from the little snippets of information, she allowed me it seemed as if that would extend to Elliot too. I started to think he had done something to her but then she dropped the Asher baby bomb. Now, I don't know what to think.

It seems in this town people only speak freely when they think they are alone. So, I stay, remain quiet and pray for some of the answers I long for.

Chapter 15

ELLE

I am soaked through but I don't care. I have been putting off coming here ever since I came back to town. It's like I thought once I came here and visited his grave, it finally made it official. Michael Riviera saved my life and paid the price with his own. No one will ever understand the guilt I feel because of that. Standing here now and seeing his life cut short and reduced to nothing but a fucking huge block of stone, makes that guilt even more soul crushing. Zack paid for his funeral and I wish I could have been there to say goodbye, but it was too dangerous.

Talking aloud to him feels silly but there was too much left unsaid, too much I had to tell him. I voice it out loud, said everything I wish I could say to him in person and pray to all the gods that the afterlife is real, and he can somehow hear me. Once I have nothing left to say I just grieve in silence until I am so cold that my body hurts as much as my heart, my own version of self-punishment.

When I think it's time to go, I place the orange roses that Cass and I picked out into the empty vase.

Orange makes everyone happy, she said when we bought them. I hope she is right.

I prepare myself to say goodbye, not knowing when the next time I will get a chance to come here will be, when the voice of the devil himself hits my body like a wrecking ball.

"I'm sure he'd love them, princess."

I repress a flinch and force myself to turn around slowly and come face to face with the devil himself. Elliot Donovan. Fuck. I feel my wrist wanting to flick out the knife at my thigh for protection, but I refuse to allow him to push me back into the fear I felt that night. Besides pulling a weapon would show me as more than the girl he once kidnapped and the longer he stays in the dark about me the better.

The way he says princess is nothing like the soft affectionate way Jace says it, but more like he wanted to say whore, but is playing nice. He hasn't changed over the years, he still has his thin blonde hair slicked back, with too much product and somehow his eyes manage to be the same blue as Asher's, yet dark and sinister at the same time. I make quick work of checking the surrounding areas by flicking my gaze across the land to see if there is anyone else here, but I come up with nothing.

"I don't go everywhere with an entourage, my men are fine waiting in the car," he says cockily, clearly knowing where my line of thought just went. I mean what does he expect me to think, he put a fucking price tag on my head, dead or alive? Who the fuck knows but I won't take any chances.

"Maybe you should, you never know who you might come across," I reply, keeping my tone flat and uninterested.

He smirks a mocking smile like the thought of me alone doing something to him is just hilarious to him. He looks me up and down and it takes everything in me not to shudder. Remember your training Elle, remember what Zack taught you, panic will get you killed.

"It's been a long time, Elle," he adds, and he almost looks sad about it, like he cares. I guess he does in a way. He doesn't care about seeing me, he cares about the pay-out he missed out on because of me.

"Not long enough, if you ask me," I respond without missing a beat. I cannot show weakness, men like Elliot Donovan feed off of it. Catalogue it and use it to grind you down. I won't allow him that benefit again.

"Visiting our old friend, I see," he replies, choosing to ignore my last statement and finally breaking his appraisal of me as he cocks his brow at Michael's headstone.

"Using the word friend, a bit loosely, I see," I grind out through my teeth. He laughs, fucking laughs. The devil really does have a sick sense of humor, eh?

"Michael and I went way back, further than you think. He just lost his way and chose the wrong side; you know that better than anyone. He's dead because of you, Miss King."

Fuck, the urge to whip out my knife and gut him like the fucking vermin he is, is strong. Sure, people would notice but would anyone actually miss him? His victims sure wouldn't and he deserves it. I don't think anyone deserves it more, except maybe Greg. I'm biting my tongue so hard I taste blood which is fitting. Blood mixed with a Donovan, it's practically their signature, they go hand in hand.

I ignore his obvious attempt to rile me up and stand my ground.

"What are you doing here? Michael didn't like you and I think you know how I feel, so just turn around and leave," I say with as much confidence as I can muster. Luckily, he doesn't know me well enough anymore to see how much his presence is affecting me.

"Don't be like that, we all know you're my favorite King," he smirks a devilish smile like we are in on some joke together, in a way I guess we are. The world's fucking sickest joke. "We could be friends?" he continues, and the way the word friends rolls off his tongue almost makes me bring up fucking bile in my throat. I know exactly the type of relationship he would want us to have and it's far from fucking friends.

"After what you and your son did, I'd say we are beyond ever being friends, don't you?"

"So, enemies then?" He inquires with a smile so big it could rival the Cheshire Cat.

"Enemies would require me caring enough about you," I quip back and the lie burns on my tongue and I am sure he can sense it.

"Ah, I see. You know someone cared enough about me to burn one of my businesses to the ground," he says, watching me for a reaction but I don't even fucking flinch. I can't. My life depends on it. I am far too aware that I am in the middle of a graveyard with the most dangerous man in town. Anything is possible at this point. When he sees that I am not giving him a response he takes one last look at Michael's headstone and then tips his head at me.

"I look forward to seeing you again soon, Miss King."

"Oh, I'm sure you will, Mr. Donovan," I gleam at him, imagining how it would feel to plunge my knife into his gut. I watch him walk away, every second imagining the different ways I could make him bleed. Every single one of them doesn't feel like enough. Fuck.

I stand there staring after him until long after he is gone and then I take a deep breath trying to push past our interaction when another voice cuts through the wind, "That was an interesting family reunion," Marcus' rough voice hits my ear.

I whip around and the sight of him almost breaks me, fuck he looks so bad. He looks nothing like the playful and lusting boy I was with in the alley last night. He looks like he hasn't slept or digested anything other than alcohol and weed. Fuck. I did this to him. When am I going to stop taking things from him? Stop hurting him?

"Marcus," my voice comes out in a raspy whisper and I don't even know if he heard me. All the confidence I held in my interaction with Elliot has completely disappeared. Unlike Elliot, Marcus knows me so well he can practically see what's written on my bones. Or at least he could until I covered myself in lies and secrets.

"Care to shed some light on that little interaction?" he says, but my mind is blank. I have no idea what to say to him or how to keep lying to him. I am just so tired of keeping him in the dark.

"I--" I start but he flicks his wrist, cutting me off.

"Save it," he says, sensing the lies burning in my mouth and he starts past me to leave.

"Marcus wait---" I begin after him and he whips around.

"I did wait, Elle, for three fucking years I waited. Look where it got me!" He yells back and I don't know what to say because he is right.

"I'm sorry," I reply, knowing that those two words will mean nothing but what else can I say? He is right.

"For which part exactly?" He huffs a mocking laugh like he can't believe I would have the audacity to even say it when it's so useless.

"All of it," I say, sadly dropping my shoulders, all of my bravado shattered, because what else can I say? Nothing more without telling him the whole truth.

He huffs out a breath and steps towards me until he is so close, I can smell his spicy scent and it wraps around me like a vice. His head drops to my shoulder and it's like he is using me to gain some strength. I don't know how long we stand like this, but I don't move, I can't. If this is the last moment, I get with him then I will savor every second before he returns to hating me. When I feel him lift his head, I still remain frozen when but then his voice hits my ear again, "I'm going to find out the truth, Ells. Whatever it is, it's the only thing that matters to me anymore."

I squeeze my eyes closed to stop the tears gathering there from falling and I feel his presence leave me, I can't open my eyes until I know he is gone. The last thing I see is his motorbike barrelling away from here.

Fuck, I need to get out of here, this was definitely more than I bargained for when I decided to pay Michael a visit. Lincoln is waiting in the SUV for me, no doubt he will have seen Elliot. I'm surprised he stayed away, unless he knew Marcus was here. Did he? Did he know I would be safe, or did he just think I could handle myself? It's not like I'm not always armed, and he has seen me fend off men twice my size.

I make my way back to the car and find him leaning against it waiting for me.

He nods as I approach, "Everything okay?"

I nod in response, unable to voice the mixed feelings I'm experiencing right now after going toe to toe with both Elliot and Marcus.

"He's gonna be heading home," he says and we both know he is referring to Marcus not Elliot.

"You should be there when he gets back," I say, finding my voice again. I consider Lincoln a friend, but Marcus is his family. I know how hard he is finding this divide between us all. I don't want to add to it any more than I already have. He looks unsure so I continue, "It's fine, Superman, honestly, just drop me home and go be there for him, he needs you more than I do."

He nods and then surprises me by giving me a hug. My shock causes me to freeze awkwardly in his arms. When he pulls back, I can tell this kind of affection isn't something he shows often. He isn't touchy and overly friendly like Jace, he is more reserved and closed off, so the fact that he is opening up to me more and more everyday warms my heart.

"Let's go," he says, and I nod as we climb into the SUV and head back to the house.

Once inside I know there is only one solution to cheer up my day and I am grateful when I find Cassie and Helen already in the kitchen.

"Mommyyyy," her little voice screeches loud and it speaks right to my heart and soothes me like it always does. It's amazing how someone so small can impact your life so greatly. She really is everything to me. I go to her, immediately sweeping her into my arms, as I come to stand next to Helen. They have a bunch of ingredients laid out on the counter.

"Sassy Girl, what do we have here?" I say, as I nuzzle into her hair stealing a cuddle, as she squeezes around my neck tight before pulling back.

"Cakes, Mommy, cakes!" She squeals excitedly.

"Want to join us, little rose?" Helen asks. I nod with a smile.

"An afternoon of baking with my two favorite girls?" I question, "There is no where I'd rather be," I tell them honestly.

Chapter 16

MARCUS

I drive around for hours trying to settle my thoughts. I am drowning in them. So many thoughts, so many questions, so many variables. I need to get to the bottom of what happened that night. That is where it all started, and it just spiralled from there. I can't sit back and keep waiting for answers. I need to take them and that starts with my brothers and hers.

It's late by the time I get home, I park my bike in the garage at our building. I spy both Jace's Dodge and Linc's SUV, so I know they are home, and an exchange with them is long overdue.

We haven't been avoiding each other, more like I haven't had anything to say to them, until now. I stalk in the door and both their gazes lift to me immediately. Neither are what I was expecting. They don't look pissed or angry at me, in fact, they look as defeated as I feel. It's time to cut the shit between us all.

I don't want to talk about what has gone on between us or Jace kissing Elle, no. I have bigger fish to fry right now and it's time I was let back into the fold.

"What did Elliot Donovan do?" I ask loudly, cutting past all the niceties and getting straight to the point.

"Erm...think you're gonna have to be slightly more specific there, Bossman," Jace snorts, while continuing to drag on the joint in his hand. Clearly, he's stoned and the itch to ream him out right here, is as fierce as him locking lips with Elle last night, which plays on repeat in my head. But I can't be distracted again.

"What did Elliot Donovan do to Elle?" I specify and they both give each other a look, it's a knowing look and it fucking pisses me off. Jace goes to speak first but I cut him off, "Jace, don't give me any bullshit right now, not today," and that is all it takes to stop him from continuing. I swing my gaze to Lincoln as he clears his throat, "You know, we can't answer that for you brother," he starts and before I can reply he continues, "But if you would stop being so reckless and thoughtless you would already know."

"Oh yeah, how's that?" I ask.

"If you put your own emotions aside, you could have figured it out or Elle would have trusted you enough to tell you."

"Oh, so she can't trust me who she has known practically her whole life, but she can trust the two of you, who she has only known for a few weeks?"

"Maybe that's the point," Jace interrupts, "Maybe, because we don't know her, we see the bigger picture." I look between the two of them and they both share the same expression on their face. "So, you both know then," I say and it's not a question so neither of them answer. "Okay then," I say and turn to leave.

"Where are you going?" Linc asks, and I don't bother stopping to answer him.

“To be reckless and get answers,” I reply, before I’m out of the door and back on my way. I don’t hesitate in going for my car instead of my bike and I am putting it in drive and flooring it away from home before I can second guess what I’m doing.

It takes about fifteen minutes to get across town to the hill and it's a drive that is sickly familiar, once I get into the North Side of town. My dad and I used to drive this way home almost every day when we lived here. I push those memories aside until I find myself on track to Elle’s house or should I say Zack Royton’s? Who even knows at this point?

I arrive at the gates and take it in properly for the first time. The house is enclosed with a huge wall that has to be at least twenty feet tall and the large iron gates look more secure than a prison. I know the only way I was able to slip in last time was just pure timing and good luck. I won’t be so lucky again. I pull up to the front of the gates and notice an intercom, so I quickly wind down my window and press it.

There is a crackle of interference before a stern voice comes through the speaker, “Name?” Is all I hear.

“Marcus Riviera.” There’s no point trying to hide who I am. I’m almost sure everyone in there will know who I am by now, after what happened a couple of weeks ago. There is a pause, and no one answers me and just when I think I am going to have to buzz again, the gates start opening up slowly. Once they are wide enough, I drive through them and down the long road until I get to the front of the house.

It's newer than most of the houses in North Hill and stands wide and tall across two floors. The front has large pillars on either side of the big black door and all the windows are trimmed in black too. I wonder mildly how long it's been here and who lived here before they did.

I park and make my way to the front door but before I can knock it swings open and reveals Zack Royton.

"Little late for a house call," he says, simply. It's only then I register that I have no clue what time it is so I just shrug. "Are you drunk?" He asks, and I laugh until I realize how serious he is.

"No," I say seriously before adding, "Hungover as shit but not drunk."

"Are you calm?" He replies, and it's then I can truly see it. I mean I felt it the day he hit me but now I really see it. That brotherly instinct. He wouldn't let me close to Elle again if he felt like I would hurt her.

"Yes," I reply, and he nods.

"Then you can come in," he replies, stepping back and gesturing for me to enter. He nods his head over my shoulder, and I turn to see two guards that I didn't notice approach us, turning and walking away. Very tight security.

I enter and stand in the hallway as he shuts the door and turns to look at me. We both silently assess each other before I break it, "Where is she?"

He doesn't respond for a few seconds before he says, "You and I should talk first, come with me," he doesn't wait before walking further into the house and I have no choice but to follow.

I follow him into what looks like a home office and as I enter and shut the door behind us, he gestures to a trolley in the corner that has a decanter, of what I presume is whiskey, and four upside down empty glasses.

"Want one?" He asks.

"Will I need one?" I reply, in return and his only response is to turn over two of the glasses and pour us both a drink. I guess that answers my question. He hands me the glass and gestures to the chair in front of the desk, as he takes a seat behind it.

"I'm sure you have questions for me?" he starts, as he swills the amber liquid around his tumbler before he takes a sip. When I just sit there, unsure of where to even start, he continues "I knew your father."

Four words I never expected. What the fuck? How the hell did he know my dad?

"How?" I force the word past my shock.

He shrugs slightly before placing his glass on the desk and clasping his hands together with a serious look on his face, like he is unsure of what to say.

"Michael found me," he says, simply.

"Why weren't you with Elle and your mom?" I ask, quickly.

He frowns, "I wasn't with Elle and Sarah King because I didn't know about them." I can tell from his tone, that me referring to Mrs. King as his mom, pissed him off. He continues, "I was adopted at six weeks old by my mom and dad," he says, before adding "Helen and Arthur Royton, you met them last time you were here."

I nod, recognizing his reference to the elder couple who were present the day I discovered Cassie.

"They were always honest with me about not being my biological parents but that didn't change anything for me. As far as I was concerned, if my biological parents didn't want me, I didn't want them."

"Is Elle's dad your father?" I wonder out loud.

"No."

"Is mine?" I panic, trying to figure out my dad's part in this.

"No," he says again, and I seem to be getting more questions than answers.

"Then how did he become involved?"

"Michael contacted me directly when I was eighteen, he told me about Elle. At first, I wasn't interested but then when I got used to the idea of her, I got curious," he supplies, with a shrug before adding, "Apparently, Michael had always kept in touch with my parents and they all decided to keep me in the dark until the time was right."

"Until the time was right for what?" I ask.

"For me to meet Elle. I wasn't interested at first but then things changed."

"And when did you meet her?" I ask, gritting my teeth, afraid I already knew the answer.

"I'm the one who took her from Black Hallows."

I huff out a breathy laugh, unsure of what to even make of this whole situation. He took her from Hallows, from me. I should be mad, but I have a loop of conversations I have heard from Elle playing on repeat in the back of my mind and it keeps me wondering.

"Why?" It's the only word I can come up with.

"Michael called me, told me--" he pauses briefly before continuing, "He told me she needed me, and I came," he says, like it's just that simple. Like he didn't change the course of things by doing that.

"Why did she need you?" I ask, warily as I replay the conversations, I've heard Elle have over in my head. I think about the day with her parents, what Lincoln has told me and how Jace has been acting. None of it makes any sense.

He remains silent so I push on, "Where does Elliot Donovan come into this? If this town was what she needed to escape, why has she come back? What happened to make her leave?" The questions barrel out of me as dark thoughts start consuming my mind, but I shut them down.

"They aren't questions for me, Marcus," he replies, grimly.

I nod knowing he means that it's something only Elle can tell me if she chooses to. I suddenly have the desperate urge to see her now more than ever. We have both walked away from one another, but that's over now.

"Where is she?" I ask, standing up.

He stares up at me, silently assessing me before he sighs, stands himself, comes out from behind the desk, and heads towards the door.

"Come with me," he says before walking out. I follow behind him in silence as he leads me through the house and towards a large set of glass doors. He puts a code into a keypad at the side and it beeps, and the doors click open. He waits until I'm next to him before nodding out the doors, it's only then I look out and across the grass at the back of the house to find another large house. Nowhere near the size of the mansion we are standing in, but still, large by most people's standards.

"Up the stairs, to the top floor, last door on the left, code for the house is 1208," he says, gesturing for me to exit.

I take a deep breath and look between him and the house before offering him a nod and making my way outside. The cold October air bites into my skin but it's a welcome pain, it reminds me that I'm alive, that I have something to live for.

I walk across the grass until I hit the path for the house, bypassing a large swimming pool. The house is dark and it's only then I look at my phone and see it's almost 11pm. Fuck, probably way too late to even be thinking about doing this, but I'm here now.

I take a deep breath one more time and then punch in the code Zack gave me.

It's only once inside and up the stairs I realize the code is my birthday. I don't know what to think of that, so I just follow the directions that Zack gave me the rest of the way in the house.

I stand in front of the door for ten minutes. When Zack gave me directions to this room, I just presumed he'd meant Elle's, but the sign on the door reads 'Princess Cassie'. *Fuck*. What do I do? Is Elle in there? I mean, she must be otherwise why would he have told me to come here. The ache in my chest appears again and the tightness of it has me rubbing at it. Can I do this? Do I have a choice? If I want answers then I have to open this door.

I curl my fingers around the handle and press down as softly as I can. I'm not sure if Elle is going to be asleep or not but I can guarantee that Cassie will be and the last thing I want to do is wake her. I push it open as gently as I can and feel relief when it doesn't make a noise. I step inside and push the door closed behind me. The room is dark, and the only light is coming from a small nightlight on the stand next to the bed, but it allows me enough light to see around the room. I was right Cassie is asleep, but so is Elle. I find the two of them tangled together, Elle curled protectively around her, in a big spoon, little spoon situation and it makes me smile for the first time in weeks. I curse silently as it really hits me, for the first time. Elle is a Mom, she has a living, breathing daughter that is not only dependent on her but also completely devoted. Just like she is to her. I don't even need to see them together to know that it's all over this room.

The walls are covered in children's' artwork and pictures of them together. There is a bookshelf on one side of the bed filled with books of all sizes, a toy chest overflowing with toys, and stuffed animals. Next to the light on the nightstand, is a framed picture of the two of them pulling silly faces and the word 'besties' is printed on the frame.

I look back at the two of them curled together and I feel such a mixture of emotions. I imagined this would be my life one day, coming home from work to my family, to

Elle. Now, here she is having it with someone else. Fuck it hurts, yet I can't bring myself to care enough to leave. Yes, she lied to me, and I have no idea what is going on. Where the truth starts or the lies end, but if I keep walking away, I am never going to find out.

I take one last look at them and gently pull the duvet to cover them more. Elle sighs, cuddling in closer to Cassie, as a lock of hair drops across her forehead. I lean in and softly brush it away from her and she turns downwards, slightly offering me more of the back of her neck. I notice something there and lean even closer to take a look, immediately wishing I hadn't.

Just below her hairline is a small tattoo of a star with the words 'make a wish' in script arched above it and an intertwined E and M beneath it. E and M, Elle and Marcus, the star, the quote, the tattoo is for me, for us.

Not wanting to linger any closer and wake her, I move quietly across the room and drop into an armchair in the corner. I need answers and the only way I will get them is if I stay. I sit there for hours watching them. I don't know when, but at some point, I must have fallen asleep, because next thing I know I am opening my eyes to be greeted with the miniature version of Elle standing right in front of me watching me sleep.

I almost have a heart attack; how did she even get over here without me hearing? Are kids supposed to be creepy? Is this like a thing they do? Are they actually little ninjas sent to scare you? As soon as my eyes lock with hers, she smiles, lighting up her whole face. Fuck, she looks so much like Elle. I open my mouth to speak when she dives onto my lap and covers my mouth with her tiny hands.

"Ssssshh...Mommy sleeping," she says, with a giggle and a not so quiet whisper. I can't help but smile. I look over to the bed and sure enough, Elle is still fast asleep, looking as peaceful as an angel. I bring my gaze back to Cassie and nod; she slowly drops her hands from my mouth. I don't say anything, one, because she told me to be quiet and two because I haven't got any fucking clue how to talk to a child.

She doesn't seem to mind my silence as she jumps off my lap and speaks again.

"Come on, tea party," she says, as she pulls on my arm and when I stand, she drags me across the room to a small table that has four child size chairs around it. She pushes me down into one before I can even agree or disagree. She rushes over to the bed and grabs a pink rag doll and an orange giraffe before rushing back to the table. She places them into the two seats on one side and then takes a seat next to me.

I have never felt awkward around a girl before, but I guess there is a first time for everything. She takes the teapot and proceeds to fake pour us all a drink and then passes one to me. I can't help but laugh at what is happening right now, the king of the South Side Rebels is having a fucking tea party. I should care, but the smile on her face squashes any other thoughts in my mind. It's a smile that makes me feel like I would willingly do anything for her, it's exactly how I used to feel about Elle. Do I still feel like that? I look into the eyes of the little girl, who is half King and half Donovan, and for the first time it feels like that fact doesn't bother me so much.

Chapter 17

ELLE

I feel myself waking and I immediately stretch out my arm to reach for Cassie, but all I find is cold sheets. Not unusual but it means something else has her attention, otherwise she would have woken me up. I keep my eyes closed, comfortable enough that I feel like I could fall back asleep when I hear them.

"Nuh uh, Mommy never lies, it's bad," I smile with my eyes closed at her statement, she remembers everything I say. I don't know another kid her age that has a memory like hers or speaks so well.

"Well, that is not what happened, and you weren't even there, I was," Marcus' voice hits me like a fucking Mack truck. WHAT THE FUCKING FUCK!?

I snap my eyes open so fast that it takes a few seconds for my vision to unblur but sure enough there he is. He is sitting at Cassie's small table, looking ridiculously oversized in one of her tiny chairs while she sits on his knee like she belongs there. They are looking at an old photo album of mine, that has a ton of pictures of Marcus and I as kids and swapping stories about them.

Cassie reciting them from hearing them during bedtime stories and Marcus reciting them from memory.

I didn't think my heart could get any fuller. Seeing Cassie with Asher is one of my favorite sights in all the world, they really do adore each other. I thought I would never match that, but seeing Cassie with Marcus, fuck, that hits me differently. Which is crazy right because I love Asher and Marcus, albeit, not in the same way, maybe that's why it feels so different. Asher is my friend, my family and Cassie's dad but in a way, Marcus is much more than that. He's my first friend, first crush, first love, what I thought would be a forever kind of love. It sure felt like it, well until the Cassie bomb dropped. I thought we would never recover but now here he sits with his arms around her like he has been here every day of her life. Fuck, why is life so complicated? I sit up slowly but clearly not slow enough because as soon as I move both pairs of eyes hit me.

"Mommyyy!" She screeches, as she struggles off Marcus' huge lap to come racing towards me. She dives onto the bed and cuddles into my side.

"Look, Mommy! It's River, he came back, you said he wouldn't, but he did, he came to play with me, tell me stories, and have tea parties," the words tumble out her mouth, so fast and mispronounced, in her excitement and I can't help but turn my gaze back to Marcus.

He is staring at us both intently. I can tell immediately this thing with us is far from over, was it ever going to be over? How much longer can I keep him in the dark? Every time I push him away, he just comes back harder. Is it time for him to know the truth? He must want something otherwise he wouldn't be here, would he? He said as much in the cemetery yesterday. Fuck, why is *my* life so complicated? Surely, this is not what an eighteen-year-old should be dealing with. What fucked up karma gods thought I was equipped enough to deal with all this shit?

Cassie bounces off the bed and runs back over into Marcus' arms and he welcomes her. It's the most beautiful thing in the world, to see him accept her like that. It's as beautiful as it is when I see her with Asher but with a twist of something that sends butterflies through me. Seeing my childhood crush, turned hot as fuck leader of the South Side Rebels interacting with my little girl should be a crime. Why does he have to be good at everything? My thoughts quickly go back to the alley on Friday night as I remember just how many things, he is good at and I start to blush, so I shut it down.

I pull the covers back and stand up and watch as his gaze falls to my body taking me in, all the way down to my feet and back up, I shift my weight feeling awkward, as his gaze settles on my torso. At first, I can't believe he would just openly stare at me like this but then it hits me what I am wearing. I went to bed in his hoodie, the same hoodie I came home in when I spent the night with him after the club. FUCK.

I never gave it back and have been secretly sleeping in it most nights with his scent soothing me to sleep. Now here he is, catching me in the act. In the past, it wouldn't be a big deal, I was always stealing his hoodies and never giving them back, but this isn't the past, we aren't those same kids. But from the look in his eye, can we be? He doesn't look mad or awkward, in fact he looks happy, smug even and something else I can't quite decipher.

This situation is way past being awkward so I say the only thing I can think of to get us out of it "Breakfast?" He smiles like he can see what I am trying to do but he just nods and stands up taking Cassie in his arms effortlessly. Holy fuck. Forgive me father for I want to sin. I feel like tearing the hoodie from my now burning skin, but considering I only have panties on underneath, I highly doubt it would help the situation. Instead, I do what any normal awkward eighteen-year-old virgin would do, I run. I grab my sweats from where I threw them on the floor last night and flee the room, quickly, in the hopes he knows to follow and make my way down to the kitchen.

Arthur spies me immediately from where he is already cooking breakfast. "Perfect timing, firecracker, this is almost done. Where's my little spitfire?" he asks but trails off as Marcus walks in behind me cradling Cass in his arms. Arthur's eyebrows practically hit the roof before he quickly schools his expression, looking at me and then back to Marcus.

He grabs a towel and wipes his hands before speaking as he walks round the counter, "Hey, it's Marcus, right?" he starts, which is a stupid thing to say, considering he knows exactly who he is. I roll my eyes as he continues, "It's great to finally meet you. Heard a lot about you, I'm Arthur."

Marcus looks at me quickly before offering his hand to Arthur. "Good to meet you too," he replies, gruffly.

"Grandpaaaa, pancakes!" Cassie interrupts them, as she squeals and they both smile.

"Of course, I made pancakes for my best girl," he says, going to take her from Marcus, but she snuggles back into him. I'm not the only one shocked, but I am the first to smile.

"I thought after twenty-five years of marriage I was your best girl?" Helen jokes as she enters the kitchen. She drops a kiss to my head as she passes where I'm now sitting at the counter and goes straight to Marcus and Cassie.

"I'm so happy to officially meet you, sweetheart. Elle never stopped talking about you," she says, and I feel myself turning red. She is playing the part of embarrassing Mom, perfectly.

"I'm so sorry about your father, he really was one of a kind," she adds, and I catch the slight flinch from him before he represses it and offers her a nod and a smile.

"Breakfast is ready," Arthur interrupts. I guide Marcus over to the dining table as Arthur and Helen carry plates over and we all take a seat. Cassie refuses to leave Marcus' lap, so he is left to eat around her.

To say breakfast is awkward, would be an understatement. For once, I'm grateful for the ramblings of a toddler. Cassie saves us all from getting into anything too deep as she talks about her love for Olaf from *Frozen*. To his credit, Marcus listens intently, as if what she is saying is the most fascinating thing in the world, it only makes me love him more. Fuck, I am so screwed.

Once we have finished eating, it's clear the tension didn't go unnoticed as Arthur begins to clear the plates, Helen leans over to Cassie.

"How about you and I take a trip to the park?" She says, and the squeal Cassie releases answers the question before she does and for the first time, she tries to eagerly leave Marcus' arms.

"Yesssss!" She screeches.

"Okay, well come on let's go get dressed," and I smile at her gratefully for stepping in.

Cassie begins to run out of the room before she slams to a halt and turns around to run back to Marcus. "Will you come play again?" She asks him sweetly and I tense.

He looks to me ever so slightly before concentrating on her fully, "You bet," he says, simply and she smiles at him and holds out her hand.

"Pinky promise?" she asks, and I see his shock. He didn't know I continued our tradition with her, but he doesn't hesitate to curl his large, little finger around her tiny one as he repeats the words back to her. She turns away and flees the room without looking back and I stare after her knowing that I have no choice but to let him in. The only person in the world I won't hurt is that little girl and keeping Marcus in the dark will do that. He needs to know the truth. As if he has direct access to my thoughts he speaks.

"I need the truth, Ells," he says softly, but with conviction and I nod, swinging my gaze back to him. "I know, River, I know."

Chapter 18

ELLE

I agreed to give him the truth, but I needed to shower first. We walked back to the main house in silence. Once there, I led him to the basement that houses the indoor pool, games room, theater, den, and gym where Ash and I usually work out. I told him to wait for me and to call Linc and Jace, he wanted to argue but I asked him to trust me. While getting ready I also text Ash to come over. If I am going to do this, then I need to do it right and it involves him, Jace, and Linc now too.

By the time I have showered and dressed in something that doesn't belong to Marcus, I make my way back to the den, where all three Rebels and Ash are waiting for me. The tension is so thick I don't even think my knife could cut through it, and trust me, it's a sharp knife.

I take a deep breath and enter the room fully and all four gazes hit mine. I'm not surprised Ash is the first to speak. "Hells Bells, you don't have to do this," he says, standing and striding over to me. I'm not the only one that catches Marcus' snort. I ignore him, in this moment in favor of Ash as I reach out and pull him into a hug.

"Yeah, Ash, I do," I whisper to him quietly before I pull back and offer him what I hope is a reassuring nod and smile.

I turn and make my way over to the sofas the guys are currently occupying and take a seat on the vacant one. Marcus and the guys sit across from me and Asher joins me by my side. My heart is beating out of my chest. I can barely take a breath, but I know I must do this. I breathe as deeply as I can manage before I start locking my gaze on Marcus who is already staring at me with an unwavering glare.

"First, I need you to promise two things," I say, mimicking what I said to Lincoln not too long ago and I see the smile tug on Linc's lips out of the corner of my eye, clearly, he is thinking the same thing.

"Okay," Marcus replies, without missing a beat.

"First, what you learn here today can never leave this room, that also needs to include what you already know in regard to Zack and Cassie," I say, and I'm amazed that I even manage to get the words out, and he just nods so I continue.

"Second, you can't do anything about it."

"What?" he laughs slightly, like I am joking.

"You can't do anything about what you learn, you can't retaliate," I say firmly.

"Why would I retaliate?" he asks, through gritted teeth, swinging his gaze to Asher and then back to me.

"Just promise me, River," I plead with him because I need that from him more than anything right now.

He sees the look on my face and looks to his brothers at his side, to Ash, and then back to me. He takes a deep breath and then says, "I promise, Ells."

I take one last deep inhale into my lungs and let Ash put his hand in mine. Taking the strength that he is offering before I let another person into my darkest secret.

"Greg Donovan is Cassie's biological father."

Six words hang in the air like poison.

He laughs looking confused, "I'm sorry what? Is this your idea of a joke? He's like five years older than us," he swings his gaze back around to all of the boys. "Are you guys fucking with me? Because that really isn't fucking funny," he asks again, as he brings his eyes back to mine and when he does his smile disappears.

He sees it then, the truth. I know he knows what I am trying to say but he must hear it. I need him to hear the words from me. I need to get it out there and strip away all the lies and lay everything on the table. The only other person in this room who knows the story I am about to tell is Asher. All three Rebels are going to get the truth today.

"Greg Donovan took me from the woods that day. He drugged me, beat me, and then raped me. Elliot knew. They were planning to sell me. They had some sort of deal with my parents that went south and the collateral damage to be paid, was me. My parents agreed," I pause briefly to take a breath and Ash squeezes my hand so tight I think he might break a finger. I know he is reliving that night all over again with me. "Asher overheard his father talking about me and followed him to where they were keeping me. He went to your father to ask for help. They both got me out of there and I left town with Zack, just wanting to forget everything."

I speak with such a monotone voice that is void from any emotion because I won't allow myself to break again for them. Asher is deathly silent beside me, Jace and Linc both look distraught at hearing the full story. Marcus is frozen as he absorbs my words. My heart is hammering hard in my chest, but I ignore it and push on, "Except, I couldn't forget when I was carrying a reminder with me."

He closes his eyes and starts shaking his head like he can rid himself of the images I have painted for him. If only life were that easy. I don't know how we are going to be after this, but it was time for the lies to stop.

"Michael died because he chose to save me. Elliot murdered him for making a move against him. I'll never be able to put into words how sorry I am. It's my fault, I'm so sorry."

As soon as I say the word sorry his eyes snap open and focus right on me. "Sorry?" He chokes out in barely a whisper before he jumps up and throws himself to his knees in front of me, clasping my hands in his. "Sorry," he repeats again, in anger, "Ells, don't let me ever hear you say that shit ever again."

He takes my face in his hands as he cups both my cheeks. He wipes away a tear I'd let drop and leans in until our foreheads touch. We remain like that until he pulls back and it's only then I realize the others have left the room and only the two of us remain.

He takes a deep breath, I can hear when it catches in his throat, the emotions of what I have just revealed flow through him. I can see the moment when the anger takes over, his eyes become wild and black and I know he is just thinking of all the ways he wants to burn the world for me, for us. I won't let them take him from me again. I reach over and grip his face in my hands until his eyes collide with mine again.

I force every bit of love I feel for him into that look and I open my mouth to speak but he silences me with a punishing kiss that steals my breath. He pulls me off the sofa until my legs go around his torso and he grips me so tight, it's like he never wants to let me go. I feel safe, loved, at home. When he pulls back, we are both breathing heavily, lost in each other, as he leans in and plants one more soft kiss against my lips.

"These lips are mine, baby," he says, as he leans in again and pulls my bottom lip between his and sucks. "You're mine, don't ever let me catch them on anyone else again," he adds, before he nips at me unexpectedly.

"And are you mine?" I ask, with a whisper.

He laughs, "Ells, I have been yours since the day we met," he says, with a pained grin. He reaches out and strokes a hair behind my ear before he adds, "we just got separated for a while as you ran and I was lost, but I won't let that happen again. If you're here, I'm here, if you run again then I will be right by your side, it will be you and me baby, and that beautiful little girl."

I pull back from him and he frowns but I push my hand between us and hold it out to him, "Pinky promise?" I ask, and his frown changes instantly.

“Pinky promise,” he replies, and for once everything in my world feels right.

Chapter 19

MARCUS

"Greg Donovan is Cassie's biological father."

Six words that just bounce around my head on repeat. Six words that are something I had thought of but dismissed as being unimaginable. Six words that have just blew my fucking world apart. Six words that are going to change the course of my life forever.

I won't ever forget them or the way she said them. With no emotion and with complete and utter finality. Something she has had over three years to know and become accustomed to. How can she do that? Have no emotion about what they did to her.

I think about the fourteen-year-old girl who was my best friend. My sweet, innocent, little King who would get mad at me if I even killed a spider. What they must have done to her. Did they hold her down? Did it happen more than once? Did she scream?

I fight with everything I have, to stop the vomit from clawing its way up my throat, as I try my hardest to focus on Elle and only Elle. She is the only thing that matters, but all I can see is images of what they no doubt did to her. So many emotions flood my body, I'm hard pressed to narrow it down to a single one, I don't know what to feel. That's a lie, I do. I feel rage. Pure unfiltered fired up rage. They took her, hurt her, fucking raped her, and to make everything worse than that, they fucking got away with it.

Just like every other crime they commit. Their criminal roster is so fucking long it would take days to recite. Yet have they had any punishment? Of course not because if your wallet is deep enough then people will look the other way.

This town. This fucking town. A town I used to love is now nothing but a fucking shell of my broken heart and grief.

A town run by Elliot Donovan and his fucking lackeys. His own son included. A son that fucking raped my Ells. Fuck. You think they have already taken so much from you and just when you think you have nothing else to give, they come back for more. My chest tightens and I try to focus on anything, other than the numb feeling in the pit of my stomach. How can you feel so much love and contentment at the same time as your heart being ripped out and stomped on?

I pull Elle close again and enclose her in my arms tightly, like my embrace alone can shelter her from the horrors she has already endured. They will pay, I will make them fucking pay. I was already planning on killing them for what they did to my dad, but now? Now, I am going to fucking destroy them. Ruin them. Make them fucking bleed until my body is coated in their blood. And lucky for me, I know exactly who is going to help me.

I stand gripping Elle and taking her with me and she squeals slightly, and it makes me smile. How? How can she still smile and laugh and just live her life after what they did to her? Cassie. That's how. She took the worst thing that could ever happen to her and turned it into the best and she did that with the help of Asher fucking Donovan.

Fuck. Asher Donovan, the little prick I have always loved to hate, saved my girl. Saved her when I couldn't and has been continuing to save her every day since. He stepped up and not only risked his life to allow her to escape but puts himself at risk everyday by being a father, to his sick fuck of a brother's little girl. Fuck if I can't feel anything but respect for him at this moment.

"Thank you for telling me, baby," I finally manage to croak out.

She shrugs like it isn't a big deal, when it is the biggest fucking deal in the world and then smiles "Figured it was the least I could do before Jace punched you again," clearly, she is aiming for a joke but the memory of what I said to her hits me. Jace was right. Now, I know the truth. I do wish he would have done more.

I push my forehead against hers and scrunch my eyes closed tight, like that will help me erase what a prick I was, "I'm so fucking sorry, Ells. Fuck, how can you even forgive me after the things I have done and said?" I puzzled.

"Easy. You're my River," she says, reaching up and stroking a hand to my face. I open my eyes to lock my stare on hers, "Everyone who isn't us is insignificant," she adds, repeating what I said to her a few weeks ago. I smile and nod because I can't say anything else.

I drop Elle to her feet and start to take a step back, but she stops me, "I have a plan," she says simply. "I'm different, stronger, and I am going to make them pay."

"Let me be strong for you," I plead with her, but she is already shaking her head at me before I even finish my sentence.

"No. They took from me, Marcus, stole from me. Stole something I can never get back and trust me when I say, I am not the only one. I don't need a knight in shining armor. You don't get to ride in here on your white horse and slay all my evil dragons. I'm not the broken little girl they ruined. I'm their worst fucking nightmare and they will bleed at my feet, no one else's."

Fuck if I'm a sadist because her words make my blood run hot through my veins. My beautiful little King is a fierce fucking warrior. If she wants to make this town burn, then I want to be the one to hand her the match.

"Ells, I would lay down my life for you without blinking, if it meant giving you justice," I reply honestly.

Her stare turns hard, "No more Riviera blood is going to be spilled on my watch." I can feel the love she had for my father shining through. She misses him just as much as I do.

We both straighten and I sense she needs a moment to collect herself. I take a step back and nod towards the door, "I'm just gonna go chat with the guys," I say, and she smiles and nods allowing me to turn around and walk out.

Chapter 20

LINCOLN

We left the room silently to give the two of them some time to talk. Keeping Marcus in the dark for so long has been hard. It's caused cracks to show in our group for the first time ever and I didn't like feeling so out of control. I guess we are a lot like real brothers in that sense, we have to fight sometime. I think about what he must be going through right now. How he must be hurting. For himself, for her. Hell, I'm hurting for her and I have only known her a couple of months, the pain he must be enduring is surely astronomical.

Jace and I are leaning on the wall opposite to the door we have just come out of. I can feel the tension rolling off him from here. I turn my head slightly to take him in. All I can see right now is pain and grief, for Elle, for Rachel. There is barely a trace of the usual flirty and easy going Jace I love. No, in his place is the dark Jace, the reckless Jace. The one who smokes too much and parties too hard. I wish there were something, anything I could do to help him, that won't end in him numbing himself with the drag of a joint and a warm female body. But that's just him. A pure soul. A soul that is bleeding, bleak, and broken.

Then there is Donovan. He is pacing the short corridor in front of us. Back and forth, back, and forth. His face the perfected blank mask. His stare cold and predatory. He looks to the outside like he doesn't have a care in the world and the only reason for his pace, is that he simply wanted to move. But I see it differently. The more time I spend with him the more I pick up on his little tells. I watched his eyes darken when Elle mentioned Greg, I saw his knee bounce ever so slightly when she talked of her escape and now, I see the slight tightening of his shoulders beneath his jacket. All giving me a glimpse of the emotions he feels whenever he thinks about that fateful night.

He is just as dark and broken as the rest of us. I know he is fighting more demons than either of us right now, but his pacing is putting me on edge.

"Can you not?" I snap at him before I can even think about it and I feel Jace chuckle beside me.

He halts and looks at me, "Can I not what?" he asks.

"Quit fucking pacing," I respond, and Jace laughs out loud next to me.

"Yeah, chill out, Donovan. They are probably gonna end up fucking in there, nothing to worry about," Jace unhelpfully adds.

His head snaps his way, "What have I told you about that fucking mouth, Conrad?" he seethes at him but Jace just laughs again.

"I don't remember, maybe we can ask Elle what she thinks of it?" he preens, wiggling his eyebrows at Donovan.

"Don't make me fucking hit you," he snaps in response, taking a step towards him and I lean up off the wall taking a step forward too. He allows his gaze to shift to me, then back to Jace before settling back down again like he can tell that I am the bigger threat. It's ridiculous really that he would think that same as the way people think Marcus is a bigger threat than me or Jace. He's not. I'm not. We are all lethal in our own right and to dismiss one of us is a deadly mistake.

"What, Blackwell? You think you can take me?" he says with that signature sinister smile.

I smile back at him pushing out my chest and broadening my shoulders, "I know I can."

He takes another step, "Now listen here, you fucking piece of --" he starts but Jace cuts him off.

"Oh, for fuck's sake, will you give it a rest? We are all on the same fucking side here, Team Elle! So just play nice and suck each other's dicks or something to relieve all this tension," he says casually, as he gestures around us with his arms.

I freeze slightly but I see Asher catch it and just when I think he will do what every typical Alpha male would do in this situation and hype the macho shit of, 'Fuck off I'm not gay,' he smirks. His eyes take me in from head to toe and darken into a stormy blue before he looks to Jace and says, "In his fucking dreams."

Oh, if only the little psycho knew the stuff he got up to in my dreams. I lick my lips willing him to play this game with me, "No, in yours, dark prince," I fire back.

He brings his blue gaze back to mine but before he can say anything, the door swings open and we all freeze. Marcus appears alone and he lets the door close behind him before leaning back against it with a sigh. He stands there in silence for a minute before collecting his thoughts and when he stands to his full height again his stare locks on Donovan's. Fuck this won't be good.

He stalks towards him and just when I feel Jace tense beside me like he is ready to intervene with me if need be, Marcus does the last thing I ever expected.

He grips Asher by the neck and pulls him towards him, "We are gonna kill every last one of them for her," he says simply. Arousal surges into my body, thinking about how it would feel if I were to grab him like that instead of Marcus. I shut it down quickly.

Asher clamps his hand onto his shoulder, "For her," he responds.

I look at Jace as he looks at me and we both speak at the same time, "For her."

Asher and Marcus look at us and we all nod before Marcus backs away and slumps back against the wall and slides down until his ass plants on the floor. He looks broken.

I take a step forward, "I know this hurts, brother" I say to him softly and he flinches.

"Hurts?" he says, with his voice laced so pure with anguish as he looks up at all of us. "Fuck. I wish it did hurt. I wish I could feel some pain. All the fucking pain she no doubt felt. I wish it would slice through my body and leave me to bleed out until I could do nothing but fucking feel." He pounds his fist against his chest, "I feel empty. Weak. Useless. Because somehow a simple dare between friends turned into the worst night of her fucking life. Changed the course of fucking everything and all I did was let it happen," his voice is so strained with the emotion he is trying to contain. I can't think what to say to make him feel better, but Donovan beats me to it.

"This wasn't your fault, Marcus," he soothes, "You were a kid, she was a kid," his voice strains a little now too. "You should have been free to play a simple game without this happening. The darkness my father and brother create would make any man sick."

Marcus' glare focuses on that statement and I can tell Elle hasn't even told him the half of what is going on yet. Before he can speak though she emerges, and we all swing our gaze to her. This girl. Four men at her mercy all willing to lay down their life for her without thought. She doesn't realize how amazing she really is.

She takes us all in, offering us a small, soft smile before she finally turns to Marcus. She crouches down beside him and presses her head against the side of him like just his presence can heal her. I'm sure it will. He pulls back and the look they give each other makes me feel like they are the only two people in the world for each other.

She stands and holds out her hand to him, "Come on, Riv," she says, as he puts his hand in hers. "Time to make them pay," she adds as she drags him to his full height before swinging her gaze to the rest of us, "together."

"Together," we all respond.

Chapter 21

ELLE

Can you be calm in the midst of chaos?

Whenever I used to think about anyone else finding out about Cassie, it would make my heart race, my throat tighten, and my palms sweat. But here I stand, surrounded by four guys who know my whole truth, and instead of worry all I feel is calm. Like a weight has finally been lifted off my shoulders.

I have no idea what is going to happen next or if we will survive the plans I have in mind, but I do know one thing. We will do it together. Marcus, Asher, and I were always like the three amigos, well to me anyway. One for all and all for one. They may have hated each other, probably still do, but one thing was always more important than that, me. Now, not only do I have both my best friends back by my side but somehow my army of two has grown to four.

Four beautiful, broken, and completely deadly boys who for some reason have chosen to have my back. Do I deserve them? Not a chance in hell. Will I do everything in my power to have their backs? Without question.

I take in each of their expressions and all of their gazes are locked on me.

Asher is holding onto his usual impassive mask that he thinks is impenetrable and it is to most, but not to me. I have seen him on his best days, his worst days, and everything in between. He hates reliving that night just as much as I do, maybe even more. I hope he understands why we had to. Things had to change. There are too many secrets in this town and not enough truths, I didn't want to keep being a part of that. He has more self-control than anyone I know, yet even I can see that psychotic pulse pumping through his body as he imagines all the ways to gut his own father and brother. All to avenge me. No one's best friend is better than mine.

Jace has his own dark look. He too is trying to mask it with his sexy little crooked smile that makes most girls fall to their knees. If only those vapid bitches could see the real prize is his heart and not his cock. A heart that is tainted and broken beyond repair but still willing to bleed for those he loves. A heart that even after all the cracks it has endured, still somehow manages to have enough space for me and my daughter. Jace Conrad. A playboy, a man whore, a party starter, and somehow the sweetest soul I have ever met.

Lincoln doesn't have to hide his emotions but that is mostly because they are always the same ones. Overthinking, calculating, and concerning. It is rare to be blessed with one of his smiles and that just makes them even more heartfelt. He is the type to think before he acts, assess before he attacks, and befriend before he trusts. Yet, for some reason that trust, he so rarely doles out, was given to me blindly and without question. He went against his own morals, his own brothers, all to keep a secret, and protect two girls he didn't even know. Something I will never be able to repay.

Then there is Marcus. My beautiful River. I wish the emotions on his face were hidden and masked as well as the others. Then I wouldn't have to see the heartache there. Ever since I came back here and locked eyes with him, I could see he was different, hardened. I knew that was partly because of me but mostly because of Michael. The look in his eyes now though, that is all for me. He looks devastated, destroyed, damaged. All because of a secret I thought I would take to the grave. But that's the thing with secrets they always come out in the end. It's better he heard it from me.

Should I have told him earlier? Maybe. But that doesn't matter now, we are here either way. I spoke my truths and he kissed me. Kissed me like he wished his lips could erase any pain I have ever felt. Who knows maybe they could? But the look in his eye now doesn't make me feel like I have him. Am I his? Yes. I always have been. But is he mine? I thought yes, but that was before. Before that night, before everything that has happened over the last few months, before all the lies. This is the after and I don't know how we live in the after.

All four of them eye me like I have all the answers. I wish I did. I wish I could just go over to the Donovan mansion right now, with these boys by my side, and put a bullet in the skull of every single one of them. That would be justice. Watching the life drain from their eyes would satisfy me. But would it be enough? Will it ever be enough?

My revenge has been delayed and derailed so many times since I returned that I figure one more day won't hurt.

"Come on," I say with a chirpier tone than I feel, and they all frown at me in confusion.

"Revenge on a Sunday, princess?" Jace asks, his tone still too far from his playful self.

"Not today, pretty boy. Today, we have some fun. Family style," I say in return.

This weekend feels like it has lasted a lifetime already, and after the dark and serious morning we have all had, I decide the best thing for all of us is a little R and R.

I lead them all back into the main part of the house and with perfect timing, Helen returns with Cassie. I ask if she wants a pool party. She screams so loud I think the whole of Hallows might have heard her, before she dragged me away to her room, so she could get dressed.

We return to the pool in matching swimsuits. She is wearing a lilac one piece that has tassels across the chest that match with my bikini in the same color. The tassels on mine come across my breasts and around my back with a couple on the side of my bottoms. We look cute as fuck, if I do say so myself. Perfect for an afternoon of family fun.

I find Asher is the only one waiting for us and when I take in his still fully dressed form and the frown on his face, I know he isn't staying.

"Daddy, no swim?" Cassie asks him and I see the pain in his eyes at having to be away from her.
He picks her up and cuddles her close, breathing her in before speaking to her, "Not today, angel. I have some work to do," he locks eyes with me on the word work and I feel rage at the thought of whatever shit Elliot has him doing.

"Okay, Daddy. Love you," she says, and he smiles.

"Always?" he asks and then it's my turn to smile.

"Always," she responds happily before she runs to climb into the small kiddie pool, we have next to the main one.

We watch her go and then I turn back to him, "Sure you can't stay?"

He takes a deep breath before looking at me, "Elliot is getting suspicious, keeps asking where I am going. I don't want to draw any attention to myself."
I am nodding before he has even finished because this is what it comes down to. Protecting our little girl, no matter what the cost. We both know that won't be complete until both his father and brother are buried six feet fucking under.

I give him a hug, "Watch your back and call me if you need to," I say to him.

"You too, baby girl," he says, dropping a kiss on my cheek before he turns and leaves.

I hate to see him go, even more than I usually do. But I'm not stupid, I know the front he must keep up, the risks he takes every time he comes to see us.

The rest of the guys are nowhere to be seen, but I know they would have told me if they were leaving, so I don't wait around before I grab Cass and get into the main pool. We play and splash around for a while in the shallow end before we start practicing her swimming. Marcus finds us first, he is still fully clothed, but I notice he has shaved and changed. I mildly wonder how. He slumps down into one of the loungers by the pool and locks his gaze with mine. My questioning stare must be obvious because he answers my unspoken question "I had a bag in the trunk of my car. I wasn't sure if I was leaving town or not," he says simply with a shrug like it's nothing. Like it would have been okay for him to have just left again.

"River," I start, but I don't know what to say. Would he really have left again? Would I have let him? Would it be better if he went? The truth is out there and still, I don't know what to do. Who said being young is the best time of your life?

I turn my attention back to Cassie and continue to hold her while she practices her paddle, but all the while I can't help but think, what I would do if I lost him again. Would I survive it twice?

Chapter 22

MARCUS

Desire. It's a funny thing, isn't it? How it can consume you, taking over your whole body until it's the only thing you can feel. No matter what emotion I feel, when it comes to Ells, I always feel in excess. Too much, too long, too fucking hard. It doesn't matter. All that matters is I fucking feel it.

Love. Hate. Rage. Passion. Friendship. Desire.

I have seen Elle King in a bikini at pretty much every stage of her life. From vacations when we were kids, to going to the swimming hole in middle school. I never really thought much about it, not even when we were fourteen and I was practically a fucking walking hard on. I mean of course I was hard; I was a young hormonal teen seeing a girl's body for the first time. Now? Well, clearly, I am still a hormonal teenage boy because I can't even see her body, and I am hard as fuck watching as she floats around the pool with Cassie. In a pool where she is in a bikini and wet. Apparently even the fact she is playing with her child isn't enough to deter my cock right now.

No, all I am thinking about is how the bikini must be clinging to her body as the water laps around her.

How it would feel if I slid into the pool with her and swam to her until I could back her against the side of the pool and wrap her silky wet legs around my body. Drag my tongue across every droplet of water until she was wet only from my mouth.

I swipe my hands across my face like that will help erase the images I am conjuring up in my head. Jesus fucking Christ, I am as hard as fucking steel. I should not be lusting over her, not when she is just being a mom. Especially not after what she just told me, but I can't help it. The image of her riding my hand on Friday night and the taste of her when I sucked my fingers into my mouth are at the forefront of my mind right now.

Jace finally comes back, dressed ready to swim. He and Lincoln went back home to grab some stuff so they could enjoy a swim with the girls. I could have done the same, but honestly there is too much pent-up energy running through me right now to be able to concentrate on anything. Even something as simple as swimming. He runs in from the direction we came earlier and cannon balls directly into the middle of the pool making the girls laugh. When he pops back up, he swims right over to them.

I would never admit this out loud but sometimes I am jealous of Jace Conrad. You'd think him kissing my girl would be the thing that makes me jealous but it's not. Okay that's a lie, the fact he has had his lips on what is mine makes me want to punch his fucking face, but that's not why. I am jealous of how he can handle himself, his coping mechanism. How he takes his heartache and pain and just mashes it all down and puts a smile on his face, like his world hasn't fallen apart. It's something I always wish would come easy to me.

He grabs Cassie from Elle and launches her into the air before catching her again and dunking her back into the pool to her shoulders. Over and over, he does this and the giggles that pierce the air, pierce my heart at the same time. I can tell by the interaction and Elle's smile, that they must have done this before.

I spent the last few weeks getting drunk and high believing some stupid bullshit because I was too fucking hurt to see the truth. All the while I was missing out on this. Missing out on time spent with Elle, her daughter, my brothers, our family. I should have been here with them. The ache in my chest returns. Just as I rub my hand to it like I can stop it from hurting, Elle looks over and catches my eye. She looks back to Cassie and Jace, saying something I don't hear, they both nod, and then she is looking back at me. She dips under the water and swims towards me until she hits the side.

She puts her hands on the side and uses the force to pull herself from the water. My eyes immediately lock onto her tits. Her perfect, fucking magnificent tits. I don't allow my gaze to linger too long and I drop my stare as she pushes out and stands. I am ready to take in the rest of her body until my eyes drop to her stomach and I freeze. The arousal I felt is doused in cold water when I take in the multiple scars on her abdomen. Some faded but there are two prominent ones that stand out against her otherwise perfect skin.

I feel sick. My skin is on fire, my heart rate increasing, and my stomach churning. My hands grip my thighs so tight; I think I could draw blood even through the fabric of my fucking jeans.

Taken. Beaten. Raped.

Those words float around my head on repeat and still my mind can't contemplate the horrors she must have endured. Why? Where? For how long? Fuck. I need to get out of here. Find that fucker and bleed him dry.

I stand from the lounger so fast that my legs push it back and I scramble to stay standing. The anger pushes through me in a way I have never felt before. I can't do this. I am going to break my promises before the day is even out. Don't retaliate. That is what she asked of me because she knew. She fucking knew her skin bore the marks of his sick and twisted crimes.

He is going to fucking die. I am going to torture him until he begs me to stop. I will not feel better until his body is cold and dead, at my fucking feet. Even then, I doubt I will feel anything other than this fucking fury.

Fuck. I never thought I would see the day where I would understand Asher fucking Donovan. He changed after Elle left, and I always just put it down to him being quiet and reserved. I thought people were exaggerating when they said he was deadly. Now I get it. That night changed him. That night made him. That dark stare, that fierce protectiveness of Ells, it all stems back to that night.

I turn and flee the room quickly pushing through the doors and smack right into Lincoln. The rage is consuming me so much, I didn't even see him. I can barely breathe. He grabs me by the shoulder and forces my face to his so he can lock eyes with me. He observes the look in my eyes and then moves his gaze over my shoulder. I see him do a quick once over and then look back to me.

"Don't be reckless, brother, not anymore. She needs you strong and by her side," he squeezes my shoulder before pulling me into a quick hug and smacking me on the back. He moves around me and pushes through the doors I just fled through.

I hear the doors again and take a deep breath again before turning around. It takes everything in me to try keep my emotions in check. When I turn, I find Elle with a towel wrapped around her, and immediately feel like a fucking prick for making her feel like she needs to cover up. She thinks I fled because of her body, I did but not in the way she thinks. I didn't run because of her body; I ran because of what he did to her body. She gestures to a room off to the side of where we are standing, and I follow behind her until we enter, and she closes the door behind us and leans on it.

She speaks before I even get the chance, "Look, Marcus," the way she says my name cuts through me, whenever I'm not River I know I'm not going to like what she is about to say. "I understand if this changes things for you," I frown not sure where she is going with this. "I don't have any expectations of you. My life is messy and complicated, and it won't be easy, so if you need an out, then no hard feelings. You will always be my best friend."

WHAT THE FUCK! My heart is beating so fucking hard I hear it pounding in my ears. *Pound. Pound. Pound.*

Is that what she wants? Have I read this whole situation wrong?

I am frozen and not really sure what to say, "Is that what you want?" I ask and even I can hear desperate confusion in my tone.

"It doesn't matter what I want," she answers immediately before she closes her eyes and takes a deep breath before opening them and taking a step towards me, clutching at the towel around her. That fucking towel, like she needs a barrier between us, like there haven't been enough fucking barriers that we've had to break through. I want to rip it from her body and burn it. Tell her to never fucking hide anything from me ever again. Peel back every layer she has built around her heart until I can grasp it in my hands and keep it forever.

"Ells," I start, but she cuts me off.

"No, Marcus, I get it I do. There are plenty of girls out there who don't come with all this baggage and a scarred body," she says, gesturing to herself, her voice getting smaller and quieter with each word. Nothing like my usual strong and confident little King.

Oh no, not today, baby.

I move quickly, until she is pushed back against the door and my body is covering hers. Not a bit of space between us. Her gaze locked on my chest.

"Baby look at me," I whisper and wait until she gives in and looks up. "There is only one girl in this world who is perfect for me and I am looking right at her. She shouldn't want me, I for sure, don't fucking deserve her, but god, do I fucking want her. I want her more than my next fucking breath," a tear rolls down her cheek and I move my hands to cup her face swiping the tear at the same time. "You are my missing piece, Ells, I just don't work without you."

"But I'm not whole anymore Riv. I'm broken and bruised. Used," she whispers, her voice breaking and the pain in her tone fucking guts me. How can she see herself like that? She tries to tear her gaze away from mine and push me back, but I fight against her.

"Then I am going to fucking put you back together, baby," I grit out, gripping her neck and pulling her forehead against mine. "Build you up until you are whole again because we won't let them win. They don't get to fucking ruin you, ruin us. They are insignificant in our lives, little King. A blip on the radar. Me and you baby, me and you are going to change this fucking world. For you, for her, for us. Because you are it for me, Elle King, always have been, always will be. I love you."

We are so close that our lips brush as I pour my heart out to her and lay it all on the line. I can't believe I just let those three words fall from my lips. I didn't even realize how fucking true they are until right this second. I love her, I am in fucking love with her. I mean I knew I had feelings for her, I always have, whether it be love, hate, friendship, fucking lust. They all tangled together in a complicated web of secrets and lies, of her being my everything, then my nothing. She came back to this town and back to my life and made it impossible to ignore her. Not like I could have ever forgotten her. Elle King is a stain on my soul that can't be erased.

"I love you too," she whispers back and the taste of her breath mixing with mine at her confession will be something I remember for eternity. Etched onto my black fucking heart.

Four words. Four beautiful words and I can fucking breathe again. For the first time in three fucking years, I can breathe without being in pain. Like I am alive and have something to fucking live for. I step back and rip the towel from her body, and she gasps.

"That is the last time you hide from me, Ells. From now on every secret you have is also mine, every tear, every pain, every fucking thought" I push back into her, "You share with me, okay?"

"Okay," she says.

I drop my gaze and take in every scar allowing my fingers to trail my gaze and her breathing is heavy.

"These scars they tell your story, our story, don't ever fucking hide them, not from me," I say before my hands move to her hips and I grip her tight, "I will return every single one of these ten-fold," I grit through my teeth. "I will bleed out every fucking person who has ever hurt you until there is no one left but us, our family."

I don't give her a chance to respond before I press my lips to hers, kissing her without restraint and regret. Pouring every fucking emotion I can into it. Hoping she feels it all. My love, my pain, my fucking grief. It all belongs to her.

This is our love story. It isn't a fairytale or happily ever after. It's fucking messy and painful. The good, the bad, and the fucking ugly. Love isn't enough, not for us. No. We need more. We need friendship, family, loyalty, and the blood of every person who has dared to hurt us.

And I want it all. Every single part of it. And I want it all for her.

I pull back and lock our gazes once again. No more words needed. I interlock her fingers with mine and pull her away from the door so we can get out and head back to the pool. She uses her other hand to grip onto the arm that is holding her hand and I have never felt more powerful. The King of the South Side finally has his Queen. Now it's time to fight for our fucking Kingdom.

Chapter 23

JACE

Three months ago, I would have woken up hungover with my dick being sucked. That's how my Sundays normally went. One girl, two, three? It didn't matter as long as it ended with me coming down their throats. It was just the standard way to end my weekend. Never in a million years would I have thought that I would spend it playing with a two-year-old. Even more than that, never would I have thought that it would be exactly where I wanted to be.

What is it they say? A Sunday well spent brings a week of content. Well, I can't think of a better way to spend my Sunday than with my brothers, by my side, and the two girls who have stolen our hearts. Albeit in different ways but getting to be part of Elle and Cassie's family day really is something special.

Now instead of being sandwiched between two girls, begging for another round with the playboy rebel, I sit around a dinner table having a true family dinner for the first time in, well, for the first time ever. I have had dinner at the Roytons' a few times now, but never like this, never with everyone I care about in one room. Those other dinners were usually just Elle, Linc, Cassie, and I, the others either absent, busy, or giving us privacy. Now, the table is full. Lincoln is sitting to my right and Cassie to my left, Elle is next to her and then Marcus, Helen, Arthur, and Zack. The only person missing really is Asher and fuck me, at this point it's weird him not being here. I have gotten quite used to the little psycho and I know I'm not the only one.

Arthur is telling the story of how he and Helen met, and it has us all laughing as we listen. It's clear they are still as in love now as they were when they met. It's rare to see a love like that, pure and untainted. Watching them with Zack and Elle, hell even the three of us Rebels, it's clear how much love they have to give.

Cassie giggles along with us, even though she probably doesn't really understand what is being said, who knows? Kids are a mystery. I find myself watching her constantly, afraid I will miss something magical. I have this fierce instinct in me, to protect her and her mother. I won't let anything happen to them.

"Mommy, do you love River like Grandpa loves Grandma?" Cassie interrupts Arthur. Elle chokes on her food. I burst out laughing at the face she makes, I'm usually the one who causes her to look like that. Who knew the kid could do it too? I move to fist bump her, but she just stares at it, hmm looks like we will have to work on that one kid.

Everyone at the table pauses like they want the answer just as much as she does. I know they have talked some stuff out and I saw them holding hands around the pool today, but I haven't had the chance to grill them about whether they are finally a fucking couple.

Elle looks at Marcus before she looks back at Cassie and pushes a hair behind her ear that has escaped her tiny ponytail.

"Yeah, baby, I do," she smiles softly, and I don't miss the blush rising up her neck at her admission, or the smiles from the rest of her family.

I see Cassie think about it for a while and just when everyone else is about to start getting back to eating she finally responds, "I love him too, Mommy."

She lets those five words settle into the air and goes back to her dinner, like it was nothing. I look to Marcus and see him frozen, fork half in the air, his gaze locked on Cassie. I know how hard things must have been for him recently. I'm sure there are many things he wondered about Elle King over the years while he was pining for her. I may not have known anything about Elle but that doesn't mean I don't know pining when I see it.

Marcus was always an impenetrable force. Nobody could ever get too close. Not even me and Lincoln. He may have let us into his life, had our backs and shit but there was always a part of himself that he held back. It was the same with girls, never showing interest in anyone. Sober or drunk, it was only ever to get his dick wet. He wouldn't kiss any of them, never went back for seconds, and probably couldn't even name the last girl he fucked before Elle showed up. It's like he knew, knew that she would eventually come back here, back to him.

He just never thought she would bring someone else with her. I'm sure he always wondered if she would have met someone else, fallen in love. I just doubt it ever crossed his mind that the someone she loved would be her child. The last few weeks have changed the course of his life forever, it isn't just him and Elle anymore. It's about accepting her as who she is now, who she has become, and that includes her daughter. If they make a go of things with each other, then it isn't just their hearts they have to worry about but hers too. And a heart so small should never be broken.

Since she came back, I have seen a whole new side to my brother. She changes him for the better and the worse. He is calm in a way but also never more reckless, possessive, protective, jealous, loving. So many things that only come out when Elle King is near. It's like he was a padlock, and she was the key, they only work together.

Elle reaches out and clasps her hands around his and it shocks him out of his stupor. She gives it a gentle squeeze and goes back to her dinner as Arthur resumes talking and we all pretend that wasn't such a big moment.

After dinner I help Helen wash up because I am not a total fuck up, and then we head to the den to wait for Elle to finish up bedtime with Cassie. It's weird seeing this side to her. The day I met her I thought she was just a hot as fuck chick I for sure wanted to bang, that didn't last long when I found out Marcus knew her, and I saw the way he looked at her. Yeah, every guy was fucking looking at her that day, but no one looks at her the way Marcus does.

I got used to her as the little badass who kept putting him in place, she was all cocky comebacks and deadly threats that I thought were jokes. Since then, I have seen her laugh, cry, clean up busted knuckles, and make up stories for Cass. Hell, I have even seen her covered in blood after slitting some guy's throat. It's safe to say we are closer than ever and having that kind of bond back in my life, a family bond outside of my brothers is something I really cherish.

I am the last to enter the den besides Elle. The den, more fucking rich people shit. It's a huge as fuck room that has two huge sofas with a large glass coffee table between them, there is a bar in one corner and a pool table in the other. A big as fuck flat screen tv and even more game consoles than we have at the loft. A few doors lead out of here, one I came through, one that leads to a bathroom, and another leads through to fuck knows where.

I walk in and drop onto the sofa by Linc and nod at Marcus, "You okay brother?" I ask, considering this is the first time it has been just the three of us all day.

He blows out a breath, "Is it fucked up if I say yeah?" he replies.

I smile, "Of course not."

"How can I be happy yet fucking so filled with rage at the same time?" he adds.

I shrug, "Easy," I reply, and he frowns, "What? You finally got the girl, the same girl your ass has been trying to lock down since you were in fucking kindergarten, from what I gathered, so course you are happy, just makes her pain all the more painful to you."

He nods processing what I said as Lincoln speaks up, "This is far from over brother, this doesn't just start and end with Greg."

"What do you mean?" Marcus asks.

"He means there are a lot more people on my list of sorry fucks who need to die," we all swing our heads as Elle steps into the room, her voice calm and collected, as always when talking about this. I honestly don't know how she does it.

Marcus gets up and she crosses the room to him immediately, "I'm gonna need that promise again, Riv," she says softly, and he looks confused, "the one where you promise not to retaliate."

He looks at us and grinds his teeth and cricks his neck before looking back to her, "I'm still here, aren't I? Not bathing in that sick fuck's blood."

She smiles, "I know," she pats his chest and looks to the two of us, "All of you, come with me," she says, before turning away from us and making her way to the door in the corner of the room.

We enter behind her and it looks just like an old, unused storage room filled with boxes and some stuff covered in dust sheets. She moves until she is on the other side of the room, and then shifts back some tarp hanging from the wall that reveals another door. It's not like the one we came through; this is steel and there is an electrical keypad next to it and Elle taps it a few times until it beeps, and she opens it.

She turns to us and gestures us inside; I look at the guys before we all move at once to enter. Fuck, this is not what I expected.

"Fuck," Marcus hisses under his breath coming in behind me.

The door closes behind us and I hear the click and beep of the electrical lock going back in place. The room isn't big, but it has enough room to fit a large table with six chairs around it. The back wall has a large screen above multiple smaller ones all connected to what seems to be one computer. There is a chair in front of the desk under the wall and multiple programs running on the screens. On the left of the room is a large whiteboard with photos stuck to it that have names underneath, few of them have red crosses across the face.

"What is this?" Marcus asks, breaking the silent tension of the room.

"This is my revenge," Elle replies simply.

"What do the red crosses mean?" I ask, a little warily because there are at least eight of them.

"Eliminated," she says mindlessly, as she taps away on the computer before she sits in the chair and spins it towards us and gestures for us to sit at the table.

We all take a seat.

"You are all here because I trust you," she says, "with my life, with my daughter's life and with my secrets." I take in the faces on the board. There are the obvious ones who I recognize; Greg and Elliot Donovan, Sarah and Jonathan King, that low life The Octopus, hell even the fucking Captain of Police is up there. What the fuck? "All the details of everything are irrelevant, so I will only tell you what you need to know," she exhales, looking between us all as we nod.

"You know the obvious. Greg raped me," I feel Marcus flinch beside me when she tosses that statement out casually. "What you don't know is, it was payback for something my parents did. They knew all about the Donovan's sick little sex ring and went against him anyway, he paid them back by taking me," she shrugs again like it's nothing and I grind my teeth.

"Elliot only used to take the girls no one gives a fuck about, the ones forgotten or left behind on the South Side," she locks eyes with me and grimaces apologetically knowing she is referring to Rachel and others like her. "Well after they took me, they realized they could keep all the other North Breds in line by threatening their children to keep them on their side."

She stands and gestures to the board, "As you can see, he has a lot of people on his payroll willing to help keep his crimes on the down low. Police, lawyers, even a politician, no one is willing to go against him," she adds, before turning back to us and that's when I see it.

Marcus speaks first, "What happened to Nate Maxwell?" he asks, and I think back to the day Elle had a black eye and little Donovan kicked our door clean off thinking Marcus had done it. Their whispered words revealed the Octopus had done that to her.

"I went after him," Elle says carefully, "I --" she starts again but Lincoln cuts her off.

"I killed him," he says calmly and both Marcus and I swing our heads to look at him.

Lincoln isn't bold or brash, he doesn't allow his actions to get the better of him. He always thinks through every scenario before doing something, assesses every threat and goes through every backup possible before doing anything. That is what makes him so ruthless. He isn't unpredictable and reckless like Marcus and I, so this shocks the both of us.

When he sees us staring, he snaps losing some of his cool, "What? It was him or her," he says, gesturing to Elle.

"Lincoln's right, he saved my life," she adds, and he smiles.

"Sorry, what was that King? I didn't quite catch that," he teases her, and it lightens the mood of this fucked up room.

"Don't fucking push it, Superman," she responds.

"I never asked what happened in the warehouse. Whose blood were you covered in?" I voice my inner thoughts.

"What fucking warehouse?" Marcus snaps.

"You were busy being a dickhead," I respond, with a smug smile and he huffs.

Elle ignores his outburst and points to another red cross on the board, "This guy, I sliced his throat," she says, like I just asked what she wanted for breakfast and then gestures to the other four red crosses next to the first adding, "Lincoln dealt with the rest," she pauses before also saying, "In what Ash tells me were some very colorful ways."

She smiles at him clearly amused by it and he rolls his eyes in response and I look between the two of them like I am seeing them for the first time. It's only now I see a whole new side to both of them, that's a given with Elle, considering I don't know her that well yet, but I thought I knew Lincoln. Yet, here I am seeing a whole new side to him, a side that is darker than I ever imagined but also filled with more smiles and jokes. He is comfortable with her, he trusts her. They don't just have a friendship between them but something else, a bond made in blood. I mean I'm not naive, we aren't the good guys, we beat on people, do drugs, drink far too fucking much but I have never gone this far. But after what they did to her, can I blame them?

Am I ready to do the same? Before Elle revealed her secrets, I don't think I would have ever been able to kill someone. But now, here I sit thinking about what they did to her, the scars on her body, and the protection of her daughter.

Would I kill for them? Without a shadow of a doubt.

"So, what happens now?" Marcus asks.

"Now?" She repeats sitting down in the chair opposite us. She looks us all in the eye before she adds, "Now we go to war."

Well fuck me, three lost Rebels have finally found our way. Death, chaos, and vengeance, a path drenched in blood and all for two amazing girls. Let's go to fucking war.

Chapter 24

ELLE

The only words to describe my weekend with the Rebels is cathartic. No more secrets, no more lies, just everything out in the open. I feel like I can breathe again for the first time since I laid eyes on Marcus that first day of school. The rollercoaster we have been on the last few months isn't something I enjoyed, yet somehow, we ended up here. Together again, by each other's side, and ready to slay the fucking world.

The guys left late last night after we spent a couple of hours going over all the information I have and mixing it with everything we know. I didn't think I could ever shock Marcus again after he found out about Cassie, but the more he learned about Elliot, the angrier he got. He knew he was bad he just didn't know how close to the devil he actually is. Not forgetting about his fucking spawn of Satan son either.

I wanted to ask Marcus to stay but I know he needs time to process everything that he has learned. So, I sent him home with his brothers and then spent the night wishing I hadn't. I ended up sneaking into Cassie's bed at 2am, where I eventually managed some sleep before my alarm woke me.

Now I'm getting ready for another week at Hallows High and for the first time I'm nervous. Which is dumb, right? I finally have all three Rebels by my side, so what the hell am I so worried about? It's just I haven't done this before, been someone's girlfriend. Am I Marcus' girlfriend? Girlfriend just sounds so insignificant. Like just a regular couple of teenagers. What we have is so much more than that. He is so much more than that, our hearts are intertwined in a way that can't be undone.

My phone pings signaling that the guys are here, so I grab my bag and head outside. I find Linc's blacked out SUV parked in the drive with the front windows down. Lincoln is driving and Jace is sitting in the passenger seat. Marcus is standing with one of the back doors open, clearly waiting for me.

He looks a lot more rested than he did this weekend, he has his usual dusting of facial hair shadowing his chin and dark sunglasses pushed up onto his head. He is smoking a cigarette and has the collar of his leather jacket popped up. He looks like temptation. Not just for me but any woman who has a pair of eyes in their head. When he sees me, he smiles sinfully, one that says I am his, I don't think I have been this happy since before I left here, over three years ago. Cassie makes me happy, ever since I heard her little heartbeat, she has been my lifeline daily but not having Marcus around always left a hole in my heart. A hole that is now filled with all things Marcus Riviera.

"Will you two stop eye fucking each other and get in the car before we are late, I wanna stop at Starbucks on the way," Jace whines, leaning out of the window like a puppy.

I break out of my appraisal and feel myself blushing as I move towards the car until I'm next to Marcus. He grabs my bag off my shoulder and throws it in the back of the car before turning back to me.

He curls a hair behind my ear that has blown into my face as he speaks in a low soft tone, "How'd you sleep?" he asks gently, it sounds super fucking weird to hear him speak in anything other than his stern gravelly tone.

"Erm, okay I guess," I say with a small smile trying to work out what is going on with him, something is different.

He smiles and it is nothing like the cheeky flirty smirk he has given me before, no, this smile is full of love. It freaks me out a little to see such a change in him.

"My little King," he says softly, "I thought we said no more lying," he cups my face and places a chaste kiss on my forehead before pulling away and gesturing for me to get inside.

I stand frozen for a second, considering I was expecting a kiss a bit more, shall we say steamy? I mean I am not experienced really, not past Marcus, but I have gotten used to the way he kisses me without restraint. How it consumes me, and I can feel it in my entire body. I shake my head to myself and climb into the back of the car and slide across the seat so Marcus can slide in next to me.

"Seatbelt," Marcus says, and I frown and Jace chokes a laugh out trying to hide it into a cough. I look up to find Lincoln's gaze in the mirror and see a smirk on his face too.

What the fuck is going on?

I pull my seatbelt on and off we go to school. Jace got his wish and we stopped for coffee on the way. I asked for an Americano and he got me a Iced Chai Tea Latte. I would have dick punched him, but the fucking tea drink was too good. I cursed him out in my head while he watched me drink it.

I am looking out the window watching as we approach the school when a hand hits mine. I look down to see Marcus curl his hand around mine. He gives it a gentle squeeze and I look up until our eyes lock. We just stare at each other; I've no idea what he's thinking but he looks like he has so much to say. I guess neither of us know what is going on with us now. Weird right? How can you confess your love to someone but have no clue how to what? Date them? Fuck knows. I'm not exactly an expert on this kind of thing.

"Erm, I hate to break up the backseat party, but your other girlfriend is waiting, brother," Jace cuts into our stare off with a chuckle.

Marcus and I break each other's gaze and look out of the front of the car to find Cherry waiting. Well, this should be interesting. I look to Marcus as he looks back at me.

"How are we playing this?" he asks, and I laugh.

"Erm, we aren't playing anything, Caveman," I reply with emphasis on the we. "You were the one who entertained Cherry, therefore that looks like a you problem to me," I say, with a smug smile before exiting the car leaving Jace and Lincoln's laughs behind.

"Morning, Cherry," I say, as I pass because now that I have Marcus, I realize my wanting to murder her was slightly over the top. I was hormonal, sue me.

"Morning, Elle," she says with a smile and I almost feel guilty. Almost, then I remember the way she slammed her lips against Marcus' on Friday, and it takes everything in me not to slam her into a wall. Not quite as bloody as stabbing her so I see that as progress. Personal growth.

I plonk myself on the wall of the steps and ready myself to watch the show. Jace and Lincoln pass Cherry and make their way to me as Marcus finally drags himself from the car. We can't hear what he is saying to her, but he looks resigned and she starts gesturing wildly with her hands, getting the attention of a few other people passing by. The slap comes out of nowhere and honestly, I didn't know anyone would dare to hit Marcus, except for maybe me, but damn she did that.

"Damn," Jace echoes my thoughts with a laugh, "And that is why I don't do girlfriends," he says, looking at me and taking in my bemused expression. "No offense, princess, but it's just not worth the drama," he adds with a shrug.

"None taken, pretty boy, but trust me when I say, the right person is worth everything," I reply and then drop my head to his shoulder.

Marcus steps back up, "Tryna steal my girl again, Conrad?" he asks with a smirk.

Jace laughs, "If I wanted to steal her, I would," he taunts with a challenging smirk, and before Marcus can reply he jumps off the wall and throws me over his shoulder and runs into the school. He doesn't let me down until we get to my locker and when we lock eyes, we both laugh.

"Thank you for the ride, pretty boy," I say with a wink and he laughs louder.

"It's the only ride you're getting," he says with a smile, but I don't get to ask what he means, as Marcus and Lincoln join us.

Marcus grabs me and pulls me to him, "Gonna need you to keep your hands off my girl, brother," he says with a tone that is only half joking.

Jace smiles wider, "Hey, she is the one who kissed me," he says innocently and gives me another wink as I roll my eyes.

"Do you honestly have a death wish, pretty boy?" I ask in exasperation.

"Nah, Marcus knows I'm only playing, he wouldn't hurt me."

I open my locker and grab the book I need for the first period and slam it shut before looking back at him, "Who says I was talking about Marcus?" I ask with a smile before I turn and walk to class.

By the time lunch rolls around the news of Marcus and I being a couple has reached the whole school and apparently there is a divide of Team Elle and Team Cherry. Fucking stupid school politics.

We sit at our usual table only this week. I am sitting next to Marcus with his arm draped around me. He hasn't stopped finding ways to touch me all day and with my newfound libido, I wish I could say that some of those touches were inappropriate. Except no, for some reason Marcus has decided our relationship is strictly PG-13. He hasn't given me more than a peck on the lips and after what we did in the alley on Friday, it is safe to say I am wanting, no needing more.

"Fuck happened to McCormick?" Marcus' voice brings me back from my thoughts and I look up to see that Chad has finally come back to school. My heeled boot didn't do enough damage in my humble opinion but the limp he is still sporting, satisfies me anyway.

"Ask Queenie here," Jace says with a smile and Lincoln laughs.

Marcus looks between the three of us, "What am I missing?"

I exhale a huffed breath, "Chad tried to make a move against you, I just politely told him that would be a mistake," I say with a shrug.

"I hear she broke his jaw and his cock," Lincoln says, casually scrolling through his iPad. His tone suggests he picked up that information from the high school grapevine when we both know he would have hacked into his medical records.

"I'm sure the female population will thank me for the latter," I take a sip of my sweet tea and scan the cafeteria again.

"The guys could have handled it, you didn't have to step in," Marcus replies, and I frown.

"I know how to handle myself, Marcus," I snap back at him.

"Yeah, but you shouldn't have to," he says, getting louder and I huff.

"It was no big deal," I shrug.

He pulls me closer to him and grabs my face until I look at him, "It was a huge deal you could have been hurt, baby," he leans in and presses his lips to mine. I sigh, opening my mouth to slip my tongue inside his. When his tangles with mine, I forget we are in the middle of lunch with an audience of a hundred students. No, the only thing that matters is me and Marcus. He pulls away far too quickly and once again I'm left wanting more.

"I'm not made of glass Marcus," I finally say, my head clearing from the kiss.

"We should finish up and get to class," he ignores me. What the fuck?

"We still have ten minutes left," Jace says, looking at Marcus weirdly, which isn't ridiculous considering he is more likely to skip class altogether than be early. However, he is already standing up and sliding back into his leather jacket. I look to Lincoln who is also watching him closely.

He leans back down and pecks me on the cheek, "Catch you later, baby," and before I can even respond he is stalking away from us and out of the doors.

I frown, "What the fuck was that about?"

Chapter 25

ELLE

The rest of the week has followed the same pattern. Marcus being overly nice, sweet, and attentive, all of which has freaked me the fuck out. I just got so used to his hot and cold attitude, one minute he was threatening me and telling me to get out of his town and the next he was slamming me against walls and using his magical fingers to fuck me. Now, I am dealing with kind and caring Marcus. One who carries my books, gets my lunch, and pecks me on the head. What's a girl gotta do to get more orgasms around here?

I mean I get it, I do, I told him my truths, and this is his way of trying to be respectful, but how do I tell him that's not what I need? I am not some broken little girl; I may carry the scars from that night three years ago, but I don't carry the fear. Not anymore. The only thing I feel when I think about what happened to me is revenge and love. How I am going to pay back all the ones involved in hurting me, and how I will do anything it takes to ensure my daughter is kept safe and never at risk.

It's the weekend now and the guys are all sitting in the cinema room with me and Cassie watching *Tangled*.

It's pretty funny to see the South Side Rebels spending their Friday night watching a Disney Princess movie. But apparently my daughter's convincing skills know no bounds. Even Asher is here and honestly it is the happiest I have ever seen Cassie and the most settled I have ever felt. It's pretty hard to feel worry or be scared when you are surrounded by four beautiful, brooding men willing to lay it all on the line for you.

I am sitting in the middle of a huge, curved sofa, Cass is snuggled into my right side with Ash next to her. I have got Marcus on my left side and the two other Rebels next to him. I lay my head on his shoulder and feel content at knowing almost everyone I care about in this world is under this roof right now, it's blissful. I drag my fingers up and down Marcus' arm transfixed on how the goosebumps break out across his skin every time. I glance up and find his gaze transfixed on the same thing and I halt causing his stare to flick to mine. The blackness I find there makes me break out in goosebumps of my own. How the fuck am I meant to control myself around him? His dark lashes cast a shadow on his cheeks and the glow of the movie just highlights his chiseled features perfectly. I want to kiss him.

He turns back to the TV but I still lift my face so I can press my lips against his neck and the shiver he lets out makes me blush. I think of all the ways our bodies will respond to each other, but he has more restraint than me because he keeps his eyes on the movie.

As usual we don't even make it to Rapunzel hitting Flynn with the frying pan before Cassie is out cold. Asher looks over at her sleeping form and then to me.

"You mind if I tuck her in?" he asks, and I smile.

"Ash, you're her dad you don't have to ask," I remind him, and he gives me the same little smile he always does whenever I tell him he is her dad. It's a smile that says he can't quite believe how lucky he is.

He lifts her sleeping frame off the sofa and bends down so I can drop a kiss to her forehead before he turns and leaves the room. I turn back to the guys and find Lincoln staring after them, he must feel me staring because he turns to me before quickly averting his gaze.

"You like him?" I say finally realizing what all the tension from him towards Ash has been about.

"What?" Jace says looking between us.

"Superman here, has a little crush," I tease him with a smile.

He rolls his eyes as Jace barks a laugh, "I do not have a crush," he replies, emphasizing the word not.

"This is fucking gold," Jace chimes in looking at Linc. "Sorry brother, but think you are shit out of luck for once, that little psycho screams big dick energy. I am sure he doesn't swing your way."

Lincoln exhales a huff like he is pissed off, but I can see the little gleam in his eye. My little Rebel has a crush on Ash. I pocket that information for future reference and make it my mission to find out Ash's thoughts. We might be best friends but something he has never discussed with me is his sexual orientation. He has too much on his plate to think about such trivial things but now I am thinking I should find out.

Marcus snakes his arm under me and drags me until I am sitting in his lap. I squeal in surprise until I realize that he has dragged me into his lap, and I decide not to waste the opportunity. I turn and throw my arms around his neck and surprise him by slamming my lips against his. After a week of gentle kisses, I am ready for more and I don't care if the fucking Rebels are here at this point. He kisses me back for a minute before he pulls away and abruptly stands effectively leaving me to fall onto the sofa.

"I erm," he panics, looking for something to say as I stare up at him in disbelief, "I just need to grab a drink," he says quickly, before he looks at me and pats my head like a dog and then leaves the room.

I sit stunned for a minute before I look at the two remaining guys and Jace bursts out laughing as I speak, "Did he just pat my head?"

"Yes," he manages to choke out before choking back into a fit of laughter again.

"What the fuck am I missing?" I say to the two of them. Lincoln looks uncomfortable so I concentrate on Jace who is wiping actual tears from his eyes the little fucker.

"He is just trying to go at your pace, Elle," he says, turning his tone slightly serious but still with a stupid smile on his face.

I frown, "What do you mean?"

"Oh Queenie, you really know nothing," he replies, shaking his head before patting the seat between him and Linc "come and let Jacey tell you everything you need to know."

His patronizing tone makes me want to dick punch him, but I am feeling desperate, so I move until I am between the two of them. "You're inexperienced Elle," he says, totally serious and I blush. Okay so we are going there, what the fuck?

"I'm gonna need you to make a point before I get stabby, pretty boy," I huff out trying to stifle my embarrassment.

"Marcus is," Lincoln starts pausing to try to find the right word.

"A manwhore," Jace finishes for him and I grimace.

"Seriously?" Lincoln asks him but he just shrugs in response so Lincoln continues.

"Look Elle, Marcus has slept around but that was before. He wouldn't do shit like that now, but now he is dealing with something he has never had to before."

"What's that?" I ask with concern.

"Blue balls," Jace pipes up with a smirk and Lincoln hits him in the head but he just laughs.

"Look, princess, Marcus wants to respect you and wait until you are ready for the next step, virgins can be tricky," he adds, with another shrug.

"I --" I start but have no idea what to say so I try again, "And if I am ready?" I ask quietly and he smiles big.

"Oh, then you have come to the right place, pretty lady, I've got plenty of advice for you to get under his skin," he winks.

I roll my eyes, “Is that so?”

“Yeah, you just got to ramp up your hotness,” he says like it's simple.

“What the fuck does that mean?”

“You know, like all this,” he gestures to my body, “but more.”

“I don’t understand,” I look down at my body and back to him and he huffs out a breath.

“Okay, Elle, how fucking dense are you? Look at you. You’re so hot you’re like fucking fire.”

I squirm slightly under his glare when Lincoln speaks, “He’s right, you’re beautiful, Elle, and you guys have history so can you imagine how hard it is for him to control himself around you?”

“So hard,” Jace says with an exaggerated wink and I laugh.

“You are such a dick,” I mock punch his arm and he laughs in return, “but,” I add pausing, “tell me what to do?” I ask and Lincoln groans as Jace starts excitedly bouncing up and down in his seat.

“Yes,” he says turning to face me fully, “first lose these,” he pulls at the fabric of my oversized hoodie. “He needs to see the skin to crave it, sweetheart,” then he tugs on my ponytail, “also this, let it down, your hair has to be down for us to pull it,” he winks again, and I blush harder, yet I can’t imagine having this conversation with anyone else.

I look towards the door quickly before I ask my next question, “Do you have any tips?” I say quietly and he smirks.

"Lincoln is your guy for that, he knows his way around a guy better than I do," he says leaning past me to pat his shoulder.

"The fuck is that supposed to mean?" Lincoln replies.

"I've seen you suck a dick, your technique is flawless," Jace says, jumping up onto his knees and leaning over me, to mimic sucking a dick to Lincoln, just as Ash enters the room. He takes one look at us and turns back around and leaves.

We burst out laughing at his retreating frame. I often wondered if I was missing out only having Marcus and Ash as friends when I was younger. People would find it weird that I never hung around with girls but all I felt was lucky. I feel that way again now having them both by my side and ever better my little group has grown and has two more amazing guys in it.

Our laughter is interrupted with an alert going off on Lincoln's iPad at the same time Marcus comes back in.

Lincoln picks up the tablet and quickly scans whatever is on his screen before cursing, "Fuck."
I immediately sit up straight at the tone of his voice and the look on his face, "What is it?"

He looks at Marcus before he speaks to me, "Movement down at the docks, we have got a couple of people watching it and they just heard a new shipment is coming in," I can tell by how serious he is being that I am not going to like what he says next.

"Twelve girls no older," he pauses, "no older than eighteen."

"Fuck," Jace curses now standing and beginning to pace and I feel a pang of regret for bringing someone else into the darkness of my revenge. Greg may have killed his sister, but he didn't have to be involved in this, probably wouldn't be if it weren't for me but there is no going back now.

I stand, "Well, what are we waiting for? "Let's go," I say but Marcus steps up gripping my arm.

"We aren't just going somewhere without checking it out properly," he lectures, looking down at me as Ash returns to the room. He looks at his grip on my arm and frowns.

"The fuck is going on?" he asks calmly, yet I can hear the undercurrent of rage in his tone.

I pull my arm from Marcus, "No offense, River, but I wasn't asking permission. I have been doing this without you for months. You're my boyfriend, not my fucking keeper, you don't wanna join the fun, cool, you are more than welcome to stay here but I'm going."

I don't give him a chance to respond before turning my attention to Asher, "We have girls down at the docks, I need CCTV images and any information you have on the guys stationed there, Lincoln will get you up to speed with anything else," I say, gesturing behind me.

I stalk away from them all without waiting for an answer. I make it to the stairs before I feel a presence and an arm wrap around me.

I know immediately from the scent that it isn't Marcus and I turn to find Jace. "Look, pretty boy, I will say the same to you that I said to Marcus," I start but he holds his hand up cutting me off.

"Wear your leather pants," he smiles cheekily. "He won't know what's hit him," he adds walking backwards away from me and I can't help the laugh that bubbles out of me. I shake my head at how ridiculous he is as I make my way to my bedroom but that doesn't stop me from grabbing my leather pants.

Chapter 26

MARCUS

I can't remember the last time I was outnumbered. Since I met the guys, we have always had each other's backs, they have been there for me no matter what. I thought they would take my side throughout anything, but ever since Elle King barged back into my life, things changed. That is how I find myself on a stake out in the car putting the girl of my fucking dreams at risk the longer we sit here.

We are parked facing the dock yard that is adjacent to the docks watching a few guards walk up and down guarding what I have been told is a container filled with young girls. There are easily over two hundred containers here, and the knowledge of what's in this one makes me wonder what might be in the rest of them. Lincoln is sitting in the driver's seat with Elle next to him, while Jace and I lounge in the back seat. Nobody has spoken in a few minutes and the silent tension is putting me on edge.

"What's the plan?" Lincoln asks, without taking his eyes away from the scene in front of us.

Elle shrugs even though he isn't looking at her, "In and out, keep it quiet," she muses simply and all it does is remind me how many times they must have done this before behind my back. This isn't the Elle and Lincoln I know, the beautiful girl next door and my quiet reserved brother, no these are different people entirely.

"Knife only," he nods, "got it."

"And keep her fucking alive," Donovan's voice hits all our ears from the tech he gave us to wear earlier and for once he and I are on the same page. I watch in the mirror as Lincoln rolls his eyes so this must be the norm also.

She ignores Asher and looks in the back at me and Jace, "You got your weapons?" she asks and we both nod.

She waltzed out of the cinema room before I could protest any further and returned ten minutes later dressed like Lara Croft. Tight ass leather pants that hugged her so snugly, I thought they might burst, and a black top tucked inside them, her tits cupped perfectly. She led us back to the secure room we entered last week and showed us a closet filled with different weapons. Watching her strap blades and a gun to her body was practically porn.

Now, here we are ready to fucking murder and not the first time for her, apparently. I wish I could say I don't know what happened to my sweet little King, but I do. I know exactly what happened to turn her into this and I wish I didn't. So, if getting her revenge is what will help her heal, then that is what I will do. We all climb out of the car silently. The adrenaline is pumping through my body as I ready myself for a fight. We use the shadows to move closer until we can hear the conversation of the two guards left outside.

"I wouldn't mind trying one. I haven't had my dick sucked in weeks," twat one says, and the other laughs.

"I doubt at that age they know how to suck a cock properly," twat two replies.

"Yeah, I'd have fun teaching them though," twat one jokes, nudging him and they both laugh.

I go to move, Elle grabs me. She looks at the three of us and uses a finger to motion shush to us. We watch as she slips out of her jacket and pulls her hair down from where she had tied it up and fluffs it out messily. She removes the gun from her thigh and passes it off to Linc before making sure the two knives she brought are hidden. One behind her back at the waist and the other at her ankle. The only thing she doesn't move is the black knuckle duster.

"Stay here," she whispers with force, putting her focus on Lincoln like she is communicating something silently with him. Before I can say anything, she is turning and backing away from us further into the shadows. I stand dumbfounded wondering what the fuck she is doing until she reappears a little further down.

"Excuse me boys?" she says in a voice that is breathy and flirty, and I am immediately irritated.

"Hells bells, what the fuck are you doing?" Asher hisses in my ear echoing my thoughts but I can't concentrate on him right now. My sole focus is on these two predators in front of me. I watch as they take her in from head to toe with a sick gleam of satisfaction in their eyes.

"What's a girl gotta do to find a good time around here?" she adds, as she confidently walks towards them ignoring the weapons, they both have on their hip.

"You shouldn't be out here, girly," twat two says and she smiles.

"How many dicks can you take?" twat one adds, and I see red but as if Lincoln can read my mind, he clamps a hand on my shoulder and shakes his head at me.

"Not now, brother, trust her."

"Oh, you would be surprised by the things I can do to two men at the same time," she replies to them, making a show of running a finger along the neckline of her top, tracing her breasts with it, forcing both of their attention to her tits. I am grinding my teeth so fucking hard I am surprised they can't hear it.

She uses their distraction to move towards them, moving a hand behind her back to grip the blade there and the action just pushes her tits out more. They are entranced. She keeps moving towards them seductively, swaying her hips and twat one moves towards her finally getting in her space. She uses her free hand to grip his waist above where his gun sits, a tactical placement I'm sure. She cocks her head to the side-tracking twat number two who seems to finally be on board as he takes a step towards her and she smiles. She leans up on her toes to whisper into the first guard's ear and I watch as his face transforms from excitement to confusion.

It happens so fast I barely catch it; her blade is embedded in the throat of twat two and she wastes no time ducking to grab the other blade strapped to her leg.

The guys and I move in sync to help her, but we barely make it a few steps before she grabs his arm and swings him away from her in a similar move she used on me when she broke my finger a couple of weeks ago. She doesn't give him the chance to retaliate before she grips the blade and slices his throat from behind and then moves back so his body can drop to the floor next to his friend's.

Holy fuck. She turns around as we get to her and is completely unphased about the two murders she just committed. She looks to Linc first and for the first time I am envious that I haven't been by her side from the beginning doing this. They communicate silently again, and he pulls his phone out and taps away a couple of times.

"Someone fucking speak to me," Asher yells into the earpiece and Elle smiles.

"Donuts," she replies, and he curses and now it's Lincs turn to laugh.

"Fucking donuts," he curses again as Jace and I look at each other confused but apparently there is no time for explanations, as she ducks down and starts searching the two bodies. She unclips their weapons and Lincoln takes them and stuffs them in a bag, I hadn't even noticed. She also removes an earpiece and walkie talkie and plugs it into the ear that doesn't have Ash in. She listens intently and then motions for us to follow her.

She moves to open the door but Linc grabs her and pushes her aside and she rolls her eyes "Don't piss me off, Superman," she whisper-shouts at him.

"Just let me check it out okay, King?" he smiles back at her affectionately and she huffs but moves back to let him get to the door fully. Just as he is about to open it Donovan speaks.

"Careful help, my intel says there are at least four more guys around somewhere," he warns into our ears with no emotion and that affectionate smile turns into a devilish smirk on Lincs face.

"Don't worry about me, dark prince. I can handle myself," he retorts.

"Want him to show you how, Donovan?" Jace cuts in with a smirk of his own and Elle muffles a laugh as Asher exhales a breath.

"Fucking Rebels," he curses and for the first time since we left the house, I find myself smiling too.

We wait as Lincoln pulls open the lock on the container and sneaks inside. He is only in there a few seconds before he comes back out pushing the door open fully so we can all see inside.

It's empty.

Chapter 27

ELLE

I stare in confusion and disbelief at the empty container. What the fuck? We're too late.

That thought doesn't get time to transform into anything else before a bullet is whizzing past my head and hitting the side of the container. I don't get a chance to react before I am being slammed to the floor with Linc's body covering mine as he pulls his weapon and fires in the direction it came from.

"What the fuck?" I hear Jace shout. I turn my head to see him and Marcus laying on the floor next to us, both with a gun in hand. They are taking shots but without training, they are sloppy and going wide, but I'm still grateful to have them here. I need my own gun back and I reach my arm behind me to pat down Lincoln until I feel it.

I whip it from his side, aim and fire without even blinking. With all four of us now shooting the fire stops coming but that doesn't make me feel better. No that only means one thing, they are moving in on us.

"Get up, move," I order quickly. Lincoln rolls off me and we all jump to our feet and slink our bodies, so they are plush with the container. "Crab Sticks," I mutter into the mic on my top and Asher curses and I hear tapping away.

"Okay, you've got six guys coming up on you, they are spread wide, fuck," he taps away some more and then adds in a pained voice, "you need to split up."

I don't think before I dash away from them as fast as I can, that was my only option, otherwise I would have had to battle with Marcus over it and we don't have time for that shit right now. I hear four sets of cursing in my ear but then it goes quiet and I know they have followed suit.

"Watch your backs," I whisper as I move into the shadows cast by the containers and pause. I remove the earpiece and listen intently. There is a slight rustle that could just be the wind, but I listen closer and it happens again. Someone is coming. I take a deep breath and put my earpiece in my pocket and prepare to fight. I need to be able to concentrate and not have Ash barking orders in my ear.

When I feel the presence get closer, I take a peek and another bullet is fired past my head. Fuck. I grip my pistol and duck low as I lean back out and fire two shots in quick succession and one hits my target right in the chest and he stumbles to the ground, but before I can feel relief I am kicked hard from behind.

"Fucking little bitch!" The hard voice hits my ear as my face smashes into the ground. Fuck that hurts. I turn at the same time he steps over me with a sinister smile on his face. He goes to take another step closer, but I pull the blade from my ankle and plunge it into his thigh, he falters with a curse. I crawl out from under him and I can hear the bullets being fired in the background, but I have to ignore that. I stand but my head is pounding, and I am dizzy as fuck, so I stumble into the side of the container.

My assailant pulls my knife out and throws it to the ground next to where he kicked my gun and locks eyes with me smiling thinking I'm unarmed. He crowds into me "Tell me if this hurts," he taunts.

"You tell me," I reply as I plunge the knife from my waistband into his gut. He gurgles and blood chokes out of his mouth. His stare goes from defiant to pleading but I don't let it deter me, I twist the knife in his stomach determined to cause as much damage as possible. When he finally gives up the fight and slumps to the floor, I lean back against the container and try to catch my breath.

I look around trying to listen for anyone else, but I can't hear anything. I move slowly and pull the blade from his gut and wipe it off on my pants before slipping it back at my waist and retrieving my other from the floor and doing the same. I pick up my gun and step back against the container to take another look around as the ringing of a phone startles me. I pick it up, ignoring my blood-soaked hands and press the answer button and place it to my ear.

"I told you not to underestimate her," Elliot Donovan's commanding voice booms down the line.

"You were right in that assessment," I reply, deciding there is no point in this game of smoke and mirrors any longer. He knew I was coming, so it's time to stop playing games. There is a slight pause before he responds.

"Miss King," he starts, and he does not sound pleased, "How lovely to speak with you again."

"I wish I could say the same," I reply, trying to slow my breathing down and calm the adrenaline rushing through my veins. I look around trying to find someone else to kill or one of my guys. Fuck, I hope they are okay, they have to be okay.

"You are making big mistakes, Elle, stop this now before it goes any further," he threatens in a sickly-sweet tone like we are talking about something as casual as the weather.

"No, Elliot," I grit his name past my teeth, "the only one who made a mistake around here is you." A noise to my left startles me and I whip my gun in that direction to find all three Rebels coming my way. I breathe a silent sigh of relief and Lincoln nods telling me all threats are neutralized so I turn my focus back to Elliot. "You made a mistake when you thought you could take from me without regret, but trust me Mr. Donovan, I will make you regret the day you were born." My tone is calm which is the exact opposite to how I am feeling right now, "All your men are dead. Watch your back, I'm coming." I don't wait for him to respond before I end the call and throw the phone to the floor and stomp on it.

I don't even get a chance to take a breath before Marcus is on me. He slams back against the container and cups my face kissing me breathless. I taste blood, I'm not sure if it's his or mine, but even the tangy coppery taste couldn't stop me from kissing him right now.

He pulls back and presses his head to mine with his eyes pressed tightly closed. "Don't ever fucking do that to me again, Ells," he says, as he opens his eyes and locks our gazes. He looks at my face and grimaces before tracing a finger across my eyebrow and a thumb across my lip and I wince, "You okay, baby?" he asks gently.

"I'm fine," I nod, hoping to reassure him when fine is the fucking opposite of what I am feeling right now. Elliot knew we were coming which means somewhere along the way we have slipped up.

"This was a trap," I say and all three of them exchange a worried glance.

"Will you please speak to your bestie, and calm him down?" Jace pleads and I remember the earpiece in my pocket.

I reach for it and place it back in my ear for me to catch the end of Ash's rant, "...if I don't hear her voice in five fucking seconds, I will murder all three of you and paint the fucking walls with your insides," he seethes, and I snort.

"Donuts," I say calmly but it doesn't have the effect I'd hoped.

"Donuts fucking donuts, don't ever fucking do that to me again, Elle, or I swear to god I will kidnap you and lock you up until every one of our enemies is dead," he yells and all three Rebels smirk.

"Are you done?" I ask and he huffs at me before he replies with a gruffed yeah. "Okay we have," I pause looking to Linc and he holds up his hand with four fingers, "Eight bodies in total that need to disappear, make sure all feeds are wiped and then go home, Elliot knew we were coming, I need to know how."

"Already on it, get out of there," he snaps, losing his cool again but I know it's just his worry about what occurred here. Before I can respond he speaks again more calmly, "Go back to the South Side with them, last thing we need is someone finding out where you live."

He doesn't have to say what he truly means. The last thing we need is for someone to discover Cassie. That is the only thing that matters to me. I could be killed here and now, and I know Cassie would be taken care of. I have so many contingency plans in place when it comes to my daughter, that I don't have to worry about anything happening to me. I could take her and run, hell, I could have never come back here, and no one would have ever found us, but then what? Could I have lived without guilt and regret? Knowing that my rapist walks free and continues to commit heinous crimes. Knowing that at any time he could accidentally stumble on us. I wasn't willing to leave that up to chance. Some things are worth the risk and for her I would risk it all. For her I would risk dying just so she can live.

"Okay," I agree, nodding looking to the guys. "let's go."

"What about these?" Jace asks, gesturing to the dead bodies.

"I have someone who will take care of that," I reply gesturing vaguely to the bodies. I don't get into the deal about the team of guys Zack keeps on standby. All I know is when I call, they turn up and clean up the mess. They are the type of people I could have got to do all my dirty work, but that would be too easy. I want to be the one to make these sick fucks bleed. So, I am happy to have them handle the cleanup and nothing else.

"Of course, you do," Jace mutters and Lincoln laughs. Marcus is silent beside me and I can only imagine the shit running through his head right now. I mean it's one thing to tell someone the things you have done and another thing to witness it. I told him I wanted revenge and how I've been getting it, but that is not the same as finding me after I killed four men without thought.

We make our way back to the car quietly, all of us continuously looking around, waiting for more people to come for us. The tension is so thick I can almost see it. When we reach the car, I take stock of us all and see none of us have escaped any bloodshed. I have blood dripping from my eyebrow and lip, it coats my chest and is soaked into my pants. Lincoln has a few speckles on his neck, Jace's shirt is damp from it and Marcus has his fists coated in it. We look like we just took part in a sacrifice together, what a team.

I look to Lincoln in concern, but he just shakes his head "Just get in we will sort it out later," he says, before opening the door and getting behind the wheel. We all follow suit except when I go to climb in the front Marcus grabs me and pulls me into him and gives Jace a look. Without a word he moves up and slides into the passenger seat. Marcus opens the back door and slides inside pulling me along with him, until I am straddling his lap and his arms cage me to his body, like he doesn't ever want to let me go. We pull out of the shadows and are on our way before Lincoln turns on the stereo and music filters into the car.

Marcus pulls back and before he can say anything, I kiss him. I push my hands into his hair and pull hard to tilt his head to mine. He groans into my mouth and I swallow it down using it to slip my tongue into his mouth until it tangles with his. The tang of blood isn't unexpected this time and I relish in the taste of it, the taste of him. His hands are splayed across my back as he tries to pull me closer, but our bodies are already so tight against each other that there is no space between us. I feel the ache in the pit of my stomach with my need for him and grind against him to try find some relief. I feel him harden beneath me and it spurs me on to know I can have that effect on him. I press into him more, moving my hips back and forth, and when he groans again the music conveniently gets louder drawing out any other sounds that might occur.

I try to roll my hips again and his hands move to grab me by the hips, my top has come untucked in all the commotion, so his touch burns against my bare skin. His calloused fingers grip me, no doubt leaving blood stains on my skin, but I don't care. He pulls back and looks at me, his stare is dark and full of desire, and it only turns me on more. He flicks his eyes over my shoulder and then back to me before kissing me again. Moving his mouth across my jaw and down my neck biting and sucking gently and I clench my thighs on either side of him. I feel his smirk against my skin as he moves his mouth up to my ear.

"Need something, baby?" he asks, I'm nodding before he can even finish speaking, he laughs "then be quiet." His hands come up and he pulls my bra down, thrusting my tits out into his face before I can even protest. Not that I would. His mouth latches onto me as he sucks one of my nipples into his mouth while his fingers pinch my other. Fuck. I can't believe what we are doing on the back seat while' Jace and Lincoln are sitting not even three feet away, but I don't fucking care. His mouth on me feels fucking divine and after how gentle he has been with me all week the feel of his teeth biting into my nipple is exactly what I need. He continues his assault on my tits as he alternates between licking, sucking, biting, and pinching both nipples until I am a writhing mess above him and without even a touch to my clit, I am coming hard muffling my moans into his shoulder as he finally slows his tongue. He kisses his way back up my chest and neck until he reaches my lips and gives me one last kiss.

When I come down from my orgasm, I realize the car has stopped and we are parked in the guys' garage at their house and the front seats are empty. I smile at that, but when I lock eyes with Marcus the dark lustful stare has disappeared and instead. I find restraint and confusion invades the post-orgasm haze. He opens the door and steps out with me gripped to him before he settles me on the floor, then turning and walking inside leaving me staring after him. What the hell?

After my shock subsides, I go after him but by the time I make it to the living room he is nowhere to be seen. However, Jace and Linc are standing by the island in the kitchen.

"We're ordering pizza," Lincoln says. "Shower and bag your clothes. We can eat and talk after," he adds and it's only then I remember my blood-soaked clothes and cringe a little at what I just did in them and I'm not talking about the murders.

"Where did he go?" I ask in response.

"He's probably gone to jack off in the shower after that back-seat performance," Jace smiles gleefully and I blush hard.

"Shut the fuck up," Linc scolds him but he just shrugs and winks at me and I shake my head even though I smile. Only Jace could get away with saying shit like that.

"You're lucky I like you, pretty boy," I tease.

"Oh. trust me, Queenie, I know, I've seen what you can do with a blade," he replies with a laugh, but I can tell tonight took its toll on him. This is just his mask in place hiding the darkness that resides inside him. I drop my smile and move until I am in front of him.

"You okay?" I say with a serious tone and he blanches slightly.

"Of course, I am," he replies, and I notice Lincoln disappearing from the room in my peripheral, giving us some privacy.

"Jace Conrad, you listen to me," I start reaching up to put a hand on his shoulder, "you never have to hide your feelings with me okay? You're happy then be happy, sad, mad, fucking horny, I don't care as long as you feel it, don't hide away behind your jokes because it's easier than dealing with this shit."

He looks off to the side breaking our eye contact, before looking back to me and grabbing me into a bear hug. His tall frame means his arms wrap around my head as mine go around his waist, “Thank you,” he muffles into my hair.

He pulls back and I look up at him making sure he is really okay.

“I’m good, Elle, I promise, now go sort your man out. We’ll save you some pizza,” he winks. I roll my eyes before turning to go fix another lost Rebel.

Chapter 28

MARCUS

The water turns my skin to ice, but still it isn't cold enough to put out the fire I feel in my body. I am burning with need, rage, desire, and pain. The panic I felt earlier as I watched Elle disappear followed by the sounds of gunshots is something I never want to experience more of. I felt like she was slipping through my fingers all over again and I fought with everything I had, to get to her. I didn't think twice when a guy stumbled across me on my way to find her. Didn't take the time to worry about my fists pounding into his face until it caved in. Didn't think about the life I took without restraint. The only thing running through my mind was that I had to get to her.

The shower door opens, I don't have to look to know it's her. Taking away the fact that out of everyone here she would be the only one to come looking for me, I just know it's her. I can feel her, like I'm a magnet and she is my counterpart, pulling me towards her at all times. She wraps her arms around me from behind and I shudder when her naked body presses against mine. Fuck. Elle King is naked and wet in my fucking shower. I reach out and turn the dial on the shower to warm the water up.

I take her arms in mine and unfold them from around me so I can spin and face her. I look down and my throat goes dry, she is naked, fully stripped bare, and all for me. Fuck. I don't fucking deserve this. She lets her gaze travel down my body taking in my own naked frame and I see the moment she lands on my cock as she sinks her teeth into her bottom lip. I am harder than fucking stone but still my cock juts at thinking about biting that lip myself. She seems transfixed on it and it's only then I wonder if this is the first time, she has ever seen a naked man. She is looking at me like she wants to memorize every inch of me. It takes every ounce of restraint I have, to allow her to continue her appraisal instead of grabbing her and fucking her against the tiles.

Her gaze comes back up slowly but catches on my chest and it's only then I notice some blood there. She frowns before looking round and grabs a washcloth and soap. She squirts some into the cloth before she begins to wash my body slowly and rhythmically. I honestly don't think I have ever experienced anything as erotic as Elle King washing me, but fuck I am barely holding on. She washes me until I am completely clean and then she goes to return the washcloth to where she got it, but I stop her movements. She looks back up at me and she swallows, as I take it from her and squirt more soap onto it. I slide it over her shoulders and down her arms before dragging it across her breasts, removing the traces of blood. I take in the bite marks I left there in the back of the car, and my cock juts out again. Fuck, she looks good with my mark on her. I drop my gaze to her stomach and grimace at the sight of the scars there, not that they diminish my lust or her beauty in any way, but they are just a reminder of what that fucking prick did to her. I clench my fist around the cloth as she steps closer, so her body touches mine and I lock my gaze back with hers.

"Don't leave me, River, stay here with me and only me," she whispers, pleading with me.

I pause and then speak quietly, "It should have been me," I whisper into the water.

"You think I didn't want that?" she whispers back taking a step closer to me, so her body is pressed completely against mine and I fight back a groan as she continues, "You think I didn't wish that. That my fourteen-year-old heart didn't beat every fucking beat for Marcus Riviera," fuck her honesty is pouring out. "Fuck me, River, my heart has beat for you ever since we were five years old. I dreamt of the days it would go further than a peck on the lips. Of what it would feel like to have your tongue tangle with mine." The water drips down her body as she continues, "Or what it would feel like for your hand to slide into my pants and find me soaked for you. How we would be each other's first and nothing and no one would ever matter again. You think this is hard for you? Well fuck you, River because you don't know shit."

She turns to leave but I don't give her a chance, she isn't walking away from me anymore, we are fucking in this together, forever. I grab her by the back of the neck and drag her back to me, "No more fucking running, little King," I say, as I pick her up and back her into the tiles. “No more fucking messing around. You’re right,” I add, and her face is shocked. “You want me, you fucking got me, baby,” I kiss her wildly and she opens her mouth for me without pause and our tongues dance together in reckless abandonment.

Fuck, never in my life will I get used to the feeling of kissing her. My cock is painfully hard and presses against her core, fuck she is wet, warm and oh so fucking tempting, but I am not fucking her for the first time against the shower wall. She grinds against me and when I pull back, she fumes and I laugh, “Patience, baby.”

“I think we’ve waited long enough for this, River, don’t you?” she rasps, and she is right, no more holding back. I reach behind me and turn off the water. I place her back on her feet before reaching out and grabbing us both a towel. I wrap mine around my waist before putting hers round her shoulders and then I scoop her up into my arms and stalk back into my room. I throw her gently on the bed, she squeals in shock and excitement. The sight is fucking glorious. My girl, naked and in my bed, looking at me like she is willing to give me everything. We both know I don’t deserve it, but I’m selfish bastard so I’m going to fucking take it anyway.

I move to the end of the bed, grab her ankles, and drag her down until she reaches me. The movement leaves the towel behind her and my eyes fucking feast on her nakedness. She is fucking perfect. Her skin is flawless even with the scars, I drop to the floor and she props up onto her elbows so she can look at me. I grip her knees and part them, leaning down to drop a trail of kisses along her inner thigh. I kiss and tease along the dream catcher tattoo and make sure I don't leave any of the marks there untouched. I move to the other thigh and continue the same pattern until I reach her pussy.

Fuck, it's perfectly pink and plumped and she already has juices coating her thighs, I lean in closer and I can smell her arousal, I fucking groan. I slide my finger down it and she takes a sharp breath, I flick my eyes back to her and she is watching me from a hooded gaze, already panting. Oh, my little King has no fucking idea what I am about to do to her. I use my fingers and part her lips exposing her clit to me, she is dripping. I take a long lick all the way from her ass to her clit before I suck it into my mouth gently and she moans. I flick my tongue back and forth across it, before motioning the number eight around it and her moans get louder.

"Fuck Marcus!" she pants and my name on her lips has never sounded so good as she releases it with a breathy moan. It spurs me on, I lick her harder, faster until I can feel her legs begin to shake. "Yes, Marcus, right there," her moans get louder and I fucking love it. Seeing her lose control in a whole different way, reacting to what I am doing to her. Letting go and not caring who hears.

"You taste so fucking sweet, baby," I say sucking her clit back into my mouth and she grinds against my lips. So, fucking perfect I groan again, "Yes, Ells, ride my face. I wanna taste your cum on my tongue, baby," I say as I continue licking her from top to bottom before I spear my tongue inside her and she breaks. I swallow her down as she comes, lapping her up like I am a starving man, and she is my last fucking meal. She tastes so fucking sweet and I know I will never get enough of her.

I don't let up as I drag my lips up her stomach and allow my tongue to tease and lick every scar there paying special attention to the two largest ones. I want her to know that these marks on her skin mean nothing to me, I don't care that someone took her first, I only care about the fact that she was hurt and making sure it never happens again.

She grabs my hair and drags me up until she can kiss me again as she tastes herself on my lips. She grinds herself against me and her wetness soaks my cock and I shudder desperate to slide inside her, but I need to make sure she is ready. I glide my hand between our bodies and tease her clit with my fingers until she has soaked them. I move further down until I can push one inside her and she groans at the intrusion. Fuck, she is tight even on my finger. I pump it slowly in and out of her before I add another, teasing her until she is panting again. I curl them inside her ensuring they stroke along her g-spot, while bringing my thumb to her clit, in quick hard circles. It isn't long before she cries out again, clenching around my fingers as she comes. The look on her face of pure ecstasy and I wish I could see it forever.

She is breathless as she grabs at me, "No more, Marcus. I need you inside please, I need you to fuck me," she begs. Fuck. I have never had an offer so fucking tempting.

"Fuck, baby, I'll come before I am even inside you if you keep talking like that," I press her body into the mattress and kiss her hard. Feeling desperate for more of her. When I pull back, I lean over and reach for a condom out of my bedside drawer but when I bring my arm back, she grabs it shaking her head.

"No River, no barriers, please, I'm clean, obviously, and if you haven't been with anyone since I came back, then I know you are too."

I blink, what the fuck? "How do you know that?" I wonder and she blushes biting that fucking lip again.

She looks away, "Erm, I may have hacked into your medical records," she says with a shrug and I grab her face and bring her gaze back to mine.

"I fucking love you, baby," I smile so wide my fucking cheeks hurt, but for her, I don't care. For her, it's worth it. I toss the condom on the floor and kiss her again before I add, "Fucking bare."

I line my cock up with her entrance and slowly slide inside. Inch by inch letting her accommodate to my size. Fuck she's tight. Tighter than anything I have ever felt. It takes everything in me not to come as soon as her wet heat wraps around me.

"Fuckkkk," I groan, unable to keep it in and look down at her, "You okay?"

She nods rapidly, "I'm fine, don't stop," she says in a tense voice.

I push all the way in until I bottom out inside her and fucking hell, nothing will ever feel this good. I regret every fucking girl before her because no one has ever felt this fucking amazing before. I wish I could erase every single one of them and only have her. I am never letting her go again.

I slide back out slowly before pushing back inside her, "Mine," I growl in her ear, slowly rocking my hips forward and giving her time to adjust. I know it isn't technically her first time but as far as I am concerned this is the only first time that counts. She gave this to me willingly and I want to make sure it's perfect.

"Marcus," she moans my name and I swear to god, I have never needed to come so much in my life but her breathy moans just spur me on. My body is humming with electricity as the pleasure courses through me. My heart is pounding hard and my breathing comes in quick huffed breaths. My whole world is fucking alive for the first time ever as I take what I have been fucking dreaming of for years.

I thrust into her in long, slow, deep thrusts, and it's fucking euphoric. Nothing has ever felt this good or this perfect and it's in this moment, that I know. I don't care what I have to do or what lengths I have to go to, I will bring this town to its fucking knees for my girl.

Chapter 29

ELLE

This is how I always imagined my first time to be. No pain, no fear, just pure fucking love. It's addictive. It's like he is a drug and I want every high he has to fucking give. I never want to come down. He trails kisses down my neck and across my nipples and it's like his tongue is erasing every affliction of pain marred against my skin. I don't feel dirty, abused, or afraid. I feel loved, empowered, fucking worshipped.

I hold onto his shoulders, digging my nails into his back causing him to moan as his body rocks into mine. His fucking body, I thought you only saw shit like this on Instagram, but he is fucking toned to perfection. The hard plains of his stomach contract with every thrust and the veins in his forearms are bulging out. It's like he was made from the mold of a fucking Greek god. He starts to pick up the pace as his thrusts turn maddening. Quick and deep making the sounds of our bodies slapping together loud. He circles his hips as he enters me smacking against my clit each time and I feel like I am ready to snap.

He has one hand with a punishing grip on my thigh. He uses it to lock it in place around his body as he continues to pound into me and I pray he leaves more marks on me, so I can remember this feeling. He uses his other hand to tease my nipple into a hard aching point before he pinches it hard and I cry out. Fuck who knew that could feel so good. I feel myself starting to clench around him as my orgasm starts taking over again. He already made me come twice but I can feel a third building.

I sense the moment he feels it because he becomes relentless. Pounding into me so hard that the headboard starts to bang against the wall. No doubt alerting his brothers to exactly what we are doing in here, but I am beyond caring. The only thing I care about right now is him, us. I want everything he has to give. I need it. Crave it. Chasing the high only he can give me.

He moves the hand from my nipple to the bottom of my throat and gives it a gentle squeeze and instead of panic all I feel is pleasure. Pure ignited pleasure. I grip the arm around my throat and squeeze it tight urging him on. His eyes darken even more as he takes me in beneath him, fucking me even harder.

"Come for me, little King," he growls and it's my undoing. My release slams into me like a tidal wave that just keeps going as he continues to fuck me relentlessly, chasing his own release.

"Fuckkkkk," he groans loudly thrusting into me one last time, emptying himself inside me, before collapsing on top of me as we both try to catch our breath. Our bodies are coated in sweat, as they come together in an entanglement of limbs, and I never want to be apart from him again. I want this always. Us naked and bare for each other.

He pulls back his head from my shoulder and kisses me again. It's slow and passionate and fucking everything I have ever wished for. It's erotic and fucking maddening and it feels like he is kissing me like it might be the last time he ever does. I hope he always fucking kisses me like this, like he needs it more than his next breath.

I feel the tears on my cheek before I even realize I am crying and when his hand comes up to cup my face, he feels them and pulls back immediately regret filling his eyes.

"Fuck, baby. What's wrong? I'm so sorry, did I hurt you?" his panicked words just make me cry more, as I struggle to respond.

Shaking my head vigorously, "No, River," I gasp. "It was just so perfect. That is exactly how my first time should have been," I admit my heart breaking for everything we should have had.

He gives me a pained smile before kissing my lips again and pulling back, "Baby, that is the only first time that matters," he whispers against my lips before adding, "for both of us."

I am immediately on high alert thinking about who else he has been with and wondering if making them bleed is over the top as I ask, "Who was your first time?"

He rolls his eyes, "No one relevant, trust me," he says before taking in my expression. "And no, you can't stab them with your pretty blade," he adds with a teasing glint in his eye.

He pulls out of me slowly and I wince slightly. He didn't hurt me, but it's been three years since that night, so I might as well have still been a virgin. He looks down between our bodies again and curses.

"What?" I ask panicking but he just bites his fist with a groan.

"Seeing my come leak out of you should be a fucking crime baby, fucking perfect," he professes, and I laugh at his dirty words with a blush.

He laughs in return palming my thigh possessively still staring between my legs, "Can't be shy on me now baby. Not when I know what it feels like to have that wet pussy coming on my cock."

"Oh my god!" I choke a laugh before I throw a pillow at him and hide my face in the blankets.

He dives back onto the bed and whips the cover off me, "Never hide, baby, not from me," he says with a serious look on his face, that is so intense all I can do is nod. He smiles and then moves to the bathroom before returning with a warm wet cloth which he uses to clean between my thighs.

"Wanna sleep?" he asks gently but I shake my head.

"Actually, I'm starving, can we go see if the guys left us any pizza?" I plead, needing to satisfy my other needs. Only cheesy carby goodness will suffice.

"They will have if they know what's good for them," he snarks and I laugh.

He makes his way into his wardrobe to get dressed as I climb from the bed and it's only then I realize I have no clothes here that aren't ruined by blood. Marcus comes back out and pauses to lean on the door as his gaze rakes over me like he didn't just fuck me six ways to Sunday.

"Damn," he whispers with a smile, "As much as I like the view baby, I don't want my brothers seeing it," he teases passing me some sweats.

"Please," I roll my eyes. "Linc has more interest in my best friend than me and Jace has become more like my brother than yours," I tease back.

"Oh yeah? Kiss your brothers often do you?" he says, giving me a pointed look.

"You deserved that," I eye him with my own look as I slip into the clothes he gave me.

He groans, "You're insufferable, come on" he drags me by the hand until I'm following him into the living room.

Lincoln and Jace are both sitting playing video games with a bunch of empty pizza boxes surrounded them. "Hey lovers," Jace greets us, wiggling his eyebrows and I groan looking at Marcus.

"See? Definitely an annoying little brother," I joke, and he laughs.

Jace snorts, "Queenie, there is nothing little about me, I can assure you," he replies with a flirty glint in his eye and I groan.

"Pizza in the kitchen for you," Linc adds, ignoring Jace, turning away from the game yet somehow still winning. Both Rebels have showered and changed into sweats of their own and I still feel humble at being invited into their safe space and getting to see the boys behind the name.

Marcus brings two big pizza boxes from the kitchen island and we settle on the sofa with the guys as they end their game.

Lincoln is the first to speak, "So, what do we think?"

I blow out a breath as I take a bite of pizza and chew it while I mull things over, "Honestly, I don't know. It's clear he knew we were coming, that *I* was coming," I put emphasis on the I because let's face it, Elliot is clearly trying to call in that bounty on my head.

"What did he say on the phone?" he asks.

I shrug, "Not much. Told me to stop coming after him before things go too far."

"I think it's a little late for that," Jace scoffs.

"It's been too late for that for three fucking years," Marcus snaps and I reach out with my free hand to give his arm a squeeze. He uses it to drag me right into his side and doesn't turn back to the guys until I am completely tucked into his side.

"What guys did we have scouting things out?" he asks them.

"None from the inner circle, a couple of the lower guys, didn't tell them why just to let us know if there was any unusual activity," Lincoln replies with a frown. I can tell he is frustrated that he hasn't worked out what happened yet.

"So, we have a rat or a traitor?" Jace confirms.

"Either way they need to be found," Marcus replies. "I want everything we have on them and we will sort them out first thing in the morning but for now we should sleep," he adds.

"You staying here, Queenie?" Jace asks, wiggling his eyebrows at me again.

"Like I would let her out of my sight after tonight," Marcus scolds him and Jace laughs.

"Oh yeah, a lot of time to make up for, right, brother?" he says with another cheeky smile.

I groan, "Pretty boy, why do you insist on making me want to practice my knife skills?" I ask him in all seriousness, but he just laughs.

"Look, Elle, if Marcus didn't satisfy you enough that you still feel the need to let off some steam then you know where my room is," he flirts.

"I will kill you," Marcus snaps at him and then it's my turn to laugh and he turns his gaze on me "Oh, is that funny, little King?" he doesn't give me a chance to answer before he launches himself at me and throws me over his shoulder as I scream with laughter.

He storms us back to his room leaving the guys echoing laughs behind us and doesn't put me down until he reaches the bed. He is on top of me hovering above me before I can even move, "I don't share, baby, even with my brothers."

"That's a shame, they're both pretty hot," I tease reaching up to kiss his neck and he groans.

"Ells," he warns, "stop."

"Make me," I whisper into his ear and it's like a break in his control because he fucking snaps pulling back and ripping the sweats off my body before pulling me into a sitting position almost against the headboard so he can climb onto his knees and pull the hoodie over my head.

The action puts his crotch in my face, I can see his hardened length straining against his own sweats, and I don't hesitate to reach out and squeeze him over the material and he moans in the back of his throat. I love having that effect on him and I crave more.

I reach into his sweats and fist his cock in a firm grip. I don't really know what I am doing but watching the goosebumps break out on the v shape, leading to his groin keeps me from stopping.

I look up and find his dark lustful stare locked on my hand before he flicks it to mine. His breathing is ragged and all I am doing is holding him in my hand. I glance back to his cock and watch as pre cum leaks from the tip, it's fascinating. I use my thumb to rub it across the head of his cock and he hisses, "Fuck."

He closes his eyes and takes a deep breath like he is trying to calm his breathing but that is the opposite of what I want right now, what I need. I want him to lose control, to break beneath my touch like I did his. His cock swells in my palm and I can't contain my smug smile at having that effect on him. I need to taste him.

I lean forward and suck the head into my mouth and repeat the same motion my thumb did but with my tongue. His eyes snap back open and lock with mine. His eyes are the blackest I have ever seen them, as he takes me in with his dark stare full of fucking lust. I swirl my tongue around the head again marveling at how smooth it is, while licking off his pre cum.

"Ells," he says through gritted teeth and I release him to speak back.

"I need to taste you, River," I say as I tease my tongue against the slit tasting more of him and it seems any restraint he was trying to keep is shattered because his hand slides into my hair and grips me tight as the other slams against the wall above me.

"So fucking taste me, baby. Put that mouth on me, I'm all yours."

I don't hesitate to take him into my mouth running my tongue along the underside of him as I put my lips as far as I can manage. Bringing him deep into my throat and hollowing my cheeks so I can accommodate him.

He grunts loudly, jerking into my mouth as he hits the back of my throat, I hold back my gag as tears gather in my eyes but the sounds, he is making are so fucking primal I don't stop. I keep bobbing my head up and down and taking him in and out of my mouth. Sucking, licking, tasting. Fuck knows if I am doing it right, but he seems to be enjoying it, so I continue.

His grip in my hair tightens as he takes control of the movements and begins fucking my mouth in short rapid thrusts. His cock hardens even more on my tongue and I glance up to find his head thrown back in ecstasy all because of my mouth. I moan around his thick length and he shudders, throwing his head forward and snapping his eyes open to lock with mine.

He moans roughly, "Baby, I am going to come, so if you don't want me in your mouth move now," his voice is ragged. I suck him harder ensuring he hits the back of my throat again. Fuck who knew sucking dick could be so fucking hot.

I pull back and suck the head into my mouth once more before gliding my lips down to his base again and sucking hard until I feel him spurt hot jets of warm cum down the back of my throat. I don't stop, I keep sucking him, swallowing down his seed, until he pulls on my hair.

I pull back letting his cock fall from my mouth and I barely take a breath before he grabs me and kisses me like he needs me to fucking breathe, not caring that his salty essence still resides on my tongue. *Why is that so hot?*

His kiss is rough and his grip on my hair doesn't move, as he tilts my head back so he can thrust his tongue into my mouth over and over again. His fingers slip between my thighs finding me soaked again just from tasting him.

"Always so fucking wet," he grits out against my mouth before he rubs in quick erratic circles against my clit until I am a screaming mess. I come within seconds coating his fingers with my come until we are both spent and breathless against each other.

Our breathing slows and he kisses me again, softly dragging us down until we lay flat on the bed. He curves my body into his and wraps my leg around his thigh until we are pressed against each other fully. He pulls the covers across us before he brushes his nose against mine.

"Sleep, baby," he whispers into the night.

"I love you, River," I reply, succumbing to the slumber of the night.

"I love you too, sweet girl," he presses his lips to my forehead, and I fall asleep feeling more content than I have ever felt in my life.

Chapter 30

LINCOLN

Tonight was a fucking shit show. What was supposed to be a simple mission from some good intel, turned into a shootout with eight dead bodies. Thankfully, they were none of ours but still it was too fucking close for comfort.

Elle added four bodies to her kill count and Marcus and Jace both made their first kill. Joined us on the dark side. I added two more bodies to my roster like it was nothing and for me, it really was. Nothing. It's hard to be affected by draining the life out of someone when you killed your first person at eight years old. The darkness slides inside of you before you even know what it means. It has been in me for years, growing, festering. I had several unhealthy ways to deal with it, hacking, fucking, hunting, but then Elle came along and gave my darkness a purpose. Now, I don't have to fight against it, I can let it out and rid the world of fucking rats at the same time.

Being able to share that with someone else is hard to find. I have my brothers but seeing Marcus with Elle, I can't help but wonder what it would be like to have someone of my own to relish in it with. But how can someone ever love you if you don't love yourself?

Everything is quiet right now considering it's been two hours since everyone went off to bed. I look at the clock and spy that it's almost 2am. I should probably try and get some sleep, but I just can't shake the feeling that something isn't right.

I have been over the CCTV footage from tonight three times and come up with nothing that we don't already know. Eight guys were sent after us, after Elle. How did they know we would come? All fingers point to us being betrayed by one of our own. I thought we had more loyalty than that but apparently not everyone believes the same thing we do.

I press play on the footage for the fourth time when my email notification pings.

From: Asher Donovan
To: Lincoln Blackwell

Help,

Here are some files that need decrypting. I trust your skill set can manage that. Be quick about it.

Short and sweet as always with him. Never using more words than necessary except when it involves dishing out threats to protect Elle. I guess he isn't unlike me in that way. I hit reply and type out a quick message in response.

From: Lincoln Blackwell
To: Asher Donovan

Anything else I can do for you boss?

My reply is petty, but his domineering email fucking infuriates me to no end. Why is it the only person to ever crawl under my skin is a fucking psycho with a devil complex? Before I can even wait for a reply my phone rings and although his number isn't saved, I know it's him.

"Dark prince, to what do I owe this unexpected pleasure?" I drawl sarcastically as I answer the phone and he huffs in contempt.

"Are you always so fucking annoying?" he snaps, and I smile at his tone.

"It's one of my many talents," I muse.

"Well, let's just focus on your talent as a fucking hacker tonight, shall we?" he says, in exasperation.

"Ah, so you admit I'm talented?" I toss back, enjoying our back-and-forth way more than I should.

He takes a deep breath, "Lincoln," he draws out my name slowly and he obviously means it as a warning but all it does is make my skin break out in goosebumps. My name should not sound so good on his lips. It makes me think of other things I could do to get him to say my name like that.

"Relax I will get it done --" the perimeter alarm interrupts me as it starts blaring into my office.

"What the fuck is that?" he snaps.

"Perimeter alarm," I huff as I quickly type into my computer to pull up the feeds to find four masked men surrounding my home, "Someone's here," I growl.

I hear him typing on his side, “How many?” he asks, his tone dark and furious.

I pull up every feed I can from every angle, “Four.”

“Where's Elle?” he snaps, but I can hear the telltale sign of panic laced with his anger.

“She’s in bed with Marcus I will go wake--” I start but get cut off by a loud bang.

“What the fuck is that?” he roars into my ear.

I lock eyes onto the bottom left feed and see smoke and flames as another firebomb goes off. BANG.

“Fire,” I say quickly, “they set fire to the building downstairs, two points,” I watch as another starts, “Three points, fuck.”

“Blackwell, I swear to god,” Asher starts, but I cut him off.

“I already told you I would die for her, so how about you let me try?” I snap at him as I strap two guns to my body, place an earpiece in, and pocket my phone so I can free up my hands.

“I need you to hack into our feeds and be my eyes,” I say quickly, entering in some code to allow him access.

“On it,” he barks, and I hear him typing away before he adds, “I’m in,” followed by a quick, “Fuck.”

I stalk towards the bedrooms across the loft and notice the smoke is already billowing under the front door. Fuck this is bad. “We need Zack,” I say but he interrupts me.

“Already on it, you have a team of six guys, five minutes out,” he says, pausing before adding “You don’t have five minutes, Lincoln.”

"Heard," I reply as I storm into Jace's room, he's already up and half dressed.

"What the fuck is going on?" he asks.

"House is on fire, they're coming," he takes in the weapons strapped to my torso and grunts before pulling up his sweats and pulling on boots. He slides on the knuckle duster from his bedside table, grabs the baseball bat from the corner and then follows me down the hall.

I bang open Marcus' door and startle both him and Elle who were clearly still soundly sleeping, not surprising after their extra curriculars. "What the fuck, brother?" he roars, grabbing the sheet to cover her naked body but now isn't the time to be worried about that.

"We're on fire, four men are on the way in," I haven't even finished speaking before they both dart out of bed and are pulling clothes on. Elle runs into the bathroom and comes out with the two knives from earlier. Her hair is wild, her clothes a mess but the look in her eye is refined and ready. I will never not be amazed by her resilience. We all stalk into the living room which is now thick with black smoke and I cough.

"Roof?" Marcus asks, I nod as I push them all into the direction as I hear crashing beneath us. There go our cars. We make it outside and up the stairs and gasp for air, which is also thick with smoke but mixing with the fresh winter air. Fuck, this is so fucking bad.

"Help," Ash snaps into my ear.

"All of us are on the roof, what's their status?" I ask, hoping he has some sort of good news.

"They pulled back without setting the last fire, can you make it down the northeast side of the building?" he asks, still typing away.

I stalk across the roof and lean over the side seeing that there is a clean drop free of flames if we can make it down. Our building isn't that high compared to others. Only two stories but it still has quite the drop. Elle joins me and looks over the side scouting out our next move with me.

"Drainpipe?" she asks, pointing to the one that runs along the corner of the building.

Probably the worst idea ever but we don't have the luxury of options right now.

"Did she just say fucking drainpipe?" Asher barks into my ear.

"We aren't exactly spoiled for choice right now, Donovan," I snap in response and he curses but remains quiet otherwise. Marcus and Jace join us and both lean over to check it out.

"I'm the lightest, I'll go first," Elle says.

"I don't fucking think so, princess," Jace scoffs before Marcus or I can protest. He swings his leg over the wall and reaches out to grip the pipe.

"Careful," I snap.

"I got this, brother," he replies as he puts his full weight on it and pulls on it to test its support. When it doesn't move under his weight, I breathe a sigh of relief. He slowly starts maneuvering down as Elle swings herself up onto the wall with a leg on either side.

"What the fuck are you doing?" Marcus snaps in a panic when she grabs for one of the guns at my side.

"Covering him," she replies, like he is stupid as she casts her glance around the surrounding area readying herself to take a shot if need be. How the fuck did we get here?

We watch as Jace carefully descends until he reaches the floor before Elle waistbands my gun and moves to take her turn. The smoke is so dark and thick now. Just as she is about to drop onto the pipe Marcus grabs her and kisses her.

"Fall, little King, and I will fucking follow you to the gates of heaven," he says with conviction.

"Don't be silly, River," she smiles. "I'll be at the gates of hell," she adds before winking, disappearing from view.

We both lean over and watch her go as Jace awaits her at the bottom with his arms up waiting for her like if she fell, he would really try and catch her. The dedication we all have for this girl is astonishing.

"Jesus fucking Christ," Asher curses into my ear and I know he must be watching her on the camera feeds.

"She's got this, don't worry," I say with as much conviction as I can manage, considering I am watching her every move like it might be her last.

"Just fucking get her out of there and home, Help," he snaps, and I roll my eyes at him even though he can't see me.

Marcus doesn't waste any time jumping over the wall and onto the pipe as her feet barely touch the ground, like he can barely stand to be away from her for even a few seconds.

I know the guys have him covered so I turn back into the roof and watch the smoke engulf our home. The only true safe home I have ever known before, going up in flames. I don't realize how long I stand there, until Asher's voice hits my ear again.

"Get on the fucking pipe, Blackwell," he grits into my ear, breaking me out of my appraisal.

I climb over the wall as I reply, "Is that an offer, dark prince?" I muse aloud and he scoffs, cursing at me under his breath again and I laugh. I get to the floor just as two SUV's come speeding around the corner towards us and we all ready ourselves for another fucking fight.

Zack bursts out of the door of the front one before it even has a chance to fully stop followed by a few more guys. They are all dressed in black from head to toe, with weapons out, ready to fight. When Elle sees him, she sags with relief and barrels towards him and he engulfs her in a hug, relaxing himself.

He pulls back nodding to us before looking down at her, "You okay, sweetheart?" he asks, with concern taking in the cuts on her face from our earlier fight.

She nods, "I'm all good, it's just been a long night," she exhales, and he nods back at her.

"Ash filled me in. Let's get you out of here," he says, looking around as the other men from the two vehicles case the area before settling his gaze on us, "You three too, come on."

Elle turns to us and smiles, "Looks like you're gonna be North Breds for a while, too," she says with a tease and how she even has the power to make a joke right now astounds me. We move towards the vehicles, but her gaze moves past us and her smile drops. Before we can stop her, she is rushing back towards our burning home.

"Ells, what the fuck are you doing?" Marcus shouts but it's too late she is already next to the flames bending over and picking something up before she rushes back towards us. She's holding a bunch of orange roses and an envelope with her name on. She rips in open and reads it quickly before grimacing.

"Fighting fire with fire only gets you ashes," she repeats what is on the page before flipping it over in her hands to see if there is anything else.

"The fuck does that mean?" Jace asks, but she looks at me and then to Marcus.

"It's a quote from Abigail Van Buren," I muse, she nods.

"Of fucking course, you would know that too," Donovan mutters into my ear.

"It means Elliot Donovan is coming for us," she states, and we are all silenced by her words. This is no longer a simple revenge mission; we aren't sneaking up on him and slowly taking his business apart piece by piece. No, that's over now. He knows we're coming, and he isn't waiting. The war is coming to us and it's time to fight harder than ever before.

Chapter 31

MARCUS

What the fuck happened tonight? No what the fuck happened in the last three years? I thought the worst thing that could ever happen to me was finding my father's dead body, murdered in cold blood. I was wrong. The worst thing that could happen to me would be to lose Elle again. Something I have been close to feeling twice in the last twenty-four hours alone, and not just her, but my boys too. Tonight, I lost my home, my bike, my car, and everything I own. At least I still have my family.

I think the only person getting any sleep tonight is fucking Cassie. The rest of us sit in silence around the island in the Royton's kitchen island. It's already 4am but I doubt any of us feel like sleeping after everything that happened. I never thought after being complicit in eight murders, that my night could get any worse. But then as usual, I underestimated Elliot Donovan.

Helen is fussing over us all as she hands out hot chocolate. She squeezes my shoulder as she pauses and drops a kiss to Elle's head. It's funny isn't it? She isn't the biological parent to anyone in this room, yet the love I see in her eyes every time she looks at Elle and

Zack is so pure. I haven't seen love like it since I lost my father, taking them out of it, Michael Riviera is the only parent between us worth a damn and he's dead. Zack's parents gave him up, Elle's parents let the devil take her, Jace's parents cared more about drugs than him or his sister and Lincoln's, well, he doesn't talk much about his past, but you don't typically end up in foster care with good parents. I know his past is dark as the rest of ours, if not more.

Zack is furious. In the few times I have met him and all the times I have spoken with him, I've never seen him like this. He is usually a blank mask of no emotion. Calm, cool, collected, someone hard to work out, a force to be reckoned with, especially in business. I never thought a man like him could have a soft spot but apparently it comes in the form of his half-sister and niece.

"Why are we even surprised this happened? It's not like we didn't know he put a hit out on her. He has wanted her gone ever since he learned she was back. I told you we should have put a security detail on her, but no one listened to me," he rants in a rage as Arthur tries to calm him down.

"No one could have imagined this, son," he says, clamping a hand on his shoulder, but Zack shrugs it off.

"Oh really? Why? Because Elliot Donovan is such an upstanding member of society?" he snorts a laugh. "Every person here knows he is the devil in disguise, he spends his spare time trafficking children and raping teenagers, in what world did we think he wouldn't come after her again?" he roars.

Elle flinches slightly as he raises his voice, but her focus doesn't move to him, even though I can tell by the frown on her face that she is listening to every word. Listening, planning, plotting.

"Zack," Arthur tries again to calm him.

"No, dad, do you not realize how lucky we are to have saved her the first time? I met my sister in the middle of the woods covered in blood. I could have gone in there and killed him with my bare hands, fucking all of them, but instead I did the sane thing, the right thing. I ran and never looked back, not until she asked me to."

I tense at the image he just painted in my head; it goes along with the others already there that I try not to fucking conjure up. I don't want to think about her like that. I look at her now, as she stares silently into her untouched hot chocolate. She has barely spoken a word since she picked up that note outside the loft. Dangerously quiet. She's barely even aware of us at this point, just stuck inside her own mind, which I am sure is a dark place to be.

"Maybe coming back here was a mistake," Helen muses, looking worriedly at Elle.

"So, what, should she leave again?" Zack responds, and his words hit me hard. Would she leave again? Pack up and run once more without looking back. I'd like to think she would never do that, but she's done it before, she could do it again.

"I think we are past that. Elliot clearly knows she is here," Arthur points out. "What good would leaving do now?"

"It would keep her safe," Helen argues in a pleading tone, looking at Elle with a tear-filled eyes.

"We kept her hidden and safe for three years, we could do it again," Zack agrees.

"I am not fucking running," Elle snaps, breaking her stoic state. Silence descends upon the kitchen.

"Sweetheart," Zack starts, but she cuts him off.

"No," she stands pushing back her stool. "None of you were there. You don't know what it was like. You didn't feel what I felt, the pain, the defeat. You didn't come face to face with not one devil but two. How can I run from that? How can I let them keep doing to others, what they did to me? What if they got me again or worse, got Cassie? I'd rather die fighting than live in the shadows, while they run free."

She doesn't wait for anyone to respond, just turns and stalks away, and all we can do is watch her go because she's right. How can we turn our backs on their crimes just to save ourselves? I look back to my brothers and see them looking after her too. She really has become one of us, the center we never knew we needed. Can we avenge her and keep ourselves intact at the same time?

"You boys should get some sleep," Helen interrupts my thoughts with a tired smile. "Take any room you like on the second floor for now. I'll have them adjusted to your tastes."

"That won't be necessary Mrs. Royton. I'm sure they are more than good the way they are," Lincoln replies.

"Nonsense," she scoffs. "This is your home now and I want you to feel that way. Whatever you need just ask, and I will sort it out for you," she says, standing as she gestures for us to follow, before turning around and adding, "And it's Helen."

How this angel of a woman wasn't blessed with a child of her own is beyond me, but at least she was here for those who need her most. My brothers and I dutifully follow her from the kitchen as she leads us upstairs and down the hall until we reach a cluster of doors.

She turns to us again, "I had Zack leave some fresh clothes for you all. They should fit okay until the shops open in a few hours. Oh, and there are fresh towels in the bathroom, which is just behind you," she points to a door over our shoulders. "No one else sleeps down this way so it's all yours. Anything you need just write it down for me, and I'll get it tomorrow, or today I guess."

Jace steps forward and throws his arms around her shoulders startling her slightly, "Thanks Mrs. R., you're the bomb," he says, pulling back with a smile and a wink.

"Yes, Helen, thank you," Lincoln adds, ever the proper gentleman.

She just nods and smiles, "Alright then, I will leave you to get settled," she says, turning to leave us as she makes her way back down the hall.

"Oh, and boys?" we all pause at the doors of our rooms to look at her, "No random girls in the house," she speaks with a smile before adding, "That means you too, Jace Conrad."

Jace mocks a surprised look, “Why me?”

“Elle told me you're the slutty one,” she shrugs, and Lincoln and I laugh.

“Oh, and Marcus isn’t?” he gestures to me and Helen follows his gaze to mine.

“I think those days are far behind him,” she winks at me and then leaves us with a laugh.

My brothers give me a nod before both entering their rooms, no doubt to probably try to get a few hours’ sleep if they can. I don’t even bother pretending that I am gonna be sleeping in here and make my way back down the hall to go find Elle.

I know exactly where she will be, so I don’t waste any time and head in that direction. I find Zack sitting in the lounge sipping from a tumbler. He looks up when I enter and gestures to his glass, “Want one?” he asks, but I shake my head and move to continue past him.

“Marcus?” the way he says my name stops me in my tracks. “How far are you willing to go?” he asks, I frown so he continues, “Elliot Donovan murdered your father practically in front of you, and you never went after him, why?” He questions me and I can tell he is genuinely interested in my answer.

I shrug, knowing the answer is simple, “I wasn’t ready.”

“Are you ready now?” he inquires, and I nod.

“So, I'll ask again, how far are you willing to go?” he says again taking a sip from his tumbler with his intense stare locked on me.

“As far as it takes,” I reply without pause and he just nods. When he doesn’t speak again, I turn and go back on my way.

I find Elle exactly where I thought she would be. I enter Cassie’s room, where she has pulled the armchair over to the side of the bed, and is curled up in it, watching her daughter sleep. I move silently across the room before scooping her up into my arms and sitting in the chair with her curled in my lap. We sit silently for a while just listening to the rhythmic breathing of Cassie's soft snores, watching the simplicity of her chest rise and fall. I wonder what she is dreaming about. Hopefully, it's of a world far better than this one.

“Hey,” Elle whispers eventually.

“Hey, baby,” I whisper back into her hair.

“Sorry about the loft,” she says softly with a touch of regret in her voice.

I reach down and grip her chin between my fingers and tilt her chin until my gaze can collide with hers, “Don’t ever apologize for the workings of the devil.”

“If it weren’t for me this would never have happened. Zack's right. I should have never come back here. I am putting you all at risk,” she says, trying to pull away from me but I don’t let her.

“I’d risk the wrath of the devil every day, for a minute of you in my arms, little King. Ever since you came back here, I feel like I can breathe again. I will die a thousand times if it means saving you once. So, don’t ever fucking apologize or think about leaving again, you hear me?”

"River," she whispers, "Look at my fucking life, how could you possibly want to be part of that? It's not like it's even just me," she adds gesturing to Cassie.

I roll my eyes in exasperation, how is she not getting this?

"I love you, Elle King, and in loving you, I will love your daughter with everything I've got. Protect her and you with all I am until the day I die. You are it for me, always have been, always will be. I don't care if I have to kill a thousand men, it will all be worth it to spend my life with you. Having Cassie be part of that just makes it even more worthwhile, even more so when we give her some beautiful little brothers and sisters to play with."

She closes her eyes, breathing a sigh of relief, "I wish I was selfless enough to let you go," she breathes into the night before opening her eyes to me, "but I can't do this without you, River, I don't want to."

"As if I would fucking let you," I scoff at her even thinking she could get rid of me now.

"Pinky promise?" she pleads lifting her finger to mine and I smile.

I twist my own around it as I respond, "On all the fucking stars in the sky, baby girl."

Elle King is the other half of my soul. She settles something inside of me that I never realized was missing, completing me in a way I never knew possible. What happens now? How do I be enough of a man for these two amazing girls?

How do you go against the devil and survive?

Chapter 32

ELLE

I barely slept an hour all weekend and arriving at school I feel like a drunk zombie. I am so exhausted it hurts. We spent the rest of the weekend laying low and getting stuff delivered to the house for the guys, so they could feel at home. They lost everything because of me, because I chose to come back here and seek revenge on those who wronged me. A plan that only a few months ago seemed so simple and easy to execute. I was going to come back, dismantle the Donovan's' empire, and leave without a second thought. Move on with life, happily knowing that I had ruined the devil's dynasty and have zero regrets. Now, not only have I not managed to be successful in my revenge, but I have also painted a target on three more people's backs.

We came away unscathed this weekend, but what happens next time when we aren't so lucky?

I feel like I did on the first day of school. As I ascend the steps into Hallows High, I feel that same sense of dread in my gut like I did the first time I took this path. That first day I was worrying about seeing Marcus again for the first time. Now I am on edge thinking that Elliot is going to send someone else to try and finish me off. I am paying so little attention that I smack right into someone as soon as I walk through the door.

"Shit, sorry," I start, until I look up and lock eyes with Cherry.

We both just stare at each other, at an impasse of how to handle the awkward situation we have found ourselves in. Of all the people I could run into, why the fuck did it have to be her? Her face is set into a grim line until she looks over my shoulder. She plasters a huge fake smile on her face, confusing the shit out of me. Until I feel him, he doesn't touch me, he doesn't have to, I just sense he is there. Like he is part of me.

"Cherry," he says in acknowledgement, coming into view and looking at me, "Everything okay here?" he asks.

She smiles wider, "What? Oh, of course it is, Elle just bumped into me, but I'm sure she didn't mean it right, Elle?" the tone of her voice is so fucking fake that all I can do is just stare at her in bewilderment.

"I'm sure it was an accident, right, Ells?" Marcus says and I swing my gaze to his to see if he is really buying this shit and it seems he is. The other two Rebels join us and sense the tension and look at me as if I'm causing it. What the fuck?

"Anyway, I best get to class. You guys all have a nice day," she says with a sickly-sweet smile, before she turns and sashays away into the sea of people who were all pretending not to watch our interaction.

I stare after her in disbelief, when Marcus cuts into my line of sight, "Don't get stabby. She deserved better than what we did to her, at least she is being nice."

"You're fucking dumber than I thought," I scoff at him and Jace chuckles beside me. I shoot him a death glare, "That was the fakest shit I've ever seen," I say, stamping my foot and Marcus smiles.

"It's really hot when you're jealous, baby," he says, pulling me towards him but I am having none of it and move from his arms.

"I am not fucking jealous of that cunt," I hiss, furious now, and my voice is getting louder but I can't bring myself to care. "You invited a snake into your life, and you think I'm mad because I'm jealous? Are you fucking kidding me?"

His flirty smile disappears, and he looks like he hasn't a clue how to handle me right now. Well, I'm fucking glad. I hope it pisses him off. "I'm sure it's nothing, Ells," he starts again, but I just scoff before turning away from him.

"Sort your fucking shit out, Riviera," I grit, turning to stalk away from them and flipping off the people who are unabashedly staring at us now. Fuck this high school bullshit.

I suffer through morning classes with barely any attention given to whatever was being taught. I am too distracted, too on edge. How is one expected to learn about American History when you have a hit out on you and spent the weekend being shot at and almost barbequed?

It doesn't help when I get a message from Asher telling me he has some stuff he needs to update me on. I have barely heard from him all weekend, which I'm sure had him on edge, just as much as me. I always notice the darkness in him is that much stronger the longer he spends away from Cassie.

By the time lunch rolls around, I am more than ready to go home, but on the off chance I survive Elliot Donovan and his fucking demons, I want to be able to graduate. The Rebels are quiet at lunch, they have been all weekend, but I guess the last few days have been a lot to swallow.

"Ash has something for us," I muse, trying to make conversation and it seems only Linc takes the bait.

"What sort of something?" he questions.

"Probably not the sort you are wishing for, brother," Jace cuts in with a wink and I laugh for the first time all day.

"Fuck off," Linc replies, losing a little of that cool he always holds on to so tightly.

"Did he say what?" Marcus asks, interrupting them both, his sole focus on me.

I shake my head no, "I'm sure whatever it is won't make me feel better," I mumble with a grim smile and then silence descends between us again. I can't stand the tension so I excuse myself and head to the bathroom so I can have a few moments alone with my thoughts.

As I am washing my hands, the toilet flushes behind me and the door opens, revealing Cherry for the second time today. She looks at me with disdain, the comforting look she offered me earlier nowhere to be seen. Ah, so I'm getting the real Cherry now that we don't have an audience. I remain silent as I finish washing my hands and go to dry them.

"I'll get him back you know," she says to my back before I turn around to face her. "Marcus, I mean," she confirms, like I didn't understand her meaning. Maybe she is stupid after all.

"Is that so?" I respond without emotion; she is so predictable.

"I waited for him, watched him fuck his way through this entire school before he finally noticed me," she says taking a step towards me, "I had him and you ruined it," she spits. "I will get him back, I won't lose him to some North bred whore who has decided to slum it," she pushes me against the wall. I allow her little show of rage, as I assess her angle, and wonder what her endgame is here. This seems like a lot of anger over just one guy.

"Go back to that rich asshole from the North Side," she adds, and I frown inwardly, who does she mean? Ash? Why would she bring him up? How the fuck does she even know about him, he hasn't been here since the first week of school and that was months ago.

I push off the wall and that move alone causes her to falter backwards.

"Listen to me, Cherry, because I am only going to say this once," I say firmly. "Marcus is mine, always has been. You may have thought you had him, but you didn't. You never could and I am sorry for that," I'm not but she doesn't need to know that. "It will always be us, and anyone who tries to come between us. will regret it," I pull the knife from my waistband and glide it slowly across my fingertips and her eyes follow the movement.

She gulps before finding her bravado, "Whatever psycho barbie, I'm out of here," she says spinning around to leave. A wise choice on her part.

I follow her out the door and shout after her, "Oh, and Cherry?"

She turns looking at me with an angry expression as I continue, "Don't make me come for you, you won't like it if I do," I say, pointing at her with my blade and she huffs at that, before turning and marching away as a laugh hits my ear.

"Naughty, Queenie," Jace says from behind me. I turn to find him leaning on the wall a few feet from the door, just casually smoking a joint in the middle of the hallway.

"Pretty boy," I acknowledge him, "Spying on me?" I ask and he smiles wider, blowing smoke into my face.

"It was me or your boyfriend," he shrugs, and I roll my eyes. Stupid, overprotective bastards.

"I don't need a babysitter," I grit at him as I stalk back to the cafeteria, and he follows me with a laugh.

"Oh, trust me I know. I've seen your creative extra curriculars," he muses taking another drag of his joint, like we aren't in the middle of fucking school, "but an extra pair of eyes on you can't hurt, can it?" He takes one last drag before stomping it out on the wall at the same time Principal Lock rounds the corner. Graham looks at him displeased, but Jace just mock salutes him and enters the cafeteria.

"Elle a word?" he asks, as I go to continue after Jace, halting me in my tracks.

I nod and he continues, "I have just heard from the school board about a Winter ball," he says with a frown.

"Okayyy," I respond wondering why the fuck I would care about some stupid school dance.

"Hallows Preparatory is inviting us to join their festivities," his face is set in a tight grimace as he talks.

Fucking Elliot Donovan. I was a fool to be on edge thinking he would attack me out in the open in retaliation. That's not how snakes work though, is it? They stalk and slither through the grass, waiting to stumble across their prey. He is using his name and connections like always to try and get to me.

"I see," I say, acknowledging what he said.

"Is there something I need to be made aware of, Elle?" he asks, looking worried.

"Honestly, at this point, Graham, I wouldn't even know where to start," I say in truth. "I have to go but I will explain everything soon, I promise," I add, and he nods.

I dart back into the cafeteria and nod my head at the guys that we need to go, they don't hesitate before rising from the table. I don't wait for them as I make my way out of school ahead of the guys and text Ash telling him to meet us at the house with whatever he has found. I make it to the bottom of the steps before someone grabs me from behind and I drop my phone to the floor. I throw my elbow back immediately hitting my attacker in the stomach, but the hardness there hurts my arm probably more than it did them.

They trap my arms down at the side of my body, in an impressive move, making it impossible to reach my knife. So, I have to get creative. I throw my head back and smash right into whoever is holding me, connecting with their nose and I smirk as they grunt in pain.

I don't get a chance to fight any further before I am slammed against the wall and recognition flows through me at the familiar face, and the last one I ever expected to find here. *What the fuck?*

"Getting sloppy, little sis," he says with a smirk as blood drips down from his nose onto his lip.

Before I can even form a response, Lincoln appears grabbing him by the back of the neck and slams him against the wall by his throat, as Marcus pulls me into his side.

"You must have a death wish," Linc says to him coolly, with a firm grip around his neck but my attacker just smiles wider, flicking his eyes back to me.

"Oh, I like this one, can I keep him?" he asks, licking the blood from his lips, and bringing his gaze back to Lincoln.

"Cut it out, Logan," I groan with exasperation and Linc frowns.

"You know this guy?" he questions, not taking his gaze from Logan's.

"Unfortunately," I reply. "You can release him," I gesture at him.

"Or not," Logan teases, "I will gladly let you show me what else that hand can grip," he says with a wink and I roll my eyes.

Lincoln drops his hand and steps back, but his gaze doesn't move as he assesses him. No doubt trying to work out everything about him, and how he can use it against him, if need be. I'm sure once we leave here, he will take his name and go all hacker on his ass, until he knows everything from where he was born to how he takes his fucking coffee.

Logan ignores him for a moment and turns back to me, “Missed you, sis,” he teases with a gleaming smile.

“Sis?” Marcus questions, looking between the two of us.

Logan takes in his grip on my hip before holding his hand out for Marcus to shake, “Ah, you must be the famous River. Nice to finally meet you,” he preens, before turning to me. “Fucking hot, sis, no wonder you came back to this rat-infested dump,” he says, holding his hand out for me to fist bump but I just shake my head at him, so he drops it.

He turns to the others, “So that must mean you’re Jace,” he asks nodding to him, “and this delicious glass of tall and handsome is Lincoln. I hear you swing for the better team, if you are interested in taking a ride?” he purrs, grabbing his crotch with a completely serious tone and a flirty smile on his face.

“Boys, meet Logan,” I say, gesturing my hand from him to the guys.

“Her brother,” he adds with a smile and I groan.

“Arthur and Helen's adopted son,” I confirm.

“The best child they ever picked,” he says with a wink.

“Where’s Lily?” I question, trying to change the subject and finding out where his twin is.

“Eurghhh, who knows where that little Satanist ever is,” he declares with a shrug.

“But she’s here with you?” I confirm.

"Of course," he rolls his eyes, like I'm the one being ridiculous.

"Why are you here?" I ask and he frowns.

"I called Mom and she said everything was fine. We all know that is code for everything is not fine, and since Lils and I haven't seen you in forever, we decided to road trip," he speaks the way he always does, matter of factly and oozing with confidence.

I've known the twins ever since I met Zack and made it to Arthur and Helen. Logan and Lily are biological siblings, they are a year older than me and have been with the Roytons since they were five and their parents were killed in a car accident. They both have smooth golden skin, dark brown hair and brown eyes, so strikingly similar that you would know instantly they're twins. Their personalities, however, couldn't be more different. Logan is confident, outgoing, laid back, and a super slutty bisexual. Lily is quiet, shy, reserved, and would rather be alone than with company. The only person she truly opens up with is Logan, she just about tolerates me and Zack although we have seen a softer side of her, ever since Cass was born which I appreciate.

I scoff, "No, dickhead, not here in town, here at my school?" I question.

He smiles and trails his gaze over Lincoln again, "Came to check out all the eye candy, of course," he teases, adding another wink.

I sigh again, "Well come on, we are meeting Ash back at the house, so we need to go."

"Ahhh, and how is the beautiful little psycho these days? Still dark, dangerous, and delicious?" he muses, biting his lip as he follows me towards Linc's SUV.

"Lincoln seems to think so," Jace offers, and that just riles Logan up more. For fuck's sake, there's two of them.

"Hmm, so I have some competition," he broods, like he is genuinely thinking about what to do next. "Good. I love a challenge," he declares with a savage grin.

I punch his arm to get his attention, "Just meet us back at the house, dickface. I will catch you up on what has been going on," I say, as I swing open the door to Linc's ride.

He walks away from us backwards towards his car, "Sure thing, sissy," he drawls at me with a menacing smile, knowing how much I hate that fucking nickname.

I flip him off before jumping inside. Just what I need around here, another fucking testosterone filled alpha male, hell bent on saving my life. This should be fun.

Chapter 33

ELLE

Is there some kind of record for the highest amount of hot teenage boys in one place? Like do they run competitions for that sort of thing. Because I'm pretty sure if they did, the boys currently standing around my kitchen island would win. I'm standing with Marcus and Logan on one side and Jace and Lincoln on my other. Like some sort of fucked up family orgy as we wait for Ash to show up. All of the boys are currently staring a hole into Logan's head, trying to work him out. They shouldn't bother, I 've known him for almost four years, and still haven't managed to work out his brand of crazy. Of course, Logan is being his typical insufferable self and making any situation more sexual, it's a true skill of his.

"Sis, how the fuck do you get anything done with these three around you all day? I've got a semi just thinking about the fun I could have with them at the same time," his tone is completely serious as he appraises the three other guys standing around me.

"She gets stabby," Jace unhelpfully replies with a wink in my direction. Logan takes the opportunity to fully check him out, just like I did on the first day of school.

You would have to be blind not to, you don't get as many girls as he does without being a walking fucking Adonis.

"Ever sucked a dick, Jacey baby?" Logan asks him with genuine curiosity. I can see he is picking up on their similar flirty natures. Lord help me, they would be fucking chaotic together if Jace swung that way. Thank the devil he doesn't.

Jace doesn't look offended in the slightest as he answers honestly, "Sorry man, I am on a pussy only kinda diet," he shrugs, "just can't beat it."

"I get it," Logan nods, "I like a bit of both myself, but I just love dick too much to commit to any one girl," he replies offering an equal amount of honesty. I already know the two of them are going to be fast friends.

Logan turns to Marcus who is still silently assessing him with a stoic look on his face, which just makes Logan smile wider, "Ooff, I bet that alpha attitude is fucking killer in bed, Elle," he comments, and I blush furiously.

"Shut the fuck up, Logan," I scold.

He barks a laugh, "Please don't tell me you are still holding onto that pesky V card with all this cock around?" he splutters through his laugh and I blush harder.

"Not after this weekend, ey Queenie?" Jace winks again. I want the ground to open up and fucking swallow me whole.

"Cut it the fuck out, brother," Marcus warns Jace in a deathly tone, causing Logan to smile.

"Oh yes, definitely hot in the sack. I can tell," he says offering me a high five which I decline, and he shrugs.

We are saved from any more awkwardness when Asher finally arrives, casting his glance around the kitchen until he notices Logan standing there and rolls his eyes.

"Oh great. Look what the cat dragged in," Ash sneers as he enters, eyes locked on Logan's. "Always a displeasure to see you, little Royton," he draws out sarcastically.

"We could easily change that to a pleasure, you little psycho, just say the word," Logan jibes back, licking his lips as he looks him up and down. He has flirted with him furiously since the day they met, much to Asher's annoyance.

Ash huffs in exasperation, "Do not start with me, Logan."

Logan holds his hands up in mock defense, "Oh, don't worry, I have my sights set somewhere else now," he teases as he slides his gaze over to Lincoln causing him to blush.

Ash snorts, "Of fucking course you've got your eye on the help," his tone completely dark and accusing, causing Lincoln to snap his gaze over to him.

"Is it so hard to believe someone would, dark prince?" he stares at him so intensely, showing his cards a little, as we all get a glimpse of how much of an effect Asher has on him. I wonder how Ash feels about that.

"Oh, dark prince, I like that," Logan wiggles his brows. "I could be the filling in this flirty sandwich you guys have going on," he gestures between the two of them. I notice Lincoln blush at just the idea of both of them and decide to jump in and save him.

"Cut the shit, we have got enough shit to be worrying about without you two jibing at one another," I fume at them.

Logan stares at Ash and Linc one more time before bringing his attention back to me, "Fine!" he huffs out, "Bring me up to speed of what happened over the weekend."

"He knows what you do?" Lincoln questions me.

Logan snorts, "I thought you said he was smart?" He turns back to Linc, "Don't let my obvious good looks and flirty nature confuse you, Mr. Blackwell. I am lethal in everything I do. Do you really think I would let my sister go off to war without being a soldier by her side?" his tone is unusually dark.

I watch as Lincoln soaks in his words, dissecting them until they process through his dark and wonderful mind. There is a tense minute of silence before Linc nods at him which is like his version of approval. Fuck me, it looks like Logan is joining the team officially.

I look at Asher who is watching Logan and Lincoln's interaction without emotion, but something in his eye is unfamiliar to me. It's like he is trying to see what makes them both tick at the same time, as trying to work out how to end them.

"Ash, what have you got?" I question him just to break the tension in the room. His eyes snap to me before he takes a deep breath and speaks.

"Elliot is officially on the war path after what happened at the docks, he is amping up his guards, and doubled the amount of money on your head for you to be brought to him alive," he looks hesitant as he speaks, and

I know there is more as Marcus curses at what he has already said.

"Go on," I encourage him.

"He has sought the help of Captain Baizen, in getting every piece of information he can find on everyone you know," he says looking at the three Rebels before adding, "Also, he threatened your parents trying to see if they knew anything about where you are."

"Well, that's a waste of his time, like those fucking assholes would know anything about me."

"You had contact with your sperm donors?" Logan interrupts with his question.

"Unfortunately," I reply with a grimace, "we followed them on a stake out. Jonathan went into a warehouse on 5th and Middleton. We still don't have any true information on it, and my mother cornered me while dress shopping."

"You never told me that," Marcus snaps, and I huff at his pissy attitude.

"It was before you stopped being an asshole," I offer him with a smile.

"Ohh, burn," Jace whispers under his breath for us all to hear and Marcus glares at him.

"Can we fucking focus?" I curse, just as Lily, Logan's twin enters the room.

"Lils," I say with a desperate smile hoping to coax more estrogen into this cock fest. She looks up taking in the five guys around me and senses the tension between us all.

"Nope," she says, before she does a complete one-eighty and leaves without another word. I can't help but laugh at her.

Jace watches her leave, "She seems…" he pauses, I'm sure trying to find the right word, 'interesting,'" he finishes.

Logan laughs, "You have no idea."

I ignore them as I press on, "Seems Captain Baizen is the most pressing issue then," I muse aloud, as the others bring their attention back to me.

I see the moment Ash knows when I've made a decision because his shoulders tense before I even speak, "Well, seems it is time for the Captain of Police and I to have a little chat." He is going to bleed for every single one of his crimes.

"I'm helping," Logan cuts in before anyone else can respond to me.

I roll my eyes, "What use is you being here, if you don't fucking help, Lo?" my tone is sniping but I have far too much coming at us right now to give a shit. The fucker just smirks at his rarely used nickname from me anyway.

"Knew you missed me," he preens with delight.

"What do we have on Baizen? Anything?" Marcus cuts in with a serious look on his face.

That gets a genuine smile from me for the first time since we all got here, "Come on, I'll show you," I gesture for them to follow me. I lead them back down to my little den of danger so we can make a plan. Once all the guys have taken a seat in there, I pull out a spare whiteboard, and start sticking information to it as I talk.

"Steven Baizen," I begin by placing a picture of him in the center, "husband of Katherine and father of Damien," I add, sticking a picture of his family up. "He is the Captain of Police and a decorated one at that," I continue, as I hand out files to each of the guys containing all his background information. "People see him as a hero, a family man, a true credit to the town of Black Hallows. What they don't see is this," I press a few keys on the computer until pictures of him start appearing on the screen, all of him in compromising positions with underage boys.

"Baizen is a predator. He preys on innocent young boys, befriending them through the system, and then raping them before making them disappear," I turn back to the guys. Asher and Lincoln are emotionless, having already known all of this. They are my information collectors after all. Logan is reading his file and no doubt committing every inch of it to memory, whereas Marcus and Jace look a little green at what they are seeing. I turn back to the screen and make it go dark, the images there aren't pleasant, and we don't need reminders of what a sick fuck he is. I take a seat and wait for the guys to process the information.

"If you have proof of his crimes, why haven't you handed him in?" Jace asks with curiosity.

"To who?" I laugh slightly. "His police buddies, who he is the boss of? Or Carter Fitzgerald the Governor who he golfs with every Sunday?" I don't mean to sound bitchy, but these guys really need to grasp that the only way out for anyone involved with Elliot Donovan is death.

Baizen is one of Elliot's inside men, complicit in all of his crimes and a master at keeping them covered. It's time for him to disappear.

"What's your plan?" Lincoln speaks directly to me. He knows this is my show, he and the others are just along for the ride.

I blow out a breath, "Honestly? I don't know yet. It needs to be discreet," I muse as I rub little circles on either side of my temples, like that will help me conjure up a solution to all my problems.

"I may have something," Marcus pipes in, looking down at his phone with a frown.

"What is it, brother?" Lincoln questions him.

He passes his phone to him as he speaks, "I just received a report signed off by Damien Baizen that the fire at the loft was an accident."

Asher grunts, "Yeah, and I'm the son of a fucking saint," he drawls, his voice brimming with contempt.

Lincoln passes the phone to me so I can read what's in the report. Sure enough, even with all the evidence of foul play that was left at the scene, the fire has still been ruled an accident. I fucking hate money, it really can buy anything. I spin on my chair until I'm facing the board again, my gaze locks onto the picture of Steven smiling down at his wife and son.

I smile when the idea hits me, "Time for us to capture a little incentive, boys. We are done playing in the shadows."

Chapter 34

MARCUS

Elle is quiet as we drive across town to get to the loft, well, what's left of it anyway. She isn't tense or even fearful, just calm. It unnerves me. Her plan seems simple but as I have come to learn, nothing is ever fucking simple. I'm running through a range of scenarios in my head and praying none of them come true. I just want something to go smoothly for once.

It's just the two of us in her jeep, the others are following behind us in a brand-new SUV that is identical to what Lincoln had. Elle gave it to him like it was nothing to just hand over a car worth thousands of dollars. I guess to her, it was nothing. She's no longer heir to the King fortune but somehow managed to find herself with even more money than before.

"Do you think this will work?" I ask, breaking the tension as we pull up alongside the police cruiser that is waiting for us. Her plan was simple, use Steven Baizen's son to get him to come to us.

"Only one way to find out," she answers simply, before turning off the engine and climbing out, so I follow suit.

Damien Baizen looks pristine in his uniform, every bit an official man of the law like you would imagine. His brow is furrowed as he looks back and forth from the paperwork in his hand, to the black vessel that I used to call a home. He looks between the two like he is trying to work something out. I clear my throat to get his attention and he startles, like he didn't even realize we had arrived.

He shakes his head like he is clearing his thoughts and reaches out a hand for me to shake, "Mr. Riviera, I presume?" he asks. I have to hold in my grunt at his fake bravado, knowing full well he will have seen my file. They may not be aware that I committed fucking murder, but I have enough of a rap sheet to be on a first name basis with most of the officers down at the precinct. Although, this is the first time I have ever crossed paths with Officer Baizen.

I shake his hand and squeeze his fingers slightly, he winces before he can stop himself and I smile. I feel Elle watching us before she thrusts out her own hand.

"Elle King," she says, casually tossing her name out. We both see the recognition in his eyes.

"Miss King? What a pleasure," he holds out his hand and I frown at the genuine tone of his voice, like he really is happy to meet her. What the fuck?

Elle's face crumples in slight confusion, but she accepts his hand, as we both clock the other guys creeping up behind him. Elle smiles a sinister smile which shouldn't turn me on but fuck me it does.

"Don't speak too soon, little Baizen," Elle responds without remorse, as Logan comes up behind him and slides the syringe into his neck at the same time that Lincoln and Jace reach out to grab him. Elle told me Logan is following in Arthur's footsteps and studying medicine at college, making him our in-group pharmacist. It wasn't hard to figure out a dosage of Flunitrazepam to get him to take a little nap. Elle doesn't react to his flailing body as he slips into unconsciousness, "Get him in the trunk," she simply requests, and the guys follow her instruction. Once he is locked inside, we all look to her as she surveys the surrounding area.

"Pretty boy take his car and burn it. Lo, you go with him. Superman, you hack his phone and get Daddy dearest to where we want him. Ash make sure any cameras that may have caught him on his way here are wiped. Marcus and I will get everything set up and keep an eye on our incentive until we get Steven," she rattles off her list of commands, we all nod our heads in unison. A queen commanding her troops.

It doesn't take long for Elle's demands to be met and before I know it we are parked outside a seedy bar on the outskirts of town in a blacked out van. Lincoln used Damien's phone to text his father, telling him something bad had happened, and that he needed to meet him urgently, away from prying eyes. Of course, the Captain of police knew just the place for that kind of conversation. I want to laugh when I think of all the officers at my house the day, I found my dad's body. All of them were so professional looking for evidence and offering me their condolences. What a bunch of fucking bullshit that was.

Logan insisted that the best plan of action was for him to go into the bar and use his good looks and charm, his words not mine, to lure our target into the bathroom. Elle begrudgingly agreed when we all decided that was a good idea. She sits next to me fidgeting with a laser focus on the bar.

I reach out and grip her hand in mine, "He is going to be fine," I say trying to placate her, but she just scoffs at me.

"You don't know that, River. Baizen is a fucking demon. I have every right to be worried," she snaps back, but I know her tone is more aimed at the situation than me.

Her phone vibrates before I can respond to her. She whips it out faster than anything, reading whatever is on her screen, before blowing out a breath of relief, and cracking a smile as she shows it to me.

Logan: Officially the saggiest balls I have ever fucking seen *gag emoji* come help me get the fat fuck out the back door he is heavy as shit.

She turns to speak to Linc who is behind us, "He needs help getting him out, can you go help him, and I will back the van around?"

"On it," he is moving before he finishes speaking and pushes past the hog-tied body of Damien Baizen that is 'sleeping' peacefully on the van floor. Elle waits until he gets out before she drives around the back entrance and reverses up to the exit there. I can hear Asher tapping away in the back, no doubt wiping any possible camera feeds. Two minutes later the van doors are flung open and Jace moves to help Logan and Lincoln heave the unconscious body of Steven Baizen inside.

We drive for two fucking hours, until we find ourselves in the middle of fucking nowhere. Like seriously, an hour of that was without seeing one other car or main road. I haven't a clue where we are, but it seems Elle knows exactly where to go. It's pitch black when we finally stop, but the headlights of the van highlight what looks like a cabin. It looks run down and deserted, like no one has inhabited it in years. It also seems to be our final destination. Elle turns off the engine and climbs out and the others follow suit.

The guys and I drag the two Baizens out of the van and follow Elle as she moves towards the cabin. She pushes open the door, coughing at some dust that escapes. She pulls a flashlight from the bag she is carrying before switching it on and moving inside. We continue after her as she approaches the middle of the room and lifts an old dusty carpet aside, revealing a door in the floor. When she opens it and disappears down it, I look at my brothers who look just as shocked as I do, Asher looks emotionless as always and Logan looks like he is genuinely enjoying himself.

We all move at once to follow her down there, not taking any regard for either of the Baizens as we drag them along. Their heads hit each step of the stairs, as we descend through the door on the floor. Elle flicks on the lights when we get down there and my mouth opens in shock. What the fuck is this place? The whole room is grey concrete, the floor, the walls, even the fucking ceiling. One wall is lined with weapons, some of which I haven't even got a clue how you would use them.

Elle seems comfortable here, so I know this isn't the first time she's been here.

"Damn sis, the improvements look great," Logan whistles his approval, confirming he has also been here before.

"Yeah, the drain is a particularly good addition," Asher draws as he surveys things and true to his psycho form, he is smiling sinisterly at some of the weapons hung up.

Elle finally turns around and looks at the five of us, ignoring the two bodies before us completely.

"This is going to be done bloody and without mercy," she warns, "if you can't handle that then now is the time to leave," she gestures to the steps behind us but no one even flinches. That satisfies her and she nods slightly before turning and rummaging around until she finds what she needs.

She hands us all plastic jumpsuits and some gloves, "Suit up, boys."

She steps into her own suit before pulling on gloves. Then she retrieves some plastic sheeting and starts lining a large area of the floor with it until it is almost fully covered and places a metal chair in the center. She waits until we are all dressed in the stuff, she gave us, before giving us another instruction.

"Little Baizen in the corner for now, put Steven in the chair," there is no emotion in her voice as she talks, just the fire of revenge in her eyes. She is right, this will be bloody.

Chapter 35

ELLE

By the time Steven Baizen starts to wake from his forced slumber, I'm practically giddy. I have thought about killing each of Elliot's men multiple times, fantasized about it even. How I would make them squirm, how their blood would squirt from their bodies and how the life would drain from their eyes. So finally having one of them in front of me, is like Christmas coming early.

He wakes slowly at first, his eyes flickering with the struggle to open them, until he tries to move his tied-up arms and startles awake, taking in his surroundings. His eyes focus in and out as he surveys the room with a panicked, confused look at what he finds. It is a bit of a masterpiece if I do say so myself.

The plastic sheeting covers almost everything, we don't want any pesky evidence being left behind. The walls also have about a hundred images of Captain Baizen in a variety of sickening and compromising positions with children. His legs are tied to the bottom of the chair, his wrists too and the chair has a high back allowing me to strap his head to it also. His eyes dance around the room frantically, until they land on his son in the corner. Damien is still out cold thanks to the extra dose from Logan, but his mere unconscious presence is enough to get Steven flailing.

The guys are all against the back wall, unseen and waiting, watching. They know this is my show to run and not to interfere unless I ask.

"Hello?" Steven croaks out in an uneasy tone and I smother a laugh. Nothing like the brave, predatory Captain now is he.

"Hello, Mr. Baizen," I answer from the shadows and even though he can't see me, his gaze still swings to my direction.

"Who...Who, who are you?" his voice trembles slightly, as he stumbles over his words. So pathetic.

I step into the light until my face comes into view and our eyes lock on one another. I watch as his shoulders relax at my presence. A mistake on his part. He recognizes me instantly. It may have been a few years since he has set eyes on me, but I look just like my mother. Steven used to frequent our house on occasion, whenever my father was looking to show off his connections to his bullshit friends.

"Miss King?" his voice sounds a little calmer but still the undertone of panic can be heard and so formal like his son, manners run in the family I see. "What are you doing here?" he adds, trying to look around but failing.

"Why, I am here to do your job for you, Steven," I reply sweetly, moving closer towards him. I see the moment his eyes drop to take in the coveralls I am wearing over my clothes, he gulps.

"I don't understand," he exclaims, and he is back to stuttering, I roll my eyes.

"Of course, you don't. Did you think you could protect him forever? That your crimes would go unnoticed alongside his?" my voice is calm, but my heartbeat is so erratic, I wouldn't be surprised if the rest of the room could hear it.

"Who?" he starts but my temper breaks slightly, cutting him off.

"Elliot fucking Donovan," I grit through my teeth with a smile. I don't want to play any games with him, "The devil who lines your pockets, so you keep his darkness hidden. You know the girls he rapes, the drugs he runs, the guns he sells." I take a step forward, my voice getting louder, "Ring any fucking bells?"

He flinches at my tone but still tries to force some bravado into the situation he finds himself in. "This isn't a game you want to play, little girl," he sneers, and I laugh. A full head thrown back, belly laugh. This fucking moron.

I move until he will be able to feel my breath on his face as I talk, "You're right, this isn't a game." I grin as I lean in further until my mouth is at his ear, "This is war, and you picked the wrong fucking side."

He doesn't notice the gun until the bullet shatters his kneecap. My silencer muffled the sound of the shot, but not his screams of pain. No, those I devour.

"You shot me, you fucking little slut," he splutters, stating the obvious as I step back and watch the blood pulse from his leg.

"Here is how things are going to go," I say, gesturing wildly with the gun. "You will answer my questions to my satisfaction, or you will find out how fucking creative I can really be with a man's body," I shrug, willing him to underestimate my skill set, so I can really make him pay.

His breaths are coming quick and fast as he pants through the pain with a groan. He looks at me with pure disdain, "Fuck you," he spits at me and I gleam with appreciation.

I shake my head with another laugh, "Wrong answer, Steven," I move before he can even register my next action, when my knuckle dusted fist connects with his face, I hear the crack of his cheek.

"Fuckkkkk!" He yells out, as tears start to stream from his eyes. "You can't do this to me, you fucking little cunt, I am the Captain of police, the law of this town," he seethes at me through gritted teeth.

"Oh yes, the high and mighty, untouchable Captain Baizen," I drawl sarcastically before I look down at him, "How the mighty have fallen."

I move towards the table at the side to assess the weapons I have laid out there. Time for some fun. I pluck some pliers first and twist them over in my hands to inspect them. Perfect.

I turn back to my prey and move until I am right in front of him again, "Let's try this again, shall we?" I smile as I slip the pliers around one of his fingers. "Tell me what Elliot Donovan knows about me?"

His focus is on his captured finger and his hesitation makes me angry, he still isn't taking me seriously. I take great pleasure in the crunching of his finger as I force the pliers together. His finger falls to the floor as he screams out in pain again.

I hear one of the guys mutter a 'fuck' under their breath while another laughs, but Steven doesn't seem to hear anything over his screams. I block them out too. I appreciate having them here with me, but they are connected to a side of me that I can't bring into this room right now. I watch the blood pour from his hand with mild satisfaction, as he tries to control his breathing and ignore the pain, but I can tell by how white he is, that he is failing. We can't have that.

"Shoot him, Lo," I toss over his shoulder to Logan and he steps forward without hesitation and plunges another syringe into his neck, only this time it is filled with adrenaline. That will keep his blood pumping and his heart beating.

I line the pliers up onto another finger ready for my question, "I'll ask again, tell me what Elliot knows."

He is panting hard but grits his teeth "He, he knows you're back. That you've got someone after him. That you are with the Rebels," he pants more trying to get his words out quickly. "He thinks you are using them to get to him, that's why he went after them," he is so breathless that he sounds like he just ran a marathon.

"And what about Asher?" I push him applying pressure to the pliers.

"What about him?" he yells, frantically trying to pull his finger away, when all it does is increase the hold against the tool in my hand. I look over his shoulder into the darkness and nod. Asher steps out of the shadows and walks to my side and Baizen's eyes go as wide as saucers.

"No, no way," he stutters over his words. "He's with you?" He asks in utter shock that only makes me happier.

Ash slides his fingers into my free hand until they are entangled together not caring about the blood on my gloves. "Always," his tone is firm and dark, leaving no question to his loyalty.

Asher turns from him to look at me, "He's a useless sack of shit, let's euthanize him," his emotionless voice fills the room without faltering and I smile at him. This is a dark path we forced ourselves on and he has been with me since the very beginning.

"Let's play with him a little first," I reply with a gleaming smile as I snap the pliers for a second time and let another finger fall from his hand.

Ash and I use a number of tools to experiment effective ways to make our Captain of police bleed until apparently, he can't take anymore.

"Enough," he cries, "Please stop, enough!" He begs but his pleas mean nothing to me.

"Did you stop?" I question him, bending down until I'm at his eye level. "When those boys begged you to leave them alone, did you stop? When those girls came and reported heinous crimes committed by your friends, did you stop?" My tone is laced with anger but unwavering as I speak, "No you didn't, you raped them, tortured them, and then covered it up just like your sick band of friends. Do you even remember any of them?" I ask gesturing to the pictures that cover the walls, "Their names? Their families? Do you remember fucking any of them? Lord, how I wish they could see you now, covered in blood, and drenched in your own piss, not so fucking tough now are you, not untouchable anymore? No, now you're just a fucking rapist who is finally getting the justice you deserve."

"Dad," Damien's voice splutters behind me and I spin to find him looking utterly shocked behind me, as his gaze bounces rapidly around the room. He looks between his dad and the pictures and then throws up on himself.

Steven can barely see through his bloodied swollen eyes, but he splutters his son's name, "Damien, don't listen to them son, they are liars," his desperate tone is grating, I watch Damien closely as he dissects what his father is saying.

He looks scared, not the guilty kind of scared that Steven looked. No, he looks shocked, confused, and downright fucking petrified. Hmm interesting. I move until I am in front of him and he removes his gaze from his father to meet mine. He looks like everything he has ever been told has been a lie, could it be that the son of a scumbag like Steven, is innocent?

"What do you know about Elliot Donovan?" I inquire, watching his face for every reaction which means I don't miss his immediate frown.

He looks past me to his dad again with the same confused frown before he answers, "He's my dad's friend, they have known each other for years," he pauses, like he is trying to think of more information. "He gives money to the police department every year, funds, uniforms, and stuff like that," he is trying and failing to hide his body shaking with fear, or nerves, I'm not quite sure.

"And what do you know of him being a murdering rapist piece of shit like your dad?" I push him further for information and he splutters in disbelief immediately, and I have my answer, he knows nothing, lucky for him.

I spin back to Steven, "Well, would you look at that Captain? You did one thing right. Kept your son out of your sick and twisted lifestyle, now your wife only has to mourn one of you," I don't even let my words register before I lift my gun and plant a bullet right in the middle of his head. My target practice is clearly paying off. Damien lets out a muffled noise as he watches his father die.

"Let what you saw here today be a reminder of what I can and will do to you, if need be," I speak in a smooth, flat tone, letting the dark edge of my mood shine through. "You will go home and act like nothing has happened, your father's crimes will be revealed to the world and you will be thankful that you weren't involved." I hope I am doing the right thing, I don't want to murder innocents, that would make me as bad as them.

Asher isn't as collected as me, shocker I know, he steps forward and kicks Damien onto his back and places his foot at his throat.

"Do you know who I am?" He asks and Damien tries his best to nod, "Good." He pushes his foot harder into his throat and I watch as he struggles to breathe.

"If you even think about speaking to anyone about what transpired here today then it won't just be you who pays. I will murder everyone you have cared about, your mother, Katherine, your cat, Mr. Sniffles, even your high school girlfriend, Josie. I will hunt every single one of them down and skin them alive until they are begging for mercy and then and only then will I show it. I will boil their bodies in acid until they are nothing but sludge for the fucking pigs to eat, are we clear?"

I can practically taste his fear as he digests Ash's words and tries his best to nod. Ash presses into his throat even more before pulling back and turning to me with a nod.

I turn to find all the guys watching us. Marcus is staring at me with a whole new look in his eye, a look that says he is impressed, frightened, and if I'm not mistaken a little turned on. Jace has a look I have never seen before, there is a fire behind his eyes like he is ready for a whole new chapter of his life. Lincoln is taking in the scene before him with a dark approving appraisal, like today is exactly his kind of day, it makes me wonder about his past. Then I lock eyes with Logan who is smirking at us as he leans on the chair that Steven's warm dead body still occupies, "I knew today would be fun."

Chapter 36

LINCOLN

It has been hours since we got home and everyone disappeared to their own corners of the house. Marcus dragged Elle off as soon as we got back, Jace got so stoned that I had to carry him to bed, Donovan stalked to Zack's office, and Logan said he was going to catch up on his extra curriculars, whatever the fuck that means.

There is no way I could attempt to sleep, I'm too wired. Today was the kind of day I long to be part of the kind that reminds me of my past, my childhood. The darkness of what we did pulses through my veins. The adrenaline courses through me like a drug. A drug I know well. One I've been addicted to since I was eight years old and watched the life drain from my father's eyes.

Some of us are born into darkness, people like Elliot, Greg, Asher, and even me. Others are molded by things that happen to them like Elle, Jace, and Marcus.

I relish in the blood that was spilled today. Reliving every blow Elle delivered to one of her tormentors. He may not have laid a finger on her that terrible night, but that doesn't mean there haven't been countless others who suffered under his hands.

Unlike us, Elle King wasn't born a dark murderous queen. No, her circumstances made her into one. She took the pain she endured and turned it into a power that grows daily. Donovan underestimates her at every turn, but he is also relentless. Every move we make from here on out, needs to be calculated, every possible outcome considered and prepared for. Elliot Donovan may have a fucking criminal empire, but we have more to lose than he does.

For the first time in my life, I have a family to call my own. People to protect and love. I won't let anything happen to them.

I can't seem to settle my mind. Contemplating and worrying about all we might come to face. I tried pulling a Marcus and drowned out the thoughts with half a bottle of whiskey, it did nothing. I tried following Jace into a weed induced sleep, all that did was make the darkness feel more decadent. That's how I find myself in the gym, my fists pound into the bags hoping I can bleed this high away. My knuckles split and bleed, finally drawing me out of the haze. I turn around and lock eyes with Logan. He leans against the door watching me with a dangerous smile on his face.

He appraises me slowly, like a predator would its prey. He's fucking delusional if he thinks he can hunt someone like me. His gaze takes in my grey sweats and lack of shirt, lingering on my sweat soaked chest before he meets my eyes and I raise my brows at him in question.

"Sorry, I didn't mean to startle you," he purrs in that alluring flirty voice of his as he enters the room fully.

"You didn't. You've been watching me for seven minutes." I don't think about how weird that would sound to someone, the fact I noticed him as soon as he darkened the doorway, felt him even. Just one of my many learned talents. Something I had to be good at to survive. Always be aware of your surroundings.

He lets out a low whistle, "Damn your perceptive. Wanna know what else I could do in seven minutes," the teasing edge to his voice gives me pause.

This isn't like his previous attempts at flirting with me, he isn't trying to show off, or embarrass me. He isn't trying to get a rise out of having an audience, there is no one here but the two of us. This is just for him, for us, he wants me for real.

I take into consideration his blatant sexual offer. I'm not blind, he's fucking sex on a stick. Tall, dark, and handsome, with a jaw that could slice you open. He looks at me with a glint in his eye. Like he's willing to do whatever I'd want him to but isn't expecting me to take him up on his offer. He doesn't know the turmoil inside me. He doesn't know how long it's been since I've had the pleasure of sinking deep into someone else. How long since I've put my cock down someone's throat and fucked their face. I've been so busy with everything since Elle got to town, that I'm itching to feel that relief and Logan might just be the perfect candidate.

I feel the smirk tug on the side of my mouth as I decide to take him up on whatever he is offering, "Come on then, Logan. Show me what you got," I sit down on the bench leaning back against the mirror and open my legs. The invitation is clear.

He licks his lips appreciatively, his gaze darkening as he takes me in once more. He wastes no time stalking towards me and sinking down onto his knees between my open legs. It's a fucking pretty sight.

"I didn't know computer nerds were this stacked," he smirks, as he eyes my bare chest.

He places his hands on my knees and runs them up my thighs with a firm touch. When he reaches my waistband, I think he's going to dip inside, but he doesn't. His fingers bypass it and skim across my abs. I flex under his touch, and he smiles as he looks up at me. His dark lashes fanning against his face, he increases the pressure as he rubs up my chest and leans closer to me.

"The quiet ones are always so fucking hot," he murmurs, leaning in to kiss my neck. His lips are soft but firm at the same time. His tongue traces a path up to my earlobe and I groan as my erection begins to strain against my sweats.

"Quiet and reserved at all times," he whispers into my ear, "just like Asher. I bet I could make you both scream." He grips my hard dick over the material at the same time he says Donovan's name and I can't help but groan again.

"Yeah, don't think I haven't noticed how hot you are for our resident little psycho." He slips his hand into my sweats and grips my length giving me a slow tug. Fuck, it's been too long since I have had another's hands on me. He strokes me slowly up and down as he kisses his way across my jaw.

His tongue flicks across my lips as his breath coats my mouth. He continues to tease me with his hand and taunt me with his words, "Have you imagined him like this? On his knees for you, ready to take you. Or would it be you, taking him?" I moan an anguished sound and he smiles, "Oh, you'd like that, wouldn't you, baby?" The word baby rolls off his tongue far too easily and sounds too good in his gravelly tone. It sounds familiar, like maybe I could get used to hearing it every day.

I take in his dark lustful stare and smile at him. It's a smile that promises dark and wicked things. He closes the distance between us, and we come together all teeth and tongue as we devour each other's mouths. Fuck, he can kiss. I can't fucking wait to feel his mouth on my cock. He must read my mind because he pulls away and starts licking, biting, and sucking his way down my body. He doesn't seem phased by the sweat lingering there, as he groans lapping it up. When he reaches my abs, he pulls back and grips my sweats on either side, motioning for me to move. I stand so he can drag the sweats down my legs and free my now rock-hard cock.

He stares at it like it's the best thing he's ever fucking seen and when he flicks his tongue across my slit, I hiss. He wastes no time in gripping my base and swirling his tongue around the head of my dick before sucking the tip into his warm, velvety mouth. I can't help the shudder that escapes me as he sucks me like a fucking champ.

He pulls back and licks the length of my shaft, coating me in his salvia before he sucks one of my balls into his mouth. He's teasing me, tasting everything, I've got to give and using it to try and own me. Doesn't he know I can't be owned?

I tangle my fingers into his hair and grip until his eyes lock with mine.

"Do I have to fuck your mouth or are you going to be a good boy, and give me what I need?" I practically growl the words at him, but he needs to know how close to the edge I am before I fucking snap.

He takes in the no doubt dark look in my eye and instead of being deterred, he looks determined. His signature cocky smile makes his handsome face just that much more fucking beautiful.

"I'm gonna rock your fucking world, Blackwell," he declares, taking me into his mouth so deep I can feel the back of his throat. Fucking hell. I'm throbbing with need and the cocky fucker knows it as he smiles around my cock.

He works me down his throat like a fucking pro, not a gag in sight. Bobbing his head up and down my length, sucking without restraint. His mouth feels sinful and his enthusiasm for my cock just makes it all the better. He takes my dick like he's never tasted anything better. No wonder his ego is so big, he's got a mouth like a fucking vacuum.

He alternates between taking me deep in his mouth and swirling his tongue around my head as one of his hands twists around the base of my shaft. It feels amazing. I get lost in the bliss he's pulling from my body.

"Fuck, Logan." I can't contain my groans or my words of encouragement, "Yes, just like that."

My cock hits the back of his throat again and I groan, throwing my head back, closing my eyes and trying not to come too soon but his mouth feels too good. When he pulls back, I feel his teeth graze against me and I almost fucking burst.

"Are you a giver or taker, Lincoln?" He swirls his tongue around the head of my dick again, lapping up the pre cum there. "Or both?" he continues, licking me furiously like I'm his favorite treat. "I bet you'd feel so fucking good in my ass," he teases, as his hand curls around my base again giving me hard, quick strokes.

He swallows me down again and I can't help but start to meet his mouth in slow smooth thrusts as I growl back at him, "I'd be the one fucking you Logan, hard and deep until you screamed my name," he hums in appreciation at my words and it feels amazing. I need to see him, watch him take my cock into his perfect fucking mouth.

When I open my eyes again to look down at him, something else catches my eye. Someone has managed to sneak up on me for the first time in years. Why am I not surprised that it's my little dark prince? Donovan stands in the doorway of the gym, one hand fisted around the doorframe, the other clutching a rolled-up stack of files. He's frozen on the spot as he takes in Logan on his knees for me, his head bobbing back and forth frantically as he uses his mouth to disarm me.

I can't help the full body shudder that escapes when I lock eyes with him. My whole-body tenses with the need to come. Logan must feel me tense, his eyes flick up to mine as I look down at him and then back over to Asher. I feel the moment that Logan spies him in the mirror, he hums around my cock and I moan as the vibrations travel down to the base of my dick. He takes me to the back of his throat and then draws back to the tip, before letting me fall from his mouth and turning to tilt his head at Donovan.

"Care to join us, Ash? I don't mind sharing, in fact I am pretty sure I would fucking love it," he purrs at him but Asher doesn't so much as fucking flinch, his eyes still locked in on the two of us.

Logan shrugs, "Suit yourself, I'll keep him for myself then," he turns back to me and takes me in his hand and strokes me again while my gaze remains on Donovan. I can't seem to bring myself to break our stare. Why isn't he moving? Does he like what he sees? Does he want in? *I fucking wish.*

I try not to conjure up images in my head of the three of us writhing naked, but it's impossible and with another hard stroke of my cock from Logan, I moan.

"Oh, my baby likes being watched," he groans as he strokes me, flicking his gaze between me and Asher in the mirror. *You have no fucking idea.*

He leans forward and takes me back in his mouth, my eyes never stray from Asher. Fuck. This is the hottest thing I've ever experienced, and it isn't even the first time I've been watched. So, why does this feel more erotic than ever?

The fantasies my head creates can't stop me now. I grip Logan's hair with both hands and fuck his mouth with hard punishing thrusts and he doesn't falter for a second. Just keeps licking and sucking me as I use his mouth to pound in and out of.

He takes my thick length easily, like his mouth was made for me. When he hums around me at the same time I lock eyes with Donovan again, I'm a goner. I come with a choked groan, shooting several long spurts down the back of his throat, which he swallows greedily.

He pulls back slowly, his eyes still locked on mine. When a drop of my come slips out of his mouth and onto his lips, he smirks. He stands, licking my essence back onto his tongue and then slams his mouth onto mine, forcing my own release onto my tongue. He kisses me like he wants to fuck my mouth and knowing that Asher is watching just makes it even hotter. He pulls back and offers me a wink before dropping back to his knees, pulling my pants up and tucking my cock away.

"If you're quite finished, we need to talk, help," Asher's cold voice cuts into the room. He flicks his gaze to Logan on his knees, "alone," he emphasizes in a tone I'm not familiar with from him.

"Sure you don't want a turn, my little psycho?" Logan teases, licking his lips like he can still taste my come on them, "I can easily go again."

I can't help the flare of jealousy I feel at his offer. Why am I jealous? Because less than a minute ago he was swallowing my come or because I want to be the one to suck Donovan's dick? What would it be like to have them both on their knees for me worshipping my cock?

"I'll pass, little Royton. Run along and find another willing dick," he tsks at him in response, before bringing his attention back to me.

Logan isn't deterred in the slightest, rising from his knees to reach up and whisper in my ear, loudly enough for Asher to hear, "I can't wait to take your cock in my ass," I'm surprised, as I imagined Logan to be a one and done type of guy. I didn't expect him to offer himself up again. Unsure of what to say, I just smile and give him a slight nod. You don't turn down a mouth like his.

He nods in return and looks between Donovan and I again, "Okay, well, I'll leave you two to whatever kind of foreplay this is," he gestures with his hands, before walking backwards to leave.

He offers me a wink before he turns as he gets to Asher. He leans in and whispers something in his ear, I see a flicker of surprise on his face before he schools his expression again and Logan leaves us alone.

He stares at me so long I start to feel uncomfortable. It's not something that is easily done so I can't help but snap at him, "What?" I reach up and run my hands through my hair which is no doubt a mess after my impromptu work out and the best blow job of my fucking life.

"Nothing," he finally breaks his silence and steps into the room with me. "I just thought Jace was the slutty one," his smile is deadly as his lips curl up around his accusation. I can't help but think about how good it would feel to shove my cock between them and punish his dark mouth.

"I'm slutty cause I got my dick sucked?" I try to confirm what he's saying because it seems ridiculous.

"You only just met Logan," he reminds me like I'm not aware.

"And?" I push him trying to work out his point. "What's the matter, dark prince. Haven't you ever wanted someone enough to put them on their knees as soon as you meet them?"

He smirks, “The only time I put someone on their knees is when I'm about to plant a bullet in their skull,” he replies coolly.

I give him a savage grin, “Well, maybe you should try it my way, I can assure you it's just as fun.”

Chapter 37

MARCUS

The ride back to the house was quiet, all of us lost in our own thoughts, including Elle. She looked completely vacant and nothing like my Ells. I didn't give anyone the chance to speak with her, knowing what she needed, I grabbed her and hauled her away. I took her to the bathroom and turned on the shower until steam filled the room. I stripped us silently and pushed her under the spray. I washed her body, memorizing every part of her. Her tattoos, her scars, even her stretch marks, everything that makes her who she is today. Someone who is strong, willing, and determined to take back her life and most importantly just a girl who wants to live her life as a mom.

Once dry, I put her in some of my clothes, something I will never get tired of seeing. Elle draped in my hoodies and sweats is the hottest fucking thing ever. Then I dragged her until we reached Cassie's room and gently pushed inside. I watched as the stress melted away from her, like a weight was being lifted from her shoulders. The light in her eyes finally returned and all for that little girl.

Cassie is something I never expected, yet now I can't imagine what Elle would be like without her. I watch them together and they're so alike it's ridiculous. It's like reliving my past and seeing Elle as a little girl again. She is so caring and attentive, the exact opposite to what I know she had growing up. She would never make her daughter feel inferior or push her to do shit that didn't make her happy.

People think because Elle grew up with wealth that it made her lucky, it didn't. She grew up in a cold household where she was nurtured more by a credit card and a bunch of servants than her own parents. The fact that she not only survived that, but is now making sure her own child experiences the exact opposite is everything.

I think about what our future might look like, about if we will have kids of our own and make Cass into a big sister. How she would take all the love and comfort that she gets from Elle and give it to her younger siblings. Other people would find those kinds of thoughts strange and premature, but how can that be when this is something that has been in the making since we were five years old. How many people can say they met their soulmate in Kindergarten?

I've been watching her sleep for hours, memorizing every inch of her. Just in case she wakes up and comes to her senses, realizing she can do far fucking better than me. The curtains are parted just enough that a slither of moonlight shines into the room lighting her up. She turns until she is lying on her side and snuggles into her pillow in the exact same way she used to when we were kids. Her breathing even and low, a sure sign she's sleeping peacefully. I curl around her on my side so her back is nestled perfectly into my chest. The curve of her ass resting neatly against my groin. Molded together as one. My arms are tight around her waist pulling her against me. It's like I think if I hold her tightly enough, I can shield her from the evils of this town. Not that she needs me to, if anyone can protect themselves it's her, I just wish she didn't have to.

I watched her kill somebody today, I watched her take his life right in front of me. That should probably make me feel different to how I actually am feeling. Scared maybe, yet all I feel is love, acceptance, just pure fucking obsession. I'm amazed by her. She took an awful situation and let it make her. Burned the old Elle King and rose from her own ashes to become who she is today. Filled with strength, love, and determination. Willing to go to war to protect her family.

I pull her in even closer if that's even possible and wonder again how the fuck we got here. We were just a couple of kids thrust together by chance, friends by choice, separated by evil, and brought back to one another for vengeance. We aren't the Elle and Marcus who used to lie under the stars and wish for miracles anymore. No, now we fight and fuck and hope our enemies don't get the better of us.

I can't sleep. So many thoughts and emotions pulse through me as I try and sort through everything that has happened. The only thing soothing me is my arms wrapped securely round Elle. Knowing that she's here, that she's mine, that she's safe. We lost our way, the love and friendship I had with her was lost in grief and hate. Yet here she is in my arms. My girl, my fucking girl. How the fuck I managed to convince her that I am worthy enough to stand by her side is beyond me, but here I am.

I don't know how we went from best friends to strangers to whatever this is. Calling her my girlfriend just sounds so insignificant, like it's not enough of a word to describe what she means to me. I don't know if such a word exists. She's a lifeline I didn't know I was missing until she came back and now, I don't think I will ever be able to function without her.

It's funny because she is still the Elle I remember from when we were young, but so different at the same time. I remember when we met, and I had to push a kid in the sand box for being mean to her. When we were eight, her pet rabbit died, she cried into my shoulder when we buried him in the garden. I think about the time she broke her arm when we were eleven after I dared her to climb a tree, I held her non injured hand all the way to the hospital and wouldn't let go even when they were putting her cast on. She curled up in my bed the night she got her first period as I rubbed circles on the bottom of her back. Always together, always there for her, except now she doesn't need me. She isn't the little girl who needs me to protect her anymore, she is a wild creature who took the darkness that happened to her and turned it into others' destruction.

She stirs in my arms until her cheek rests on my chest and her hand flattens against my heart, if she were awake, she would feel my rapid heartbeat. I look at her hand, the same hands I watched her kill a man with today and not just any man, but the fucking Captain of Police. Except he wasn't spending his life to protect and serve like he should have been, no instead he was a fucking child rapist.

I watched her walk into that cabin and turn into a different person entirely. She tortured him, made him bleed, and all I could do was stand and watch in fucking awe. The way her lips curled in distaste at every word he spoke, the way she rolled her eyes at every scream, the way the blood dripped through her fingers, and she didn't even care. It was fucking stunning.

I wanted to help her, show her that I am in this with her all the way, but I know she needs to do this herself. To take back what they took from her and so many others. It didn't stop me from wanting to bend her over the fucking table of weapons and fuck her until the only screams in the room were ours. Blood or no blood, I wouldn't fucking care.

I just want to take her in my arms and tell her that I know she doesn't need me, but I need her, want her, fucking crave her. Not that she would have given me a chance, she wouldn't even look at me, like she couldn't bear too. I fucking hated it. I wanted that rage filled gaze locked on mine so she could have seen the way my eyes filled with pride. The way she handled herself, the way she handled that fucking piece of shit, fuck, it was magnificent. I shift slightly, trying to ease my growing erection, thinking about her like that shouldn't make me hard, but fuck it does.

She stirs in her sleep and the wiggle of her body against mine causes my half hard dick to awaken fully.

Not that it's ever really asleep with her around, her body is like an accelerant to the lust in my veins. Always present and waiting to be ignited. If a kiss from Elle was the lighting of a candle, then fucking her is like the eruption of every fucking volcano on the planet. Fiery, explosive and completely unstoppable.

She moves again and I can tell the moment she wakes up, the relaxation of her body melting away. I feel her try to turn around so I loosen my arms enough that she can roll over until she is facing me. She stares up at me and I can see the numerous questions swirling behind her eyes.

"Hey," she whispers, like she doesn't know what else to say. It fucking kills me to hear the uncertainty in her voice. What is she thinking?

"Hi, baby," my voice is quiet but steady as I plead with my eyes for her to not overthink anything, to not worry about what she did last night, to know that I love every part of her, including the darkest parts.

"Did you sleep?" She sounds like she's wishing I did, but I can't lie to her. I shake my head indicating and she frowns as she squeezes her eyes shut with a sigh.

I can't bear it. I uncurl my arms from around her and cup her cheeks, causing her to open her eyes, "I couldn't sleep because no dream would have been better than my reality, my girl safe and asleep in my arms," I watch her take in my words and feel the blush color her cheeks. The heat of it searing into my palms making me smile and lick my lips.

"You're cute when you're embarrassed," I tease.

"I'm not embarrassed," she snaps.

"Oh yeah? Then why are you blushing? You only blush when you are embarrassed, horny, or angry and I don't think you're angry. So, which is it little King?" She leans in to kiss my cheek, her lips grazing across my jaw until she reaches my ear, "Maybe I'm horny," she murmurs, and I growl.

"Don't play games you can't win, baby," I grit out as her tongue licks my ear.

She pulls back and looks up at me through her lashes, "And who says I can't win?" She lifts her leg and wraps it around me, using the momentum to push me onto my back. She swings her leg across me until she straddles me. She looks down, her hair falling on either side of her face, the strap of her top slipping off her shoulder, she looks like a fucking goddess. My fucking goddess. *Mine.*

She is only wearing a long, baggy t-shirt and a pair of panties. I can already see her nipples poking through the thin fabric of her shirt. She smiles at me coyly, before she rocks her hips against me, causing my half erect dick to stand to attention fully. When she feels my thick length against her she grins and rubs against it gently. There are two layers separating us, but I can still feel her heat burning through them. Fuck, I need her.

I reach up and kiss her, letting my tongue caress hers in perfect synchronization until we are practically fucking each others' mouths. She continues to grind against my dick and moans into my mouth when she hits a certain spot.

I reach out and grip her hips tightly to pause her movements. "If you wanna ride my dick, baby, then I am gonna need you to do it without the barriers," I growl and she laughs, the sound of it hitting me like a fucking drug. I want more of that, more of her lighthearted fun side, more of her fucking laughs, and definitely more of her moans. She is an addiction of the very best kind.

I slide my hands beneath her shirt and relish in the goose bumps that cover her skin at my touch. I move until I can cup both her breasts and her nipples harden further. I pinch them both and then roll them around in my fingertips and she gasps, arching into my touch. It's exactly what I am looking for, but I need more. I slide my hands back down and she groans in protest while I laugh.

I reach her panties and grip, "I hope you aren't attached to these," I murmur before tightening them within my fingers and pulling until they rip. She startles slightly before giving me a sinful smile. I slide my hands back across her thighs until my thumbs can tease her lips, lips that are already dripping and I grit my teeth when I feel how wet she already is. I slide my thumb up and down her, teasing her until she begins to arch into my touch again, begging for more. More of which I am willing to give her. I move my grip back to her waist and she fumes at me.

"River," her tone is pleading, only fueling my addiction to her.

I pull her up by her waist, so she is on her knees on either side of me and use her distance to allow myself to slip my shorts down and free my hard aching cock. She looks down at it and licks her lips and I feel myself throb. I need her on my cock now! I shove my shorts down my legs until I can kick them free and then drag her back down onto me until her heat coats my cock.

"Fuck, baby, you're already soaked," I drag her along my length until I am covered in her, something I have never had before, and it sets off something primal inside of me. "Ready to ride me, baby?" I grit out, almost begging her.

She reaches out her hands to lean against my chest and lifts herself slightly. I waste no time in lining my cock up with her entrance. She lowers herself onto my aching cock so fucking slowly that I can't breathe. When she reaches my base she curses, "Fuck." *Fuck indeed.* She rolls her hips allowing herself to adjust to me before she rises slightly and comes back down. She is trying to find a rhythm that works, and I am her willful fucking servant. I grip the sheets and let her have control, I want her to fuck me how she needs, taking what she wants from me. She leans down and kisses me hard, pushing her tongue back into my mouth and letting it dance with mine.

When she starts to slide up and down me, her wetness grips me in the most perfect way, I can't hold back anymore. I grab her hips and pick up the pace. Pounding up into her, until she is moaning loudly into my mouth. She pulls back when she can no longer kiss me through her groans. I move one of my hands until it grips the back of her neck, holding her against me, our foreheads locked against one another. She stares deep into my eyes, my fucking soul, as I fuck her relentlessly. Nothing will ever beat this feeling, the feeling of her consuming me as she rides my dick like it was made for her. Hell, it fucking was made for her, like I was made for her. She couldn't escape me now even if she tried, I would stalk to the ends of the fucking earth to find her.

"Yes, Marcus, yesssss," the only time my name on her lips sounds good. "Don't stop, right there," Like I could stop, does she not know how good she feels?

She starts to shake, and I feel her clench around me as her orgasm wracks through her body, her pussy like a vice around my cock. When I feel her coming, I can't stop my own impending orgasm and I fuck her in fast, shallow thrusts until I am flooding her with my release, "Yes, baby, I'm coming," I growl loudly, not stopping until every drop of come has been drawn from me.

Fuck. Our bodies are covered in sweat as we both struggle to catch our breath, eyes still locked on one another. I bring my hands to cup her face again and kiss her. This time slow, steady yet still as fucking sinful before pulling back. "You are so fucking perfect, baby," I whisper, nuzzling into her hair as she collapses onto my chest.

"Thank you for being here," she whispers into the night and I can't help but startle at her words as she adds in a sleepy tone, "I need you more than you know."

I curl my arms around her and drag the blanket to cover us, "I've always needed you Ells. Now that I have you, I am never letting you go."

Chapter 38

ELLE

I fell asleep in Marcus' arms after we had what I can only describe as the best fucking sex ever. Now, I am no expert when it comes to that scale, but I am pretty fucking sure Marcus Riviera is a ten out of ten when it comes to fucking. After what I went through, I always thought being intimate with somebody would be too hard, yet Marcus isn't just anybody. He is the light in the dark, the guy who was always there for me until he couldn't be. There wasn't a day I was away where I didn't think about him, miss him.

We may not have had the best start a few months ago when I came home, but we are slowly finding our way back to each other. He consumes me in a way I can't explain. His joy is my joy, his pain is my pain. That is how he knew what I needed today when I didn't. From the shower to Cassie to the sex. It was just the release I needed after the blood shed at the cabin. Marcus and I didn't discuss what happened there, but things have changed between us. I can feel it. I knew he was committed to helping me, that he loved me, but now he is part of me in a way I never imagined. We are entwined deeper than ever before and if I ever lost him again, I don't think I would survive.

I know he is awake before I even open my eyes. I am still encased to his chest where we both fell asleep a few hours ago. He drags his fingertips up and down my back in featherlight touches. When I move his strokes pause as his hands splay across my spine in a possessive touch that is scorching, addictive, and completely fucking obsessive. When I look up, I find him staring down at me, his smile is fucking beautiful.

We take our time getting showered and dressed and that may have something to do with him bending me over and fucking me against the shower door until I came with a scream. His hands never really leave my body, but once we are both ready, we make our way down to the kitchen. I dance ahead of him with a giggle as he catches me multiple times, tickling me before letting me go again. He grabs me into his arms for the last time as we enter the kitchen with a laugh until he halts in his movements. I turn to find Asher, Logan, Lincoln, and Jace all paused in what was clearly a heated discussion, their grim faces burst my happy bubble. What the fuck has happened now? Marcus loosens his arms allowing me to slide down his body until my feet hit the ground.

"Can this wait until I've had my coffee?" I grumble as I move towards the island and I offer Jace a small smile as he slides a cup filled with the black magic over to me.

"We got this in our inboxes first thing," Linc says as he pushes a piece of paper over to me. I look down and take in the invitation to the Fire and Ice Ball. My mind flicks back to what Principal Lock told me about Hallows High joining forces with Hallows Prep for their winter dance. I snort at the irony of the name. *Fire and fucking ice indeed.*

"So why the long faces? It's not like we didn't know this was coming," I shrug.

"Does anything ever rile you, sissy?" Logan teases with an amused smirk.

"Your pissy attitude first thing in the morning," I preen back at him, but he just smirks wider, flicking his gaze over to Lincoln.

"Oh, trust me, I am nothing but relaxed this morning," he says with a wink and I see the tell tales sign of a blush creeping up Linc's neck as Asher grinds his jaw. What the fuck am I missing there? I see Jace look at them and then turn to me with a shrug like he hasn't got a clue what is going on either.

"I just think we should come up with a plan," Linc clears his throat and brings my attention back to the invitation. "Prepare for the worst."

"The worst already fucking happened," Marcus seethes at his brother and I slide my hand in his under the table and squeeze.

"Regardless, we should always expect more from my father. He won't stop until he gets his hands on Elle," Asher grunts in animosity, his eyes locked on the invitation.

"Well, that's not fucking happening," Jace spits in an angry tone and I flinch slightly. I hate hearing anything but his teasing, flirty tone. It just reminds me of the sadness he has endured. It makes me feel the need to avenge his sister even more than I already do.

"Don't worry about me, pretty boy. I can protect myself," I reach over and grip his hand, giving it a little squeeze before sitting down and blowing on my coffee while I take a moment to think.

Asher is right, this party screams Elliot and his wicked ways. I know he wants me; I know he is coming for me. He has too. It isn't just about saving face or me knowing too much. No, it's more than that. I got away, escaped the pits of hell he created and came out stronger on the other side. He can't let such a sin go unpunished. Well, unlucky for him, neither can I.

All the guys start talking game plans as I pick up the invitation and note it's only two weeks away, not a long time really, but enough to ensure we come up with a plan, and cover all our bases. We need to come up with multiple plans for every possible scenario to ensure our safety but first I need something.

"Let's go shopping," I say, interrupting all of them.

"Shopping?" Lincoln repeats, pulling his face like I've gone crazy.

"Yes, shopping," I repeat. "I need a dress for the party, and I know just the place," I smile already thinking about the perfect dress with a gleam in my eye. "Let's get ready."

Two hours later, we are pulling into a parking lot on the edge of Havensgrove. It's two towns over from Black Hallows effectively marking it a safe territory, meaning I am able to have Cassie with me. I drove over with her, Marcus, and Ash leaving Logan to ride with

Lincoln and Jace. It's basically a family day out.

Marcus is getting his first experience of what we call a Cassie concert as she belts out *Do You Want to Build a Snowman?* from the backseat. To my amusement Marcus tries and completely fails to sing along with her but she appreciates the effort and so do I.

By the time we make it to Havensgrove, Cassie has talked Marcus into a movie marathon of both the *Frozen* films and insists that we pick up popcorn while we are out. I climb from the car and move to get Cass, but she screeches at me.

"No, Mommy! River get me, River get me," she pleads excitedly.

I stand back slightly worrying what to do but Marcus doesn't even falter in stepping up and getting her out of her seat. He easily lifts her up until she is sitting perched on his shoulders. The smile on her face is infectious and I notice Asher also trying to hide his smile. He may act like enemy number one to Marcus and all the guys, but I know how much he appreciates their efforts and discretion when it comes to her.

The guys pull up in the other car and get out and Cassie yells out to them.

"Look, Superman, I'm up high," she waves her hands frantically in the air at them.

Jace reaches out to tickle her leg, "I thought I was your favorite, little one?"

"No, River and me best friends," she says proudly.

Jace takes the challenge, "Right, that's it," he grabs her from Marcus' shoulder and flies her around like she is actually Superman, her giggles pierce the air like a bolt of lightning.

"Careful," Ash and Linc both snap at him at the same time.

Logan snorts, "Oh, look how in sync you two are. That could really be fun, you know?" he wiggles his brows at them and they both give him vastly different looks. Asher looks pissed off, but Lincoln looks, dare I say intrigued?

We all move as one over to the row of shops here and I lead the guys over to the only place I ever enjoy shopping and push the door open. The bell dings signaling our arrival. The shop owner comes out of the back room and when he sees me his face lights up immediately.

"Ma belle fille," he cries in his French accent barreling towards me and engulfing me in a bear hug. "It has been too long."

"Sorry about that, I have been keeping a low profile," I say pulling back and behind me one of the guys snorts. *Dicks.*

"Construire en harem?" he asks, taking in the wall of muscle behind me and I choke on my breath.

"No. *Non*, definitely not, no," I shake my head furiously, spluttering over the words but he just laughs at me.

I gesture to them one by one, "You remember Logan, Ash, and Cass," he nods, "This is Lincoln, Jace, and Marcus. Ma Rivière," I add, and he smiles wide when I gesture to Marcus having heard so much about him.

"Ah, yes," he holds out his hand for Marcus to shake which he does. "Very nice to meet the man who stole ma belle's heart," Marcus just nods at him before continuing to cast his eyes around the shop.

They are all clearly wary of him and I can see Linc taking in everything about him including the shop, so I cut in to help him out. "This is Robert Abreo, he is a designer from France, he does a lot of special work for me."

"How special?" Jace muses with a smile.

"He sources most of my weapons and tech," I reply with a shrug before turning my concentration back on Robert. "That's why I'm here, I need something."

He tsks, "Of course you do, ma belle," he mumbles more in French as he rounds the counter to his computer and slides his glasses onto his nose to await my instructions.

I look at Ash, who is leaning against the wall and I don't even have to say anything he just nods. He reaches out, taking Cassie from Jace's arms.

"Come on, angel, let's see what dresses we can find for Mommy," he tells her.

"Yes, Daddy," she beams at him, "Orange ones," she almost yells, and they turn to take in the rest of the shop. Once I know she is out of ear shot I turn back to Robert.

"I need a dress," I start. "Red," he starts to type away rapidly, "Spaghetti straps, a hard bodice and a floaty skirt with a slit up one side that reaches the thigh."

"Armes?" he asks, and I nod immediately.

"I'm thinking Glock, two blades, knuckle dusters, and a couple of syringes," I'm pretty much thinking out loud, unsure of whether it can be done but he just keeps tapping away on his keyboard unphased by anything I have said.

Once he has finished typing, he pulls out a tablet and a stylus and starts designing a rough draft. While he does that, I turn back to the guys who are all looking at me expectantly. Except for Logan who has been here with me a few times and is already looking through a rack of suits.

"Baby, what exactly is this place?" Marcus asks, flicking his gaze between me and Robert.

"I told you Robert is a designer, just not your typical one," I try to sound casual, but I can't. I am more than a little obsessed with this place, it's cool as fuck. I sigh before continuing, "He designs clothes, weapons, clothes with weapons in them," I say gesturing around.

Logan pulls a suit jacket off the hanger and shrugs into it before checking himself out in the mirror, "How do I look, hacker boy?" he asks Lincoln with a wink.

He looks undeterred by his flirting now as he replies, "Looks like you need a size down," he says mildly, Robert agrees with him without even looking up from his tablet.

"Glad to see you checking out my size, Lincoln," Logan responds with a wink.

"I need you all to get measured so I can have you fitted properly for the stuff we are going to need."

"Like what?" Jace asks.

"Making sure your shirts fit over a vest and you can get a holster under your jackets without it being obvious," it feels like common knowledge to me, but I can tell from their faces they had never thought about it before. I am saved from having to go any further when Robert speaks.

"I outdo myself," he gleams, and I turn around to find him smiling down at his design. I move back to the counter and he hands the tablet over to me. He's right, he's outdone himself.

I tell him what I need for the guys and he takes the Rebels' measurements having already gotten Ash and Logan's and then as always, he pulls out a beautiful dress for Cassie. She squeals in delight begging to put it on to go home and of course, I say yes.

I pay Robert and as always, he refuses payment for Cassie's dress. He tells me he will have my order done by next week, a couple of days before the party, so we head out.

We hit a few more shops, picking up some more stuff for the guys to ensure they feel at home in their new rooms. Cassie somehow manages to coerce the guys into more than a few new stuffed animals she didn't need but according to Marcus and Jace, she definitely did. She already has them wrapped around her tiny fingers. Once we are all shopped out, we stop for ice cream.

We are sitting in a booth by the window watching Cassie stuff her face with chocolate ice cream. It's the calmest and happiest I have felt in a while. I know we have a fuck ton of shit going on but sitting here with Cass and the guys, I can breathe easily.

I relax into Marcus' arm which is slung around my shoulder, while I play with Cassie's hair. I look over her head to where Ash is sitting on her other side and find a familiar look in his eye. Family days are the best.

Once she has eaten enough to make her little stomach push out, I get up from the booth and head to the register to pay. I ask for some tubs to take home for Helen who is addicted to their fudge brownie and when the cashier heads in the back I lean on the counter and look out the window.

I freeze. *What the fuck?*

I swing my gaze to Asher who just happens to look over at me at the same time and takes in the look on my face and dives from the booth stalking towards me.

He cups my face, "Baby girl, what's the matter?"

Marcus is by my side in the next second looking worried as the rest join us, Cassie in Logan's arms. I push Asher aside and look back out the window, but I don't see anything. Did I imagine it? Was I just so content in my day that my subconscious was reminding me of my monsters?

I shake my head out and put a smile on my face before turning back to everyone not wanting them to worry, "Nothing, I'm fine, just thought I saw someone." I scrunch my eyes shut and open them again before adding, "I'm just tired and on edge after yesterday," and they all relax a little, understanding what I mean. Marcus puts his arm around me, "Well come on, baby, let's go home," the word home hits me right in the heart. *Home.*

As we leave the store, I can't help but feel like we are being watched but casting my glance around I see nothing. Maybe the devil on my shoulder is just forcing me to not relax after the sins I have committed. The people I kill, might deserve to die, but it still makes me a killer all the same.

Chapter 39

JACE

I've never been good in other people's houses, it's not something I'm used to. You can't relax within something you've never had. I didn't grow up in a nice, big mansion with a picture-perfect family. A fucking run-down trailer with a pair of crack heads is a more accurate description.

The only salvation I had growing up was Rachel, she made everything better. From our shitty shared mattress on the floor, that she covered with a stolen blanket, to the ramen noodles we were lucky enough to eat most days that she always gave me more of. We may have been cold, starving, and fucking abused, but at least we had each other.

When I lost her, I lost myself too. Her disappearance and murder eventually sparked CPS into taking action, I was taken and placed into foster care. I hadn't seen my parents since the day I was taken. I heard a while back that they had both been killed in a car accident. When Rachel died, I felt everything, guilt, rage, hate, love, abandonment. When I heard my parents died, I felt nothing. A feeling I had become so accustomed to, so used to that when I met a fierce and fiery girl on the front steps of our shitty school, my first thought was how I couldn't wait to fuck her without even knowing her name. How fucking stupid was I? Like you could ever fuck and forget someone like Elle King. She rocked up in her fishnets and no bullshit attitude and put me and my brothers in our fucking place. I knew she was on a mission the first time I laid eyes on her; I just never imagined our mission would collide so fucking perfectly. How could I have ever imagined that the devil on her shoulder was the same as mine?

She could never replace Rachel, no one could, but having her around makes that hole in my chest a little less fucking big. I'd do anything for her, like I already have, and I won't stop until we have our justice. For her, all the others, and for Rachel.

I take a drag of the joint between my fingers, inhaling deeply, praying the effects will numb the dark feelings raging inside of me. I killed a man and before this is over, I plan on killing more. I'm a killer and I feel no regret or remorse. Does that make me a bad person? Is killing murderers and rapists still a sin? I don't know where I land on the scale of right and wrong anymore.

How would Rachel feel about the man I have become? I am not the little boy who she tried so desperately to save anymore. Now, I'm a man on the path of death and destruction. A fire of revenge burning inside of me and the only fuel is more blood. Will it stop? Will I stop? What happens when I finally have Greg Donovan bleeding out at my feet? Will this aching crater in my chest finally fucking heal?

The cracking of twigs beneath someone's foot has me snapping to attention as my head whirls around and my gaze locks with Mrs. Royton's. *Fuck*.

I scramble to stub out the joint in my hand and waft away the remnants of smoke praying she isn't on to me.

"Are you really trying to hide the stench of weed from a Mom of two boys?" Her tone is light and teasing but I still feel like a fucking shit for her catching me.

"Sorry, I know I shouldn't," I start but she cuts me off.

"Some things are needed to tame the demons inside one's head." She sits down next to me and looks out into the distance, studying the dark of the night with me. I don't respond because I don't know how to. She saves me from answering as she continues, "What troubles you this evening?"

"The same thing as every other evening," I reply without a thought. I frown. *What the fuck?* Why the hell did I say that? I don't do this, sit and talk about my fucking feelings, especially not with someone I barely know. No one wants to dig into my black mind and see the damage painted there. They want the fun Jace, the flirty Jace, no one is ever interested in more than a fuck or a good time. But that isn't Helen, her motherly instincts pour out and wrap around you, so no matter what, you just feel safe. Like you could tell her anything and there would be no judgment so before I can talk myself out of it I add, "Regret."

"For Rachel?" She says her name so easily, it's weird having people know about her and speak about her. It has been a long time since anyone has used it so casually and I find myself hating it, yet also craving it. Emotions clog my throat and I barely trust myself to reply, so I just nod.

"She's in a better place than this awful world, she would just want you to look after yourself now."

"And how do I do that?" I whisper hoarsely, trying not to let my emotions pour out more than they already have.

She laughs, "You're already doing it, look around," she gestures wildly to the house.

I sigh slightly, "Yeah I see a house that isn't mine, family that isn't mine, wealth I can never even hope to amass," I start listing off things.

Her frown is instant, "If you think that the people inside that house aren't your family then you haven't been paying attention. Those brothers of yours would die for you, Elle would kill for you, Zack would give you his entire fortune if he felt you needed it," she pauses. "And well, Arthur and I are more than used to being blessed with children we don't deserve but love them anyway. You are part of this family whether you like it or not, Jace Conrad."

An unfamiliar feeling floods my body as I try to process her words. I have never had this, an adult that cares, it's weird. My parents were more interested in their next fix than their own kids, and while the foster homes I were in weren't terrible, they weren't caring either. More interested in the paycheck than the kids they housed. So, having someone like Mrs. Royton show any kind of affection well, I don't really know how to react.

She looks over and must-see whatever emotions I am unsure of on my face because she curls her fingers around my forearm and squeezes, "Give it time, it will come. You will feel it, you belong here, you just haven't processed that yet," she gives me another squeeze before she stands dusting off her pants and looking down at me. "Now go on, get to bed, it's late and you have school tomorrow."

I can't help but smile at her light scolding, not once in my life has anyone ever given a shit if I make it to school or not. I stand up immediately, "Yes, ma'am," I tease with a smile.

"Don't sass me, boy. Don't think Elle is the only Royton lady who knows how to brandish a blade."

My eyes hit the roof at that, but she just smiles, winks, and then turns and walks away. Well damn. Momma Royton is also badass. I better watch my back with the girls in this house.

I'm still thinking about what she said at lunch the next day. We sit at our usual table except our new usual, now includes our little Queenie. She is sitting across from me quietly picking at her lunch and tapping away on her phone, that serious little frown she does on her face. Marcus is staring at her, she's got his balls in a fucking vice grip, poor guy doesn't even know how far gone he is for her. I mean I love the girl like a sister, don't get me wrong, but what they have is the last fucking thing I want. I will keep my endless string of girls. Who would give up threesomes for one pussy? Not me. I am happy for the both of them, but I couldn't imagine letting one person have that kind of power over me.

I flick my gaze around the cafeteria just as Marcus' biggest mistake starts stalking towards us. Elle and Marcus are too engrossed in whatever is on her phone to notice but Lincoln has spotted her just like I have. His back tenses as he awaits whatever bullshit she is coming over here to start.

"Exciting isn't it?" Her shrill voice causes Marcus to snap up straight, while Elle just smirks into her phone, before continuing to tap. A few quiet moments pass before she sighs, making a show of putting it away and turning around to greet her, pushing herself into Marcus as she does. *I see you, Queenie.*

No one responds to her and I watch as Elle assesses her and whatever angle this is before sighing again, "I'll bite. What's exciting, Cherry?" The way she says her name has me smirking.

"The Fire and Ice Ball, of course," undeterred by Elle's tone she gushes back at her. "I can't believe we are finally getting to have a school party; we are so lucky the board of Hallows Prep decided to include us."

I snort, "Yeah, if you like dirty money." She looks at me with a slight frown and a look I can't decipher in her eyes when I speak. Hmm what are you thinking about, little Cherry?

She schools her features quickly, but I can tell Elle saw it too when she looks over at me as Cherry and I continue to stare at each other. She puts on what she must think is a flirty smile and turns her voice breathy, "Well, what do you say, playboy, wanna be my date?" Now, it's Elle's turn to snort.

I don't even miss a beat before responding, "I'm already going with someone with a lot more class than you. Sorry, darling." I sound like a patronizing fuck, but there is just something about her that irks me, unsettles my stomach. I can't put my finger on it.

The bell rings but we remain seated as she glares at me before she smiles that sickly sweet smile again, "Your loss, I got a beautiful dress from Havensgrove," she remarks, and I feel Elle's flinch from across the table. *Fucking Havensgrove.*

What the fuck would someone like her be doing shopping somewhere like Havensgrove? It can't be a coincidence. I feel Lincoln pull his tablet out and begin tapping away next to me. I keep my bored mask in place as I respond, "I'm sure it will look good on some douche bag's trailer floor."

She smirks an evil sort of smile before she turns back to Elle and Marcus. "Marcus, we have Chem together now, wanna walk together? You've got Bio, right, Elle?" She sounds so smug but all I am focused on is how well she seems to know our schedules.

Elle smiles wide with a glint in her eyes and I don't miss the possessive grip Marcus encases her hip in before he responds, "Sure thing, Cherry."

They both stand and Cherry looks like she just won the lottery. Until Elle goes to move, and Marcus grips her by the back of the neck, spinning her into him and kisses her like he is ready to fuck her right there on the table. A couple of the football douches holler but shut it down quick when Lincoln and I glare at them. Cherry looks murderous as she watches them, but quickly smiles when she finds me glaring at her again. *I see you.*

Elle pulls away and licks her lips, a slight blush to her cheeks as Marcus whispers loud enough for all of us to hear, "To be continued later, my little King."

"Later," she responds before looking at Linc, "Come on, Superman, you can walk me to class."

Lincoln looks at me offering me a nod before he meets Elle on the other side of the table, and she takes his arm as they leave for class.

Cherry is practically preening now that she is gone and giving Marcus what I can only assume are fuck me eyes, except her face looks fucking weird doing it.

"Come on then, Mr. King of the Southside," she purrs before turning and walking away putting as much sway into her hips as she can manage.

Marcus moves to follow but I grip his arm tight and pull him back, "Please don't tell me you are buying that little miss nice bullshit. Something is off about her."

He smiles at me, "Why do you think I am keeping her so close, brother? I won't let anyone close to my girl and that's exactly where Cherry's eyes have been since we got together. Keep your enemies close and all that."

"Marcus," she snaps across the room. He winks at me before pulling away to follow her. Well, fuck me, my brother has finally pulled his head out of his ass. *Finally.*

Chapter 40

MARCUS

The news of Captain Baizen's disappearance made headlines every night on the 8 o'clock news for four days straight. When the news of his own crimes came to light, it made national news, morning, noon, and night. Everyone in the country is talking about what a sick, sadistic fuck he was.

If you would have asked me a few months ago if I was capable of killing a man, I would have said no. Yeah, I had hurt people before, broken bones, made them bleed, but I always stopped before I crossed that line. Now, I pray I get to do it again. Every time I hear Baizen's name on the news, I feel a mixture of glee and pride flood my veins. Taking out our enemies gives me a high I never knew I needed, and never thought I would crave. I already can't wait for my next fix.

I think about Greg Donovan every day, it used to be Elliot and what he did to my father that plagued my mind, but that is nothing compared to the rage I feel towards his son.

Elle has us training daily, from basic hacking skills, to fighting, to weapons. All of which, I now know she started at fourteen, thanks to Zack. He gave her back what they tried to take from her. It made her come back stronger than ever. Elle leaving broke my heart but knowing what she went through, what she did while she was gone. Well, in a way, I am glad she left.

We pretty much spend our days going to school, coming home, playing with Cassie, family dinner, bedtime stories, and then training. Asher hasn't been around much, he is trying to stay close to Elliot in case, he hears any plans in regard to the party. Logan had to head back to college, but is coming home for the party, so we have a little more back up.

After training is the best part of my day, taking a worked up and sweaty Ells to bed is fucking cathartic. We fuck in the shower, on the floor, against the wall, even in her walk-in closet. I can't keep my hands off her, the fact that she feels the same after what she went through is something that will astound me until the day I die. The girl is a fucking walking miracle, and she is all mine.

The party is tomorrow and even though we have everything ready, have run through countless things that could happen, and have more weapons than I would have thought possible, Elle is still worried. She denies it, but I have known her too long for her to try and hide it from me.

We came to bed over an hour ago and she is still restless and nowhere near sleep. I get up from the bed and head into her closet and when I return, she is sitting up in the bed watching me. I throw one of my hoodies at her as I pull on my own before holding out my hand out to her. She takes it wordlessly and doesn't speak as I lead her out of her room and down the stairs. I don't stop until I get to the doors that lead out to the patio and then I enter the code to let us out, closing the door behind us.

I walk past the outdoor pool, tugging her along by her hand, and stop when I reach the big oak tree in between the pool and the guest house. I slump down against it and pull her until she is in my lap. From where I have positioned us, we can't be seen from the main house or the guest house and we have a perfect view of the stars.

She is still tense, so I lean forward and whisper into her ear, "Make a wish, baby."

She sighs, "I wish I could give you another life."

"Why?"

"So, my darkness didn't leave you so shaded," she admits into the night. I can't bear the pained tone of her voice. I grip her by the hips and spin her in my lap until she is straddling me, nose to nose.

"Ells," I start, and a tear slips from her eyes. The look on her face, the most vulnerable I have ever seen. I swipe the tear with my thumb, "Another life would not be this life. Another life would not have Zack, Helen, Arthur, or Cassie. In another life, I wouldn't have my brothers, they wouldn't have you. I wouldn't trade this life for anything. I would sacrifice anything to take away the shit that happened to you, but how could I wish that when it brought you so much good? I've told you before and I will tell you again. You and I are inevitable. In this life, in another life, in every fucking life. You are mine, forever."

She opens her mouth to speak as more tears caress her cheeks, but I won't allow her words of self-doubt. I grab the back of her neck, the place that fits my hand so fucking perfectly and drag her mouth to mine. As always it feels like fucking home. She is everything, my home, my love, my life. Her tongue dances with mine in an erotic battle of devotion.

She pulls back breathless, her eyes still glistening with emotion, "I'm scared."

"Me too," I admit, knowing I don't need to put on a tough guy façade with her, "But that's okay, we can be scared together," I add, and she nods, taking a deep breath.

"I need to feel something other than this despair; I don't want to worry about tomorrow," she brings her mouth back to mine and kisses me like she needs me to breathe. She molds herself to me so fully that we might as well be one person.

We are like fire and water. Apart we both cause chaos but mix us together and you create the perfect balance.

Her kiss turns reckless, messy, as her hands explore my body until she reaches my sweats. She fumbles with the waistband until I lift up so she can move them. At the same time, I bunch the hoodie around her hips and when she comes back down against me, I rip her panties to the side. I groan when I feel her dripping onto my fingers.

"Always so fucking ready," I growl as I drag my fingers through her lips until I can coat my cock in her juices. I line up to her entrance and she impales herself on me and we both groan. She isn't shy as she takes what she needs and rises and falls onto me, fucking me the only way she can.

This isn't about love, it's about pure carnal need and release. We don't have time for soft touches and gentle caresses. I grip her hip so tight I know it will bruise and use my other hand to thumb her clit until she starts to shake, her pussy gripping my cock.

"Fuck, River," she gasps. "Don't stop, I'm gonna come," she moans, and I pick up my pace.

"I'm not fucking stopping until your come is dripping down my cock, Ells. Until I can feel your cream fucking covering me," I growl at her, thrusting into her wildly, taking over our movements.

My words push her over the edge. I flick my thumb harder and faster as I feel her clench around me. She comes with a loud groan and I can't hold back when her fingertips dig into my neck as she rides out her release. I come with a grunt.

Her head falls to my shoulder as we attempt to catch our breath when she whispers, "I don't think I will ever get used to this feeling."

I smile and kiss her hair, "Me either, baby."
She pulls back and gives me a shy smile which I find adorable and ridiculous at the same time, considering my cock is still inside her and my come is leaking down her thighs. "I think I'll be able to sleep now," she whispers.

"Well, if you can't, I'm sure I can find more ways to tire you out," I tease, and the sound of her laughter pulses through me.

When she stops, she stares at me intently, "Thank you, River."

I frown, "For the sex?" I ask with a laugh and she punches my stomach and I grunt.

"No, you fucking asshole. For knowing what I need when I don't even know it myself. You have always been the best at reading me," she admits.

"That's because you have always been mine. You just forgot for a while and I guess so did I, but that doesn't mean I ever stopped knowing you or loving you."

She smiles again, "I love you too."

No four words have ever been more perfect and I just have to pray I will keep hearing them every day for the rest of our lives. Lives I hope we get to fucking live, with whatever tomorrow brings.

Chapter 41

ELLE

I barely recognize the person staring back at me from the mirror. I look nothing like the young girl who was kidnapped and raped. Nothing like the girl who came back to this town with a mission for revenge. I look like a woman, a woman who is ready to get her vengeance.

The silk red gown almost touches the floor, the straps are thin but tight, holding up the corset top. The corset is honestly the most beautiful and brutal thing I have ever seen. The breast part is cupped and encrusted in red diamonds that distract you from the ruby knuckle dusters hiding there. The bones of the corset hide a syringe filled with a heavy sedative and two thin blades. Both blended perfectly into the design. The dress then floats around my ankles, a huge split up my right thigh touching just below the red leather thigh holster strapped there, my Glock sitting perfectly inside of it. Robert really has outdone himself. I am only wearing a red lace thong underneath and I have finished the look off with a YSL stiletto heel. I had a stylist come in and do my makeup in an old Hollywood style type of way with my hair waved and pulled back on one side. A matte red lip to finish off the look perfectly.

I feel powerful, dangerous, and for once, willing to use my looks as a weapon. Considering I am walking into a lion's den tonight, I think that is a good feeling to have. I try not to fidget but I can't help it, as powerful as I feel, it doesn't seem to stop my nerves. A constant scenario of things that could go wrong is playing in my head on repeat. It doesn't matter how much we have prepared, how many back up plans we have concocted, I am still brutally aware that anything could happen.

I pick up the red diamond encrusted clutch that Robert made to perfectly match my dress and slip in my red lipstick, keys, and phone. It's showtime.

I leave my room and make my way down the hall. The carpet keeps the click of my heels from sounding out. As I near the staircase, Zack's voice floats up and I smile.

"Just because she knows how to handle herself, doesn't mean she should have to. Watch her fucking back, or I will make you all disappear without a trace," his voice is cold but completely sincere and my heart aches for the brother I didn't grow up with but became part of my whole world.

I round the corner, "Can we not threaten my Rebels? They're sensitive little souls, really," I tease, and all of their gazes snap towards me at the sound of my voice.

Oh, holy hotness. The South Side Rebels in fucking tuxes should be illegal, or like, I don't know an attraction you have to pay to see. They look glorious. They're all wearing black tuxedos, with black bow ties, a red pocket square, and shiny black shoes.

Lincoln is wearing his black rimmed glasses, his lean frame looking completely beautiful encased in a suit, and his dark stare just makes him seem that much more stunning, yet dangerous. Jace has smoothed his hair into a neat man bun and apart from that and the perfect fit of the suit, his usual messy style pours out. He has the top button of his shirt open, his bow tie hangs loose around his neck, and there is a joint perched on his ear.

They both have big smiles on their faces as they take me in. "Holy shit, Queenie. You look fucking gorgeous," Jace says, offering me a playful wink.

I move down the stairs, not yet looking at Marcus, as I know he is going to floor me. Instead, I focus on Zack.

"He's right, sis," Zack says, taking me in at arm's length before pulling me in for a hug. "You look beautiful," he drops a kiss to my head.

I smile and then finally let my gaze collide with Marcus'. I feel that familiar inferno inside of me flare, just like every time our eyes connect. He is staring at me intensely as he takes me in. He has got his dark hair slicked back neatly and to one side, his suit is molded to him like a glove. He looks like a fucking movie star. He's frozen to the spot as his dark stare drinks me in.

"Marcus," I barely whisper his name, but he snaps out of his head and steps up to me.

"Ells," he swallows thickly. "You look so fucking stunning, baby," his voice is filled with pride until he leans in and whispers into my ear. "I have a lot more thoughts, but they're inappropriate for your brother to hear."

Jace snorts a laugh so I know he heard him. I hide my blush in his chest. His scent wrapping around me as I inhale deeply, taking one last moment of calm before we descend in the pit of devils for the night.

"Mommy," Cassie's little voice squeaks into the room.

I turn to find her little body already housed in her pajamas padding towards me. "Wow, Mommy. So beautiful like a princess," she says in awe and when she reaches me, I scoop her into my arms and snuggle her close. Throughout all of this, she is my safe place, my base, and the reason I do any of this. I would be nothing without her. She took a broken little girl and made me into a strong and independent mom, willing to take on the world just to keep her safe.

"Eskimo?" I whisper and she immediately rubs her nose against mine before pulling back and looking at Marcus and the guys.

"Is Marcus your prince, Mommy?" she wonders.

I smile, "No, baby. He's my King."

She frowns confused, "I thought you were the King?" she asks innocently, and we all laugh. If only we could all see the world through the simple and wondrous eyes of a child.

"I am," I start. "It's a long story," I end with a laugh.

She wiggles to get down and rushes to Jace and gives him her fist which he then brings his too straight away in a fist bump. Of course, he taught her to fist bump. She high fives Lincoln, hugs Marcus' legs, and then runs over to Zack and holds her arms out to be picked up.

Arthur and Helen are having date night for their anniversary, so Zack is on babysitting duty for the night. "Don't let her run you wild, Z. Or bribe you into a late night," I tease, and he smirks.

"Hey what happens on Uncle watch stays on Uncle watch. That's why I'm her favorite," Zack says.

"Now, we all know I'm her real favorite," Logan states, as he saunters in from down the hall. He looks just as devastating as the guys do in his tux and I don't miss Lincoln quickly checking him out, unfortunately neither does Logan.

"What do you think, Linc? Wanna go for a spin?" he does an obnoxious twirl and wiggles his brows at him as he walks right up into his space. He leans closer to him whispering loudly, "Love the glasses by the way, you look even more fuckable than usual."

Zack coughs loudly covering his crude words from Cassie, but I can't keep in my smile. Especially when I see the little blush on Linc's cheeks before he steps back and croaks out, "Come on, we don't want to be late."

"Oh, I always come on time," Logan responds with a smile.

"We are gonna go start bedtime," Zack cuts in, giving a death glare to Logan at his crudeness.

I step towards them and nuzzle another kiss into Cassie's hair. "You be good for Uncle Z, okay baby?"

"Always, Mommy," she replies, and her words instantly hit my heart. Zack gives me a half hug and they both turn and head towards the movie theater room. I watch them until they are out of sight before turning back to the guys.

Logan takes me in and lets out a slow whistle, "Fucking hell, King. You scrub up nice, if only we weren't related, ey?" he mocks with a wink.

"Careful now," Marcus warns but Logan just laughs in his face.

"Oh, don't worry, River," he replies with a huge grin. "I'm all about sharing my toys," he adds the last bit with another wink to Lincoln.

"Yeah, well, I'm not," Marcus grits back, gripping me until he can pull me close into his body. Logan just holds his hands up in defense, "Calm down Alpha dog it was a joke."

"Jokes are usually funny, Lo," I muse, trying to ease the situation.

"Oh, you want to be funny? How's that gun on your thigh? Got the safety on? Wouldn't want you accidentally shooting anyone," he teases me sarcastically, as he brings up the time I shot him during our training a couple of years ago.

"That was one time and barely a graze. Trust me, my aim is a lot better now, so if I shoot you now it's on purpose," I snap back at him as Marcus and Jace laugh.

"You shot him?" Lincoln asks to confirm, and I nod not taking my eyes off Logan.

"You're lucky I don't wanna ruin my look or I'd suggest a spar," I toss out with a smile.

He rolls his eyes, "Like I'd take you now with the three guard dogs on your back, hardly fair," he snorts.

“All's fair in love and war,” I smile a smug grin, before adding, “Now, let’s move.”

He salutes me mockingly, “Yes, King,” before he turns towards the garage. He won’t be driving with us tonight, no one knows Logan or my connection to him. He is acting as a bit of a so he can hang around our enemies and see what he can pick up. We will be there if he needs us and vice versa. Hopefully, it won’t come to that, but even if it does, he will have Ash close by.

We make our way to the garage and get into Lincoln's SUV. He starts the engine and then clocks me through the mirror, “You ready for this?”

“Only one way to find out,” I shrug and Jace laughs, lighting up his joint.

“It sure is fun having you around, Elle King,” he says taking a long drag.

I preen under his appreciation, “Right back at you, pretty boy.”

Chapter 42

MARCUS

The drive over to Hallows Preparatory is quiet. I guess we are all mentally preparing for whatever is going to happen tonight, if anything. I'm replaying every drop of blood I have seen Elle spill and the other stuff I've heard about. I need to run through those thoughts to remind myself that she can handle anything. She's armed to the teeth, so are we, and I won't fucking hesitate to hurt anyone who gets in our way.

When she appeared at the top of the stairs, I thought I had died and gone to heaven or maybe hell. Surely, it's a sin for someone to look as fucking stunning as she does tonight. The red silk clinging to her perfect frame like a second skin, like she had shed the innocent little girl I came to know and love and transformed into a badass, avenging angel.

She took the flames of sin that licked her skin that terrible night and let them burn her to ash until she was a fucking phoenix, spreading her wings into the path of vengeance. She won't stop until all of the sins she has uncovered are repaid.

I turn to look at her as she takes in everything we pass on the way to the party and when we roll through the gates of Hallows Prep, I don't miss the slight sneer in her face. There was a time where we did nothing but talk about how great it would be when we went here for high school, it feels like another lifetime now.

We pull up to the valet, yes, the fucking valet, and Lincoln exits looking around until he spots someone in particular. He hands the keys over with some folded up bills and a whispered threat. I jump out at the same time Jace does and rush around to open Elle's door for her.

She smiles when she looks up at me, "Oh, did I get the gentlemen version of you tonight? Is it the tux?" she teases me as I help her out and shut the door behind her.

I pull her until her back is pressed against my chest and whisper low in her ear with a growl, "I could show you how not gentlemanly I am by fucking you on the hood of the car until everyone sees who you belong to," before quickly letting her go. I don't miss the thick swallowing of her throat or the blush that covers her chest.

She turns around and starts walking backwards, "In your dreams, Riviera" she smirks and turns to walk into the school but not before I yell out to her, "Nah, in my dreams we do it on my bike."

We're ushered by fucking wait staff to the Great Hall. When I see it, I roll my eyes. It's fucking grotesque. Every table is alternated with a small fire pit or ice sculpture in the center and there are literal fire breathers in the middle of the dance floor. I can't believe the shit these cunts choose to spend their money on.

We are barely in the door when I spot Jonathan King and Elliot Donovan in the far corner, surrounded by their fake fucking cunty friends. No doubt all fighting to get their tongues further up Donovan's ass. I wonder how many of them know his true face. Have any of them sold him their fucking children? I think about the guns strapped to my torso underneath either side of my jacket. Oh, how it would feel to reach inside and grip them and plant every bullet inside him until he's sporting more fucking holes than a golf course. Would it tame my pain? Curb my grief? Would I feel repaid for the sins he committed against my father and my girl? *Only one way to find out.*

Elle curls her arm around mine, "You know you can't kill him here right? Even I can't clean that up," her tone serious and teasing at the same time. I love that she knows me well enough to read my mind. Like she is fucking part of me.

Lincoln and Jace arrive besides us as the latter snorts, "Like we give a fuck about the cleanup." The sad thing is how true that is and how dark the tone he is using to say it. There isn't a trace of my carefree jokester brother when he locks eyes on Elliot. Just another casualty of their sick twisted games. Their victims aren't just the ones they touch with their darkness, no that darkness spreads touching everyone around them until it's like the aftermath of a fucking natural disaster. People bleeding and broken everywhere in sight, some literal, some metaphorical.

Elle and Jace are like two sides of the same coin. Both touched by evil but in completely different ways and yet their grief so perfectly intertwined. Just like mine.

"Yeah well," Elle says slowly, "Trust me when I say, I have extremely specific plans for Elliot Donovan."

When she speaks his name, he looks at us, like he heard her across the crowded room. His smile is slow and sinister as he drags his gaze across the four of us, until it settles between me and Elle. He raises the glass in his hand at us in a toast before taking a sip. Fuck, I want to bleed the cunt dry. I can feel my rage pouring out of me and into my brothers, but when I look at Elle, she is smiling just as sinister as him. She snags a glass of whatever is on the tray the passing waiter holds and tips it towards him. Tossing his toast right back at him and he fucking glimmers at her with respect in his eyes. Yeah right, like he has any fucking idea how to respect another human being let alone a woman.

Jonathan King finally takes notice of what has stolen Elliot's attention and when his eyes land on his only daughter, he falters slightly, but my girl just offers him the same toast before knocking back whatever is in the glass before throwing it aside and giving them her back.

"So, which of my favorite boys is going to give me a spin first?" she cocks one eyebrow at us expectantly as she challenges us to dance. I don't think any of us have ever fucking danced in our lives. I almost die of shock when Lincoln is the first to hold his hand out.

She gleams at him, "Oh, Superman, how did I know it would be you hiding more hidden talents?" she places her hand in his and I nod at the two of them as they descend onto the dance floor.

Jace lets his attention wander from Elliot just as Taylor Kennedy enters the room with a couple of friends, and I finally see that signature sparkle in his eyes. “Excuse me, brother, I spy myself a princess of my own,” he stalks away without another word.

I find a table that allows me to have my back to the wall while also keeping Lincoln and Elle firmly in my sight and take the opportunity to stake out the rest of the room.

Despite the mixture of two schools, it really doesn’t seem busy but it’s more to do with the size of the room we are in and not the fact that people aren’t here. They are, I recognize students from both schools, the divide between us and them easily noted. You can pick out the cheap untailored suits and rack bought dresses a mile off, but that isn’t stopping the girls from trying to bag themselves a guy with a net worth longer than their phone numbers. It’s pathetic really.

Speaking of pathetic, the fucking leach that is Cherry steps in my line of sight to Elle. “Looking a little lonely without your queen there Marcus,” she says with fake pleasantry. Allowing her to latch herself to me, even for such a short period of time, will go down as one of the stupidest fucking things I have ever done.

“I was actually enjoying the view you're blocking,” I toss back, and she arches her thinly shaped brows at me before taking a seat next to me.

“What view is that? The one of your current fuck buddy grinding on your brother’s dick?” she says in what she must think is a joking tone, but I hear the jealousy underneath. She continues as she slides her hand onto my thigh, "How about I show you how a true South Sider can fuck? Unlike your preppy little princess, I can go all night. Does she even know how to get on her knees?"

She attempts to brush her fingers further up my thigh, but I grip them tightly and twist them off my leg as she whimpers slightly at the sting of my hold. I can see the pink of her skin turning white in my restraint, but I don't give a fuck.

"Are you fucking suicidal as well as a dumb slut, Cherry?" I ask her in a low, threatening tone and note when she swallows.

"She's a North Bred, Marcus. You said it yourself when she first got here. She isn't right for you," her tone has turned pleading, but I'm too fucking pissed at her to care.

"What, and you are?" I scoff a laugh. "Do you even know anything about me, Cherry? About my past?" I interrogate her and she frowns further so I spell it out for her. "I was born and raised right here in town, up on North Hill." Her eyes widen in shock when I mention the most elite real estate in town, "Side by fucking side with that girl over there. She is my fucking reason for everything I have ever fucking done and will be until the end of time. I suggest you stay the fuck away from both of us, otherwise I won't hesitate to make your miserable, little life even less desirable," I release her fingers from mine, and she pulls them back clutching them to her chest dramatically.

I turn my gaze back to Elle who has a smile on her face, but I don't miss her sharp eye taking in what is happening here, so I offer her a slight tip of my chin. I still feel Cherry's presence next to me. "That was a command to get the fuck away from me, Daniels," I snap, and she rushes out of the seat and disappears into the crowd.

If only all our enemies were that easy to deal with.

Chapter 43

ASHER

The bow tie is like a fucking noose around my neck. Like the strings to the puppet, I have to pretend to be under the watchful eye of my father. The presumed prodigal son, the dutiful little brother. I am a fraud, a fake, a fucking master at this game of lies. It's a complicated weave of smoke and mirrors that I'm constantly battling to ensure my mask stays in place and my true family remains safe.

I would never be considered a threat, they don't pay enough attention to me, at least my father doesn't. Even now, as I stand here with his hoard of loyal followers, I might as well be invisible. It allows me to easily cast my gaze around the room as I swill the clear liquid in the glass I'm holding. I note Logan sitting lazily at the bar, I watch as an angry girl storms away from the table against the wall where Marcus sits alone, his gaze glued to Elle. She is on the dance floor with the help. They have been dancing together since I walked in about three songs ago. Why she allows him so much time of her day is fucking beyond me, he is like an infuriating gnat you can't rid yourself of. Now, not only has he got her entranced, but he got his claws into Logan too. I don't see the fucking appeal. Fuck knows where that little manwhore, Conrad, is. Probably already fucking one of the Prep girls in a closet somewhere.

I continue my appraisal of the room ensuring I don't linger on Elle or any of the guys when I find the last pair of eyes I expected to see here. Greg is staring at me before my eyes even reach his, he has an unusual smile on his face. It's the same smile he has been wearing for the last couple of weeks. We have barely exchanged more than two words, but that smile has been ever present every time we crossed paths. Like we are playing some game that I am unaware of and with Greg, you know there will be no rules. *What the fuck is he doing here?*

I don't hesitate to cross the room to him, playing my role and putting my mask in place.

He speaks before I even have the chance, "Little brother," he spits at me in a sweet tone.

"Greg," I smile. "Still looking for more underage girls to play with?" I ask smoothly and it only makes the grin on his face stretch wider. I wonder how it would feel to take a knife and make that smile a permanent fucking emotion, ensuring he felt anything but fucking happy about it. Knowing him, the sick fuck would probably get off on me scarring him.

"Oh, on the contrary," he muses, casting his gaze back into the room. "I know exactly who I want to play with," his tone is both charming and threatening as I follow his gaze to Elle. I will fucking murder him where he stands with all two hundred fucking witnesses, without a single regret if the next words out of his mouth are about Elle.

I'm quiet, controlled, and completely unassuming, most would consider me an unworthy opponent. That is what makes me so dangerous. Not my name or my bank balance. Not the fact that my father is a killer. No. None of that. I'm dangerous because people look at me and see a quiet, polite, and respectable young man. A child yet to step up and take his place in this family of murderers. They don't know I was thrust into that role three years ago and haven't looked back since. Looking back would mean having regrets. I have none. Yes, I wish what Greg did to Elle could be erased, but that would also mean erasing my daughter. Something I would never wish for, no matter how dark her creation. She took something sick and depraved and made it good, made me good.

My daughter is the purest thing my world will ever know. I don't feel emotions like normal people do, don't indulge in lust, sex or even friendship outside of Elle. They are all things that are of no concern to me, my one and only priority is ridding this town of its fucking sinister sick bastards, so my daughter only knows love and light.

"Oh, I thought father was dealing with her," I attempt for an uninterested tone but falter slightly trying to contain my rage.

He brings his sick, gleaming stare back to mine, "Oh yes, brother, he is but tonight is all about family business," he says the words with a slap to my shoulders before he slithers off back towards our father.

Family business. Isn't that a pleasant way to describe the kidnapping, the drugging, the raping, the torturing, and sometimes murdering of young girls. I purse my lips as I watch him infiltrate my father's group of friends with his presence, the pride in my father's eyes, the fear in his friends'.

"Well, he is about as pleasant as I imagined," Logan drawls from beside me. I loathe the fact I didn't notice his approach. I pride myself on being aware of my surroundings and yet I just let someone slip past my defenses without so much as a flicker of awareness.

"What do you want, baby Royton?" I snap in annoyance as I throw back the remainder of the liquid in my tumbler, before I stalk over to the makeshift bar for a refill. Only a board my father is a member of would allow for a party full of seniors to include alcohol. I slam down the glass and signal for a refill as Logan appears at my side.

The bartender fills my drink efficiently and Logan dives for it before my hand touches it and takes a sip with a smile.

I fucking hate people touching my stuff, "Can you get your own? You fucking neanderthal," I growl, snatching my drink back from him.

But my glacial tone does nothing as he licks the remainder of liquid from his lips, his eyes meet mine, "Why? Are you remembering where my lips have been? Thinking about whose taste might still be lingering there."

Of fucking course, he would bring up that night from a couple of weeks ago, where I caught him on his knees for Blackwell.

Why the fuck would I be thinking about that?

I ignore whatever the fuck he is trying to reference and ask again, "What the fuck do you want, Logan?"

"Relax, my little psycho, I was just ensuring the two brothers weren't going to gladiator it out. It looked like a possibility with the way you two were glaring at each other," he shrugs before adding, "Not that I wouldn't enjoy seeing you shirtless, sweaty, and bleeding," he winks, before making a show of checking me out.

I roll my eyes, typical Logan bullshit. He's made a game out of attempting to flirt with me since we met, no matter how many times, I ignore his attempts at affections, he still continues. I thought maybe with what happened between him and Lincoln I'd be free from his ridiculous notions. A joke or not, he is more than wasting his time with me.

"Why don't you take your affections to the help and see if you fare better? Some of us are actually taking tonight seriously," I tsk.

He grabs my drink back and necks the remainder before leaning in at the same time I catch Lincoln's eye over his shoulder. All three Rebels are now sitting at the table where Marcus was alone before. I watch as Elle pulls out her phone and gestures out the doors to the guys and leaves the room.

"Oh, I take everything seriously, baby," he whispers before turning to leave as my gaze is still locked with the other fucking asshole. The only thing that makes me break it is seeing Greg in my peripheral stalking across the room towards the exit with intent.

My gut screams at me like it has been doing for weeks. When I look back to Lincoln, I note he's seen the same thing I have, hmm, so he is good at certain things. When he watches Greg, he looks back to me and we share an unspoken communication.

Something isn't right.

Chapter 44

ELLE

I put the phone back into my bag after I tried calling Z back. I take a moment to myself in the stupidly large music room I came across. Such a far cry from what they have over at Hallows High. I let my fingers dance across the skin of a drum set as I try to imagine what life would have been like if that night never happened. Would I have met the same fate another time? Would Michael still be alive? Would Marcus and I be what we are now?

"Well, look here, it seems I've found myself a lost princess again. Or should I say Queen?" The blood in my veins turns to ice as the last voice I ever wanted to hear again pierces through the room. The goosebumps that dance across my skin no longer have anything to do with the cool December air filtering in through the window and I can't suppress the flinch I let out.

"I thought I'd never get you alone," he continues, and his words crawl over my skin, his tone dark, demonic and completely giddy at his findings. I turn and come face to face with Greg Donovan. My best friend's brother, my child's biological father, my rapist.

I don't speak straight away, I can't. I won't allow him the satisfaction of hearing the tremble that will shake my voice. No amount of preparing or training could make me ready for this. To come face to face with the man who raped me.

He hasn't changed in the almost four years since I've seen him. He is still as handsome as he ever was, beautiful and blonde, just like his little brother. The only difference between them is the look in their eyes. Asher might be dark and corrupted by everything he has seen, jaded by it, but he still knows how to feel, how to love. It might have been limited by his trauma and the demons he calls life, but it's there. He shows it to me, Cassie brings it out of him every day, and I'm sure one day the right person will make it fucking shine.

Greg wasn't just born into the darkness, he was made with it, it seeped into his bones until his very essence was nothing but black. That blackness pours out of him and mars his features until all you can see is pure fucking evil.

He is watching me, assessing me, as he starts to slowly circle the large room, somehow still managing to move towards me at the same time. Casually, carefully, stalking what he thinks is his prey. I steel myself, taking comfort in the feeling of the pistol strapped to my thigh. Relish in the two blades buried into the corset of my dress and find peace in knowing my Rebels are somewhere close by. *They will have my back.*

When I'm finally confident enough that I can speak without my voice shaking I force a bored tone into my voice, "Gregory, to what do I owe this unfortunate interaction?" I offer him the fakest, sweet smile I can manage.

He smirks at me, like my uninterested tone is exactly what he wanted, "I had been looking for you for sometime, Elle," he puts emphasis on my name, and the way it sounds on his tongue makes me want to never hear it again. Change it until he can't ever say it again. Every step he takes brings him an inch closer and makes my fear increase tenfold, fear I am pushing down. Hiding as well as Z has trained me to.

I smile a taunting grin ensuring to show not even an ounce of the fear that infects my insides "Sorry, I didn't realize the devil looked for people. Don't they just fall at your feet?" I make a gesture to the floor before him, disguising my aim at bringing my fingers close to the slit in my dress just a breath away from the grip of my gun.

His smile widens, "Oh, the princess has a sense of humor now?" he moves towards me again, but still, I remain rooted to the spot and the glint in his eye turns my stomach.

"I have a lot of things I didn't on our last encounter," I say hoping the blank look on my face is enough to convince him he isn't affecting me. It's a lie. The fear is pulsing through me, forcing its way into me, and trying to take over my body. I hear Zack's voice in my head telling me not to panic.

"Oh, trust me, I've noticed," his words slide under my skin and cause it to prickle. I don't like his tone and my fingers itch to just pull out my gun and end him right fucking here. Paint this pretty cream floor with his fucking organs. He deserves it, I don't think anyone deserves it more. No one would mourn a sick, sadistic fuck like him.

He ascends upon me, slowly, quietly. He thinks I'm the prey, and he is the hunter. Fool me once, Gregory. Shame on you. You don't get a fucking second chance. If he came for me now, I'd welcome it, beg him to. Just so I could feel the relief of gutting him and allowing his blood to drench my skin. It would feel cathartic. Like an artist creating a masterpiece, except my Sistine Chapel would be his dead fucking body.

I watch his every step, assessing the risks of him getting close to me but I don't move, not even a fucking inch. *Show no fear.*

"How about I make you a deal?" he offers, like anything he could do for me would be a favor.

"I don't make deals with the devil," I toss back without pause.

"The devil has nothing on me," he smiles, all fucking teeth like it was a compliment. Yeah, don't I fucking know it, you psychotic little freak.

My fingers burn to curl around the pistol at my thigh, or to whip out one of my knives. My blades are a part of me as much as my fucking limbs. He makes one wrong move, and I don't give a fuck about who is here or what the clean-up would be. I won't fucking hesitate to gut him here and now, until his intestines spill on this pretty marble floor.

He continues, "I am heir to a fucking throne that is finally within reach. I don't need some fucking scorned bitch on a mission messing all that up. You think I don't know what you've done?" he taunts me, his smile finally turning truly sinister instead of charming. Ah, finally his true face, the one I know better than anyone. "You would be surprised by what I know, princess. You want to survive? Then run, fucking disappear before I catch you and finish what I started three years ago."

I laugh, "What makes you think that isn't exactly what I want?" My fingers dance along my holster, willing him to come for me now. There is a flash of surprise across his face for the first time since he stepped into the room, so I push on.

"You wanna make me bleed again, Greg? Then bring it the fuck on, I'm not the scared little girl you took from the woods anymore."

"Oh, I can see that," he licks his lips, as he drags his gaze down my body lingering on my breasts before flicking his eyes back to me, "What does the princess desire?"

"What I want, you can't give me," I spit at him, I'm done holding back. I will take my fear and turn it into fucking fire and then enjoy watching him fucking burn.

For the first time, I advance towards him letting the venom seep into my voice, "I want to look down into your cold, dead eyes as they stare back at me, Gregory. I want you to feel so much pain that you wish you never laid a fucking finger on me. I want your fucking rapist body bleeding out at my feet, you sick son of a bitch."

He takes a step forward, his excited glare sparkling once more, "Ohh, temper temper," he muses. "I thought I'd fucked that out of you, maybe we should go again."

He's so concentrated on me that he didn't notice the dark shadow enter the room. That was his second mistake, his first was thinking I would ever give him the chance to get me alone.

"Take one more fucking step, Donovan. I dare you," Marcus' voice wraps around me like fucking silk. Soothing me instantly and reminding me of the power I have. Greg turns and takes in Marcus' form and his brothers standing next to him.

He tuts, "Not one, but three Rebels by your side, ey princess? Not surprising, after all I know how sweet that cunt is," he winks at me like we are on the same side and bile floods my throat.

Marcus moves so fast that none of us see him until his fist is smashing against Greg's jaw, forcing him to the floor.

Lincoln drags him back with force and Jace helps him, he needs too. Greg stands, wiggling out his jaw with a sinister smile on his face like he is really enjoying himself. He spits blood to the floor tarnishing the pureness of it, "You'll regret that Riviera. Just like your dad did."

Marcus roars trying to escape the guys, "I will fucking kill you," but before he can get past them Greg grabs me and pulls me into his body. Dragging me against him and I almost gag when I feel his cock hardening against my ass. The pleasure I will feel when I chop it the fuck off will be unparalleled. His hands on me flood my brain with nightmares I wish I could forget, memories I try my hardest daily to suppress. He inhales my hair just like he did that night, closing his eyes, like he is trying to memorize my scent once more.

Losing control of his urges is another slip up on his part. The click of a gun hits his head at the same time Asher rushes the room taking in the scene. Thankfully, Greg's is too focused on Lincoln to notice the despair on Ash's face. Despair that turns to pure fucking acid.

"Get. The. Fuck. Away. From. Her." Lincoln speaks each word slowly putting emphasis on each one. His cool and calm tone sounds completely detached and deadly, I've never seen him look so intense and I've seen him after he committed four murders. His green eyes now a shade of black I am unfamiliar with. I have no doubt that he will blow Greg's brains out right here if he doesn't obey. I have a feeling this is a truer version of Lincoln to what we are used to, he looks too calm, too comfortable, too ready.

Greg doesn't move, just cocks his stare to the side to take in Linc's form and he smiles before looking back at me. "Oh, don't worry, Rebel," he says stepping back and away from the gun before turning and locking eyes with Ash, "I got everything I came for," he smiles wide at his brother and I can tell from Ash's face that he is close to the edge right now, so I subtly shake my head and pray he sees it.

Greg makes a show of fastening his tuxedo jacket before continuing, "Now, if you'll excuse me, I've got some family business to attend to," he moves confidently towards the door on the assumption we won't fucking murder him. To be honest, it's a close fucking toss up right now with the rage drowning the room. But in true psycho form he doesn't seem bothered, just nods his head at Asher on the way out, "Brother, they're all yours."

Asher watches him leave and nobody speaks until he turns back to us, "Something's not right,"

"Yeah, your brother is a fucking murdering rapist," Lincoln spits and I flinch at his dark, murderous tone.

"I wasn't fucking talking to you, help," Asher grits back at him before looking to me. "You okay, baby girl?" I nod before answering, "Yeah, I'm fine." I am far from fucking fine, but I try my hardest to control my breathing and work to center myself.

He doesn't look convinced, "Something's not right. I can feel it," he says looking around at the other three before coming back to me. "I'm going to follow him, you guys go home, I think we've had enough fun for one night."

He turns to leave, "Ash," I call out to him and he pauses looking over his shoulder, "Be careful."
His smile is tight and forced, "Always."

Chapter 45

ELLE

I try to take a breath but I can't, they come in short pants, as I struggle to deal with the aftermath of seeing Greg. The adrenaline that kept me going head-to-head with him is nowhere in sight. All I feel is fear, panic, grief. I need something, anything, to stop me from sinking into the void of my past. I struggle to take a deep breath, as I stare off at the door that Asher just exited.

"Baby," Marcus reaches out to caress my cheek. "Stay with me," he pleads, as he pulls me into his arms. I close my eyes and try to let his words soothe me.

I feel him turn slightly to speak with the other guys, "Can you give us a minute?" Neither Lincoln nor Jace say a word, but I hear the door open and close. I know the instant we are alone. His grip goes from careful and tentative to possessive.

He grabs my chin and tilts my head back, when I open my eyes his dark stare is locked on mine. Waiting. Wanting. He feels it too. The despair, the loss, the grief, the pain. He needs me just as much as I need him. To remind ourselves that we are here and this thing between us is real.

"Whatever the fuck he said to you, forget it," his voice is gritted, laced with the darkness I know is coursing through him. "Whatever he thinks he took from you, he didn't." His arms circle my waist as he lifts me, walking backwards until we hit a desk against the wall. He places me onto it effortlessly, parting my legs and stepping between them.

"You're Elle fucking King and Greg Donovan is rapist scum who deserves nothing more than to be fucking blood on your blade."

He is as close to the edge as I am. I can feel the string holding him here with me and not going after Greg, it's ready to snap. Being that close to the person who ruined everything and yet doing nothing. I see it in his eyes, in his fucking soul, he wants to go after him, attack him, fucking ruin him until he is nothing but fucking bone dust. Only then will he feel relief, I get it, I feel it too, more than he could ever know. He may have taken so much from me, but he took from Marcus too, took our friendship, our future, our fucking meant to be. He ruined everything.

Marcus Riviera was my first friend, my first crush, my first love, and if it wasn't for Greg Donovan, he would have been my first everything. The only person who hates him more than me for that is Marcus. It doesn't matter what we share, he will always have taken that from us. I need Marcus to know that this thing between us is everything, that Greg Donovan is nothing, and that together we will fucking shine.

I grip his shirt and start un-fastening the buttons and surprise flares in his eyes. "I need you, Marcus." I ensure that my tone is smooth and serious, even as pleading as I am, he needs to know how much I want this, how much I need this, need him.

"Make me forget," I tear his shirt open. "Take away his words," my hands brush up his chest. "His touch," I drag my nails down his abs. "Just fucking everything that isn't you and me, right here in this room." His skin is warm, yet goosebumps appear at my touch. "I want you to take me, Marcus, right here on this desk, mark me, fucking claim me the only way you can."

My words snap him into action as he growls. *Fucking growls.*

He attacks my mouth with unrestrained lust. Lips, teeth, tongue, I feel him everywhere, yet I still need more. He slides his hands along my thighs until my dress is parted fully and he drags my ass to the edge of the desk. He looks down and gets the first glimpse of what I'm wearing underneath. The red lace already soaked in my desire.

"Fuck," he grunts out like he is in pain. "So fucking sexy," he practically spits.

He drops to his knees immediately, ripping my thong aside and plunges his tongue between my folds. There is no teasing kisses or slow licks, no, he fucking feasts on me, ravishing me like I am the very air he needs to breathe. Every lash of his tongue against my clit feels like a flame licking my body. My legs start to shake as he brings me to the edge so fucking fast, I can't do anything but grip his hair, and fuck his face, chasing my release. It doesn't build, or creep up on me, it just bursts out of me full force, ripping a scream from my throat as he pushes me into the fastest fucking orgasm I've ever had.

I am barely finished coming when he stands, gripping my thighs in a vice like hold as he takes out his cock giving it two quick pumps before lining it up and thrusting inside of me. I stretch around him, deliciously, as he begins to pound into me at a wicked pace. The desk bangs loudly into the wall and I know for sure the other two will know exactly what we are doing in here.

His cock pistons in and out of me and every thrust hits my clit hard. He drags my right thigh around his waist by the leather holster wrapped around it and the angle allows his cock to drag across my G spot in rapid succession. Fuck.

"You feel so fucking perfect wrapped around my cock, Ells," his gravelly tone has me groaning, "You are fucking mine."

I move my hips to meet his thrusts as he continues his vicious assault with his devilish dick and dirty words. "Yeah, baby, take it. Take my cock in this perfect fucking pussy," he is gritting through moans as I clench around his cock at the sound of his rough voice coaxing me towards another orgasm.

"Marcus," I half scream out, as I feel myself getting ready to come again.

He moves his grip back to my waist, gripping it so hard I know it will bruise but I don't care. He lifts me by my hips drawing back before slamming back into me, thrusting deep one last time. His cock throbs inside me and he fills me with his come.

He growls my name as I scream his, as we both go over the edge together. *Holy fuck.*

Even after he has spilled in me, he continues to move slowly inside me, like he can't bear for us to be finished. We are still catching our breath when there is a hard rapid knock on the door and we both smile slightly. It's time to go.

Chapter 46

ELLE

Once Marcus ensures I am presentable again, we pull the door open and find Lincoln there alone. If he heard us, he is polite enough to pretend he didn't.

"Where's Jace?" I ask, the panic that Marcus had erased starting to creep back in, but Lincoln just rolls his eyes and nods over my shoulder.

I turn and find him with Taylor backed against a locker as he curls a lock of her hair around his finger. *Sweet lord.*

I move towards them and catch her words, "And what makes you think it wouldn't be me rocking your world, playboy?" she asks him, and I have to squash a smile.

"Oh, I am more than willing to let you show me," he teases her with a savage grin.

"Pretty boy," I call him, and he scrunches his eyes up like he is a child about to be scolded.

"Hey, Queenie, thought you were busy," he teases, confirming he knows exactly what Marcus and I were doing in that room. I ignore my blush and turn to Taylor.

“We are heading out for the night, let us drop you off?” I ask and pray she takes me up on my offer because after my meeting with the devil I don’t want to leave her in their grasp. She looks between me and the guys and then to Jace, noting the serious expression on all our faces before she nods.

Jace throws an arm around her, “Might have to sit on my lap, little vixen,” he teases and now I roll my eyes.

“Ignore him, he’s probably stoned,” I toss over my shoulder as Marcus curls his arm around me and we exit the school. Lincoln already has our car from the valet, and I presume that is thanks to the obscene wad of cash he slipped him on the way in.

The drive home is quiet, apart from Jace’s relentless attempts at flirting with Taylor, much to all our amusement. Good on her though because she takes it in stride, even though he is trying to bed her with his full charm. Seems she isn’t that immune though. When we pull into the gates of her house, Jace jumps out and lets her out of the back seat where she was sitting next to me. He shuts the door after her and just as she goes to leave, she turns back and slams her lips to his. He seems startled at first before he curls his arms around her waist and kisses her back. When she pulls away, she smiles shyly and says something we can’t hear before she heads inside.

Jace climbs back in and we are silent for about thirty seconds before we all burst out laughing.

“Fuck off, you buncha assholes,” he jeers at us, turning the music up to drown us out.

The rest of the drive we are all lost in our own thoughts. I have no idea what is running through each of the Rebels' minds right now but, for me, I can't get the look in Greg's eyes out of my head. It's a look I have never seen before. He looked smug, satisfied even, like he had achieved something within our interaction. I didn't show any fear, no matter how much of it I felt being that close to him, so what else would have had him gleaming like he was? I'll call Ash when I get inside and see if he came up with anything that might shed some light onto things.

We pull up to the gate and buzz but there is no answer. Not totally unusual considering it's pretty late. Zack must have fallen asleep with Cassie but there is usually still one of the security guys around to answer. I roll down the window and lean out until I can reach the keypad and enter the code, so the gate opens.

It's dark and quiet, calm. Just how I like it. I can't wait to get into the house, out of this dress and into bed. Lincoln pulls up to the house and moves to park in the garage in what has become his spot. Just as he goes to turn off the engine his ringtone blasts through the sound system, the caller ID says Jack Hanson. I know outside of the three of them, he is their eyes and ears out on the streets. I know he was aware of us having plans this evening, so whatever he is calling for must be important. Marcus looks at me, but I shake my head and motion for him to stay with the guys and gesture to the door leading into the house.

I get out of the car so they can deal with whatever business they have in peace. I move towards the entrance to the house taking my shoes off as I go. I drop them on the floor inside and make my way to the center of the house. It's so quiet, my earlier estimation must have been correct, everyone has gone to sleep. The guards must be doing their hourly perimeter check, overkill I think considering the security system Z invented but hey what do I know?

As I get near the kitchen, I hear soft music playing, jazz, so Zack is awake somewhere it seems. I head to the kitchen first and grab a bottle of water, unscrewing the cap, and taking a sip as I head towards the living room. When I round the corner the first thing, I see is blood, so much fucking blood.

WHAT THE FUCK?

The bottle of water falls from my grip, spilling onto the bottom of my dress as it hits the floor. I have my pistol in my hand quicker than ever before, as I flatten myself to the living room door. I want to call out to Marcus and the guys but the water bottle hitting the floor may already have given away my spot if someone is here, even if it didn't, I can't risk it.

My hand shakes, for the first fucking time ever. I instantly think of the praise Zack gave me the first time I ever held a gun and didn't falter; he praised my confidence, and ability right off the bat. I was never nervous. That training feels fucking worthless at this moment in time.

I move silently as I enter the room further, taking as much effort as possible to steady my breaths and keep the panic at bay. I reach the sofa and when I find the source of blood, my whole world falls apart.

Zack is lying in a pool of his own blood with his eyes closed.

Please don't be fucking dead.

I don't hesitate to go to him and the relief I feel when I press my hand to his neck and his eyes snap open and hit mine. The look in his eyes shatters my whole fucking world. We may not have grown up together, but our circumstances meant our sibling bond grew quick and strong. I know that look, it isn't just pain, it's pure and unfiltered grief and that's when I know. He doesn't have to say the words, but he does, he knows I have to hear them.

He chokes, a mix between a breath and a gurgle as he says three words that crush my soul, "They have her."

My daughter is gone.

TO BE CONTINUED...

Well, that was fun wasn't it? All the blood and murder and ooofff that steam. Marcus and Elle all happy and finally together, all the Rebels on the same team. Some new characters and relationships to sink your teeth into.

Oh, and that cliffhanger? Super fun, right? No? Well, sorry not sorry.

Thank you so much for reading the second installment in Marcus and Elle's crazy story! I hope you enjoyed it and aren't too mad at me.

If you did enjoy it then I would love it if you could leave me a review. They make my little indie author heart beat!

Wanna talk, then come stalk…

Facebook Page - G.N. Wright
Readers Group: G.N. Wright's Rebels
Instagram: @authorgnwright

Marcus and Elle's story will conclude in Rebellion of a Kingdom!

Acknowledgements

Damn let me start this by saying this book was a freaking journey. A fast, crazy, whirlwind of a journey that took me in so many directions that I didn't plan. So, like if you wanna yell at me then yell at the characters, it's all their fault.

I still can't believe this is my second book because I still haven't gotten over the fact, I released the first one to be honest. The last few months have been crazy weird for me. For people to be picking up a book that I wrote and not only reading it but loving it too. Just insane.

So, first, thank you to my readers. Every single one of you. I love you all! Thank you for taking a chance on such a newbie author and loving these characters as fiercely as I do. From the reviews, comments, and stunning edits! You guys are the freaking bomb!

Sammie, where do I even start? You are my rock girl! I would not be on this journey if it weren't for you and I love that even with half a world between us, we grow closer every day. Thank you for being the best alpha a girl could ever have. For every time you loved Elle, every time Marcus pissed you off and every time Asher made you swoon. Just from the bottom of my heart, thank you for being the best book bestie a girl could ever wish for.

Dean, thank you again for reading something that's definitely not your thing and loving it anyway. Oh, and as agreed we will never discuss the steam.

Mum, let's also never talk about the steam! Let's just focus on what a superhero nanna you are to my girl. Thank you for every extra sleepover you gave her to allow me time to write in the midst of a freaking pandemic. You rock.

To my husband, thanks for not reading my first book or this one either but loving and supporting me anyway.

To my awesome beta readers! Andrea, Sam, Jess, Brianna, Laura.... What would I do without you? Thank you for the time and patience you gave me and devouring the words I wrote. Your comments always make me smile. You're the best!

And finally, to my street team!!! You guys are awesome! Thank you for being part of my team and hyping up my books and loving them.

COMING SOON...

Rebellion of a Kingdom

Jace's Book

Lincoln's Book

Printed in Great Britain
by Amazon